TriQuarterly

TriQuarterly is
an international
journal of
writing, art and
cultural inquiry
published at
Northwestern
University

TriQuarterly

issue 116 *summer 2003*

Editor
Susan Firestone Hahn

Associate Editor
Ian Morris

Operations Coordinator
Kirstie Felland

Production Manager
Bruce Frausto

Production Editor
Vincent Chung

Cover Design
Gini Kondziolka

Assistant Editor
Eric LeMay

Editorial Assistant
Cara Moultrup

TriQuarterly Fellow
W. Huntting Howell

Contributing Editors
John Barth
Lydia R. Diamond
Rita Dove
Stuart Dybek
Richard Ford
Sandra M. Gilbert
Robert Hass
Edward Hirsch
Li-Young Lee
Lorrie Moore
Alicia Ostriker
Carl Phillips
Robert Pinsky
Susan Stewart
Mark Strand
Alan Williamson

Guest Editors
John Kinsella and Susan Stewart

Acknowledgments

John Kinsella and Susan Stewart would like to thank Susan Hahn, Ian Morris, and the artists who generously contributed, often without fee, such distinguished work for this issue. John Kinsella also thanks Kenyon College and its English department, and Churchill College, Cambridge, for their supportive environments. Susan Stewart would like to thank the students in her graduate seminar on pastoral at the University of Pennsylvania. And as a final word, the co-editors thank each other.

John Kinsella and Susan Stewart

An Epistolary Pastoral/
An Introduction

JK,

   Calling for the poems and essays and art works that make up this issue, I've hoped we could work in new ways with an ancient realm of thinking about the practice of poetics as making. In place of the military term of the "avant-garde," or the objectifying scientific term of the "experimental," I would like to return to—that is, I would like to cultivate—the term *pastoral*, rooted in care, ecumenism, and a symbiosis between human life and nature. I hope the issue is consonant with your own idea of *radical* pastoral and your motives for reviving pastoral concerns in contemporary culture.

   Throughout its long tradition pastoral evokes idyllic landscapes, especially in the eclogue, and agricultural practices, especially in the georgic. The works we have gathered here open up and extend the possibilities of pastoral into the present. They wander across various kinds of territories and so break open the merely territorial. The garden, the forest, the meadow are in a definable relation to urban spaces and spaces of waste or wilderness. When we first began talking about this project, I described to you the small-scale raspberry farming in vacant lots, the goats and chickens being raised in plywood pens on sidewalks, in North

Philadelphia, displaced immigrants cooking over open fires in abandoned apartment buildings in West Philadelphia, the gatherers of urban detritus throughout this city who build shelters from whatever materials have been left behind. Nomads, feudal lords and servants, industrial workers, white-collar workers—everywhere in urban spaces, rural peoples continue their earlier ways of life, for better or worse, while rural spaces become gentrified by suburban growth, tourism, and the enclosure of estates. Within a geography of center and periphery, intensity and dispersal, pockets and diasporas, the pastoral is relevant to, and in view of, all other spaces. What is uninhabitable is not only the wilderness, but also industrial wastelands and sites of poisoned soil, water, and air. Now in this era of unprecedented pollution and denigration of the earth, pastoral writers must stake their claims to insight and ethical judgment under terms of crisis.

Imagined from the perspective of time as well as space, the longing characteristic of the pastoral idyll is inseparable from projections of desires and future hopes. In the end, these works call for new ways of thinking about what kind of work artists do: will we merely produce art commodities, or will we also take responsibility for the past and future—a responsibility not manifested in things alone, but in the more profoundly material consequences of human thought and action? The occupation we turn to here is therefore that of the artist/poet as a person who shepherds forms of life. Yet, as in the first idyll of Theocritus, the place where most histories of pastoral begin, the poet/shepherd sings at noon, the hour of Pan and rest, when ordinary chores are in abeyance and the supervisory eye of the god is falling elsewhere. In this moment of suspension, poets and listeners are free from contingency and begin to invent a new economy: my song for your cup; my account of the tradition that has brought me here in time in exchange for your account of a landscape you carry within the space of your imagination. If pastoral only grows where there is leisure, or *otium*, then the pastoral dream of an idyllic landscape must include the democratization of leisure itself—a world where artistic practice is an element of every person's moments of freedom from necessity. In *White Writing*, J. M. Coetzee emphasizes the misguided Puritanism of the georgic, in its approach to work and productivity, as a factor in what makes the Western pastoral untranslatable into a South African context. William Kentridge, to whom we are indebted for his important contributions to this issue, has developed a parallel critique of the consequences of technological determinism in the South African context. It is part of the myth of North American settlement that aboriginal ways of life could serve as models for acknowledging the demands of the environment—and such a myth is often revived at moments when the means of production go haywire. Nevertheless, what is "learned from" the aboriginal models remains motivated by utilitarianism.

William Empson and others have suggested that pastoral has a particular relation to simplicity and simplification and that historically the genre of pastoral was key to the development of "minor" and "major" characters. Pastoral is also inseparable from a process of democratizing speech that extends from Wordsworth to William Carlos Williams to recent discourses on dialect poetry, but this effort toward a "real" diction will be merely condescending if it is not accompanied by extended access to expression. Eighteenth-century and Romantic pastoral mark the split between the agricultural and industrial worlds; the poet dreams speech will overcome this separation, yet in singing a "major song," the poet separates himself from the *natural* singer. Pastoral constantly studies this spectrum between ease and artifice, perhaps an inherent quality of work in general and of our somatic relation to tools and skills. The roots of pastoral are not in the imitation of shepherd's song, but in the shepherd's song itself. Until recently the history of pastoral as a continuity doesn't necessarily admit of this disruption, yet already in georgic there is a need to make explicit knowledges that would otherwise be tacitly held. Perhaps this dynamic between the explicit and the tacit is itself a way of extending the audience for the work, particularly into the future. There is an ethos of conservation in pastoral, but also an ethos of innovation. The singers are engaged in contest and judgment is valued in itself; in the *Georgics*, Virgil explicitly counsels that it is often wise *not* to follow the practices of tradition.

From Virgil's eclogues forward, the historical opposition between pastoral and violence is inseparable from a concern with the interface of morality and necessity. Returning veterans of war and the crisis of hospitality they evoke can be found in Virgil and Wordsworth alike: such veterans wander in pastoral landscapes that are their source and eventual refuge. In more recent centuries technologies of war have been developed that destroy the landscape itself for generations and for the World War I poets pastoral, like thoughts of home, was saturated with irony. The history of hunting and fishing is also bound up with pastoral, forcing the question of the boundary between necessity and sport. As an artistic form, pastoral is not tied, as tragedy is, to a demand for sacrifice, yet pastoral is shadowed by the slaughter of animals and, as is evident in *carnival*'s etymology, communal, or village festivity is often organized around a plenitude of meat. Today industrial agriculture, vicious cycles of disease and abuse of antibiotics, and over-consumption of over-consuming animals in first-world countries accompany cycles of starvation in many third-world countries. What will constitute significant art works about the forms of what Allen Grossman has called in his essay "significant work" in such a world? Pastoral has always borne a connection to loss and elegy, and as well a connection to epithalamion and fertility; can it help re-aggregate the power of considered judgment? And can it help us imagine a relation to land freed of the landscape tradition and the morals of ownership?

Michel Serres has proposed in his *Natural Contract:* "We must add to the exclusively social contract a natural contract of symbiosis and reciprocity in which our relationship to things would set aside mastery and possession in favor of admiring attention, reciprocity, contemplation, and respect: where knowledge would no longer imply property, nor action mastery." Such an ethic suggests taking the pathetic fallacy to be far from a fallacy: Serres describes us as parasites who, in destroying the earth, destroy ourselves. A pastoral relation to nature would neither romanticize nature as an otherworldly place of the sublime, nor merely anthropomorphize it. What Serres is suggesting is that we anthropomorphize *ourselves* by acknowledging we are part of nature. Even in its most parodying and ironic forms, pastoral art always bears a utopian element, projecting in opposition to the artificial a kind of natural stance. How might the history and contemporary practice of pastoral be a resource for forming a natural contract—a covenant with the future, a covenant securing the continuity of human nature in nature?

S

by the Schuylkill, Philadelphia, June 6, 2002

ᴥ

S,

Can "pastoral" as both a super-rarefied genre-form and an historical political vehicle—of a problematical variety—have any relevance in the age of factory farming, consciousness of land destruction, cloning, genetic modification, pesticides, herbicides, the citification of the rural, the de-landing and disenfranchisement of indigenous communities (nomadic, agrarian, civic, urban, etc.)? Traditionally, pastoral worked as a vehicle of empowerment for the educated classes through the idyllicizing and most often romanticizing of the rural world. The relationship between the rural workers portrayed and the manner of their presentation represented a huge gap.

One possible turning point in this approach to things was Wordsworth's "Michael," in which a consciousness of the collapse of the idyll found expression as part of popular poetic and dramatic culture in English. The Elizabethan court wits could invest their Italian-inherited pastorals with ironic relief, and utilize an arcadia as a playground for aristocratic or land-owning sensibilities, but ultimately they stayed firmly grounded in the hierarchies of control—of the divine right, the hierarchy of relations that played with the pagan hierarchy of Gods and humans, and the ladder of authority that entailed using this as a vehicle for Christian hierarchies. The goatherd or shepherd or rural worker in general could only transcend his place on that ladder through lyrical skills—specifically oral (singing)—or shows of strength. And in the Greek and Roman worlds, these usually turned out to indicate some noble lineage that had been lost or obscured through fate— usually pollution or hubris. Ironically, instead of distancing pastoral from modernity, such a world-view increases its relevance. Just look at the way Monsanto sells genetic modification—it is for the urban consumer, but appealing also directly to farmers. Or pretending to, for what it really appeals to is the idea of profit.

Traditional pastorals were basically not read or heard by the "kind" of characters they purported to be about, whereas contemporary "pastoral"/"anti-pastoral" writers expect that their work might be read by all who can read in the language they write from. It's the paranoia of the poet that far fewer people will ever read a poem than might be hoped for. Do the pastoral poems in this issue speak to rural workers, to farmers, to those who make the pesticides? Maybe; maybe not. This is an issue about intent and reception. Does audience define pastoral? Do the educated Greeks enjoying Theocritus, or the Romans reading Virgil, constitute the idea of pastoral audience?

A poet like the rustic John Clare, who might be seen as more of a nature poet than a pastoral poet, is nonetheless appealing to the same audience in terms of publishing demographics, but he actually came out of the place, felt angered by enclosure, and in the process wrote a subtextual anti-pastoral. The pastoral isn't really about nature, except insofar as it's about landscape, the mediation of nature through human interference and control. There is a critical language that is deployed to discuss these issues, which in a sense becomes part of the pastoral construct itself, so that pastoral is about the language of presentation as much as about the language of place. Terms like "pathetic fallacy" become in this context a self-conscious critique of the anthropomorphizing of place and nature, yet pathetic fallacy is itself one of the weapons of pastoral.

For pastoral has been military, despite claims of serenity and peace. The masque performed in the seventeenth-century English country mansion is a violence against workers and might be seen, in Marxist terms, as a strategy of class warfare by the bourgeoisie or ruling classes. But this is where the pastoral has grown and changed in the twentieth century. Post- Eliot's *Waste Land*, just to cite one obvious example—or maybe just post-the first world war—a brutal awareness, a trauma in the relationship between language and place, have meant a re-evaluation of what constitutes the idyll. Of course, people will always try to use the construct to configure some sweeter alternative, and that's as much the case in poetry now as it ever was. However, there are many more pollutants in there, and a lot more meta-critical awareness of the absurdity of idyllicizing anything at all. The configuration of the bucolic in terms of the weekend getaway, the vacation, or the desensitising of urban consumerism, have to be taken into consideration.

One must be aware of the "new pastorals" of the vacant block and city-fringe wastelands, the most "legitimate" of urban pastoral constructs equipped with their quota of gardeners, and the worked allotment, in which the small urban farmer grows his or her own vegetables. Ironically, the cemetery too is a scene of pastoral, or conveyance and maintenance of pastoral relationships between the sanctity of the providing earth and its keeper. The earth accepts the body and is enriched by it; the keepers of the cemeteries become "goatherds" and "shepherds" just as unreal as those in the literarily and culturally mediated world of Theocritus.

Pastoral has always been about the tensions within morality, and a moral guidebook for behavior. Hesiod's *Works and Days* presents the right things in the right order, as they should be. The cemetery, often with nationalistic as well as religious symbolism (segregation, apportioning), does exactly that. The pastoral should also be thought of in terms of its social and spiritual evocation, for the two are inseparable. The protection of the flock is seen as a noble thing, but the flock is being preserved only for human use: at best shearing, at worst eating. So works the priest or rabbi or imam, the social worker or the teacher—guidance becomes a form of social and spiritual control. We hope that some of these constructs are questioned and examined in this special issue.

Pastoral is a vehicle for the linguistic dynamism of the language as well—of all languages. Though primarily concerned with Western pastoral tradition, we hope that some of the pieces broaden and challenge this tradition. Pastoral in the specific case of Australia is twofold—a construct to recreate European, specifically English, rural power-structures, the reconfiguring of "home" in an alien landscape. Such language-usage comes out of a politics of oppression and degradation of indigeneity. A new pastoral must come out of this that re-examines what constitutes the rural space and how that is mediated.

Another concern is gender—is the pastoral a patriarchal tool? Its traditions certainly suggest so, but some of the most interesting and challenging pastoral poetry being written in English today is by women. Paul Alpers in his contribution mentions Lisa Robertson and others in this context. In short, the modern pastoral should be about challenging conventions—an engagement with the "traditional," yes, but also with the innovative. It's always been political, and has remained so. The pastoral of orbital roads, railway tunnels, the window box, the back-garden—they're part of it. But it is, possibly most significantly, a process for comparison—of producers, fetishizers and consumers, of destruction and profit, of the gaps and similarities in the way cultures discuss their use of space, of the use of nature and a concern for environmental preservation. The rights of animals—wild and domesticated, free and farmed—are pivotal.

Pastoral belongs in the realm of the gesture—of the meeting-point between drama and lyric, inseparable as they are. But it's the silences and absences that need exploring as much as anything else, and the use of visual art in this issue is a way of addressing that. Visual art works as "words" as well, as the poems and texts are visual experiences. The pastoral is about how land and the people within the land are marked—where the signs of authenticity and belonging are imposed or laid. The presentation of a pastoral drama in the court of Elizabeth I was a costly and complex act, mixing rural-estate realism (*in situ*) with decoration and allusion. So you'd be in the park and be in Arcadia as well. Allusions to contemporary political issues, to social concerns, were often comically played out. And maybe that's something that also marks the radical pastoral of now—the humor is dark and ironic, but still there. But don't doubt it wasn't always like this, especially in the history of the anti-masque. So what we have is a lineage of the radical combined with the safe, the constant. The seasonal cycle, love, marriage, and death.

The problem now is that even the seasons are dramatically changing, and doubt plays a major part in the construct of pastoral. Nothing can be taken for granted. It's that paranoia of form and intent again. So, as we read through this selection we are looking for ways of interpreting the sign—of place, presence, and spirit. A crisis is often invoked, but redressed. Closure is always an issue. Players in the field might be ciphers, but there's an awareness of this. And maybe there always was, certainly in the "western tradition." The challenging of this by indigenous peoples is the key to the radical redressive pastoral, and one with which all those interested in the genre should concern themselves. Multi-sensed, the cornucopia may be full of rot and doubt, but it is still there in the full array of colors and living for presentation!

JK, LAX, 6th Sept, 2002

Ann Hamilton

CONTENTS

**Cover art: "Colonial Landscape" by William
Kentridge, pastel on paper 120" X 160"**

Paul Alpers

Modern Eclogues

"Modern eclogue" may seem to be something of a contradiction in terms. But from their very beginnings, in the pastoral poems of Theocritus and Virgil, these dialogues between herdsmen (or, sometimes, monodies uttered by a herdsman) were conceived as modern—that is, as attempts to find a viable poetic form in specific historical and cultural circumstances, particularly in relation to prior, prestigious cultures and forms of poetry. Like other kinds of poetry by his Alexandrian contemporaries (third century B.C.E.) Theocritus's "idylls" are self-consciously belated, to use Harold Bloom's term. Written in the same meter, dactylic hexameter, as the Homeric poems (and thus claiming to belong to the same genre), the Idylls are what David Halperin calls "inversions" or "subversions" of heroic poetry (219-37). In subject and theme, they concern the lives of ordinary people, the ups and downs of love, and minor or marginal episodes from myth and heroic poetry; in poetic handling, they are short, sophisticated, and playful or comic in tone. Their claim to literary authority lies in their self-aware modesty and sense of limitations.

Theocritus's "bucolics" are more wide-ranging and various than the idea of pastoral will lead you to expect. The development of pastoral as a coherent genre, with the herdsman as the central representative figure, was the work of Virgil. Separated even more than Theocritus was from the Hellenic epics and tragedies that were the measure of poetic achievement, he set about being a Roman poet by selectively imitating Theocritus's poems in a collection of ten *Bucolica* or *Ecloga* ("selections"). The same pattern of poetic motive and self-consciousness appears in the European Renaissance, though now it is Roman poetry which has become the measure of poetic accomplishment. Eclogues were among the founding works, in the sixteenth century, of modern vernacular literatures in Italian (Iacopo Sannazaro's *Arcadia*), Spanish (the eclogues of Garcilaso de la Vega), French (eclogues by Clément Marot), and English (Spenser's *Shepheardes Calender* and Sidney's *Arcadia*). Centered on the figure of the herdsman-poet, aware of his vulnerabilities yet trusting his skills, eclogues capture the tension inherent in the classicizing project—between the boldness of emulating and appropriating ancient poetic forms and the anxieties of belatedness, the felt inadequacies of one's language and culture, as well as oneself.

But although the eclogue emerged in antiquity and was reinstated in the Renaissance as a modern form, it strikes us now as highly traditional, both because it deploys a discernible repertory of conventions and because consciousness of predecessors is part of its essence. (To suggest the matter schematically, just as shepherds conventionally come together to exchange their songs, so the poems that so represent them incorporate the songs of other pastoral poets.) The way in which "modern eclogue" now makes sense to us is due, in English poetry at least, to Wordsworth's transformation of the form. Several of Wordsworth's poems can be considered, to use a contemporary's phrase about "The Brothers," "a local eclogue, of a new, and original species" (Alpers 260). One of his greatest poems, *The Ruined Cottage*, is a version of the traditional pastoral elegy: two country dwellers meet at noontime to lament and commemorate a dead "shepherdess." And yet everything about *The Ruined Cottage* makes the poem a different kind of revisionary eclogue from *Lycidas*. Whether or not one regards Milton as exploding the conventions of pastoral elegy or as regrounding and revivifying them, their presence in the poem, along with constant allusions to earlier pastorals, is indubitable: it is these conventions and modes of allusion that are themselves at stake. *The Ruined Cottage* is committed to the traditional values of pastoral elegy, notably the way commemoration at a scene of loss sustains the lives of mourners, and the power of poetry to sustain a link between past and present. But it breaks with traditional usages, replacing them with contemporary modes of representation and utterance—the realistic and historical conception of the dead Margaret, the attention to the physical remains of her dwelling and the remnants of her household, the fact that retelling her story is the central form of lament and commemoration. Hence even in so clear a case of continuity of poetic form, the form itself has lost its earlier generic identity. Many of Wordsworth's poems have clear filiations with traditional eclogues. "Resolution and Independence," for example, begins with reminiscences of Spenser's *Prothalamion* and can be seen to combine two Renaissance eclogue types, the encounter of courtier and rustic and the dialogue between a young and an old shepherd. But such a genealogy, unlike those of older eclogues, is not an active element in the poem or in the conceived reader's grasp of it. As in the case of other Wordsworthian pastorals, the most important contexts of "Resolution and Independence" are the poet's own writings and his poetic project, as we understand them.

This is the case with all modern eclogues. However linked to past eclogues and however much they deploy their poetic usages, their interest is not in finding a place or making a significant adjustment in the order of similar poems that precede them. Rather their points of engagement are contemporary, and they characteristically make sense in relation not to other poems of the same "kind" but to other poems by the poet him/herself. Yeats's "Shepherd and Goatherd," MacNeice's "An Eclogue for Christmas," and Frost's "The Death of the Hired Man" are acutely aware of what can be done with the eclogue as a form, but they do not speak to each other. They and the several other poems we shall examine exemplify Auden's observation:

> If we talk of tradition today, we no longer mean what the eighteenth century meant, a way of working handed down from one generation to the next; we mean a consciousness of the whole of the past in the present. Originality no longer means a slight personal modification of one's immediate predecessors . . .; it means the capacity to find in any other work of any date or locality clues for the treatment of one's own personal subject-matter. (Grigson 4)

But even if modern eclogues do not constitute, so to speak, a freestanding genre, they are not without generic awareness and filiations. Each poet, as we shall see, turns to the eclogue for a reason and finds resources in it—most notably the way dialogues between "herdsmen," often formalized as responsive singing, mediate first-person utterance and complicate its status and rhetorical authority. Traditional eclogues tend to be suspended between lyric and drama; their ambiguity in this respect extends to and is fruitful for their modern descendents. The element of dialogue makes self-styled eclogues different from modern lyrics that are titled "pastoral," which tend to be short, highly scenic, and often ironize the idyllic suggestions of the title.

Unlike its companion poems, "In Memory of Major Robert Gregory" and "An Irish Airman foresees his Death," "Shepherd and Goatherd" has never been central to anyone's idea of Yeats's achievement or his development as a poet. At first glance, the lines about Robert Gregory's "crook" and "pipe" may make the reader impatient with this exercise in an older form. But it seems to me a strong, interesting poem, canny and resourceful in using its older models. Yeats wrote to Lady Gregory (Feb. 22, 1918) that he was trying to write a poem about her son "in manner like one ["Astrophel"] that Spenser wrote for Sir Philip Sidney" (646). Presumably it was Yeats's idea of Robert Gregory as "our Sidney" that prompted him to emulate Spenser's poem. "Astrophel" is a rather long-winded narration, all under the figure of a shepherd and his world, including the hero's love for Stella (here a shepherdess) and his death, like Robert Gregory's, on foreign soil. Yeats does not retain much of this pastoral representation. His emulation of Spenser lies rather in his tribute to aristocracy, in lines expressing gratitude for Lady Gregory's patronage and representing her moving through her household, bearing her grief with dignity. Despite the reference to her watching "shepherd sports," there is nothing here of Astrophel's pastoral family (his mother a nymph, his sister a shepherdess). The important convention is herdsmen as poetic speakers, which enables Yeats to praise Lady Gregory for sustaining the social cohesion of her country world.

If "Astrophel" suggested representing Gregory's death as a loss to a pastoral world, it was another pastoral elegy that enabled Yeats to give "Shepherd and Goatherd" an adequate form. A month after his first letter, he wrote Lady Gregory that the poem was finished and that it was modeled not only on "Astrophel" but on Virgil's Fifth Eclogue.[1] In this poem, which more than any other established the conventions of pastoral elegy, a younger and an older herdsman lament and celebrate the heroic shepherd Daphnis. The song of the younger herdsman represents his "cruel death," the lamentations for him, and the loss his world has suffered. The older herdsman responds with a song of exactly the same length, celebrating the elevation of Daphnis to the heavens (the apotheosis, most familiar now in the ending of Lycidas) and the promise of his continuing life as a local deity, celebrated annually by the rural world he has left. Following this scheme, Yeats ends his poem with two songs (unlike Virgil's, they are formally different from the rest of the poem, which is in blank verse)—the shepherd's providing images of Gregory's brief stay in the rural world, the older goatherd's representing his transformation in death, his soul unburdening itself of earthly experience and recovering what a later poem would call "radical innocence." In length and rhetorical force, the goatherd's song tops the shepherd's. Yeats would seem to have unsettled the symmetry of Virgil's framework in order to stage a lyric in which he had a lot invested—both a defiance of natural decline and death and an expression, firm but suitably bracketed by the context, of some mystical doctrines in which he was beginning to take an interest.

If we view the poem this way, the poet seems to identify himself with the goatherd, who speaks as an older man looking back on youthful experience, as the poet himself does throughout *The Wild Swans at Coole*. (Also it is the goatherd who expresses gratitude for Lady Gregory's patronage.) But as in Virgil's poem, the voice and perspective of the younger shepherd have equal weight. It is he who most directly expresses the feeling of loss to his world, nowhere more strikingly than in an extraordinary adaptation of an old pastoral topos. When the goatherd asks what has brought him to the hills, the shepherd replies:

> *I am looking for strayed sheep;*
> *Something has troubled me and in my trouble*
> *I let them stray. I thought of rhyme alone,*
> *For rhyme can beat a measure out of trouble*
> *And make the daylight sweet once more; but when*
> *I had driven every rhyme into its place*
> *The sheep had gone from theirs.*

This device for bringing a herdsman on the scene, which comes from Virgil (Ecl. 7) and is rife in Renaissance pastoral (e.g. *Winter's Tale* 3.3), becomes here, what it never was before, an image of the poet's work. It is not mishap or incapacitating grief, but precisely the mastering of grief, ordering one's feelings and words, that leads to neglect of the flock, i.e. separates self from world. A different kind of separation has already occurred for the goatherd, dwelling in the hills and claiming to be beyond wishes. But his image of "measur[ing] out the road that the soul treads" is not enough: the poet's work, as the shepherd represents it, is equally central to Yeats. "Shepherd and Goatherd" gives form to tensions endemic to his poems—between contemplation and action, between the stages of one's life, between a commitment to this world and a desire to transcend it. If it is more than a curiosity, it is not despite its pastoral form, but because of it—specifically because of what Yeats found in Virgilian pastoral, an equal exchange between two representative voices.

Where for Yeats the Virgilian eclogue was a one-time experiment, for Frost it was the foundation of some of his best and best-known poems. *North of Boston* was originally to be titled *New England Eclogues*, and Frost later said that the poems were written "in a form suggested by the eclogues of Virgil."[2] The trouble is that what seem to us the greatest of these poems—"Home Burial," "A Servant to Servants," "The Fear" (these are the *North of Boston* poems Randall Jarrell named in identifying "the other Frost")—are more dramatic, realistic, and troubled, not to say tragic, than any of Theocritus's or Virgil's pastorals. There is therefore a certain difficulty in saying just how Virgil's eclogues enabled Frost's, even though we know this to have been the case. Reuben Brower, the critic of Frost best acquainted with Greek and Latin poetry, said "the relation is so deep and pervasive that it is nearly impossible to describe" (156). The following paragraphs are an attempt, despite the warning of my great teacher, to provide such a description.

Frost's most specific statement of his debt to Virgil—that he "first heard the speaking voice in poetry in Virgil's *Eclogues*" (Brower 157)—raises as many questions as it answers. The speaking voice and what he called "sentence sounds" are the idea about poetry that he most insisted on throughout his career. But in the *Eclogues?* They are not the first Latin poems one would think of in this way: Catullus's lyrics (included by Frost on a solicited list of five "books that have meant the most," 852) and Horace's satires and epistles would both seem more Frostean. Furthermore, at the time he was writing his eclogues, Frost wrote his friend Sidney Cox that "the living part of a poem, . . . the intonation entangled somehow in the syntax idiom and meaning of a sentence, . . . is not for us in any Greek or Latin poem because our ears have not been filled with the tones of Greek and Roman talk" (670). Still, we should try to follow up Frost's remark, and if we want some factual solidity, we might reflect that he could have *first* heard the speaking voice in poetry in the *Eclogues*, because he would have encountered them in his Latin course in high school—a subject in which he excelled and which, unlike English, he took seriously (Pritchard

35). Where then might Frost have heard the speaking voice? First of all, in the opening lines of several Eclogues—the Third, with its imitation of Theocritean rough talk, the Fifth (the meeting of Moeris and Menalcas before they settle down to sing of Daphnis), the Seventh, in which Meliboeus tells how looking for his lost goat he was brought to the site of a singing contest, and most strikingly the Ninth, in which two herdsmen meet on the road and discuss events that trouble the countryside.

However, in the absence of any reference as specific as in Yeats's letter to Lady Gregory, the First Eclogue is my candidate for the poem that most revealed the possibilities of this form to Frost. This poem is a dialogue between two herdsmen who have been differently affected—one allowed to remain on his farm, the other dispossessed and sent into exile—by the civil wars that afflicted the Roman world after the death of Julius Caesar. It is one of the most dramatic of the *Eclogues*, and one can imagine Frost admiring many things in it—the way, for example, both the larger historical situation and the foreground details of country life emerge as the two herdsmen speak of their situations. There is even an element of country gossip, a taste for which, Frost said, was part of what went into his New England eclogues (685). Most important, Eclogue 1 displays the modulations of voice that Frost prized. It begins with an exchange of speeches which modifies, by dramatic differences, the perfectly symmetrical exchange it imitates, the opening speeches of Theocritus's Idyll 1. The different voicings in this exchange emerge less clearly in translation than in the Latin the young Frost read. But David Ferry's translation brings out what he would have responded to in the next speech, Meliboeus's response to Tityrus's account of his good fortune:

> It's not that I'm envious, but full of wonder.
> There's so much trouble everywhere these days.
> I was trying to drive my goats along the path
> And one of them I could hardly get to follow;
> Just now, among the hazels, she went into labor
> And then, right there on the hard flinty ground,
> Gave birth to twins who should have been our hope,
> Back on our farm.

Frost would have heard not only the colloquial element in these lines but their flexibility, the capacity for modulation evident when, at the end, the speaker's bitterness and sense of pathos intensify. Such modulations exist on a larger scale, one equally important for Frost. For all its apparent drama and realism, Eclogue 1 has equally characteristic moments of lyric expansiveness, like Meliboeus's celebration of Tityrus's rural bliss:

> Lucky old man! here by familiar streams
> And hallowed springs you'll seek out cooling shade.
> Here as always, the neighboring hedge, whose bees
> Feed on its flowering willows, will induce
> Your slumber soft with their sweet murmurings.
> The hillside pruner will serenade the air;
> Nor will the throaty pigeons, your dear care,
> Nor turtledoves cease moaning in the elms. (tr. Alpers)

The music that Tennyson heard in these lines—"the moan of doves in immemorial elms/ And murmuring of innumerable bees"—was not Frost's. But he emulated such eloquent moments in his own way. "The Death of the Hired Man" turns on lyrical heightening: "Part of a moon was falling down the west,/ Dragging the whole sky with it to the hills," etc. The minister of "The Black Cottage," reflecting on the way truths go in and out of favor, imagines a desert island where home truths could be preserved and is moved to eloquence and visionary description utterly unlike his garrulous speech or the poetry of the world in which he dwells.

The relation between dramatic and lyric elements is one of the central questions about eclogues. Even in Eclogue 1, which is as dramatic as Virgil gets in these poems, the best known passages are the lyrical expansions, which have something of the character of set pieces. Nowhere is this more evident than at the end of the poem, when Tityrus's invitation to supper opens out into lines in which, as Panofsky memorably said, Virgil discovered the evening (300):

> et iam summa procul villarum culmina fumant,
> maioresque cadunt altis de montibus umbrae.

> Already, in the distance, rooftops smoke,
> And lofty hills let fall their lengthening shade.   (tr. Alpers)

In Virgil the potential tension between lyric and dramatic is made stable by the underlying pastoral fiction—the shared situations in which herdsmen find themselves and their corresponding sense of shared losses and pleasures. So conceived, pastoral figures are responsive to each other's words and vulnerabilities ("Who would not sing for Lycidas, he knew/ Himself to sing"). This responsiveness is formalized in the social ritual of singing contests (Eclogues 3 and 7) and in the pairing of solo utterances that concern a shared plight, as in the matching love laments of Eclogue 8 and the symmetrical songs about the death of Daphnis in Eclogue 5. Even in the more dramatic eclogues, 1 and 9, the speeches are modulated and the poems shaped by the sense of responsive song.

How does the relation between lyric and dramatic play itself out in Frost's eclogues? If we come to them from the conventions and practices I have just sketched, his most Virgilian poem is "West-Running Brook." This dialogue between wife and husband consists mainly of the poems each improvises on the fact that the brook by which they find themselves, unlike all others in the neighborhood, runs west. The wife makes this contrary motion a metaphor of their love and of nature's responsiveness to it; the husband, resisting her fancifulness, makes it instead a symbol of the nature of human life, conceived as resistance to the obliterating rush of time. Whether or not Frost actually had the Virgilian model in mind, it certainly illuminates "West-Running Brook"—the balance between the two impromptu "poems," the set-piece nature of the husband's, and an ending which, as in many traditional eclogues, reconciles two disparate speakers. The wife first responds to the husband's grandiloquence:

> 'Today will be the day
> You said so.'
> 'No, today will be the day
> You said the brook was called West-running Brook.'
> 'Today will be the day of what we both said.'

It is not surprising that for the classicist Brower this is a "culminating poem" in Frost's work (188). But although many admire it and much as I would like to point to so strong an example of Virgil's modern presence, I find myself agreeing with Richard Poirier and William H. Pritchard that "West-Running Brook" is a flawed poem. Both argue, contra Brower, that it fails to integrate dramatic and lyric expression. Poirier, irritated to the point of scorn, says "there is a pretense of conflict" (222) and that the differentiated tones of speech are "broadly and fatuously obvious" (110). The justice of this critique is spelled out by Pritchard's observation that "having experienced the passionate speech of different female characters in *North of Boston*, [the] reader may be disappointed by the perfunctory and rather 'feminine' language given the wife in 'West-Running Brook'" (188). One sign of these inadequacies and of the "relative complacency" (Poirier 225) of the poem is the ending, which backs off from the most troubled aspects of the husband's speech and, in its tone of each making nice to the other, fails to convince us that their marriage is an example of what he says most defines the life men and women find in themselves—the "strange resistance" to "the universal cataract of death."

Lyric and dramatic expression are better integrated in "The Death of the Hired Man," the finest of Frost's eclogues that has a manifest relation to the Virgilian form. This poem has been so admired over the years that it has come to seem a known quantity, both in its style, representative of Frost's realistic dialogues, and its subject, which is taken to be the relation between husband and wife, the way they come to terms with each other in considering what to do about the hired man. But much of the poem is devoted to the hired man himself and his life, and if we think of it as an eclogue, it is a pastoral elegy. In the traditional pastoral elegy, herdsmen come together to memorialize one of their number; their laments for and celebrations of the dead herdsman enable them to absorb their loss and confirm the sense of community that has brought them together. "The Death of the Hired Man" brilliantly accommodates this model to Frost's sense of rural and domestic drama. Instead of two speakers finding appropriate speech to memorialize a dead shepherd (the model Yeats followed), Frost's husband and wife negotiate appropriate ways of representing Silas and his impending death. Indeed, putting it this way is too simple, for the status of "the death of the hired man" changes in the course of the poem and determines the way it is shaped. At the beginning, Silas has simply returned to the farm, looking for work or a handout. The initial drama is the disagreement about what to do with him—Mary's concern for the old man resisting Warren's insistence on sending him on his way. Silas's impending death only emerges in the middle of the poem, in its best known passage—the narrator's representation of the moonlight and the tenderness of the night and the alternative definitions of "home" that are prompted by Mary's, "Warren, he has come home to die." The poem moves from the initial realistic conflict to this lyrical center by means of an anecdote about Silas and a college-educated fellow worker. Mary introduces the story to convey the old man's weakened condition: he keeps running on about what happened years ago, almost as if "he was talking in his sleep." A dozen lines later, she says, "Those days trouble Silas like a dream." This turning his physical condition into a metaphor signals the way the dramatic tension between husband and wife has been suspended to provide, in the manner of a Virgilian set piece, space for remembering what the hired man was in his good days. This includes his country values, his conflicted solicitude for the college boy, and his skill as a worker—for Mary's anecdote prompts Warren's recollection, in a striking passage, of the way Silas built a load of hay. The point is not simply that these forty lines memorialize Silas, but that what happens between husband and wife, their recovery of mutual tenderness, is enabled by their recollection—which, because they think he is still alive, is a present recognition—of the third person who, willy nilly, is part of their life. The human capacities they find in themselves are thus of a piece with the poet's, just as, in the older pastoral, the poet's representation of herdsmen is a form of self-representation.

None of the other great *North of Boston* dialogues can be so directly associated with Virgilian eclogues. But our understanding of "Home Burial" is, I think, enhanced by viewing it from this perspective. Though this poem is intensely dramatic, its formal disposition owes something to the eclogue model. The drama at the beginning gives way to two long speeches—the husband's, trying to coax his wife back into a marital relation he thinks is reasonable, and then the wife's, first depicting the scenes of the burial, in which the man's actions and physical presence make him an offense to her, and then more and more extravagantly committing herself to an enduring grief. The poem is far more painful and tragic than seems possible for an eclogue. But its tragedy can be said to lie in the drastic failure of responsive, mutually sustaining speech—what older pastorals represent as implicit in, or at least available to, the dialogues of country people. There are of course other ways of representing the couple's inability to hear and find words for each other. Randall Jarrell's long account of the poem powerfully imagines the story implicit in it; Poirier shows the power with which it plays out the double meaning of the title (124–35); for Joseph Brodsky it embodies antagonistic powers of language (*Grief and Reason* 252–61). But thinking of the poem as a profoundly ironized eclogue helps us understand how its human truth is connected to its formal accomplishment—the range of expression in the speaking voices, the intensifying and summarizing effect of the descriptive vignettes, the dramaturgy of the whole. The eclogue model that "West-Running Brook" adapts too complacently underlies the poetic achievement of "Home Burial."

We now turn to two poets, the Anglo-Irish Louis MacNeice and the Hungarian Miklós Radnóti, who were born early in the twentieth century and emerged as consequential poets in the 1930s. Their eclogues have little in common, aside from the dialogue form itself, but for both the form, as Seamus Heaney said of MacNeice's, was "an enabling resource" (180).

Radnóti is best known in the English-speaking world as a poet of the Holocaust. When Germany invaded Hungary in order to impose the Final Solution on its recalcitrant ally, Radnóti, like other able-bodied men, was sent to a labor camp in occupied Serbia. He endured a long forced march after the camp was evacuated in late 1944, but finally, unable to go on, was shot and buried in a mass grave. When the grave was dug up, sixteen months later, his corpse was recovered and a notebook with ten poems was found in the pocket of his coat.[3] One of these poems, the much anthologized "Seventh Eclogue," would seem to be about as anti-pastoral as a poem could be. In the barracks at nightfall, surrounded by his sleeping fellow prisoners, assaulted by fleas, writing in darkness "blind, like an inchworm," the poet addresses his hopelessly faraway wife, while he, like "all of these tattered and feverish bodies," waits for a miracle.[4] Within the scope of this essay, I think the most useful way to present Radnóti is to explain how he could have called such a poem an eclogue and indeed, in the wretchedness of the Lager, have written yet another eclogue, more recognizable as such.

Radnóti began to write his eclogues in 1937, after being asked to contribute to a translation of Virgil's *Eclogues* by several hands. He would have embraced such an assignment both because of his conviction that Hungarian poetry, for all its linguistic distinctness and patriotic fervor, also was part of European poetry, and because some Hungarian modernists were committed to traditional meters and verse forms. (In "The Seventh Eclogue," when the poet cries out for home, wondering whether it is still as it was "when they marched us away," he asks, "Say, is there a country where someone still knows the hexameter?") In addition to these motives, Virgil's Ninth Eclogue, which he either chose or was assigned to translate, was the one that would most show him the possibilities of the eclogue as a contemporary form. Like Eclogue 1, this poem concerns the effects of civil war on the countryside; one of the interlocutors, like Meliboeus, has been thrown off his land, and other threats and dangers are more vaguely indicated. But now there is no assurance that anyone's life can go on as before; instead of the beneficent political power of Tityrus's "god" (1.6, clearly Octavian), there is only the hope that the master singer Menalcas will return to the world he has mysteriously left. As this suggests, Eclogue 9 concerns the power of poetry in circumstances in which ordinary citizens feel powerless, and what is impressive about the poem is that it does not present this question as simple or obvious. At the beginning of the poem, the young Lycidas, who had heard that Menalcas's songs had saved the countryside, is disabused by Moeris, his older companion. In the words of the most recent translator, Seamus Heaney:

> That's what you would have heard. But songs and tunes
> Can no more hold out against brute force than doves
> When eagles swoop.

But as the poem continues, a measure of poetry's power seems to be restored. As they walk to town, the two herdsmen recall songs by Menalcas and others, and the last of these, with its celebration of Julius Caesar and its pointed correction of the despair of Meliboeus in Eclogue 1,[5] seems to hold out some hope for the troubled situation in which it is sung. Yet this song, recalled by Lycidas, is followed by Moeris's expression, in the poem's most moving lines, of his failing powers:

> Time takes all we have away from us;
> I remember when I was a boy I used to sing
> Every long day of summer down to darkness,
> And now I am forgetting all my songs. (tr. Ferry)

None of the *Eclogues* better exemplifies the poise with which Virgil's pastoral mode registers felt possibilities and the considerations against them. The ambiguities of the poem carry through to the final lines, in which Moeris dissents from his companion's proposal that they keep singing as they walk:

> No more, my boy, let's do what must be done,
> We shall sing all the better when he [i.e. Menalcas] comes. (tr. Alpers)

We might take as a motto for Eclogue 9 Frost's lines about "The Oven Bird": "The bird would cease and be as other birds/ But that he knows in singing not to sing." This is not what Radnóti heard in the poem. What he emulates is the double shock at the beginning—the harsh dispossession of the tenant farmers and the dismaying possibility that Menalcas might have been killed. (The different register of Radnóti's poem is indicated by its stern Virgilian epigraph, which comes from the *Georgics*, not the *Eclogues*.)[6] A dialogue between Shepherd and Poet, "The First Eclogue" sets an ambiguous pastoral scene (emerging spring, which may revert to winter), which is disrupted first by news of the brutalities of the Spanish Civil War and then by the outrage of Garcia Lorca's murder and the pathos of the death (by suicide, though that is not specified in the poem) of the Hungarian poet, Attila József. The poem ends by directly addressing the question at the heart of Eclogue 9. The Shepherd asks, "And how do you live? does the age give an echo at all to your words?" The Poet replies:

> *In the thunder of gunfire? the burnt-out ruins? the desolate villages?*
> *Yet I write on, and live in the heart of this crazy world like*
> *the oak in the forest, knowing it is to be felled, with the cross*
> *of white that stands as a sign to the woodman, tomorrow*
> *to cut his wood there—yet it never stops putting out leaves till the end.*

Given its topicality, one might imagine that this eclogue, like Yeats's, would have been a one-time imitation. Instead, Radnóti returned to the form, after war broke out in Europe, as a way of expressing his commitment to poetry in the face of all that marginalized or threatened it. "The Second Eclogue" (1941) is a dialogue between "Pilot" and "Poet." The pilot, more independently imagined than the shepherd of "The First Eclogue," begins by representing the excitement of warfare in the skies. He then turns to the poet and asks, "Did you write since yesterday?" The poet replies:

> *Write—what else could I do? The poet writes, the cat*
> *will mew, dog howl and have his day, . . .*

This is a more ironic image of the poet doing what he has to do than the oak tree at the end of "The First Eclogue." Yet despite its self-mockery, the poet rises to an eloquent depiction of the insane destructiveness of bombing. When he then accuses the pilot of having become his machine, the pilot acknowledges that he has lost his ability to experience life on the ground: he is "an exile between the earth and sky." The strength of the poem lies in the representation of the pilot, the plausibility with which Radnóti imagines that this is what a man could become, and the corresponding modulation—consistent with his ironic self-image and with his emulation of Virgil—of his claim that the poet can speak truly for humanity.

These two eclogues set the terms for "The Fourth Eclogue" (1943), a dialogue between the Poet and an internal Voice, and "The Eighth Eclogue," written in the Lager, a dialogue between Poet and Prophet (the Old Testament prophet Nahum). This latter is an amazing poem. It speaks with increasing vehemence and authority of the outrages of human destructiveness, and it ends when the poet, feeling his life ebbing away, yields to the prophet, who nevertheless calls forth the life that is in him:

> *Take to the road, let us gather the people, call thy wife to thee,*
> *cut thee a staff, a companion unto the feet of the wanderer;*
> *give unto me a staff, even that one there that is knotted;*
> *that should be mine, for I love best the staff that is knotted.*

Touchingly reminiscent of Virgilian endings (Eclogues 5 and 9), these lines are Radnóti's final witness to what he found in the *Eclogues*—a representation of the plight of the poet and the enduring authority of the complaints he utters.

"The Seventh Eclogue" is so called because it too concerns the situation of the poet. As compared to the superficially similar "Letter to My Wife," the next poem written in the Lager, it is more impersonal and is centrally concerned, through experiencing his own and imagining his companions' dreaming, with the persistent, though enfeebled, life of the imagination. But unlike the dialogues we have examined, it does not represent the Poet or his situation in general terms. Its power as first person expression is more like that of the two monodies that preceded it in what Radnóti came to conceive as a book of eclogues. "The Fifth Eclogue" (1943, in memory of the poet György Bálint), imagines his friend's death as a forced laborer in Russia in terms that are more immediate and pained than similar passages in the dialogue eclogues. "The Third Eclogue" (1941), rather strikingly different from the others, brings out still more of what Radnóti found he could do with this form. Written as he embarked on a love affair, the poem invokes the pastoral muse at the beginning of each of its six sections. In the last three sections, the poet's passionate thought of his lover turns into an eloquent, perhaps overwrought, outcry at the impending doom of his world and his writing. But it is in the first three sections that we encounter a less familiar strength. "Be with me, pastoral muse, in this sleepy café in the city," the urban pastoral begins, and it proceeds to represent not only the natural world, as we find it in his other eclogues, but the lives of other men—fishermen in their boats and the salesmen and lawyers chattering and smoking in the café. This down to earth representation of others sharing his world was no doubt prompted by the self-irony one finds in the third section: "Be with me here! I just dropped in between teaching my classes/ to muse on the wings of the smoke about love and its miracles!" Among the several continuities (notably, love empowering the imagination) between this poem and "The Seventh Eclogue," none is more important than the poet's capacity, in the later poem, to represent his fellow prisoners and his likeness to them: "Snoring they fly, the poor captives, ragged and bald,/ from the blind crest of Serbia to the hidden heartland of home!" For all the extremity of the situation in which it was written, "The Seventh Eclogue" is so called because it is of a piece with what Radnóti found in Virgil—the poet's representation of "herdsmen" being interchangeable with his self-representation, because all are conceived under the aspect of a shared plight.

Like Radnóti, Louis MacNeice wrote with a sense of impending crisis in his society and doom in Europe, but in every other respect, turning to his poetry is like entering another world. Beleaguered personally and in his sense of national identity, Radnóti was able to reach out imaginatively to the poets of modern Europe and over time to Virgil and the prophet Nahum, and to write poems that convert real desperation into an idea of the Poet that transcends time and place and that represents something essential in humanity's idea of itself. MacNeice, coming from a world of privilege (his father was an Anglican bishop in Ireland, he took First Class honors in classics at Oxford) but never fully at home in either of his worlds, Ireland or England, found his way as a poet through constant attention, ranging from mordant irony to entertainingly performative listing, to the details and texture of his own and his family's life and of the world around him—the cities he lived in, domestic spaces, styles of living, social disparities and injustices. His poet is determinedly lower case and—to invoke the most pertinent heroic predecessor, whom Radnóti would have hailed as an ally and on whom MacNeice wrote an excellent book—distinctly post-

Yeatsian. Hence his eclogues are not only unlike Radnóti's and Frost's but cannot be usefully compared with them, except in such overall terms as I have sketched. But for just this reason, they show the "great possibilities" that MacNeice said he found in the form (Marsack 25).

MacNeice wrote four eclogues, rather strikingly unlike each other; he never intended them to be a separate volume, like *North of Boston* or the eclogue book for which Radnóti wrote a prefatory poem. In his autobiography, *The Strings are False*, he describes the first of these as the product of two sides of his inner life—his resistance to joining up with the English Communists, whose "hatred of the *status quo*" he shared, and the cozy domesticity, appealing but self-inhibiting, of his first marriage:

> During Christmas of 1933 Mariette performed her usual rites— the rustle of colored paper—and I sat down deliberately and wrote a long poem called *Eclogue for Christmas*. I wrote it with a kind of cold-blooded passion and when it was done it surprised me. Was I really as concerned as all that with the Decline of the West? Did I really feel so desperate? Apparently I did. Part of me must have been feeling like that for years. (146)

The poem MacNeice wrote is a dialogue between A, a town dweller, and B, who lives in the country. It is called an eclogue because of the dialogue form and because the interlocutors represent (in both senses) town and country. But the way MacNeice uses the form rather belies his account of the poem. There is certainly a sense of desperation in the face of cultural decline ("I meet you in an evil time," it begins). But by dividing its account of the way we live now between two self-mocking speakers and by maintaining, eclogue-wise, a formal balance between what each of them says, the poem distances itself from full or integrated first-person expression of the poet's ultimate concerns. It is not like those Renaissance eclogues in which a country person utters home truths to a courtier and can thus be thought to speak for the poet. Right at the outset, MacNeice's countryman says, "Analogue of me, you are wrong to turn to me,/ My country will not yield you any sanctuary," and the poem proceeds in its sardonic portrayal of two styles of privileged English life. What is impressive—and this is characteristic of traditional eclogues, with their representative herdsmen— is the way the speeches of A and B, with their knowing irony, are poised between public critique and troubled self-representation.

Of MacNeice's other eclogues, the last, "Eclogue from Iceland," also looks in two directions, public and private. In this poem, which first appeared in his and Auden's *Letters from Iceland* (1937), the poet's personal dilemmas are more explicitly put on the stage of the declining West. The two contemporary speakers, the English Craven (Auden) and the Irish Ryan (MacNeice) are joined by the ghost of the saga hero Grettir, whose wild vigor, archaic and anarchic, is an obscure call to moral firmness, and a "Voice from Europe," which issues temptations to self-indulgence. The longest of MacNeice's eclogues, the poem, to use one of its own phrases, is rather "maundering, meandering." But in its length, variety, and self-representational range, it looks forward to *Autumn Journal* (1939), MacNeice's most enduring poem (paradoxically, in a way, for its achievement is to capture the mood of a historical moment). In his preface to this book length poem, MacNeice called it "something half-way between the lyric and the didactic poem," and its many admirers have echoed the praise in Delmore Schwartz's review: "the circumference is always social and the center is always personal" (Marsack 32). "An Eclogue for Christmas" and "Eclogue from Iceland," both trying to represent a social and cultural situation with a poet's truthfulness, were clearly preparing MacNeice for the later poem.

Autumn Journal most obviously surpasses its predecessors in the way the fiction of a journal allows for a flexible, varying "I," who absorbs the first-person postures which in the eclogues are attached to separate speakers. But there is another way in which the eclogues were enabling experiments. One of the striking aspects of *An Eclogue for Christmas* is that the speakers' mordant self-irony sometimes leads to a more positive lyricism. A's ambiguous statement of allegiance to the city—"But yet there is beauty narcotic and deciduous/ In this vast organism grown out of us"—turns into the kind of urban poetry at which MacNeice was expert:

> On all the traffic-islands stand white globes like moons,
> The city's haze is clouded amber that purrs and croons,
> And tilting by the noble curve bus after tall bus comes
> With an osculation of yellow light, with a glory like chrysanthemums.

Similarly, in the eclogue-like ending, the two speakers joining to find a way to face their uncertainty, B concludes with a signature statement of MacNeice's lyric aesthetic: "Let all these so ephemeral things/ Be somehow permanent like the swallow's tangent wings." Such lyric moments and passages are important elements in the variegated discourse of *Autumn Journal*, and they were clearly part of what MacNeice understood the eclogue to offer as a poetic form. The second of these poems, "Eclogue by a Five-barred Gate," is a dialogue between Death and two shepherds, who, after a few gestures at rustic lingo, acknowledge that they are "of the Theocritean breed," and it concludes with each shepherd narrating a dream for Death's consideration. (This version of performing a song for a judge is MacNeice's most direct imitation of traditional eclogues.) The poem does not concern a public situation, but is rather a version of older poets' self-representation as herdsmen. The eclogue impersonally stages one of MacNeice's characteristic lyric modes—the detailing of quotidian life, in such a way as to convey both its involvements and its sense of waste—and thus serves as a form of authorial self-interrogation. Similarly, "Eclogue between the Motherless," the only other poem in this form, gives dramatic form to some of MacNeice's most personal themes (his failed marriage, his love affairs, and, in the rather anomalous title, the loss of his mother at an early age). Though there are no explicit set pieces, the form allows for a lyric fullness in the long speeches that anticipates the way MacNeice made autobiographical passages and moments of personal feeling compatible with the more reflective, satirical, and moralizing aspects of *Autumn Journal*.

If the traditional eclogue was an "enabling resource" for some modern poets, it is less clearly so for poets of the later twentieth century, whether or not we choose to call them post-modern. There is, to my knowledge, one eclogue book comparable, in intrinsic value and its importance in the poet's work, to Frost's and Radnóti's—the *IX Ecloghe* (1962) of the Italian poet Andrea Zanzotto. Turning to these poems after Radnóti and MacNeice is, for an American reader, like entering the poetic world of Stevens and Ashbery. Their central concern is the "I" of poetry—the "pronoun forever waiting to become noun" which will encompass "things worthy of an eclogue."[7] Virgil is continuously present in this project, as is clear from the prefatory poem, from which I have just quoted and which derives from two famous Virgilian beginnings (the *Aeneid* and Eclogue 4). Of the nine eclogues, four are monodies, two of them love poems with Virgilian intertexts. The five dialogues might seem to have a fairly attenuated relation to the traditional eclogue. Only two have ongoing and equal exchanges of speech, and the interlocutors of all five are simply *a* and *b*, except in Ecloga IV,

where an earthy Polyphemus emerges from Theocritus (Idyll 11) to re-
sist *a*'s talk of man as "phenomenological bubble." Yet each of these di-
alogues takes up, in post-modern terms, one of the main endeavors of
the Virgilian eclogue—to explore the capacities of poetry and, in par-
ticular, the way the divided voices of pastoral dialogue complicate the
status of the poetic first person and its relation to the social and phe-
nomenal world.

If we were to conclude this essay with Zanzotto, we would have be-
fore us three eclogue books (Frost's, Radnóti's, and Zanzotto's), which
among them "make new" three main endeavors of Virgil's *Eclogues*—
representing rural experience, seeking to assess and mitigate the harsh-
ness of political realities, and self-consciously staging questions about
the powers and limitations of poetry. To this conclusion, we could add
an attractive coda—a glance at the three eclogues (one a translation
of Virgil's Ninth) in Seamus Heaney's most recent volume, *Electric
Light*. Far from being a means of poetic exploration and self-discovery,
these eclogues are assured performances by a master poet, in a volume
that is often retrospective and elegiac. However one estimates them in
relation to Heaney's work, they are very interesting in the context of
this essay. "Glanmore Eclogue" is a surprising and witty version of the
Ninth Eclogue, the opposite of Radnóti's imitation. Written not from
within a historical crisis, but on the far side of it, it in effect imagines
that Menalcas returns to a countryside no longer torn by troubles and
asks what kind of singer he can now be. The interlocutors are Myles, a
local farmer, and the Poet, who is one of the outsiders who have taken
over the land—not forcefully, like Octavian's returning soldiers in Vir-
gil, but as part of the transformation of Ireland "with all this money
coming in/ And peace being talked up." As in Virgil, both speakers re-
call a master poet, a man of the countryside: "Glanmore Eclogue" most
directly cites Eclogue 9 in the lines recollecting his songs, just as two
of the remembered songs of Virgil's Menalcas are based on poems by
Theocritus. But Myles and the Poet are not anticipating this admired
singer's return. Their world has changed, and Myles states at the out-
set the question it puts to the poet: "You've landed on your feet./ If
you can't write now, when will you ever write?" (The Poet's implicit
answer is the Heaneyesque "summer song" with which the eclogue
ends.) It is hard not to see in all this an attractively ironic self-repre-
sentation, what we might call the Nobel Laureate bemused. The poem
recognizes the poet's good fortune, with gratitude as well as bemuse-
ment, but is willing to ask, by its difference from its Virgilian source,

what relation his poetry now has to the Irish troubles that once haunted his memory of persons and events. "Bann Valley Eclogue" has a similar relation to Virgil's Fourth Eclogue, the so-called "messianic" poem that for centuries was thought to have foreseen the birth of Christ and that is still famous as a pastoral in what Milton called "a higher mood." Writing at the end of the millennium and thinking of a child who is soon to be born, Heaney hopes to "sing/ Better times for her and her generation." He establishes a cannily belated relation to the Fourth Eclogue by turning Virgil's monody into a dialogue between Poet and Virgil, by putting the grandest lines in Virgil's mouth, and by ending with speeches that derive from what is often forgotten about Eclogue 4, its humorous and rural vein.

Because "Bann Valley Eclogue" is a millennial poem, it prompts us to put a question to some other recent poems: is the eclogue still an enabling form for poets writing in English? If it is, it is not so clearly the Virgilian form. We can take our cue from the 1990 volume of *The Best American Poetry*, for which the guest editor, Jorie Graham, selected two self-styled eclogues. Anthony Hecht's "Eclogue of the Shepherd and the Townie" is a debate poem, in which the first exchange, satiric and mutually mocking, is succeeded by the speakers' positive claims about what makes us human: this second exchange offers, for all its modest scale, competing *artes poeticae*. This immensely attractive poem, which derives "from such earlier practitioners as Virgil, Marvell, and Frost" (Hecht's note, Graham 247) could nicely round out this critical survey. But Robert Hass's "Berkeley Eclogue" is a quite different matter. This is an anecdotal poem, characteristic of Hass, in which a couple are represented in a charged situation. But here the narrator is continually interrupted by an internal voice, whose italicized words question poetic motives and choices and induce in the narrator an unusually clipped style. Compare some lines from "The Apple Trees at Olema" with the treatment of similar motifs in "Berkeley Eclogue" (both poems are in *Human Wishes*):

> *She is shaken by the raw, white, backlit flaring*
> *of the apple blossoms. He is exultant,*
> *as if some thing he felt were verified,*
> *and looks to her to mirror his response*
> *If it is afternoon, a thin moon of my own dismay*
> *fades like a scar in the sky to the east of them.*
>
> *("The Apple Trees at Olema")*

The nights were difficult.
No doors, no drama. The moon ached aimlessly.
Dogs in the morning had their dog masks on.
It did not seem good, the moths, the apples?
The gold meander in her long brown hair
cast one vote then, sinuous as wrists. He attended
to her earnestness as well—and the child liked breakfast.

"Berkeley Eclogue" seems to be a refracted, as if cubist, version of the other poem; it has the same relation to such other poems in *Human Wishes* as "Privilege of Being," where the poet imagines angels observing and feeling dismay at human love-making, or "Santa Barbara Road," with its coherently narrated scenes from family life. It is certainly a distinctive poem, but why call it an eclogue? Hass's note (Graham 247) mentions eclogues' "stylization in poetry of a certain dynamic of thinking through another voice or voices"; specifically the poem, consistent with one aspect of traditional eclogues, problematizes the poetic first person and its modes of representation and self-representation. One of its tricks, conceivably prompted by older eclogues, is shifting from third- to first-person narration, the "he" of an anecdote suddenly becoming "I." We might then say that "Berkeley Eclogue" gives a post-modern twist to the internal dialogue of Radnóti's Fourth Eclogue, in which "Poet" and "Voice" have the coherence of the persons or personifications of older eclogues. We might also think of Hass's poem as an American analogue of Zanzotto's eclogue project, with its roots in Virgil, Petrarch, and Leopardi.

It is the American quality of "Berkeley Eclogue" that directs us to eclogues that are more recent and of a different character from those we have discussed. Two sets of these go together—Joseph Brodsky's "Eclogue IV: Winter" and "Eclogue V: Summer" and Derek Walcott's "Italian Eclogues," written in memory of Brodsky. The work of both poets has extensive filiations with European poetry, but neither set of eclogues has the formal links and likenesses that indicate why the generic title has been adopted. In Brodsky's two poems, the poet's moods and self-discoveries are tied to and manifested by details of townscapes and natural life. The interaction of scene and sensibility is a hallmark of pastoral, as modern poets have understood it. But not all such poems count as pastoral, even when the term is loosely construed, and Brodsky's eclogues—in their length, concreteness, and proliferation of detail—strike a reader of English poetry as closer to eighteenth century georgics, like James Thomson's *The Seasons*. What most connects them to traditional eclogues is the thematics of humility.[8] This emerges in "Summer" in the representation of small, even grubby natural phenomena and the poet's witty humanizing of them. In "Winter" the emphasis is on natural life, including that of the human body, slowing down. This leads, in the poem's conclusion, to an explicit poetics:

> *Still, all the rivers*
> *are ice-locked. You can put on long johns and trousers,*
> *strap steel runners to boots with ropes and a piece of timber.*
> *Teeth, worn out by the tap dance of shivers,*
> *won't rattle because of fear. And the Muse's*
> *voice gains a reticent, private timbre.*
> *That's the birth of an eclogue.* (81)

"Eclogue IV: Winter" is dedicated to Derek Walcott, who may therefore have cast his memorial tribute as "Italian Eclogues." Formally these six poems are indistinguishable from most other poems in *The Bounty*: all but the title sequence are in blank verse (unrhymed, often hypermetric, pentameter or hexameter) and are roughly twenty lines long. Walcott's eclogues are entitled to their title because of their close relation to Brodsky's. They could take as their motto lines from "Eclogue IV: Winter": "From these signs alone one would compose a climate/ Or a landscape." Like Brodsky's eclogues, Walcott's represent various scenes and imagine the human presence(s) in them. The most important presence is Brodsky's, felt both in his poems, as they actually and potentially imagined Italy, and in the new fact of his death and absence. One of the finest things about "Italian Eclogues" is the way they weave into their texture some telling moments from "Eclogue IV: Winter"—the claim that "the North is the honest thing" and the concluding lines (which follow those just quoted):

> *Instead of the shepherd's signal,*
> *a lamp's flaring up. Cyrillic, while running witless*
> *on the pad as though to escape the captor,*
> *knows more of the future than the famous sibyl.*

In this respect, Walcott's poems are like older eclogues, in which herdsmen recall the songs of prior and absent masters and in effect bring them into the present gathering. One of the main motives of these poems is to join Brodsky with poets who have already shaped our sense of Italian scenes—Virgil, Horace, Ovid, Quasimodo, Montale, Auden. But this gathering of poets, though it recalls the thematics of pastoral, is dissociated from the basic representational convention, that poets are herdsmen. Though "Italian Eclogues" is an elegy, it is not an eclogue or a pastoral elegy in the sense that Yeats's "Shepherd and Goatherd" is.

At this point it looks as if time and what we may call the Americanization of Western poetry—a process embodied in the migrations of Brodsky and Walcott—has led to the disappearance of the (Virgilian) eclogue as a recognizable form. But no genre, it seems, ever wholly dies, and the question is left open by two recent eclogue books, both published in the last decade.

Frederick Turner's "Texas Eclogues" (the only poems so called in a volume of lyrics and lyric sequences entitled *Hadean Eclogues*) are the work of a transplanted Englishman who embraces his new landscape— which includes human constructions and detritus—as "the hadean arcadia of the twenty-first century." "An eclogue is a sort of picnic in words . . . and [these poems] are picnics beside the cavern mouth of Hades."[9] They are not all that picnic-like. What the reader finds is not Marie Antoinette on her *petite ferme*, but Wordsworthian engagements with "the landscape nobody wants." The six eclogues, all but one in blank verse (pentameter or hexameter) are conceived as "restless" journeys around and into the lakes, marshes, prairies, and thickets of "this disregarded Texas." The harsh details of these locales are registered with continual vividness and so make convincing the poet's sense of being "entangled" and "entrapped." Wordsworth's "Nutting" comes to mind, and Turner is like Wordsworth too in his vatic moments, which seem to me less convincing than the struggles through which he arrives at them. Turner calls his eclogues "eclectic" and says their "classicism" is neither European nor Western but derives from the poet's "conversations with shamans, living and dead, from every corner of the world." Accordingly, these poems have no formal likenesses to older eclogues. Given their project—to speak from the rawness of Texas with a voice of the new century—this would not be in the least surprising, were it not that Turner is the translator of Radnóti, who is one of his artistic heroes but whose Virgilianism has left no traces, either formal or thematic, on his own eclogues.

Just when we might be concluding that American modes of poetry distance themselves from the practices of the European past, a recognizably Virgilian eclogue book comes out of the Pacific Northwest. *XEclogue*, by the Canadian feminist Lisa Robertson, looks at first to be a more antagonistically ironic use of the form than the "town eclogues" of Lady Mary Wortley Montagu, which were, Robertson says, her introduction to the genre. The book consists, like Virgil's, of ten eclogues, but the unusual form of its title suggests "ex-eclogue" or "X-ing out the eclogue." Its polemic is against the way pastoral conventions represent women to themselves, and its project can be called an unwriting of pastoral. Stylistically, this unwriting (syntactically clear sentences, studded with semantic and imagistic oddities) is playful, occasionally hilarious, sometimes in your face. But its ostensibly plausible purpose—to break through pastoral representations to a (female) realm of nature—is thwarted by the dilemmas of representation itself (even nature must be mediated by language) and by a certain attachment, on the part of the book's female figures, to the older sense of themselves. An on-line review, by a male admirer of Robertson's work, asks whether she is "satirizing the pastoral form or trying to renew it" and complains that "the book gives mixed signals" (Friedlander). What puzzles the reviewer is, to my mind, precisely the book's accomplishment. Good pastoral writing has always been self-aware, capable of reflecting on and ironizing its enabling conventions. Robertson, we might say, ironizes conventional *anti*-pastoralism and does so by the practices of traditional eclogues. The authorial voice, which appears in prose "monodies" (sometimes polemical, sometimes descriptive) is frequently divided between the figures of "Nancy" and "Lady M," whose dialogues are the main means of questioning feminist versions of pastoral and playing them off against each other. (One of these eclogues is a deft and entertaining version of Virgil's First.) Their voices are augmented and complicated by a chorus of "Roaring Boys," whose quatrains—translations, infused by rock lyrics, of the *Pervigilium Veneris*—periodically represent Robertson's "shepherdesses" to themselves. There are no such choruses in Virgil, but this kind of enlarging the cast of characters is reminiscent of the way Renaissance pastoralists, both in printed eclogues and in pastoral dramas, discovered new possibilities in Virgilian eclogue.

Over half a century ago, William Empson, whose *Some Versions of Pastoral* is the profoundest consideration of its subject, justified the explanatory notes to his poems by rejecting "snob interest in poetry" ("That delicious thing old Uncle Virgil said, you remember"): "There is no longer the field of 'general knowledge' that old Uncle Virgil used to be in, because there are now more interesting things to know than anybody (or any poet) knows" (Empson 113). The *Aeneid*, so aware of the burdens of history and the cost of empire, will surely continue to be read, as the new century plays out the dismaying heritage of the last. The *Eclogues*, indeed, may fall by the wayside. But we may hope that these poems devoted to finding a voice in a shared plight or situation, however that plight is conceived, will continue to find readers and poets who make them new.

Notes

[1] Yeats's assertion is not as clear as I here suggest. He wrote, "I have to-day finished my poem about Robert, a pastoral, modelled on what Virgil wrote for some friend of his" (647). This would seem to refer to Eclogue 10, a metaphorical elegy for the poet Gallus, who is "dying" of love and who is represented as the poet's friend. But it is clear from "Shepherd and Goatherd" that Yeats's formal model is Virgil's unmetaphoric pastoral elegy, Eclogue 5. Eclogues 5 and 10 are frequently associated by critics and scholars, because both derive from Theocritus, Idyll 1, a lament for Daphnis.

[2] From an unpublished preface to an expanded *North of Boston* (Frost 849). For the original title and references, by Frost and others, to these poems as eclogues, see Pritchard 74-5, 89, 103.

[3] My knowledge of Radnóti and the information about him in this essay come mainly from George and Osváth.

[4] The translation I cite is *Foamy Sky*, tr. Osváth and Turner. I have also consulted *Complete Poetry*, tr. George. Radnóti's last two eclogues are numbered 7 and 8, though no Sixth Eclogue exists, for reasons scholars have been unable to discover or decide.

[5] Meliboeus's bitter line, *insere nunc, Meliboee, piros, pone ordine vitis* (Go graft your pear trees, Melibee, plant your vines!, 1.73) is echoed and given a hopeful turn in the last line of the quoted song celebrating the appearance of Caesar's star in the heavens: *insere, Daphni, piros: carpent tua poma nepotes* (Graft pear trees, Daphnis; your sons will pluck the fruits, 9.50).

[6] *Quippe ubi fas versum atque nefas: tot bella per orbem,/ tam multae scelerum facies* (For right and wrong are turned upside down; so many wars throughout the world, crimes in so many guises, *Georgic* 1.505-6).

[7] Zanzotto 147. This volume (Italian text, with facing translation) includes seven of the nine eclogues (1, 2, 3, 4, 5, 6, 9) and the "Epilogue," subtitled "Notes for an Eclogue," which in effect brings the total number to the Virgilian ten. The reader can find full texts of Eclogues 7 and 8, with an English translation, in Allen 223-7, 233-8.

[8] Brodsky discusses "Home Burial" as a Virgilian eclogue in the title essay of *On Grief and Reason* (esp. 234-6). But the Virgilian elements he discerns in Frost are not evident in his own eclogues. On the other hand, the epigraph of "Eclogue IV: Winter" is from Virgil's Fourth Eclogue, of which Brodsky's can be seen as an ironic reduction. Perhaps

that explains its number, because there are no eclogues 1, 2, or 3 in Brodsky's collected poems in either English or Russian. I am grateful to my colleague Robert Tracy for information about the Russian poems.

[9] These quotations are from Turner's preface, p. x, as is the last quotation in this paragraph, concerning the "classicism" of his eclogues.

Works Cited

Allen, Beverly. *Andrea Zanzotto: The Language of Beauty's Apprentice.* Berkeley: University of California Press, 1988.

Alpers, Paul. *What Is Pastoral?* Chicago: University of Chicago Press, 1996.

Alpers, Paul. *The Singer of the Eclogues: A Study of Virgilian Pastoral. With a New Translation of the Eclogues.* Berkeley: University of California Press, 1979.

Auden, W. H., and Louis MacNeice. *Letters from Iceland.* 1937. New York: Random House, 1965.

Brodsky, Joseph. *On Grief and Reason: Essays.* New York: Farrar Straus and Giroux, 1995.

—. *To Urania.* New York: Farrar, Straus & Giroux, 1988.

Brower, Reuben A. *The Poetry of Robert Frost: Constellations of Intention.* New York: Oxford University Press, 1963.

Empson, William. *The Complete Poems.* Ed. John Haffenden. London: Allen Lane, 2000.

Friedlander, Benjamin. "Nature and Culture: On Lisa Robertson's Xeclogue." 1995. Available: http://home.jps.net/~nada/xlogue.htm.

Frost, Robert. *Collected Poems, Prose, & Plays.* Eds. Richard Poirier and Mark Richardson. New York: The Library of America, 1995.

George, Emery. *The Poetry of Miklós Radnóti: A Comparative Study.* New York: Karz-Cohl, 1986.

Graham, Jorie, ed. *The Best American Poetry, 1990.* New York: Collier Books, 1990.

Grigson, Geoffrey, ed. *The Mint: A Miscellany of Literature, Art and Criticism.* Vol. 2. London: Routledge & Kegan Paul, 1948.

Halperin, David M. *Before Pastoral: Theocritus and the Ancient Tradition of Bucolic Poetry.* New Haven: Yale University Press, 1983.

Heaney, Seamus. *Electric Light.* New York: Farrar, Straus and Giroux, 2001.

—. *Preoccupations: Selected Prose, 1968-1978.* New York: Farrar, Straus & Giroux, 1980.

Jarrell, Randall. "Robert Frost's 'Home Burial.'" *The Third Book of Criticism*. New York: Farrar, Straus & Giroux, 1969. 191-231.

MacNeice, Louis. *Collected Poems*. Ed. E. R. Dodds. London: Faber & Faber, 1966.

—. *The Strings Are False: An Unfinished Autobiography*. Ed. E. R. Dodds. London: Faber & Faber, 1965.

Marsack, Robyn. *The Cave of Making: The Poetry of Louis Macneice*. Oxford: Clarendon Press, 1982.

Ozsváth, Zsuzsanna. *In the Footsteps of Orpheus: The Life and Times of Miklós Radnóti*. Bloomington: Indiana University Press, 2000.

Panofsky, Erwin. "*Et in Arcadia Ego*: Poussin and the Elegiac Tradition." *Meaning in the Visual Arts*. Garden City, NY: Anchor Books, 1955.

Poirier, Richard. *Robert Frost: The Work of Knowing*. New York: Oxford University Press, 1977.

Pritchard, William H. *Frost: A Literary Life Reconsidered*. New York: Oxford University Press, 1984.

Radnóti, Miklós. *The Complete Poetry*. Trans. Emery George. Ann Arbor, MI: Ardis, 1980.

—. *Foamy Sky*. Trans. Zsuzsanna Ozsváth and Frederick Turner. Princeton: Princeton University Press, 1992.

Robertson, Lisa. *XEclogue*. Vancouver: New Star Books, 1999.

Stallworthy, Jon. *Louis MacNeice*. New York: W. W. Norton, 1995.

Turner, Frederick. *Hadean Eclogues*. Ashland, OR: Story Line Press, 1999.

Virgil. *The Eclogues*. Trans. David Ferry. New York: Farrar, Straus and Giroux, 1999.

Walcott, Derek. *The Bounty*. New York: Farrar, Straus & Giroux, 1997.

Yeats, W. B. *The Collected Poems*. Macmillan, 1989. Ed. Richard J. Finneran. New York: Scribner Paperback Poetry, 1996.

—. *Letters*. Ed. Allan Wade. London: Rupert Hart-Davis, 1954.

Zanzotto, Andrea. *Selected Poetry*. Trans. Ruth Feldman and Brian Swann. Princeton: Princeton University Press, 1975.

John Tranter

Notes from the Late T'ang

for Jeremy Prynne

On the mountain of (heaped snow, boiled rice)
I met Tu Fu wearing a straw hat against the midday sun
distant bridge, restless parting, rain (in, on) the woods
[line missing]

willows among white clouds (shirt, chemise, ghost)
(to take the long view) parting
away moving, mobile telephone handset
[Bob: perhaps that's "grief at parting"]

my humble (borrowed, not inherited)
cottage (pig-sty) perspective
there is a misty view (of, from?) bridge
the storm took three layers of thatch, so

rain through the roof, porcine lucubrations
(something?) pig oil study
[Bob: "pig oil" can't be right]
burning the midnight oil in my study

phantom liberty, ghost freedom view
great ancient poet wrote for radio
(would have written) had he known
(subjunctive) radio receiver, milkmaid attitude

silkscreen pastoral, pants metaphor
looking back, sorrow (shopping) lady
parting (hair) long voyage
light and green woods, little pig woman

[Bob: I think that's "young swineherd girl"]
she questions (annoys) the lonely traveler
unfortunate view (of, from)
pig liquid telephone handset

Steve McCaffery

Some Versions of Pastoral

Preface

Et in Arcadia ergo points to everywhere. Semantic stability laid smooth across

its cyclic thin bone ridden epoch pages

of remainders.

It is the theorized ambrosia and all that's deaf against light

among the swamps of somewhere.

Chapter gathers gray   did I live in it? The fleece of the place

changing name to four-footed high-forehead country chin. The Pleistocene in discourse law of moulds surprised by the dash half-past Pan ideology ellipsoid fragments seen in the water as

Cuddy,

Mopsa

Blowzibelle ex-sensual

course to evolve through

etching sideways into the text material avalanche idyllic thought through bogs of dewlap steering a race to the tunnel shore.

Went into walking wearing eyes on the heart because splash
accumulation hints its history Against the helmets wards off war.
The thistle oval apertures a tree food glassed into morning.
Un detachment de la troupe sous le conduit de Monsieur Logique c'est arrive.

"And in such manner progression meadows Need's balm." The queen
here takes walks together.

Cart-paths hand Truth a palimpsest of leveled bridges versions of
pastoral

and the lightest possible stake in this: is speech. Comes round on the
road

      from reading

      etching spheres as continents then strolls with a flute into

      dialect

and signs it.

   I

             for Robert Stacey

When I awoke I saw sheep eating people, small children actually, on
an iron ground, executive summers populating landfills with a quote
beauty unquote turned to dust when written about.

That's it. For stanza one.

The man takes a walk from dictionary to landscape turns away in
Old French

      nothing happens.   Afraid of death Arcadia's withheld
'til stanza three.

2

Cloister my lady the mind's back

but psychologically speaking actually a parlor space with its pet dog
additive to sky line-top lit   room-tombs to the modern junque
tub at the age of seventy-five

Dulce est desipere in loco   coming via Horace as

the pleasantry of non-sense in
due place

3

Sunny black-eyed Susan with orange tongue and disappearing rail
tracks for your eyes
what a surprise melts the disproportionate esteem of dream-team
cupboard laundry thinks
a shirt needs dirt to really matter knows
the temperature a kidney melts at shuts the book
plumps turkey cook-mark snows
to make the park become a photograph by Manet signed by Blake

5

The bridge is a heaviness across itself the bridge must cross
                so not to choke   the river.

Eventually, Mom became late with supper, and Dad
made HIS appearance between Eleanor's dictatorship and Robert's
microsoft democracy.

The front lawn is where all the language stands in Bermuda shorts.

                But the sprinkler system   still remains unthought.

6

Sweet milk white snow
thy winter's in a pail

I have a night once called the tongue for rhymed quatrains the
station vacant from the stain.
And plantains too! sweetened by a legacy of transit-trust must in
the rigid wind stained, changed tympani regency of stars

banana baas.

7

Go figure it
the bearded man in a cup

ending it not until now

in a shroud-snow with the sheep

occurring in

the shepherds

8

Perhaps Paul Celan is the crematorium built especially for Language
Poets. Perhaps

no things but in ideas. Synaesthesia, the history of rhyme, the
geography of rhythm: a snowdrop offered to a sixth sense

and having signified Mount Monad changes

to a pledge, a promise not to dis-locate the hooves of that animal
whose origin names speed the pathos ad infinitum   in the Muse's
neck exalienated now inwardizing

across the negativity exposed by the slipper on the footnote

under the difference between an elasticity and a language.

A thing is a place in the touch of the world.

But all the hands are long gone here, in the orange sector

and should it not be posited it should not appear

in itself, as a face, a city's eyes, the pectoral episodes before being, the curl

in a kind of chance yet not random in its own interpretation of the execution.

"Imagine someone pointing to a spot in the iris in a face by Rembrandt and saying 'The walls in my room should be painted this color.'"

Eye into art even sense into language

the technique of the details suddenly a stop-gap calculation half-zoned between the finite and somebody else, not visible yet scalar and in geometry

a force flooding

all the transits to the promise of a different world than place

something less visual and yet vital

in arranging a sonorous life as speech and power its friendly fate concrete

as God is damaged and sanctified

in the metonymy named Auschwitz

almost a place to call cosmos in the short quartet of which there
never can be

a discussion.

Afterword

An hour through this clock is an absolute urban urge for a
sitting rung
voice to metaphor meat becoming scarves at a bullfight later belief as
power still lodged in familiar groups pretending night falls a
quadruped authority escritoire artillery follows years to pools where
sheep as relay in relaxing
stipend for genre
The luxury if arms where guns blow off comparison divisible as
unique find when sounds miss traffic
night drizzles out event by spot of big spit thing agronomized.

The second landscape:
cabbage blisters in a final ambiguity
community diggers ingesting disappearance
a doctor's note in faded Latin as the all-extending fossil calls up
object moment brick fails thinking penetrates the same unknown

Would you agree?

Led by consideration of a necessary principle of
retroactivity?
A scheme-bend altering the dominant?
Or is project simulacrum still the Eastern Star?
Sky coils completed actions writing words?
Mathematics in a folded cloth fed silence into chair?

No. Anatomy is Fauvist.
Seeds enervate then think.

Transposed umbrella to the negative space known as rip shore
sleet Asia calling
sulphur tendency to piss in exact streaks of virtue neurosis in a bottle
rack atelier composure to the opposite directiv
that I have sensed whenever the pizza comes a white wireless warms
the stove.

The Voice coughed then put itself in brackets
(Ate in Acadia Eggo?)

Mentality's the flat I've never moved from[.]

John Bull

From Illyria to Arcadia: Uses of Pastoral in Modern English Theater

In an early Howard Brenton play, *Revenge* (1969), the would-be super-villain, Hepple, and his gang take to the countryside in a vain attempt to escape the clutches of their arch enemy, Assistant Commissioner MacLeish. In a scene that consciously recalls Rosalind's meeting with Corin in the Forest of Arden in Shakespeare's *As You Like It,* they stumble across a comic cowhand complete with cow. Expecting the countryman's anticipated pastoral charity, Hepple, like Rosalind, appeals for food. On this occasion he learns not that "I am shepherd to another man," but that the only thing on offer is a "bit of bread":

> Hepple: Meat, meat, what about meat?
> Cowhand: That's a bit tricky. We not got a Sainsburys in the village.
> Hepple: But you're surrounded by meat.
> Cowhand: Ain't processed, is it. Maybe I could get you a tin of spam.
> Hepple: And a tin opener.

Already Hepple has expressed his unhappiness to his fellow gangster, Bung: "I hate the country. Listen to the bleeding birds twittering. Shut up, can't you? (*They don't.*). . . It's not my natural habitat and it's not yours, mate. We belong to the streets and pubs and back doors, and Leicester Square and the Elephant and Castle."[1]

This deliberate placement of the city as the preferred location for contemporary drama is, for all its caricature here, entirely typical of drama post the first new wave conventionally dated from the first production of John Osborne's Look Back in Anger of 1956, a play that is, itself, entirely rooted in urban experience. Where the occasional play by a new wave writer was given a rural location—Arnold Wesker's Roots (1959)[2] and David Rudkin's Afore Night Come (1962),[3] for example—the news was unremittingly bleak. The introductory stage direction to Wesker's play gives a good idea of what is in store, for there is nothing of the pastoral about the description of the cottage where the action will take place: "A rather ramshackle house in Norfolk where there is no water laid on, nor electricity, nor gas. Everything rambles and the furniture is cheap and old. If it is untidy, it is because there is a child in the house and few amenities so that the mother is too over-worked to take much care".[4] In an introductory note to the published text, the playwright emphasises the point about his depiction of rural life: "And though the picture I have drawn of them is a harsh one, yet still my tone is not of disgust . . . I am at one with these people—it is only that I am annoyed with them and myself." No pastoral counter, idyllic or otherwise, to the problematics of urban living is on offer.

Now, in part this insistent emphasis on the urban as the locale for evaluating the state of the nation is a direct reaction to the drama that had preceded the new wave. If Shakespeare's deployment of the pastoral model as both object of satire and as a vehicle for plot resolution had effectively signalled the end of the potential for a Renaissance version of the strain to be offered seriously, a new "Gentry" version of pastoral, centered on the country house, had already been emerging—from Marvell and from Jonson on, in particular—one that moved the emphasis away from the strictly courtly and towards the dreams and aspirations of the new contenders for political supremacy. It was to be a version of this that dominated just about all earlier twentieth century stage accounts of English rural life, and the continual conjuring with versions of the country house only served to reinforce the way in which, prior to the emergence of the successive new waves, the English theater had been hijacked by the interests of those audiences for whom the country-house served either as actual or—more usually—appropriate ideological location for their social status. Kenneth Tynan famously summarized the situation in 1954:

If you seek a tombstone, look about you; survey the peculiar nullity of our drama's prevalent *genre*, the Loamshire play. Its setting is a country house in what used to be called Loamshire but is now, as a heroic tribute to realism, sometimes called Berkshire. Except when somebody must sneeze, or be murdered, the sun invariably shines. The inhabitants belong to a social class derived partly from romantic novels and partly from the playwright's vision of the leisured life he will lead after the play is a success—this being the only effort of imagination he is called upon to make. Joys and sorrows are giggles and whimpers; the crash of denunciation dwindles into "Oh, stuff, Mummy!" and "Oh, really Daddy!" And so grim is the continuity of the thing that the foregoing paragraph might have been written at any time during the last thirty years.[5]

Tynan's invocation of the threat of "realism" is a telling one. As was argued in the "Introduction" to *The Penguin Book of Pastoral Verse*[6], it is when the tension between an interest in realism and the attempt to present an idyllic account of rural life is at its strongest that the model of a contemporaneous pastoral is most under strain. The single most characteristic feature of British drama from the end of the First World War to the mid-1950s was its commitment to an essentially unchanging sense of the social function of "serious" theater and of its appropriate dramatic forms. But if this perpetuation of a dramatic tradition had originally reflected accurately enough the dominant cultural concerns of its times, it was increasingly clear that it was not doing so post-1945. What was anyway already decodably nostalgic—a sighting of a past vision of England always just over an historical horizon—became ever more transparently unreal, connected neither with the realities of life for the class with which it was associated, nor even with its fantasies. Viewed with the advantage of historical hindsight, the theater "revolution" of the mid-1950s comes as no surprise. The earlier drama's resistance to change can be seen in its unwillingness, or inability, to adapt to internal cultural and political developments, and its matter was drawn largely from the environments of an identifiable audience, the drawing-rooms *et.al.* of the upper middle and professional classes.

Furthermore, what dynamism the theater then possessed derived entirely from the brilliance of its wit, the cleverness of its plot organization. It was inward-looking, self-obsessed, reflecting an insularity that was both class and geographically based. Its central concern was with questioning the details of a settled moral order—with the ruling classes of England securely at its center—and not with subjecting the very foundations of this moral order to examination.

The failure of the theater to respond to the challenge put it in an increasingly entrenched position. The attempt by such writers as Terence Rattigan to discuss larger social and moral issues was always doomed by the limitations of social locale imposed upon them by the established theater. The traditional audience was well satisfied with both the level and the narrowness of the debate—but this audience was looking evermore non-representative of the changing order of society. So, however complacently it might view the situation, a crisis point had been reached, and had the British theater not belatedly moved towards the articulation and analysis of a larger social *milieu* it would have reverted to the essentially irrelevant cultural role it played throughout most of the nineteenth century—and from which it was rescued by, amongst others, George Bernard Shaw, in the wake of the continental "revolution" usually associated with the influence of Ibsen.

However, the emergence of the new wave writers and subsequent further generations of playwrights did not, and could not, create a total break with the past. In what follows I want to consider two comparatively recent plays, David Edgar's *Pentecost* and Tom Stoppard's *Arcadia*, the products of two writers who represent diametrically opposed political positions. In these plays the historically rooted, and supposedly outmoded models of pastoral—the Shakespearean and the Gentry—are excitingly reanimated, though to very different ends. Pastoral's ability to conjure with worlds real and imagined, in the past, the present and the future allows the two writers to offer a vision of the world that takes us back to the Utopian roots of the kind.

In 1902 J. M. Barrie had resurrected an old model for his play *The Admirable Crichton*. Lord Loam, who is fixated with theoretical ideas of social equality, is landed with his family and servants on a desert island after a shipwreck. The social roles are reversed, with the servant, Crichton, assuming the role of governor; but, once rescued, everything returns to normal, and Loam, having Barrie have him learn through hard experience that social equality is a pipe dream, abandons his "foolish" ideas in a reactionary return to the status quo. It is a telling example. This particular pastoral model—society as it is; the retreat to an alternative, more innocent world; the return to the original society which is in someway made better—is a conservative one; it suggests a pattern of evolution within the original parameters of social structures rather than a possibility of "revolutionary" change.[7]

The obvious and inevitable parallel with Shakespeare's *The Tempest* (a play in which a set of characters are also landed on an island following a shipwreck in order to go through a process of moral reformation) might alert us to further connections; for what Barrie is doing is borrowing from a more general Shakespearean pastoral model. *Twelfth Night* is preceded by a shipwreck before the action opens in Illyria; and both *A Midsummer Night's Dream* and *As You Like It* have at their center an alternative pastoral world through which the major characters pass in order to emerge better and wiser people. With his deployment of the pastoral model of an alternative world, Shakespeare both uses and satirizes the conventions of the form, so that the narrative is happily resolved but many questions about the social fabric are left open; to the extent, indeed, that later dramatists found it extremely difficult to continue to play with this version of the pastoral model, a recognition that it was associated with an essentially court-dominated world that was looking increasingly less plausible.

It was the later *A Winter's Tale*, however, that really provided the structure for Barrie's play. In this play the baby princess Perdita is abandoned on the shores of Bohemia, a victim of the father's (King Leontes) obsessive conviction that her mother has been unfaithful to him. There she is brought up by shepherds who, knowing nothing of her origins, still seem startlingly unbothered by the fact that, whereas they speak in colloquial dialect, she speaks in a courtly blank verse appropriate to her social status. The parallel use of two distinct languages is mirrored by Shakespeare's use of two separate locations, the world of the corrupt court of Leontes' Sicily, and the alternative pastoral world of Bohemia through which many of the Sicilian characters will pass before returning home to spread a spirit of redemption and reconciliation that will allow, amongst other things, the reuniting of the King with his wife and daughter.

During the course of the pastoral retreat, Perdita, as Queen of the Feast, gives out flowers to Prince Florizel and a disguised Polixenes, refusing to pick carnations and gillyflowers (hybrids), "which some call nature's bastards." This allows Polixines the opportunity to give her a brief lecture on man's involvement in horticultural improvement, crossbreeding the "baser kind" and the "nobler race," in a transparent argument for a mixture of the two languages and all that they represent in terms of different class positions. Of course, the theory will not be supported by the practice in this play, and the narrative is resolved with both classes staying securely in their place.

Shakespeare's critique of the inherited conventions of the pastoral kind that he has inherited is lent further weight by a further anomaly. Quite deliberately, he has put the sites of the corrupt court and the alternative pastoral world the wrong way round. Sicily, which is an island, was the home of Theocritus, the father of pastoral poetry, whilst Bohemia had no obvious pastoral associations at that time and certainly no seacoast.

However, unlike the majority of Renaissance pastoral locations, Bohemia did have a physical existence, both in Shakespeare's time and subsequently. After a troubled history, it formed about two-thirds of what in 1993 become the Czech Republic, having been previously relieved of its autonomy, and assimilated into Czechoslovakia, in 1918 after the collapse of the Austro–Hungarian Empire. For nearly fifty years it had thus been a part of the Soviet Empire. Shortly after its most recent incarnation, David Edgar's play, *Pentecost,* opened at the Other Place, Stratford-Upon-Avon (12 October 1994). Set in the midst of the conflict following the collapse of the Russian Empire—not, perhaps, many miles from Sarajevo—the play is concerned with the implications and aftermath of the discovery in an old church of a painting of Christ's deposition that, if authenticated and more precisely dated, would significantly anticipate the "invention" of perspective in art in Italy. In the context of the play, this discovery of perspective has also more specifically contemporary significance, offering realism in place of idealism politically.

In the opening scene a local art curator, Gabriella, brings an English art historian to view her find, and to discuss the fact that its existence may necessitate an entire rewriting of art history.

> Gabriella: Because if I am right that painting with perspective even kind of painted before Giotto born, then I think I make pretty damn substantial finding here.

The art historian's skepticism arises in part, as Gabriella notes, from his inbuilt prejudice that something of such monumental importance should have occurred in a country that "make such botch of everything it touch." The response to her bitter retort is interesting:

> It's just basic British insularity. It's suddenly the papers are full of places one had vaguely thought to be made up. If not Slovenia, then certainly Slavonia. And then suddenly concentration camps start springing up all over pastoral Shakespearian locations.

With something of a shock we realize that we are, in fact, in what is essentially contemporary Bohemia, a Bohemia not of "alternative" shepherds but of bloody fighting, massacres, ethnic cleansing, and internment and torture camps. That this is not just a passing witticism on the part of Edgar (or of his character) is made evident at the end of this first scene when Gabriella asks why he has suddenly agreed to help her prove her case: "Because . . . because . . . This is Illyria, lady." This second reference to Shakespearean pastoral (in this case to *Twelfth Night*) is given further point when we belatedly realize that just as the two principal women in Shakespeare's Illyria, Olivia and Viola, have names that are virtually anagrammatic, so does our art historian, who is called Oliver.

At this point in the play the pastoral intrusions seem merely ironic. The blood bath of Eastern Europe hardly squares with the spirit of reconciliation invoked by Shakespeare. The narrative continues with arguments about the painting's provenance, the efficacy of restoration and the possibility of removing it to a museum to be venerated as a target for cultural tourism. Although we are always aware that there is a didactic debate going on, both dialogue and characterization conform to a broad model of naturalism. Towards the end of the first half of the play the church is suddenly broken into by a bunch of deliberately representative political refugees in search of asylum, and our sense of the presence of two languages on stage, the educated English of Oliver (the intruding Court figure) and the mixture of her own language and of an imperfectly learned American English of Gabriella (the native "shepherd"), is further disturbed by a whole host of different languages all competing for attention. It is a cacophony of language that clearly refers back to the biblical Tower of Babel, as is stressed by one of the quotations that precedes the published text: language as evidence of division, rendering communication and mutual understanding impossible—as if Perdita and her shepherd hosts not only spoke different languages but could not understand each other's.

The disputing assembly in the church is taken hostage by the refugees and forced to change clothes with them. It is a literal pastoral switch: "you should know—you are a different people now," the Palestinian refugee tells them; and the first half ends with an off-stage loudspeaker appealing to the hostages to come out. The second act opens with the beginning of a dialogue between the refugees and the hostages, intermingled with plans to escape and accounts of atrocities, the debate about the fate of the painting being interwoven with one about the fate of the intruders.

What follows is an extraordinary scene in which the surface naturalism of the play gives way to a dream-like sequence in which music and dance create a completely different mood. It is placed as the equivalent scene to that of the sheep-shearing feast in *The Winter's Tale*, and like it—although in a functionally quite different way—it offers hope for the future. More vision than reality, it conjures with the events of the day evoked by the play's title, Pentecost, when the apostles met together after the resurrection and spoke in tongues. However, these are not the tongues of Christian apostles, but of the various languages represented in the church, a church, furthermore, which has historically served many different functions, and which cannot be neatly tied to a Christian significance. A story is told that crosses language barriers, a story of suffering, torture and murder that leads to the possibility of an optimistic ending—mirrored in the painting on the wall—where belief in the existence of a common humanity might lead to a better world. In the published text translations are given after each speech, but these are there solely for the assistance of the actors, to guide them towards the gestural articulation of the various strands of the story in a way that will be decipherable not only for the characters on stage but for the audience in the theater:

> Tunu: Ithin anthimata, Rama saha Sita, thamange ratate gos hondin rajakamkela. [And so in the end Rama and Sita return to claim their kingdom and live happily for all eternity.]
> Yasmin: (*trying to be harsher than she feels.*) Oh yes, of course. And they live happily for ever afterwards.
> Oliver, *caught up in the story, whispers to* Gabriella.
> Oliver: Or, as we might more readily remember it: a God forbids his child the forest fruit . . . [8]

The specifically spiritual connotations of the sequence are given a more material substance not only by Edgar's appropriation of the name of the archangel Gabriel (who brought the news of the forthcoming birth in the Gospels) for Gabriella (who is given one of the final two words in the play, "Yearning?", followed by the American scholar's "Free"); but by the playwright's inclusion in the published text of the account of the Day of Pentecost from the *Acts of the Apostles*, an account that concludes, "And all that believed were together, and had all things in common; and sold their possessions and goods, and parted them to all men, as every man had need."

It is a vision that is specifically communist, but not by reference to the discarded ideologies of Stalinist and post-Stalinist state communism. Edgar's pastoral interlude allows him to think the impossible, with Pentecost replacing the image of the Tower of Babel, with a deployment of language that embraces hope rather than conflict. It is a use of pastoral that offers a potential hope of unity, and its invocation remains long in the consciousness after the inevitable storming of the church and a narrative resolution that offers a very different vision of the future, as one of continued strife and disunity. Thus, in this play, the thread of realism that leads to the shattering of the pastoral interlude means that there is a break with the Shakespearean pattern in a way that was not the case with Barrie's play: for, in Edgar's there is no return to an improved *status quo*. The material realities are consciously deployed to destroy a pastoral vision that was, in its careful staging, always seen as a kind of a dream of how things might be, a subversive account of an alternative world. Edgar thus insists on a simultaneous presentation of the pastoral vision at the center of his play, as both desirable and currently impossible. Instead of the "happy ending," in an impressive *coup de theater*, "there is a sudden explosion. . . Armed Commandos in black uniforms and balaclavas burst through a gaping hole that has appeared in the painting," and the harsh realities of political struggle break through the pastoral episode. Oliver, forcibly dressed as a refugee, no longer passing as a "courtier," is shot dead along with the other refugees. He is, significantly, the figure closest to the perspective of the English audience.

Tom Stoppard's *Arcadia* is almost contemporaneous with Edgar's play, having opened at the National Theater in London in April 1993. Stoppard's deployment of pastoral motifs in *Arcadia* is markedly less Shakespearean, and his choice of title takes us first to Sidney's pastoral work and, through that, to Penshurst where *Arcadia* was written, a country house alliable with that in which his own play is set. However, this being a Stoppard play, there are almost inevitably a number of Shakespearean allusions,[9] the most significant of which comes late in the play. However, at first a little contextualization is in order.

In *Arcadia*, Tom Stoppard's stance is completely opposed to that of Edgar, for now we are returned to England and to the model of the country house that allows the playwright to connect the past with the present. It opens in "a room on the garden front of a very large country house in Derbyshire in April 1809. Nowadays the house would be called a stately home."[10] A tutor, Septimus Hodge, is teaching his young charge, Thomasina Coverly, the daughter of the house's owners. She will turn out to be a mathematical genius, unfortunate enough to be living before the invention of the computer that would allow her to follow through her calculations to prove her thesis, "a truly wonderful method whereby all the forms of nature must give up their numerical secrets and draw themselves through number alone."[11] As is explained later the full implications of her theorizing both anticipate a mathematical model that allows the future to be constructed from the past, but also one that prefigures chaos theory: translated philosophically they embrace both determinism and free-will. At the beginning of the play she is more interested in having the mysteries of sexual attraction revealed to her, however—"Septimus, what is carnal embrace?"—and it is a theme that will assume greater importance as the play develops.

Sidley Park is about to be re-landscaped in the Gothic style by Richard Noakes, a man whose attributes are summed up early in the play by Septimus: "He puts himself forward as a gentleman, a philosopher of the picturesque, a visionary who can move mountains and cause lakes, but in the scheme of the garden he is as the serpent."[12] The tutor's casual reference to the Garden of Eden under threat from a Satan who is seen as a modern landscaper is an early reminder that the chosen location for the play will carry a large ideological payload: for it suggests a parallel threat to the continuity of a vision of England in which the country house is seen as the central organizing point both culturally and politically. It is a point picked up later by the lady of the house, Lady Croom, who argues against Noakes' desire to introduce irregularity as "one of the chiefest principles of the picturesque style." "But," she counters, "Sidley Park is already a picture, and a most amiable picture too. The slopes are green and gentle. The trees are companionably grouped at intervals that show them to advantage. The rill is a serpentine ribbon unwound from the lake peaceably contained on which the right amount of sheep are tastefully arranged—in short, it is nature as God intended, and I can say with the painter, *Et in Arcadia ego!*" Here I am in Arcadia."[13] It is important to note that the argument is not one that concerns rival versions of social reality. Lady Croom's carefully counted sheep are to be as aesthetically placed as the hermitage that Noakes will introduce to the garden.

In the second scene the action is confined to the same, essentially unaltered room, but we have now moved to the present day. The house is inhabited by the descendants of its nineteenth-century owners, who have as guests a garden historian, Hannah Jarvis, and a literary historian, Bernard Nightingale, intent on uncovering the possibly scandalous truth concerning the poet Lord Byron's visit one hundred and eighty years earlier, when the play had opened. The play subsequently moves between past and present until, in the final scene, the two sets of characters occupy the same space in simultaneously realized time zones, a coming together that is made the more significant as the contemporary figures are all dressed up in the same kind of Regency costumes as their nineteenth-century counterparts, fancy dress being *de rigeur* at the party. During the course of this final scene, Septimus and Thomasina's discussion about the validity of her mathematical theory is interrupted by Valentine (the contemporary scientific counterpart of Septimus) explaining to Hannah that the young girl with the aid of her tutor had stumbled across a discovery that was not only historically improbable but could not be tested without access to modern computers.

> Valentine: Whatever he thought he was doing to save the world with good English algebra it wasn't this!
> Hannah: Why? Because they didn't have calculators?
> Valentine: No. Yes. Because there's an order things can't happen in. You can't open a door till there's a house.
> Hannah: I thought that's what genius was.
> Valentine: Only for lunatics and poets.

Now, Valentine is here misquoting *Midsummer Night's Dream*. The passage comes from the beginning of the fifth act, immediately after the lovers have reappeared in court after the pastoral episode. Theseus casts doubt on the stories they have to tell about the past night, saying that such "antique fables" are the products of "the lunatic, the lover, and the poet," who are "of imagination all compact." He deals briefly with the madman, who is able to conjure up devils, and the lover, who "sees Helen's beauty in a brow of Egypt." before considering in far greater length the role of the poet (which must include not only Shakespeare but Stoppard in the context of his play) in the construction of such stories:

> *The poet's eye, in a fine frenzy, rolling,*
> *Doth glance from heaven to earth, from earth to heaven*

And as imagination bodies forth
The forms of things unknown, the poet's pen
Turns them to shapes, and gives to airy nothing
A local habitation, and a name.

In essence this is just what Stoppard is doing in *Arcadia*, giving a "local habitation" to an "airy nothing." The country-house becomes an idealized setting in which the playwright can conduct a debate about, among many other things, the continuity of a tradition of "English" cultural values in ways that relate to his work immediately prior and subsequent to this play, in particular *The Real Thing* (1982), *Hapgood* (1988) and *The Invention of Love* (1997).[14] Stoppard's play contains a central argument that seeks to establish that the past and present are inextricably linked. This obviously relies heavily on the way in which the twentieth-century characters attempt to reconstruct events in the house from the previous century, as well as the deliberate parallel pairings of characters in potential relationships. It is the set, however, that makes the largest case for continuity. Apparently the same, though differently named, tortoise remains on the desk in both periods and at the end of the second (twentieth century) scene the love-struck and desperately shy young man, Gus, offers a freshly picked apple to the object of his affections, Hannah. The apple—with all its associations of the fruit of the Tree of Knowledge picked in the Garden of Eden—remains on the desk as the third scene, back in the nineteenth century, opens.

For the depiction of the landscaped estate as one of pastoral perfection is both central to Stoppard's intent and continually brought into question by his characters. In scene two, Hannah rebuts Bernard as they look through the landscape gardener's drawings:

Bernard: Noakes . . . the painter?
Hannah: Landscape gardener. He'd do these books for his clients, as a sort of prospectus. Before and after, you see. This is how it all looked until, say 1810—smooth, undulating, serpentine—open water, clumps of trees, classical boat-house.
Bernard: Lovely. The real England.
Hannah: You can stop being silly now, Bernard. English landscape was invented by gardeners imitating foreign painters who were evoking classical authors. The whole thing was brought home in the luggage from the grand tour. Here, look—Capability Brown

doing Claude, who was doing Virgil. Arcadia! And here, superimposed by Richard Noakes, untamed nature in the style of Salvator Rosa. It's the Gothic novel expressed in landscape.[15]

Hannah's explanation is almost immediately somewhat qualified, however, as she goes on to talk of the changes in the garden as representing the shift from the Enlightenment to Romanticism (the under-current in the discussion being that she believes in the supremacy of reason, where Bernard puts his trust in passion):

> There's an engraving of Sidley Park in 1730 that makes you want to weep. Paradise in the age of reason. By 1760 everything had gone—the topiary, pools and terraces, fountains, an avenue of limes—the whole sublime geometry was ploughed under by Capability Brown. The grass went from the doorstep to the horizon and the best box hedge in Derbyshire was dug up for the ha-ha so that the fools could pretend they were living in God's countryside. And then Richard Noakes came in to bring God up to date. By the time he'd finished it looked like this (*the sketch book*). The decline from thinking to feeling, you see.[16]

Her use of "Paradise" and the reference to "God's countryside" are slippery terms. What she has demonstrated in her account is that no single version of the garden can claim to be the ideal, the real Arcadia, the Garden of Eden configured in the English shires. The history of landscaping, like that of the pastoral itself, is one of continual nostalgia, in which the present owners can always look back, like their counterparts—the sad shepherd, Roland, in Drayton's Pastorals, for example—to a time when things were supposedly really perfect: a reaction made the more problematic in that the main thing to be seen when looking back is a further set of sad shepherds, or their equivalents, looking still further back—Drayton's Roland to the "Golden Age" of Spenser, whose eclogues are peopled by shepherds who are again looking back nostalgically.

What is important for Stoppard, then, is not the establishment of a single perfect pastoral moment but a tracing of the links between the various stages of what he can still construct as an English Arcadia. It is the third figure, the lover, from Theseus's list, omitted by Valentine, who is the most important in Stoppard's construction of this quasi-pastoral model; and the omission only serves to highlight the point. The lover is the key figure in this play in the battle between freewill and determinism that has preoccupied Stoppard throughout his entire writing career. "Stoppard's suspicion of logical constructs is predicated on a belief in the supremacy of the individual and the particular over the determined and the enforced; his fascination with them comes from his firm sense that there must be order for the aspirations of the individual to flourish."[17] At the beginning of the final scene, Stoppard has Chloe, the young daughter of the household, spell out to Valentine the connection between the mathematical model and life. She first rehearses the settled model:

> Chloe: The future is all programmed like a computer—that's a proper theory, isn't it?
> Valentine: The deterministic universe, yes.
> Chloe: Right. Because everything including us is just a lot of atoms bouncing off each other like billiard balls.
> Valentine: Yes. There was someone, forget his name, 1820s, who pointed out that from Newton's laws you could predict everything to come—I mean you'd need a computer as big as the universe, but the formula would exist.

But, as Chloe immediately points out "it doesn't work," and not just because as Valentine argues "the maths is different."

> Chloe: No, it's all because of sex.
> Valentine: Really?
> Chloe: That's what I think. The universe is deterministic all right, just like Newton said, I mean it's trying to be, but the only thing going wrong is people fancying people who aren't supposed to be part of the plan.
> Valentine: Ah. The attraction that Newton left out. All the way back to the apple in the garden. Yes.[18]

The "apple in the garden" (present in material form on the desk) is both Newton's and that of the Garden of Eden, the original pastoral location in Christian mythology. The link between the original Garden and the unseen and changing one of Sidley Park allows Stoppard to establish a continuity that both constructs the country-house as an abiding center of *social* organization (functioning as the very antithesis of Cotta's Villa in Pope's "Epistle to Burlington," for example) and allows for the exercise of *individual* free will and non-determinism through the always available decision to eat of the fruit of the tree that is both that of knowledge and Eros. That the dominant pastoral model used is that of the Gentry country-house tradition bringing with it an inevitable strain of class privilege helps to stress the essentially non-egalitarian nature of Stoppard's pastoral vision, in stark contrast to that of Edgar, which is precisely concerned to look prophetically towards a united world. In 1979, Stoppard declared, "I'm a conservative with a small c. I'm a conservative in politics, literature, education and theater."[19] This conservatism—and his particular deployment of pastoral motifs—is rooted in a sense of tradition that predates modern *laissez-faire* capitalism, hence the replaying of earlier history, and places the emphasis on the exceptional individual, rather than on the rights of the masses.

What this comparison between *Pentecost* and *Arcadia* points to is the ability of the pastoral tradition to reassert itself in what is the most apparently barren ground. What it best illustrates is its continuing potential to adapt to such divergent political programs. That two of the most important English playwrights of their generation should draw upon strands of the pastoral in the construction of what in the opinion of many critics are their best plays to date might also cause some qualification to be made to the confident conclusion of John Barrell and myself in 1974:

> The Pastoral vision might still have some life elsewhere—in the Third World, or in North America perhaps—where there are still occasional frontiers to confront the regulating effect of urban development: but now and in England, the Pastoral, occasional twitches notwithstanding, is a lifeless form, of service only to decorate the shelves of tasteful cottages, "modernized to a high standard."[20]

The frontiers might need to be reconfigured in ways that are concerned less with the minutiae—idealized or not—of rural life, and concentrated more on the ideological potential of differing pastoral models to construct different ways of reading the past, the present and the future.

Notes

[1] Howard Brenton, *Revenge* (London: Eye Methuen, 1970).

[2] Arnold Wesker, *Roots* (Harmondsworth: Penguin, 1959).

[3] David Rudkin, *Afore Night Come*, in *New English Dramatists* 7 (Harmondsworth: Penguin, 1963).

[4] *Roots*, p.15.

[5] Kenneth Tynan, *Curtains* (London: Longman, 1964): pp.83-4.

[6] (ed.) John Barrell and John Bull, *The Penguin Book of English Pastoral Verse* (London: Allen Lane, 1974): 7.

[7] Interestingly, a variant on this pastoral model was used by Barrie in his very next stage play, *Peter Pan* (1904).

[8] David Edgar, *Pentecost* (London: Nick Hern Books, 1994): 88.

[9] On this, see Jill Levenson, "Stoppard's Shakespeare: textual revisions," in (ed.) Katherine Kelly, *The Cambridge Companion to Tom Stoppard* (Cambridge: Cambridge University Press, 2001): 154-70.

[10] Tom Stoppard, *Arcadia* (London: Faber and Faber, 1993): 1.

[11] *Ibid.*, p.43.

[22] *Ibid.*, p.4.

[13] *Ibid.*, p.12

[14] See John Bull, "Tom Stoppard: Open to the Public," in *Stage Right: Crisis and Recovery in Contemporary British Mainstream Theater* (Basingstoke: Macmillan, 1994: 192-206) for a more detailed consideration of the attempt by Stoppard to construct a contemporary model of an essentially nostalgic, pastoral even, English culture.

[15] *Arcadia*, p.25.

[16] *Ibid.*, p.27.

[17] John Bull, "Tom Stoppard and Politics," in *The Cambridge Companion to Tom Stoppard*, p.136.

[18] *Arcadia*, pp.73-4.

[19] (ed.) Paul Delaney, *Stoppard in Conversation* (Ann Arbor: University of Michigan Press, 1994): 133.

[20] *The Penguin Book of English Pastoral Verse*, p.433.

William Herbert

The Pastorauling Parole: Scottish Pastoral

One of the received notions about Scottish poetry is that it is predominantly in the pastoral mode. Our notional national poet is the ploughman bard, Robert Burns, and his output would seem to be limited to a rural focus: "Tam o' Shanter," "To a Mouse," "Comin' Through the Rye." His distinctive language, Scots dialect, was described as the "Doric" to indicate its relative lack of sophistication and implied suitability for such subjects. A second glance (and who gives us that?) might take in our more complex relationship with the pastoral without essentially disturbing this impression: the georgic prologues to certain books of Gavin Douglas' *Eneados*; James Thomson's sometimes bucolic *Seasons*; James Hogg's depiction as the "Ettrick Shepherd"—even Hugh MacDiarmid's oeuvre with its predominant concentration on the small "touns" and islands at the hearts of farming and fishing communities: Langholm, Montrose, Whalsay, Biggar. But what a closer study of Scottish literature reveals is that the pastoral has always been just one component in an energetic and ongoing cultural antiszyszygy (to employ one of MacDiarmid's favored pieces of jargon)—with the urban, or with the London-centric viewpoint—and, throughout its long history, the effects of this agon have been transformative.

So we have the Douglas prologues, with their vivid sixteenth-century country scenes, but they are in trans-cultural dialogue with the first translation of Virgil into any form of English (and, at least in Pound's opinion, one of the best). So we have Thomson's *Seasons*, a "British" bestseller when that political entity was new, but its elegant *paysages* are closely tied in with Enlightenment concepts of the sublime, and were—since Thomson abandoned the Scots language for his own particular brand of English—an acceptable influence in Wordsworth's terms on his own notions of the "true language" (and landscapes) "of men." So, too, Hogg's persona of the "Ettrick Shepherd" must be set against the urbane figure of "Christopher North" (John Wilson) in the *Noctes Ambrosianae:* the author of that extraordinary (and narratorially experimental) book, *Confessions of a Justified Sinner,* being patronized by Edinburgh's pan loaf and rather sub-Wordsworthian professor. Similar complications affect our reading of MacDiarmid, whose mastery of pastoral terminology in the Lallans of *Sangschaw* was driven by a desire to match the linguistic experiments of Khlebnikov and Russian Futurism; and whose exploration of what he claimed to be the Scottish psyche in *A Drunk Man Looks at the Thistle* was inspired more by Dostoevsky than Galt—less *Annals of the Parish,* more *The* (village) *Idiot.*

And so, to return to Burns, we must recast this archetypal Scottish poet less as a gifted tcheuchter and more as an autididact whose large library was packed with European literature. The small-holding farmer in Ayrshire and latterly Dumfriesshire was trying to continue the linguistic and formal experiments of the Edinburgh poets Allan Ramsay and Robert Fergusson, producing a radical yet populist poetry for a well-read nation, re-imagining its literary tradition at a time when it appeared in danger of being subsumed into an English literature that would ignore and belittle it. The subsequent danger has become that discerned by MacDiarmid in *A Drunk Man:* "No" wan in fifty kens a wurd Burns wrote/But misapplied is a "body's property . . ."—that of Scottish literature being subsumed into Burns: Carlyle's "Hero as Man of Letters" being the only acknowledged representative of our culture. For that reason, Burns plays a ghostly role in this essay: like Hamlet's father, he is a "worthy pioneer," beneath or behind the argument in order to give space to other authors.

Scottish pastoral is deeply involved with Scottish literature's perceived role as a kind of bumpkinish by-product of the English canon: a by-culture. In response to this limiting definition of it as engaged in a one-sided eclogue with English, it has produced a series of critiques and transgressive testings of the pastoral mode itself. It has been engaged for centuries now in a species of "pastorauling"—that self-conscious dressing up as shepherds and shepherdesses we find throughout Western culture whether in Shakespeare's *As You Like It*, Mozart's *Il re pastore*, or in the affectations of the French court at Versaille before the Revolution. But, in the Scottish case, some of those who explore the roles and language of pastoral may themselves be, like Burns, from poor rural backgrounds: they are playing at being themselves. Or, as with John Davidson, we find a poet writing from an indigent but defiantly urban context, subverting the role of the privileged Spenserian pastoralist. In this essay I will examine some of the different forms this transgressive notion of the pastoral has taken from pre-Reformation Scotland to the post-modern era.

It is a paradox that one of the most distinctive pieces of pastoral writing by a Scottish poet, the "Monologue Recreative" in *The Complaynt of Scotlande*, should be in prose. And this becomes doubly paradoxical when we consider that this mid-sixteenth-century text is virtually the only substantial prose work extant in Middle Scots—or any Scots. And yet its author, Robert Wedderburn (who also wrote a proto-Reformation songbook, *The Gude and Godlie Ballates* with his brother John), is a highly paradoxical figure.

It is known that he "took assurance" of the English who invaded Dundee in 1547, meaning that he, like many thousands of Scots during Henry VIII's "Rough Wooing," was obliged to swear some degree of loyalty to England—and yet the *Complaynt* is one of the most sustained pieces of anti-English rhetoric in a literature not over-fond of Southerners: "there is nocht tua nations vndir the firmament that ar mair contrar and different fra vthirs nor is inglis men and scottis men . . ." The fact that they burned his house whilst retreating from Dundee—despite their claims to protect the city—couldn't have endeared them.

It is also known that he shared some of the pro-Lutheran sentiments of his two brothers, both of whom had to flee the country and that ruthless prelate, Cardinal Beaton. Robert was among those fined for destroying images in the town's monasteries in 1543. And yet the chapter reproving the church for misdeeds and corruption is the mildest in the book. However, in the few copies remaining from the first edition, it is evident that this chapter replaces an earlier version. It is a reasonable conjecture that his betrayal by the English had a spiritual as well as a practical aspect: the English officer in charge of the garrison at Dundee, Sir Andrew Dudley, wrote to his superior requesting, "a good preacher and good books, for they desire it much here, and I think it would do more good than the fire and sword."

The realization that the English were using religion as a tool of subjugation may have brought on either a reaffirmation of Wedderburn's Catholicism, or a sudden grasp of *realpolitik*. Perhaps the expunged chapter had been as blistering as the rest of this angry masterpiece. Whichever, within two years of the *Complaynt's* publication in 1549, and presumably not hindered by its religious orthodoxy, he became Vicar of Dundee. And the section of the *Complaynt* which interests us here, the "Monologue," was added to at the same time as that suspicious chapter was removed: it would therefore appear to represent the pastoral as a retreat from or bulwark against spiritual and temporal crisis.

Although the literary model for the *Complaynt* proper is, as Douglas Dunn points out, Alain Chartier's *Quadrilogue Invectif*, an example of fifteenth-century French prose's rhetorical capabilities, the model for the "Monologue" is more obviously poetic, and may be more native. Its structure follows that of the most popular and flexible of medieval forms, the dream vision. The "actor" is exhausted by his initial labors, or as he more graphically puts it:

> The solist ande attentiue laubirs that I tuke to vrit thir passages befor rehersit, gart al my body be cum imbecile and verye, and my spreit be cum sopit in sadness, throucht the lang conteneuatione of studie, quhilk did fatigat my rason, and gart my membris be cum impotent.

He takes a refreshing walk, but is unable to stave off sleep long, and experiences the allegorical vision of Dame Scotia reproving her three sons, the three "estatis" of Nobility, Church and Commons, over their feebleness and mendacity at this time of national crisis.

> Before he falls asleep, however, the author lists with inappropriately tireless zeal the birds he hears, then reports a naval encounter which may or may not be an eyewitness account of military action on the Tay. Next follows the learned disquisition of a shepherd on the heavenly bodies, and a compendious catalogue of literary texts, songs and dances the shepherds recount or perform. Finally, "I maid me reddy to returne to the toune that I came fra," but before he does he has to mention another list of the herbs and

plants he walks through. After exhausting himself with such a fouth of facts, he falls asleep.

In effect, the "Monologue" is a kind of mini-encyclopaedia of mid-sixteenth century Scotland. It is a website on which many of the links are now inactive, but which we might imagine its first readers could have used to affirm and refresh their threatened sense of Scottishness. Scholars have indeed used the booklist to examine what texts were extant in Scotland at that time, and to speculate on works that only survive, if at all, in later editions. It may be nothing more than a catalogue of a portion of Wedderburn's library (or his wish list), and in that it anticipates the list of Burns' books, as well as his labors in gathering songs and (as with *The Gude and Godlie Ballates*) setting lyrics to music. It seeks to express a cultural totality.

But the lists of birds and plants also have specific antecedents and successors. This prologue to a political vision parallels the use of cataloguing in Gavin Douglas' prologues to his *Eneados*, a work circulating in manuscript form at the time. We know, for instance, that John Bellenden, the translator of that prominent historian (and Dundonian), Hector Boece, had a copy. Whether Wedderburn had a look or not, the parallels are intriguing.

Wedderburn was educated at St Leonards College, St Andrews, which was founded by Alexander Stewart, illegitimate son of James IV and pupil of Erasmus. Under Gawin Logie's principalship, it was a hothouse of humanist theory and radical theological speculation. The section about the creatures encountered by the author displays an extreme version of the humanist emphasis on rhetoric, in this case the principle of decorum: each bird is assigned a specific verb appropriate to its cry:

> the ropeen of the rauynis gart the crans crope, the huddit crauis cryit varrok varrok, quhen the suannis murnit, be cause the gray goul mau pronosticat ane storme. the turtil began for to greit, quhen the cuschet 3oulit. the titlene follouit the goilk, ande gart hyr sing guk guk. the dou croutit hyr sad sang that soundit lyik sorrou. robeen and the litil vran var hamely in vyntir. the iargolyne of the suallou gart the iay iangil. than the maueis maid myrtht, for to mok the merle. the lauerok maid melody vp hie in the skyis. the nychtingal al the nycht sang sueit notis. the tuechitis cryit theuis nek, quhen the piettis clattrit. the garruling of the stirlene gart the sparrou cheip. the lyntquhit sang cuntirpoint

quhen the os3il 3elpit. the grene serene sang sueit, quhen the
gold spynk chantit. the rede schank cryit my fut my fut, & the
oxee cryit tueit. the herrons gaif ane vyild skrech as the kyl hed
bene in fyir, quhilk gart the quhapis for fleyitnes fle far fra hame.

The effect of this varied but relentless listing is to focus the reader in-
tently on the processes of language—an effect redoubled for the mod-
ern reader by the unfamiliarity of much of this language and the pecu-
liarities of the printing ("v" had to stand in for "w"). We leave the
environs of normal English, whether that be the spoken dialect of the
day or our own presumptions about natural speech, and visit instead a
vocabulary and attitude of mind separated by its own heightened con-
sciousness from general usage. The pastoral is here an artificial zone
constructed by and consisting of language, a rhetorical territory. Scots
may be peculiarly suited to such a definition of the pastoral, not be-
cause it is a rural idiom, but because it is an idiom as conscious of its
difference from English as it is of its borrowings from French and Latin.

That this cataloguing was in no way unusual is demonstrated by a
similar list in Gavin Douglas's Prologue to Book Twelve of his *Eneados*.
Its ultimate origin is, of course, Virgil's *Georgics*, I, where the birds' be-
havior presages a storm just like Wedderburn's "gray goul mau." A sim-
ilar feat of language is accomplished in Wedderburn's list of plants and
herbs, about which Murray comments: "One may suspect . . . that his
botany was rather book-knowledge than field work, as he includes in
his list several plants not native to Scotland or even Britain, as, for in-
stance, Anise seed, Cypress, coriander, and fennel and hyssop." It
might be rejoined that he has good authority for this, as Douglas, in
the same Prologue as above, not only includes a thirty line list of flow-
ers, but refers to grapes and olive trees, apparently growing in Scotland
in May. But these writers were combining vivid natural observation
with learning, which was, for them, just as vivid a part of the aesthetic
effect their catalogues were intended to secure. Such a list declared by
analogy that the remoteness of their nation put no check either on its
beauty or their knowledge. Sixteenth-century Scotland was, for Dou-
glas and Wedderburn, fully contiguous with the first century Naples of
Virgil—but only through the power of language.

This is most clearly demonstrated in the list of tales, songs and
dances. These are given an equivalence to his other lists by the device
of having the shepherds tell "ane gude tayl or fabil": in other words the
author claims to witness no distinction being drawn between print

("the meruellis of mandiueil") and performance (one song, "pastance vitht gude companye" is by Henry VIII, which is a curiously apolitical choice under the circumstances). The shepherds, those proper inhabitants of the pastoral realm, grant all texts equal status, and equal standing with the other catalogues.

These four sections—the bird and plant lists, the astronomical lecture, and the list of texts and songs—have far-reaching implications for any study of Scottish pastoral. They establish the peculiar continuity of this genre, which might be better described as a habitual return to old tropes, by writers not only historically distant from each other, but, in several cases, not apparently familiar with each other's work. The recurring influence, say, of Virgil's *Georgics* is attested to not only by Burns' famous endorsement (.". . . the best of Virgil . . ."), but by Priscilla Bawcutt's comments on Gavin Douglas: "Douglas not only imitated Virgil but learnt from him, and seems to have been the first to introduce the *Georgics* into the English poetic tradition. In this he anticipates Thomson, but seems not to have influenced him."

Someone Douglas certainly influenced was the young eighteenth-century poet Robert Fergusson, educated in Dundee and at St. Andrews. Not only did he plan at one point his own translation of the *Georgics*, but he was seen by his contemporaries as the natural successor to the sixteenth-century poets: Walter Ruddiman said after his early death that Fergusson "would have revived our antient Caledonian Poetry, of late so much neglected or despised . . ." and F. W. Freeman comments "Fergusson . . . with his friends and editors, whose projects similarly exhibited a blend of Latinism and vernacular poetry, helped keep alive the old Scottish Latinist culture of Johnston, Buchanan, Wedderburn and Leech, while promoting the genuinely classical vernacular of Douglas's *Aeneis*."

Wedderburn's pastoral ended with the author's return to "the toune that I cam fra, to proceid in the compiling of my beuk." This use of the pastoral, as a space set aside not only from the city, but from the intellectual labour of composition, finds a significant echo in Fergusson's poetry. He had depicted a conventional type of pastoral in "The Farmer's Ingle," where the authenticity of language (Fergusson had lived on his uncle's farm outside Aberdeen) is combined with a politically reactionary bucolic note derived from Thomson or Gray:

WHAN *gloming grey out o'er the welkin keeks,*
whan Batie ca's his owsen to the byre,

When Thrasher John, sair dung, his barn-door steeks,
And lusty lasses at the dighting tire:
What bangs fu' leal the e'enings coming cauld,
And gars snaw-tapit winter freeze in vain:
Gars dowie mortals look baith blyth and bauld,
Nor fley'd wi' a' the poortith o' the plain;
Begin my Muse, and chant in hamely strain.

The influence of this on the opening of Burns's "The Cotter's Saturday Night" is apparent, demonstrating that the technique of *imitatio* did not die out with Douglas and Wedderburn. Fergusson himself followed the model of Allan Ramsay's decorous pastorauling drama *The Gentle Shepherd* in "An Eclogue," though his adaptation of the form in "A Drink Eclogue," where shepherds are replaced by a trio of "Landlady," "Brandy," and "Whisky," shows the distinctly urban focus of his poetic. In two poems, "The Rising of the Session" and its companion piece "The Sitting of the Session," Fergusson uses Horatian references to the country retreat to satirize Edinburgh's legal world:

Tir'd o' the law, and a' its phrases,
The wylie writers, rich as Croesus,
Hurl frae the town in hackney chaises,
    For country cheer:
The powny that in spring-time grazes,
    Thrives a' the year.

There must have been an ironic contrast for Fergusson, who eked out a living copying legal documents, between these "writers, rich as Croesus," and himself—and of course, Horace, rich only in his benefactor, Maecenas—as he says, seeming to echo Johnson's famous remark, "What writer wadna gang as far as/He cou'd for bread." In "The Sitting of the Session," however, he turns the Horatian model on its head. Now the legal business of the city is conducted employing the terminology of the country:

Weel lo'es me o' you, business, now;
For ye'll weet mony a drouthy mou',
That's lang an eisning gane for you,
    Withouten fill
O' dribbles frae the gude brown cow,
    Or Highland gill.

The lawyers, as they fleece those "country fock" who come to them for "business" speak in bucolic Scots rather than anglicised legalese: "'Come, shaw's your gear; / Ae scabbit yew spills twenty flocks, / Ye's no be here.'" This is Fergusson's anti-pastoral, where, by bringing the serene language of his "Farmer's Ingle" into the law courts, he indicates their perversion of the natural justice dispensed by the likes of Wedderburn's shepherds. As with Wedderburn, it is in language that Fergusson locates the pastoral, and in the play of registers and rhetoric, the latinate and the dialectal, that he finds its energy. And this paradoxical placing of pastoral at the heart of urban experience, to indicate anomie and dislocation, is precisely the device deployed by that most neglected of nineteenth-century Scottish poets, John Davidson.

Arriving in London in 1889 with a trunk full of poems and plays (including his *Unhistorical Pastoral*), John Davidson had to adjust to a constantly-faltering career as a literary journalist, something his pugnacious but withdrawn temperament never acclimatized to. Almost from the start he was in a one-sided debate with Fleet Street, as the opening stanza of the first of his *Fleet Street Eclogues*, "New Year's Day," indicates:

This trade that we ply with the pen
Unworthy of heroes or men
Assorts ever less with my humour:
Mere tongues in the raiment of rumour,
We review and report and invent:
In drivel our virtue is spent.

His first volume, *In a Music Hall* (1891), had been practically ignored (Yeats thought its spirited rewritings of popular songs lacked "dimness" of all things), and his domineering father, an evangelical preacher, had dropped dead in the same year. Davidson's response to both events was the first series of his *Fleet Street Eclogues*, based partly on Spenser's *Shepherd's Calendar*, and partly, as he says in an interview in 1894, on reading a copy of Gibbon's *Decline and Fall* he inherited from his father.

There are two methods Davidson employs in his early poetry to declare his apartness from the London scene: one is his choice of genres and the manner in which he treats them; the other is his choice of language. He takes advantage of the *fin-de-siecle* fascination with foreign and minor forms to rework the ballad, rondeau and eclogue into his own idiosyncratic shapes, by applying them to outre or "unpoetic" subjects. Thus a rondeau in his first volume is cast as an epistle from an artist making a start in Grub Street to his wife, still at home. And thus we find journalists cast as figures in a Spenserian eclogue, where the disjunction between the genre and their situation matches that between the realities of their lives, and the aspirations by which they try to live them. In "St Swithin's Day" Menzies, having published and been damned, says, "Doubting of all things, disbelieving much / I come to him who sang the heavenly hymn . . ." and Brian's reply posits the pastoral as an almost spiritual resource in times of personal crisis: "Already you have cast aside the wrong, / And solace found in Spenser's noble song."

Not surprisingly, several of the characters are Scots, or have visited Scotland. Sandy and Menzies are named after Davidson's two young sons, and in the second eclogue it is with a characteristic irony that Menzies curses "the father who begot me poor," before complaining "Of uncouth nauseous vennels, smoky skies; / A chill and watery clime; a thrifty race . . ."—not without a certain note of nostalgia. There is a frequent use of Scots vocabulary and settings, which only emphasizes the sense of dislocation they feel. In "New Year's Day," Sandy refers to "the drumlie Thames," and the unfamiliar adjective must be set against the epithet of Spenser's "Epithalamion," "Sweet Thames," also re-examined thirty years later by Eliot. Menzies toasts the daisy ." . . in Highland style . . ." on "Good Friday," while in "Lammas" Sandy drinks an ." . . amber spirit that enshrines the heart / Of an old Lothian summer . . ."

The pastoral, as with Fergusson and Wedderburn, is defined as the excursion from a metropolis, and trips to and tales of Scotland abound. In these Scotland would appear to have been redefined and, whether the settings are urban or rural, is seen almost in its entirety as a pastoral zone. In "St Swithin's Day," Sandy recounts a visit to Glasgow with a sense of arcadian epiphany, "In Sauchiehall Street in the afternoon / I saw a lady walking all in black . . ." whose beauty inspires him to praise love above politics and religion. On "Midsummer Day" he gives an account of a trip to the glens as a child who ." . . only knew of tarnished trees, / And skies corroding vapours stain [sic] . . ." where, as a " . . belated faun . . ." he discovers love.

But, despite the success of Scots like J. M. Barrie, Davidson's pastoral is intellectually distinct from the untroubled pastoral world of the "kailyard" novel. In "Mayday" he puts a ballad into Menzies' mouth, "Of a lowland town, a lowland hill, / And a lowland woman's lot."

This turns out to be an exploration of the survival of folk traditions in an age "When railways hacked and scored the land," and the heroine is depicted as "The martyr of romance": "They found her on the green hill-side / At home, and sleeping fast / Her endless sleep . . ." And, in "Lammas," Ninian gives a long description of Edinburgh as a phenomenon that overwhelms the self, a theme Fergusson explored in "Auld Reekie," concluding, "Surely to strive to please and still to fail / Is to be wretched in the last degree . . ." The retreat from the urban, Davidson suggests, is short-lived and becoming rare if not momentary.

Davidson uses the Scot in London as a modern archetype of the placeless man, "The Man Forbid," uprooted from his native city but stifled in his adopted one: "Oh, for a northern blast to blow / These depths of air that cream and curdle!" In "St George's Day," he goes as far as to depict the crushing of such nationalist sentiment as a necessary tragedy, in which the most powerful unit must overcome the lesser: " . . . By bog and mount and fen, / No Saxon, Norman, Scot, or Celt / I find, but only Englishmen . . ." However much Davidson believed in this quasi-Nietzschean philosophy (which came to dominate his later poetry), the different journalists in Davidson's eclogues are able to present opposing points of view: Sandy sardonically replies to Basil's celebration of "merry" England:

Oh, now I see Fate's means and ends!
The Bruce and Wallace wight[s] I ken,
Who saved old Scotland from its friends,
Were mighty northern Englishmen.

Fleet Street Eclogues are an intriguing example of a proto-Modernist text in their self-conscious manipulation of genre. As with his predecessors, Davidson looks to language to underscore his points: his journalists constantly introduce tensions between their Spenserian register and its industrial referents, ("Where hawkers cry, where roar the cab and 'bus"). The social analysis of the eclogues, derived in part from Gibbon, seems at times to predict the collapse of cultural hierarchies. In "New Year's Day," there is a memorable image of the spread and influence of what we now term tabloid journalism: "Newspapers flap o'er the land, / And darken the face of the sky; / A covey of dragons, wide-vanned, / Circle-wise clanging, they fly." But Davidson is able to resolve these tensions in an encompassing theory of irony. As Sandy declares in "Queen Elizabeth's Day":

Anachronists! I rest on this,
Whoe'er may count it schism:
Mere by-blows are the world and we,
And time within eternity
A sheer anachronism.

As Fergusson was seen in relation to Burns, Davidson has sometimes been seen as Hugh MacDiarmid's strongest precursor. There is a significant distinction between their aesthetic viewpoints, however, encapsulated by Empson's comment, that marks the emergence of Modernism:

> The essential trick of the old pastoral, which was to imply a beautiful relation between rich and poor, was to make simple people express strong feeling (felt as the most universal subject, something fundamentally true about everybody) in learned and fashionable language (so that you wrote about the best subject in the best way) . . . This was not a process that you could explain in the course of writing pastoral; it was already shown by the clash between style and theme, and to make the clash work in the right way (not become funny) the writer must keep up a firm pretence that he was unconscious of this.

As we have seen, this is the pretence, which from the outset was stretched almost to breaking-point in Scottish pastoral, and yet was always grounded in reality. In Wedderburn's prose pastoral, a highly-learned disquisition on astronomy is made by "the prencipal scheiphard," and yet the shepherds are accurately described: "eueryie scheiphird hed ane horne spune in the lug of there bonet." In Fergusson, the lawyers bicker like farmers at a mart, yet always have recourse to their "proper" speech: "When scalding but and ben we see / *Pendente lite*." And Davidson's journalists, no matter how transported by their encounters with nature, are always aware of their actual situation: "God has no machine / For punching perfect worlds from cakes of chaos."

In MacDiarmid's work, there is at first a similar tension: the early lyrics, with their focus on the expressive power of a lost rural vocabulary, borrow extensively from Jamieson's *Dictionary of the Scots Language*, implying that the pastoral is above all a matter of recovered vocabulary. MacDiarmid goes as far as to assert, in "A Theory of Scots Letters," that the recovery of disused language can initiate a recovery of forgotten habits of thought, attempting a kind of linguistic resurrection of the psychology of pre-Union Scotland. Pastoral Scotland is posited as the dictionary itself. But there is a distinction here between theory and practice, in that MacDiarmid, initially, rarely drew attention to his practice. As he puts it in "To One Who Urges More Ambitious Flights": Here are ferlies nae yin sees / In a bensil o' a bleeze. These borrowings, as with later examples where MacDiarmid was accused of plagiarism, perhaps form a bridge between *imitatio* and modern forms like the found poem.

In the later poems, however, the artifice is confronted head-on: indeed, in *In Memoriam James Joyce* and *The Kind of Poetry I Want* it forms part of the subject-matter:

> [I] have spent many of my happiest busman's holidays
> In books like Leonard Bloomfield's Language,
> Happy as most men are with mountains and forest
> Among phonemes, tagmenes, taxemes,
> Relation-axis constructions,
> The phrasal sandhi-type and zero-anaphora . . .
> (What? Complaint that I should sing
> Of philological, literary and musical matters
> Rather than of daffodils and nightingales,
> Mountains, seas, stars and like properties? . . .)

Here MacDiarmid's explicit rejection of Romantic subject-matter would seem to align him far more easily with the heightened rhetorical artifice of Douglas and Wedderburn. The fact that his "poetry of fact" borrows not from Virgil but the *TLS* (essentially, from that strand of literary journalism which gave rise to the *Fleet Street Eclogues*) indicates the ground-shift which has occurred. For MacDiarmid, cultural authority has been in equal parts augmented and undermined by the modern media and by scientific methodology: for the first time since the Renaissance it seems possible for a poet to know (or, rather, sound like he knows) everything:

> Hence this hapax legomenon of a poem, this exercise
> In schlabone, bordatini, and prolonged scordatura,
> This divertissement philologique,
> This Wortspiel, this torch symphony,
> This "liberal education," this collection of fonds de tiroir,

This—even more than Kierkegaard's
"Frygt og Baeven"—"dialectical lyric,"
This rag-bag, this Loch Ness monster, this impact
Of the whole range of Weltliteratur on one man's brain,
In short, this "friar's job," as they say in Spain
Going back in kind
To the Eddic "Converse of Thor and the All-Wise Dwarf"
(Al-viss Mal, "Edda die lieden des Codex Regius," 120, I f)
Existing in its present MS form
Over five centuries before Shakespeare.
You remember it?

Of course we don't remember it, and we might venture a doubt that the supposed addressee, Joyce, would have heard of it either, but MacDiarmid's purpose here is to open his reader to the possibilities, not just of accessing such texts, but of considering this particular text as poetry. There seems a strong parallel here with the methodology of William Carlos Williams in *Paterson*, if not with Olson's theory of the open field: the text has become a pastoral space in which, as with Wedderburn, all forms of knowledge may be explored for aesthetic resonance. Even the borrowing of a prose tone from journalism and academic criticism seems part of the challenge: to extend our sphere of reference to meet the rapid expansions in and increasing availability of scholarly (and unscholarly) information, which has only increased in momentum since the late 1930s when this was written.

The uses to which this expanded prose tone and fact-obsessed late style were put are themselves strongly reminiscent of Wedderburn's original lists in the "Monologue Recreative." Not only are we treated to book lists and discussions of scientific theory, but in "Scotland Small?" MacDiarmid returns to the flower catalogue to present once again the analogy that the variety of our flora indicates the diversity of our culture:

Sitting there and resting and gazing round
[One sees] not only the heather but blaeberries
With bright green leaves and leaves already turned scarlet
Hiding ripe blue berries; and amongst the sage-green leaves
Of the bog-myrtle the golden flowers of the tormentil shining;
And on the small bare places, where the little Blackface sheep
Found grazing, milkworts blue as summer skies;

And down in neglected peat-hags, not worked
Within living memory, sphagnum moss in pastel shades
Of yellow, green, and pink; sundew and butterwort
Waiting with wide-open sticky leaves for their tiny winged prey;
And nodding harebells vying in their colour
With the blue butterflies that poise themselves delicately upon them;
And stunted rowans with harsh dry leaves of glorious colour.
"Nothing but heather!"—How marvelously descriptive! And
incomplete!

There is a paradox which soon appears in any examination of Scottish pastoral: the poets keep returning to the same few tropes, and have the same focus on language, and yet few of them seem aware of this, or, more exactly, few seem aware of all their predecessors. It is as though we are describing a tradition, which is partly invisible to its practitioners. In the case of poets like James Thomson or John Davidson, this may be because they are caught up in an attempt to secure acknowledgment from English literature, rather than locate themselves within any specifically Scottish tradition. Another element in this might be the choice of language: a Scottish poet who does not engage with Scots will not be as conscious of the intellectual and aesthetic decisions which are or have been taken in deploying that language. But this uncertainty as to how clear such continuities are is itself a recurring element, a signpost indicating that bycultural quandaries are nearby. In the case of a contemporary figure like Don Paterson, we see not only a possible example of continued *imitatio*, but a new variation on the flower catalogue.

Paterson is much influenced by Northern Irish poetry—Muldoon, Heaney and, in a case of pastoral transplanting, by a Belfast poet with Scottish ancestry, Michael Longley. Longley's elegy, "The Ice-Cream Man," is a stated influence on Paterson's poem, "14:50: Rosekinghall," but where Longley's list of flowers is a funereal wreath for a shopkeeper murdered by sectarians on the Lisburn Road, he has transformed his into a list of fictional railway stations which might have served a community undermined by Dr Beeching's report, which led in the 1960s to the closing down of local lines and hit small communities in Scotland particularly hard. The fact his fictional stations are based on actual place names presents a new twist on the peculiarly Scottish version of pastoral where language constantly challenges and redefines the reality it is grounded upon:

Carrot—Clatteringbrigs—Smyrna—Bucklerheads—
Outfield—Jericho—Horn—Roughstones—
Loak—Skitchen—Sturt—Oathlaw—
Wolflaw—Farnought—Drunkendubs—Stronetic—
Ironharrow Well—Goats—Tarbrax—Dameye—
Dummiesholes—Caldhame—Hagmuir—Slug of Auchrannie—
Baldragon—Thorn—Wreaths—Spurn Hill—
Drowndubs—The Bloody Inches—Halfway—Groan,
where the train will divide

Whatever the situation historically, it is possible to assert that those modern poets who engage most consciously with the problematic, under-acknowledged continuities of Scottish poetry tend to be those who engage most with the issue of language. Robert Garioch's interest in the verse of both pre-Reformation and Enlightenment Edinburgh is evident in his translations into Scots from the Latinist George Buchanan, his use of the Christis Kirk stanza in "Embro to the Ploy," and of the Standard Habbie in his masterly "To Robert Fergusson." His work perhaps demonstrates the influence of humanist theories of rhetoric reinterpreted as a continuity of poetic forms. The intellectual crises involved in the use of Scots in the present day have been confronted with great sensuous delicacy in the work of David Kinloch, a Glasgow poet who, like Wedderburn and his fellow humanists, has made the journey to Paris to view Scots and Scotland from a European perspective. His "Apology of a Dictionary Trawler" makes the case for continued use of Scots in the era of Language poetry:

> it seemed to me as I laboured with my dictionary, as I tried to link its words up and make poems, that there was far more poetry in them when I left them in their squat paragraphs that when they swarmed forlornly about my white page looking for some connective to hold onto. And it seemed to me also that this strange, poignant feeling . . . that I was more alive in some of these words than in their English equivalents, that I "knew" them and "recognised" them as my own even as I came upon them for the first time, it seemed that this too was true and that this truth was perhaps unreachable and inexpressible. Finally it seemed that the kind of "Scots" poetry I could write would be an attempt to link these two perceptions up. . . .

What this means in practice for the art of the poet is that his "Scots" poetry will sometimes not look or even sound like "Scots" poetry. It will incorporate a great variety of voices and textures, dialects and accents and may even, occasionally, sound like criticism.

It may indeed, to come full circle back to Wedderburn's example, be in prose. Kinloch's interest in contemporary French poetry has furthered his exploration of the prose poem as a suitable medium for a poetic much concerned with slippage between registers, with loss, and with the particular momentary clarity of recovered language, which both possesses and is aligned with instants of erotic freedom:

> Habbacraws! the Renfrew Ferry throws up its glass bonnet. She nods. Tonight she sails: blackfisher of the Clyde. Far out beneath the Kingston Bridge an illegal banquet cups its ears and jumping to its feet says "Can you hear them? I hear people in the air but cannot see them. Listen!" We strain (with every pore) until we hear invisible brothers, whole words against our flesh. And they are: greengown, dustie-fute, rinker, rintherout, set, abstraklous, alamonti, afftak, baghash, amplefeyst, let-abee for let-abee. It is Homer's bounding, flying and consequently alive words. It is Plato thawing in the Glasgow air. It is the head and lyre of Orpheus.

Scots as a pastoral language gains a further edge when it is deployed through the sensibility of a gay man in contemporary Glasgow. As in Edwin Morgan's "Glasgow Green," Kinloch's relocating of the pastoral within such urban experiences recalls the fraught ambiguity of that classical inscription, "Et in Arcadia ego":

> *Now I am out on the heath*
> *Examined orally again*
> *Beneath a conference of trees,*
> *Answering, as always,*
> *Slightly beside the point:*
> *"What do you like?*
> *"What are ye intae?"*

In the final section of his 1994 collection, *Paris-Forfar*, "Dr David Kynalochus in Le Pensionnat D'Humming-Bird Garden," David Kinloch brings together Scots, English, prose, verse, herbalism, speculations on language, and elegies for AIDS victims in a manner which recalls but critiques the totalizing approach of MacDiarmid: language may provide balm but it cannot cure. In the post-modern humility of this approach

Kinloch suggests the latest variation on the Scottish definition of the pastoral—as a space in which the poet cares equally for language and the users of language.

The example of poets like David Kinloch (a list of which would include figures as diverse as Robert Crawford, Drew Milne, Ian Bamforth and Peter McCarey) may indicate that Scottish poetry in its present diversity and good health is at last capable of synthesizing the different approaches to pastoral over the past five hundred years. Restrictions of space mean I have only been able to point to a few of the ways in which Scottish poets have explored this genre—I have explored elsewhere the heritage of the Christis Kirk tradition, for instance—but it is evident even from a cursory examination like this that in Scotland pastoral will continue to provide a nexus where linguistic difference and cultural complexity produce a poetry that redefines this ancient mode by challenging both it and the assumptions we bring to it.

Virgil:
Translated from the Latin (lines 259-350) by David Ferry

from First Georgic

When the cold rains come and they have to stay indoors,
The laborers are able to get things done
That in better weather they'd have to hurry to do:
One hammering on the share where it was blunted;
Another hollowing branches, making wine-troughs;
Others sorting out and labeling
The heaps of garnered corn; branding the beasts;
Sharpening stakes and two-pronged forks; or making
Willow-shoot ties to bind up sagging vines;
Weaving new baskets, using pliant twigs;
Roasting corn on the fire of the household oven;
Or grinding it on the hearthstone. There are many
Tasks that are right and proper to do, no matter
Whether that day is a holy day or not.
There's no observance that says you're not permitted
To irrigate your plantings or put in a hedge
For their protection, or lay down snares for birds,
Set fire to brambles, or bring your baa-ing flock
Down to the stream to give them a healthy bath.
Sometimes, on such days, too, a farmer will load
His donkey's sides with bargain fruit, or oil,
And drive the recalcitrant beast to town to market,
And come back home with pitch he'd traded for,
Or a new millstone to use to grind his grain.

Luna has so commanded that there are days
That are right for doing certain kinds of work
And days that are wrong. Avoid the fifth:

The day pale Orcus and the Eumenides
Were born, and with horrible labor Earth
Brought raging Typhoeus forth, and Iapetus, and Coeus,
And the Giant Brothers who conspired together
In league to bring down Heaven. Three times they piled
Mount Ossa on Mount Pelion, and on Ossa
Leafy Olympus. Three times the lightning bolt
Of Jove the Father God was hurled; three times
It split the mountains apart and spoiled the Giants' plot.
The seventeenth is good for planting vines,
Breaking in oxen, preparing the loom for weaving.
The full moon on the ninth is good for those
Like runaways, who need to find their way,
And bad for thieves, who need not to be seen.
There are many tasks it's better to perform
Early in the morning, just at sunrise,
When the dew is everywhere, or in the night
When it's certain to be cool. Nighttime is good
For mowing the dry meadows or shearing the stubble;
The moisture makes it easier then to do so.
A farmer I know of sits up till all hours
In front of the fire in winter intently using
His knife to fashion torches out of branches.
Meanwhile his wife is doing winter chores,
Singing a song to solace her as she works,
Running the shrilling shuttle through the web,
Or boiling down the sweet must on the fire,
Or using leaves to skim the overflowing
Foam of the liquid in the bubbling pot.
The heat of summer noon is best for cutting
Ceres' golden grain and threshing it.
Work naked in the fields in the heat of summer,
Plowing the earth and scattering in the seeds;

Wintertime's the time for idleness.
Cold weather's when the laborers can rest
And feast together on what they'd labored for:
The winter festiveness unravels cares—
It's as when a ship at last comes into port,
With a full cargo, the voyage finally over,

And the joyful crew bedecks the decks with garlands.
But winter's also the time for gathering acorns
For mast to feed the beasts, and for gathering berries
Of blood-red myrtle and laurel to scent the wine;
And the time for pressing olives for their oil;
For hunting long-eared hares; and putting down
Snares for the unsuspecting legs of cranes;
Setting out nets that the stags get entangled in;
Whirling the Balearic hempen slingshots
To stun and kill the does; while the snow is deep
And the ice accumulates on the frozen rivers.

How shall I tell of autumn and its changes
And its changing constellations as the days
Grow shorter than they were, and summer's heat
Grows less than it had been? How shall I tell
Of all the things the farmers must watch out for?
Of spring and springtime rains downpouring on
The fields of bearded greening stalks of corn,
Its young ears swelling with their milky juice?
I myself have often seen the farmer
Lead his laborers into the yellow fields
To gather the ears of barley that are ready
To be stripped from their brittle stalks, and I have seen
How, all of a sudden, the warring winds came down
And ripped the plants up by their very roots
And carried them aloft into the sky
And swept them all away, light stalk and stubble,
Flying off somewhere on the black whirlwind,
The whole promising crop, lock, stock, and barrel.
Sometimes, too, there advances in the sky
A tremendous congregated mass of waters
Gathered from the topmost of the heavens
Into a hideous tempest of black clouds;
Then suddenly this wall of sky falls down
Upon the earth, and all its flooding water
Washes away the joyous crops and all
The work that men and oxen did together.
The spuming inlets seethe and overflow;
The steaming ocean waters rock and heave.

When Jupiter himself in the midnight storm
From his right hand hurls down his thunderbolts
The shocked world shakes; the wild beasts run away,
And all men cower in terror everywhere;
Mountains collapse under his terrible strokes,
Acroceraunia, Rhodope, or Athos;
The winds and the rain redouble and redouble;
The woods and the sea-cliffs wail under the storm.

Fearing such things, pay heed to the months and stars
And what they have to tell you: where in the sky
Saturn's cold star retires to; where in the sky
The wandering fires of Mercury can be seen,
And at what time of the year. Above all else,
Be sure to pay due reverence to the gods.
When spring has come and winter is over and done with,
Yield to great Ceres the yearly rite you owe her.
Spring is the season when the lambs are plump,
The season when the wine is mellowest,
The time of year when sleep is sweetest of all,
And the shadows on the hills are at their softest.
See to it that your laborers all join in
The rituals of the worship of the goddess:
Let the offering of honeycombs be washed
With milk and with soft wine; lead the propitious
Sacrificial victim thrice around
The fields the sacrifice is for, while all
The laborers follow along, joyfully shouting,
Calling on Ceres to come in under their roofs;
Let none of them use his sickle to cut a single
Ear of the ripened corn before he's wreathed
His brow with an oak-leaf garland and danced his artless
Dance and sung his song in honor of Ceres.

Reginald Shepherd

Narcissus to Echo

That summer was remarkable
for its emptiness, fool's gold or freckles
spangling my tensed arm. I'm tired
of all those poems that ventriloquize you backtalking
me, shoving someone else's words into your mouth
again. You never had anything to say, nothing
that hadn't been said before. You said it
yourself: *before*. Always babbling in someone
else's voice, as if you were a river
or a stream. Those less consumed than I
with seeing through the scrim of susurrus and foam
to see things through might have been taken in
by your agreements, the way this fishing spider
riding surface motion just to stay
still is taken in by the carnivorous small fry
it was waiting to take up: but I was determined
to get to the bottom of this shifting point
of view, this water-soluble refraction that tilts
my head to the side and down to keep the picture
bent on what's beneath the surface
tension's picture plane. Can't anything learn
to sit still? Repeat this after me: *still here*.
I'm never sure if that's a question or reply.
Impatient water posed a challenge:
to find the still uncluttered thing under what moved me so
to sit on that muddy bank for days
of staring into something nothing
like my face, constantly passing by, going
but never gone. I found such constancy

moving. We Greeks have always had a taste
for paradox, even ephebes like me. To long
too long for what doesn't change changes you. Still,
I kept hearing music I couldn't place,
that tried to sell me so much seem
for nothing, tangled branches flashing
current-like, sky glinting under
my liquid gaze. (Now I am was
and "where was I?," water and
what now.) Your omnivorous assent
was no use either: I sought
a tone more skeptical, a something
-isn't-right that just might be
correct, correcting all this lush and damp
to clean gravel, stone stream bed
that isn't going anywhere, the ground
of all those fluent propositions I refused
so many times. I wanted
to come clean, to set things straight,
and bent closer to true the line.
I heard every word you said.

Snowdrops and Summer Snowflakes, Drooping

The river is silted with sentiments, Ophelia
sings flowers in hell to all the goodnight
ladies martyred to plot, rosemary, pansies, fennel
and rue, columbine, wormwood and oxeyed daisies:
wilting litanies of no consequence. She scatters
handfuls of snow in no tense, returning
to the same spot she brings her spotless
suffering, called Candor, or Covert.

I'd give her trillium and yarrow, wild
carrot or white sweet clover,
some roadside blossoms less
historical: invasive wood sorrel, dame's
rocket, handfuls of designations,
names of names; stems broken, weeping
sap to sting her fingers, draw the flies,
make her drop her bottle of virginity.

I'd give her brambly honeysuckle
and dogwood bushes to shred her
wedding dress in passing to a proper
shroud, a weed or three to stain her white
with theirs, goodnight sweet lady,
wake up. What I wouldn't give
to hear her shut up that infernal singing,
walk out of sullen water open-eyed.

Mark Levine

Old Poem

Abstract sky, scored by
The coals we set in you: simplify us.

There; have said it. Now can turn to
The mere sparrow—an involved specimen, it

Turns out, scrounging a flecked insect
From its presumed underside—turning on an upper branch

From which flutters a few dried pods and a pair
Of yellowed leaves, heart-shaped, say, in two dimensions.

Sparrow gone as I report on it.
Won't chase this one into the sky.

Unfolded our wares before
the man, him
in the nettles
with his piercings.

Stepping from box
to box, stepping through.
Air between our legs
in which a fear

Deposited its spore.
Took a break from our heavings to report on it and

Were dusted in the glade with elements.
Me I have lost count of the heavenly.

—Was examining the scissored shadow
Of a wasp when the lights went out.

—Was putting a few of my fingers through a fabric
When the lights went out.

Moon grew empty in the old curved
Poem of war and nature.

Alan Singer

Bog Pastoral

from *Dirtmouth*, a novel

Field Inventory: Specimen # 1, Crate #1

Female of childbearing age. 1 meter, 64 centimeters. Wrists lashed in posterior position. Knees locked beneath chin. Ankles lashed together beneath buttocks. Hemp cord drawn up tightly through cleft of buttocks, along the spine to fasten, first at the hands, and then at the neck. No evidence of strangulation. Torsion of shoulder against pelvic axis marked in the asymmetrical orientation of the breasts. Toes flexed occipitally. Jaws awry. Mouth and trachea engorged with peated earth. Excavator notes: "the earth about the head is already carved out, as if the victim had attempted to eat her way out of the grave." Accompanying plaster cast of the cavity surrounding cranium exhibits striations consistent with human mandibular action and dental architecture.

I call it pastoral. Say it. The word sucks the past to its sibilant grain, as soggily as the kiss of bog meal fastens on the bodies held in its dank keep. But you would be wrong to imagine that their day is past.

Pastoral is no sentimental lament for the past in this place.

I say pastoral. But where, you will implore me, are the green trees, the lambent grasses scintillated by the breeze, the birdsong that sweetens the already honeyed air with its staccato sugars, freshly sucked from the blossoms, the blossoms twining around stalwart trunks, whose colors make the light seem prismatic and the air to tremble with the thickness of the light as if we were wrapped within it, chrysalides ourselves, luxuriating in the fermentation of our most colorful existence which will bloom no less spectacularly than the wild rose if our patience preserves us? Who are we kidding?

This place tells the truth. Bog. And it says what it has to say in a single ravenous syllable. Here all vegetation is ingestion. I do insist that the brown grain of the land is as dense as any towering trunk. The heather as tensile as any budding leaf. Its purple flower as fragrant as any footstep in the springing meadow. But none of it titillates our yearning for the picturesque.

The bog knows—as if to remind us how much better we should know this about ourselves—that its nature is not green.

Only remember how it came to be a bog. How like a murder. Almost eight thousand years before we gasp for our own breath. There was the fecundity of the lakes deposited like spawn of the retreating glaciers. The arrival of the Mesolithic fisherman. The reed communities. Their sediment, piling from the lake bed, poorly decomposed, the ground raising its dry hump, until only a few bubbles of lake water appear on the surface of the land. The water table rising with the landscape, gloomily acidic, airless, choking off the process of decomposition until its lungs are full and blue.

Trees of the forest, fabled in birdsong, have spread their shadows over this ground. We find perfectly preserved specimens of them from when a drier climate cast its golden seeds of light upon the blackest humus. But when the damp returned—was it only a 1000 years ago?— the oak, the elm, the ash were toppled by that tide. The thick mats of brown mosses took their places, an atavistic, pubic, fur sprouting on the burly hump of peat. The dome of undecomposing earth. Ever rising, ever arching, feeding gluttonously on the indigestible midden of the fallen forest and only at its edges leeching out the iron rich ochre like ingrown maidenhead.

Bogdom. And the rulers of this domain today are princes of exhumation. But their faces painted with the ochre do not disguise their pathos.

Think of it. From the time of the first souring rise of the water table, the last days of the reed communities, when the wooly headed fishermen marveled at the miraculous appearance of land in the midst of waters that had hitherto only reflected their hungry, their dirty faces, this has always, always, been a place of punishment.

Yes, there are other pastorals. I have admitted it. They lie soft and green at our feet, but as far away from us as any distant valley. Only a leap into thin air—the sensation of shredded wings whistling about our shoulder blades—would bring us to that paradisal homeland. No. I think here we are closer to home, just because we are closer to the condition of punishment. Because here our pastoral is no mere ethereal dream of eternity. Here the uncompostable fact marks our time. Where decomposition has ceased, the composition of the natural world becomes more undecipherable than a human scrawl on the bark of a primeval forest. That is the end of any yearning to be green. The bodies in the bog are neither one thing nor the other, are they not? Neither Nature nor culture. You might even say, the natural and the human are blessedly unknown to one another when they so densely embody the haste of time. I'm telling you, the bodies in the bog endure without any yearning at all. Do you know any pastoral as unsentimental as that?

Think of it. The hump of dry land having risen leviathan-like from still water. Maybe 1500 B.C. Visible but not approachable. Ringed with the feral tide of acid waters that sucks malevolently at trepidatious footsteps, the natural wonder of the bog-dome draws a helplessly introspective congregation. Who would doubt that it could stir the deoxygenated depths of some religious feeling?

Think of the throngs gathering at the water's edge, with each step feeling for the collapse of the earth beneath their feet. Think of the sensation tingling in their toes, the nails cracked and blackened as worn flints. They squish on the shrinking perimeter of the lake. These toes fringed wide, short feet, shod with calluses as impervious to the wet as gooseflesh, but attuned to the shallow immersion nonetheless. They know in their toes, as if the knowledge were an ingrown hair bristling toward the center of the brain, that as the water goes deeper it coagulates with the animus of something that can swallow hard. Everyone knows a bog to be a dangerous place. I tell you, the foot that fathoms such fear takes an initiate's plunge into the gurgling pool of prayer.

So, no sooner do the Mesolithic fisherman become Bronze Age farmers than the spongy domes of miraculously risen land—girdled as they are with waters chastened of any living organism—become sacred places. So why should it surprise you to learn that in the archeological record the evidence of religious worship at these sites is indistinguishable from the rites of punishment?

I am the archeologist. I say so.

For centuries on the congregants gather at the lip of this embittered shore. See the tall, Viking-framed priests, lifting long arms above their davening heads to stir the vapors of a settling mist. The reach of their arms sounds a clacking of wooden mallets above their heads. The glutinous weave of the robe material hangs shapelessly from their outstretched limbs, as though their entire bodies have been dipped in cooling oatmeal. Their eyes are coarse pits in the goat skulls that are lashed to their faces with leather thongs. They feel the pressure of the thong on the back of their heads like the grip of a violently forced kiss. But their lips are barely a cud, chewed in the wet, breathy, recess of the snouted skull. Bowing their heads together they touch gnarled goat horns, like tapers passing a flame, igniting a siren-like chant. It pierces the thickness of the settling damp. It whistles about the victim's naked body—of course she stands shivering in the center of their circle—like the biting end of a lash, primed against writhings of the very thin air from which the sufferer's first cries will burst at the commencement of torture.

But you would be wrong to expect such visual gratification.

The suffering of the victim will be invisible and relished all the more for its choked silence.

Oh yes, you can see her forced to kneel. The brutish hands pressing the delicate shoulders toward the wavering shoreline where her knees are lapped by the ring of breathless water, blue as the face of a still born fetus. You can see the faces of the crowding spectators, eyes jostling for the better view of these priestly rites, hair stood on end with gouts of animal fat, cheeks streaked with ochre, tongues lurching against what might be the sound of words being ejected like a loathsome taste from the mouth.

And you can see her bound. The hands twisted like loose threads behind her back. Ankles lashed beneath the buttocks. A cord drawn, sharp as a blade, through the chrism of the buttocks, made taut along the spine, cinched tighter to fasten a noose around the neck. You can even imagine how the struggle to free those limbs will be her self-strangulation.

And then you can even see the expression on her face change like wind-blown water itself. The fair skin, smoothed to translucent paleness by fright, suddenly wrinkling with rage. Watch the lines around the eyes and mouth whipping up a froth. And then the lips protrude in a wave action of their own.

You have no language to taste the meaning of these words on your own tongue. But you know the curses curdling on her lips, like the heaving of your own stomach. Think of the most bilious imprecation, meant to evoke the most abject sullying of the mind in the filth of the body. You know the force of the tongue that wants nothing more than to smear the face that feels the stinging breath of your hatefulness upon it, with the feces of the most bestially imagined bodily grunt. Who does not recognize how the angry contortions of the human mouth, when so vehemently aroused, are miming the most savage extrusions of an animal anus? The word shite is no substitute for such knowledge.

You can see all that. And you can even see the helpless body being hurled out of priestly arms, beyond the ring of blue water, into the darkest fermentation of the bog.

But now you realize that your eyes have not enough light in them—even stoked by the incendiary sights burning there—to illuminate what follows. The weight of the body when it lands is felt by the victim like the very swallow reflex that has already throttled the screams in her throat. The slightest tremor of resistance to the clutch of mire quickens its peristaltic action and pulls her deeper into the gruel-like dark. A thin but grainy broth holds the compressed curds of deciduous plant life in curious suspension while she plummets in slow motion.

Imagine the blackness of the forest grave at night, darkened more blindingly by the furious footstep of time imprinted upon it. To be so trodden upon is her fate. For all the gloom you contemplate in your knowledge of this fact, you might then imagine that her eyes are closed. They are not. She stares belligerently at her foe.

And what is more appalling than those open eyes is the open mouth. She never ceased her cursing. For every mouthful of invective she disgorges, the tongue with which she whipped the air is forced to carry a lump of dirt inside her, to suffocate the thoughts that gave her oathing breath.

Silence beyond contemplation.

You think the violent moment has passed because you can see no more of it. You imagine the unimaginable to be like a hood pulled over your own head and the drawstring knotted about your throat. Perhaps, by the grace of this image, you are even relieved.

But this is pastoral, where nothing passes away.

When the tip of the spade unseals the airtight chamber from

which the victim drew her last breath, in the form of an unswallowable clod, we know—I'm speaking for Science now—that she is as undying as the leveled forest. It stands as tall on her tongue as she is compressed within it. All the bodies in the bog are creatures of this forest, if only by the corpuscular magic that renders them shriveled and sere. Sunlight and shade mottle them as thoroughly on the inside—should a blade be handy—as on the out. Their color is like the turning of the worm, passing through what it ingests. While the breeze that stirred every leaf is as tight-lipped now as the faces it might have sucked dry then, the flutter of birdsong, the golden buzzing of the bee, the silvery dart of the fly through that unremembered air are all still sibilant in the squeaky texture of the turf when we pry against it to un-mold a shoulder or an elbow from the garment-like fit of this land. It makes a sound against the cusp of the shovel blade like a loose floorboard. And it is explicable. For the remarkable compression of the elements of the forest floor—still bark flake and seed casing, still molted snake skin and dragonfly wing, still petal and frond—contains the spring of the very footstep that is blackened almost beyond recognition in the mummified foot filling its imprint. Root ball and bud are grown together in the dark. When we unearth them, the bodies from the bog are no less earthbound than the rocks and the stones.

What makes this specimen different from the others is that the spastic gash of her open mouth, still cursing, refusing to give up the grievance of a single moment in time, makes an itchy noise in our ears. It is our attunement to the fact that her endurance is our own experience of time. We will even mark it off in our faithful exhumation of the bodies—tendered by this otherwise unmerciful ground—in a state of such uncanny preservation.

And when we do cut them out of the turf, true to the minutest detail of what is preserved, don't we carry the tune of that cursing voice, as if we had picked it up from the lips of a comrade toiling rhythmically in the trench beside us? In the fields of excavation we archeologists are laborers first, after all, spades and pitchforks wearying our calloused hands and our foreheads gilded with an honest sweat. If we hear the cursing voice are we not sworn, comrades in song, to be faithful to such harshly tuned rage, in all the ceaselessness of its expression?

When we close them in their glass museum cases we realize, as clearly as we can see through the glass, the transparency of time itself. Our victim's scourging tongue rings out on a resonant stage, if we have set the stage well.

How natural the scene! The arrangement of the limbs by means of invisible pins and wires floats the bodies in air as they rested—of course they struggled!—upon peat. We see between the splayed fingers the light they are scratching to attain. We see the heads cocked on the straightened necks, the lips puckering towards the unforming bubble, on a surface beyond reach. We see the legs drawn up in the torsions of a frog propelling itself beyond the jaws of a cat, the hips knotted by a frenzied twist, wringing pond water from the air, toes pointing away like drops of water, shed from the density of the body. That we see them through the very air which denied them breath—the diastole of our inhale is the systole of their exhale—raises the pulse of our empathy.

Unlike the taunting rabble, long dispersed on the crumbling lake shore—they preferred the invisibility of the death because it more darkly bruised the blackness of their thoughts upon the victim's suffering—we who have crossed the glaring threshold, bask in the footlights of the museum spectacle, knowing that it sees us as luminously as we see it. We feel the aching alertness of vision through such a limpid medium. The probing beams of light prickle the eye muscle as delicately as slivers of glass. The pupils are narrowed to steel pinpoints. The sheen of polished metal solders us to the view.

Staring ever harder with eyes that watch ever more closely—focus tensile as picture wire—we await the moment when, if only by the unsteadying blink of the eyelid itself, a limb will seem to twitch.

Rebecca Seiferle

Ruined Pastoral

At first the amber
seeping out
of the ancient
fireplace tearing free
from the foundation
seemed only a mystery,
a river of gold light
that you could plunge
your finger into
and taste, but then
you noticed
the cobwebbed
filth of mice,
their tiny droppings—
how ancient
the hive was
and how dangerous
in that desert
where lungs could fill
with the waters of
hantavirus—
the sound of nothing
filling the house,
invisible bees and
death in the sweetness—
your finger to
your tongue.

Eleanor Wilner

The Fossil Poet, a Post-Pastoral

—for David Lee who read me the petroglyphs at Parowan Gap

It was long after his time on earth
when they found him, the New Ones,
on a dig in the The Place Where
the Sun Sets. They guessed that ash
from some catastrophe had caught him at his work,
for a machine, archaic, was found beside him,
open, a set of small extruded squares in rows
bearing ancient letters, and what might have been
a primitive code of numeration. Seeing him—
here in the Museum of the New Ones, themselves
extinct these many years—I found myself
strangely moved, rare in these decades of drought;
as if the dust of the world has muted our senses,
even our antennae delay their signals,
letting the moments pass, seconds empty
as the ruins of the human world.

It must have been the way time opened
its deep shaft into distance as I gazed at him,
so many eons ago this creature turned
his life to words, even as I word mine.
For as I looked, it seemed I heard
that sweet hum begin again: the sound
of my first summer, when we had just
burst humming from our shells, leaving our
perfect images clinging to the walls, and stretched

our still damp wings to dry in the dying sun.
Our larval period underground, longer
than our full-grown lives in what is left
of light, allows us to survive, and makes
our faded days seem almost bright.

But as I stared into the case in which the fossil-poet
lay, I felt some memory stir, and half revive—
a brighter sun, high pastures, gorges, rivers,
towers of rock, landscapes unlike ours
where everything is worn down flat, the dust
keeping the air a fine scrim of yellow-gray.
As if the fossil-man himself were dreaming
me, I saw his vision of the world
that used to be—alive with contours, moving
shadows at the feet of cliffs, running streams,
pine scent, a wind to make the branches sing—

but then the dream began its slow retreat
into the dust-filled air, and though I bid it stay,
it grew more dim, and what I felt
along my body's length, was the ice cold wall
of glass to which I clung. Inside, the fossil-poet
dreamless lay, petrified, unmoving in the clay.
Bearing away the loss of what he knew—with a thrust,
I pushed off, spread my wings, and flew.

Sheenagh Pugh

The Garden of the Last Nizam

In the garden of the last Nizam
bare, unpruned rose branches straggle

to a single bud. The fountain is choked
with leaves. Weeds force apart

the wall's cracks, overgrow the paths
that are going back. No one walks here

any more. The old man has forgotten
what once he cared for: the tame fish

he liked to feed, the fruit warmed
by sunlight, the scent of flowers

at dusk, the rusting carts, laden
with rubies that glint through brambles.

Jennifer Clarvoe

In Solution and Dependence

I

There was a humming in the house all day;
The flood subsiding into dampness, vapor;
But now the sky is gathering into gray;
The Mind's descending into closet stupor;
Under the cloud's deep voice the Heart sinks deeper;
The Soul won't answer as the cardinal warbles;
And the water drags down the air like a sack of troubles.

2

Where can they go, the things that live outdoors?
The ground despairs after nightlong destruction;
The grass is smeared and wrenched;—and while it pours
The raccoon and three pups race in distraction
Towards and away from the house, and the opossum
Weaves, despairs, and worries through the mud
Some groove the water's worn; all things are flood.

3

I was a Prisoner then, my flood indoors;
I saw the hare outside, flattened with fear;
I heard the woods and distant waters roar
Even when they were still, sad as before:
The unstill season did my heart impair;
The present moment cracks the present torment
As lightning downs the pine—not punishment

4

But chance. Not punishment at all. How late
The light in minds that can no further go;
As low as we have sunk in our sad state
This slow solution lifts us—weary, slow
And wavering with the evening. Even so
What rises from torn root and residue,
Releasing resin, tastes both sharp and true.

5

The wren inspects the ground beneath the pine;
Alert at the edge of the farthest bed, the deer
Acknowledges my presence. No design
Affords us these companions. We are here
In the green world by accident together—
Each day is accidental—accident
All friends, heart's bliss, and peace and nourishment.

6

My whole life I have ached for happy thought
As if I were a prisoner in a flood,
As if all needful things must still be sought
Outside myself. How bright and far the good
Flares in the lightning, seams and veins that should
Feed and inform the earth, and yet the pine
Is riven to the root. That charge is mine.

7

What is thought? The Marvelous is human,
Even when sleeping deep beneath the word,
Beneath the river that a silly woman
Watches and would follow. Unknown bird
Another poet wrote about who heard
You singing questions, sing into eternity
Of accidental happiness and sanity.

Mount Auburn Cemetery

for Margot

Another level grave: bright sun lights up
        the loving rhyme engraved in its stone face—
we wonder, briefly cheered, what life they knew,
        which one chose the rhyme—the first to go,
the one who followed after? And would we choose
        that life, that death. We are not cheered enough—

we're alive, aren't we? Neither relief nor despair
        opens for us here. These aren't our grounds:
fierce light, near-neon snow, lush moss & grass
        & rushing thaw. Which way do we go now—

that path away from the wind, uphill or down?
        Whatever we want—*really*, whatever we want.
I've been here before—the restlessness dies down,
        but I'll stay restless, if you like, even get pushy,
get us lost in the twisting paths. The city
        where we live and work still lifts its face

up over the next hill, impassive. We don't slow
        its approach; it could (one of these days) love us.
I don't try to put anything behind me—what, and fall *backwards*
        into something deeper? Even what I can't accept, I like to see.
Look there! A robin in February! And up the short slope, its red
        trumped, yet, by a cardinal! I've never learned anything

hard; forgetting is hard enough, and now the light's gone like a thought-
        less lover. This is still the beginning of the game of forgetting
I was a wife, awake, sated, warm,
        saying his name. What's left to say . . .
I don't wait for weakness to wear itself out. And stubborn care
        jostles me, prompts me, like the dumb, faithless birds.

Martin Ball

Pastoral and Gothic in Sculthorpe's Tasmania

> Omni fert aetas, animum quoque . . .nunc oblita mihi
> tot carmina
>
> *Time bears all things away, even memory . . .So many*
> *of my songs are forgotten now*
>
> Virgil, Eclogue IX

It's a long way from Virgil's Italy to present-day Tasmania. There are
many miles and many years. There are fundamental differences in lan-
guage, landscape and culture. Virgil wrote from the center of civiliza-
tion; Tasmania is *"ultima Thule,"* it is the very antipodes, lying off the
south coast of Australia. But across the gulf of such contrasts, there are
also unexpected connections. Some of these can be traced through the
history of European colonialism, and the cultural traditions of western
civilization, whereby Latin poetry came to be read in far-flung British
dominions. But equally there is the circularity of historical coinci-
dence, which sees the same concerns with land and memory played out
in divers epochs and places. And in those post-colonial settler societies
where land ownership is an intensely political issue, the pastoral dy-
namic that Virgil explored so appositely in his *Eclogues* becomes once
again a genre for the times. One place where these themes of land, cul-

ture and poetics meet is the work of Australian composer Peter Sculthorpe, a native of Tasmania, who grew up reading Virgil.

Sculthorpe is one of those few composers whose music is instantly recognizable. His compositions are characterized by a distinctive blend of European traditions, fused with Asian influences from Bali and Japan. Sculthorpe first came to international prominence in the 1960s with his *Sun Music* series, and gained further recognition with works like *Mangrove* (1979), *Earth Cry* (1986), and *Kakadu* (1988). His string quartets have also received much attention, particularly through performances and recordings by the Kronos Quartet, and more recently the Brodsky Quartet. He has been categorized as *avant-garde*, though when asked about his compositional style he says he is a melodist: "I like writing tunes."[1] Landscape is a significant theme throughout his writing, together with the related notion of Place. Another theme which recurs in his compositions is that of the Pastoral—which is where the tunes tend to appear.

The pastoral aesthetic has often been the domain of sentimental nostalgia, in which the pure innocence of rural life is contrasted with the corrupt experience of the town. It's a story as old as Cain and Abel. This classic dyad of pastoral and urban is the subject of Raymond Williams's *The Country and the City*. Williams takes as his point of departure George Evans's pronouncement in *The Pattern under the Plough* (1966) that, "A way of life that has come down to us from the days of Virgil has suddenly ended."[2] Williams describes how the "vanishing pastoral" is a constant theme throughout English history. He charts how successive societies have lamented the passing of a rural way of life, which many writers like to trace back to Virgil, whose idiosyncratic *Georgics* give advice on farming after the manner of Hesiod in *Works and Days*, and whose *Eclogues* extol the virtues of rural life and the music of the shepherd's reed-pipe, in the style of Theocritus's *Idylls*.

Equally however, the pastoral can be the site of political dissidence and radicalism. This too can be found in Virgil, whose first and ninth *Eclogues* allude to the soldier settlement scheme engineered by Octavian in 41 B.C.E. after the Civil War, when farms were confiscated under a scheme to provide land to returning veterans. *"Nos patriam fugimus,"* wails Meliboeus; "I must flee our homeland" (Eclogue I: 4). "Patria" here functions like *Heimat* in German, a potent melding of the ideas of home, land and country. But whose homeland is it—theirs who live in it, or theirs who fight for it? In Australia, after the Great War, returned soldiers were granted land (previously Aboriginal) to establish farms. And a similar scheme to Octavian's has recently re-surfaced in Zimbabwe, where the government has encouraged confiscations of white farmers' property, in order to provide land to soldier veterans.[3]

Virgil's themes find a ready echo in Tasmanian cultural poetics, for the history of modern Tasmania is in many ways the history of European colonialism in microcosm. Following the invasion of the Australian mainland in 1788, the British moved south to Tasmania in 1803. While the government established penal colonies at Hobart, then Macquarie Harbour, and later at Port Arthur, free settlers pushed inland, creating a rural idyll of European imagining wherever they could. When interest in the colony dissipated in the mid-nineteenth century, the initial development was left to age gracefully, not to be superseded. Much of this beauty still remains, in the avenues of golden poplars, hedgerows of hawthorns, and the pale glinting of old sandstone walls.

But for the indigenous inhabitants, the Tasmanian Aborigines (or Palawa), the story was less appealing; a tragedy of colonial history with land dispossession at its root. Those Palawa who survived the initial onslaught of exotic diseases and random violence, were rounded up in a military campaign of ethnic cleansing and exiled to Flinders Island in Bass Strait. There is a very heavy irony transposed from Virgil's first Eclogue here, where Meliboeus complains that, after his land is confiscated he will be forced into exile, "even to Britain, that place cut off at the very world's end" (Eclogue I: 66). With the death of Trukanini in 1876 it appeared that the Tasmanian Aborigines had simply died out, like a doomed race. In truth, just as happened throughout the Americas, the Palawa culture was obliterated by the European colonizers. As Moeris says to Lycidas (IX: 12), where the claims of soldiers are involved, poetry and songs have as much chance as doves against eagles.

And yet, the trope of extinction was pre-emptive, for the Palawa remained and in recent decades have re-established for themselves a place in the cultural framework of Tasmania. But the narrative of Tasmanian genocide persists, and with it attendant mythic structures that continue to shape the telling of the island's history.

·◌·

Peter Sculthorpe was born in 1929 in the sleepy rural center of Launceston, northern Tasmania. In his autobiography, Sculthorpe describes how he read much poetry in his youth. The young schoolboy would sit in the garden studying Virgil's *Aeneid* with his Latin teacher, living out the idyllic reminiscences from *Eclogue IX:* "Often in boyhood / I would sing the long summer's day to sleep"—*et in Arcadia ego* indeed.[4] Here is the epitome of the bucolic ideal: the shepherd at one with nature and poetry, with soft music and a clement climate.

Most of the music Sculthorpe wrote at this time was inspired by verse, and by the local countryside around him. The first string quartet (1944–47) commemorates Longford, a town nearby to Launceston. The third quartet grew from Robert Herrick's autumnal lyric *To the Meadows*, and includes a pastorale. The fourth string quartet (1947–50) is subtitled "Recollections of holidays spent in a country village in Tasmania." Such works demonstrate a rather naïve and sentimental outlook, motivated largely by personal nostalgia. In the late 1940s Sculthorpe moved to Melbourne, on the Australian mainland, and in 1958 he left the country altogether to study in Oxford. He would subsequently come to regard as his mature work only those compositions written after his return to Australia from England in 1960. And as he left his juvenilia behind, so did he cease to write music about his native Tasmanian countryside, and look more broadly at the wider landscape of the Australian mainland.

It was not until the mid 1990s, when the composer was in his sixties, that Sculthorpe's muse returned to places in Tasmania. This time however, his composition went beyond the merely sentimental and engaged with the complex history and politics of the landscape. This is most obvious in the work *Port Arthur: In Memoriam*, written in response to the inexplicable murder of 35 people at the former penal colony (now tourist site) in April 1996. *Hill Songs* (1992/3) commemorates his brother's family in Launceston. But a more deliberate and sustained engagement with the composer's birthplace is the *String Quartet No.14* (1998), a work concerned with "feelings about mountainous landscapes in northern Tasmania," and which interlaces opposing narratives of settler and indigenous cultures.[5]

The quartet has a well-wrought form, with its main themes adumbrated in the first movement, "Prelude." The writing here is characterized by sustained contrasts, with strong and measured melodic lines set against an insistent background of broad arpeggios. In the second movement, "From Legges Tor," the music is descriptive, with dense and close harmonies evoking the mists on the craggy summit of the Tor. The third movement, "On High Hills," sees Sculthorpe in typically sentimental vein, recalling the township of Whitehills on the outskirts of Launceston where he grew up. The manuscript notes describe the music as "calmly lyrical, a recollection of much-loved places, its melody originally conceived in my schooldays." Finally, the last movement "At Quamby Bluff" returns to the restless themes of the Prelude. It begins *inquieto* but ends *calmato*, finding a sort of resolution.

Quamby Bluff lies at a liminal zone in the physical and poetic geography of Tasmania. It forms part of the huge buttress of the Great Western Tiers in the center of the island. At the foot of the Bluff, gentle pastures and arable land spread north and east. Behind spreads the vast uninhabited wilderness of South-West Tasmania. Janus-faced, Quamby Bluff expresses the two dominant readings of Tasmanian landscape: utopian pastoral versus Gothic horror.

Discussing literary representations of Tasmania, Amanda Lohrey suggests that the Gothic genre is characterized by "a tendency in the individuals who construct it to invest nature with their own trauma."[6] The twin narratives of convictism and genocide provide a rich vein for writers of Gothic inclination, and each year brings new examples. "Tasmanian Gothic" is familiar in the novels of Richard Flanagan and Christopher Koch, and especially in Peter Conrad's memoir *Down Home* (published in the U.S.A. as *Behind the Mountain*). It also informs Robert Hughes's history of convictism, *The Fatal Shore*, and Marcus Clarke's account of the same in *For the Term of His Natural Life*. All these books focus on Tasmania's brutal history, its remoteness and cultural insularity. Such feelings are then transferred onto the landscape, which often becomes a character in its own right, and functions as a metaphor for whatever particular historical or cultural travesty is being depicted.

In Peter Conrad it is Mt. Wellington, "a brutal, bad-tempered eminence" that sets a frown upon the young Peter's childhood. In Hughes it is the water of Macquarie Harbour, stained "tobacco-brown with a urinous froth" by the peat washed out of the wilderness: "Fish could not live in Macquarie Harbour; the peat poisoned them," claims Hughes—the same water now supports numerous salmon farms. In Richard Flanagan it is the wild Franklin River taking revenge on all who have degraded it, slowly drowning a scapegoat river guide.[7] And in Sculthorpe, it is Quamby Bluff, site of an alleged massacre in the early nineteenth century.

In the notes to *String Quartet No. 14*, Sculthorpe indicated that the fourth movement concerns "the tragic killing of Aborigines at the bluff's edge." When he subsequently re-scored this string quartet (in an orchestration for strings, horns and flutes), naming the work *Quamby*, Sculthorpe explained more fully the resonances in his title:

> When I was very young, my father told me a story about Quamby Bluff, a rather forbidding mountainous outcrop in the highlands of northern Tasmania. There, according to legend, colonial government soldiers once drove a tribe of Aborigines to the bluff's edge. The Aborigines had the choice of being shot, or jumping. They chose the latter, and as the jumped they cried out "Quamby! Quamby!" meaning Save me! Save me![8]

This story about Quamby Bluff is one that circulates in modern Tasmania as just one of the many acts leading to the genocide of the Aborigines. Yet there is no contemporary account of such an event. Neither Lyndall Ryan in *The Tasmanian Aborigines* nor Lloyd Robson in his exhaustive *A History of Tasmania* make reference to this alleged massacre. Nevertheless, both writers attest that in January 1828, thirty members of the Peerapper community were shot and thrown off a hill at Cape Grim in the far northwest of Tasmania (some 200 miles from Quamby Bluff). The details of both the Quamby story and the Cape Grim massacre are vigorously disputed in Keith Windschuttle's *The Fabrication of Aboriginal History*.[9] Whatever the facts, such a narrative displays potent mythic elements. The same fabula drives Judith Wright's poem "Nigger's Leap: New England," and Peter Carey rehearses it again in *Oscar and Lucinda*, where "Darkies' Point" is the site for an identical action: "Horace Clarke's grandfather went up there with his mates . . . and pushed an entire tribe of aboriginal men and women and children off the edge."[10]

According to both Robson and Ryan, "Quamby" was the name of a Palawa resistance leader in the north Midlands (south and west of Launceston), who was shot in 1832. But in Sculthorpe's version, Quamby's identity and fate has become subsumed within a folkloric conflation of various narratives, compounded by the attendant romanticized meaning of quamby as "save me."[11] Windschuttle traces the archeology of these contradictory accounts. He identifies the source of Robson and Ryan's histories as the diary of George Augustus Robinson for 12 August 1830, and traces the Schulthorpe story to a newspaper account in the Hobart Town Courier of 14 March 1829. There may have been a massacre at Quamby Bluff—undoubtedly many tragedies of European settlement went unrecorded—but this story seems less a case of historic testament than one of Gothic restatement. The lasting tragedy is that the Palawa themselves could not tell their own story, for their songs fell silent as their language lost its voice. As Virgil writes (Eclogue IX: 51), "Time bears all things away, even memory . . . So many of my songs are lost to me now."

The treatment of landscape in the Quamby pieces is interesting for a number of reasons. In his early period, Sculthorpe often wrote in response to his experience of actual places, though he avoided ascribing direct correlations between his music and those places. For example, the movement in the first string quartet (1944–47) inspired by the graveyard of the Anglican Church at Longford is naively titled "Little song." In the final movement of the fourth string quartet (1950) depicting the village green at Westbury, the specifics of the location dissolve into "Country dance." In *The Fifth Continent* (1963), a work inspired by D.H. Lawrence's novel *Kangaroo*, the seaside village of Thirroul becomes simply *Small Town*.

This sublimation of the specific to the generic radically changes with *Port Essington* (1974), which the composer describes as his "most Australian work." *Port Essington* is so named from the location of a failed British settlement on the Cobourg Peninsula in far north Australia, which lasted from 1838 to 1849. Across the work's six movements Sculthorpe juxtaposes European court music of the period with an Aboriginal tune, the first time the composer directly quotes an indigenous melody. Equally important, however, is that this piece represents the first occasion Sculthorpe acknowledges a real place in his title. This naming symbolizes a sense of history and socialization of the land; it transforms Landscape into Place.

This shift in consciousness provides an index to Sculthorpe's changing engagement with Tasmania. The juvenile pieces see his surroundings in a synchronic dimension, relating all through personal subjectivity. When Sculthorpe returns to the same physical locations as a mature composer, he is able to expand his vision along a diachronic axis, to historicize the landscape. Such an approach conforms to the postmodern poetics of space enunciated by John Agnew and James Duncan, who argue that, in contrast to the isotropic space of modernism, "postmodern space aims to be historically specific, rooted in cultural, often vernacular, style conventions." The various parts are often unrelated to the whole, and the historical associations are maintained through renovation and recycling.[12] This is precisely what Sculthorpe is doing with the landscape in *Port Essington* and again in *Quamby*. He has learned that the felicities of the present are not always as they seem. This is the lesson that Simon Schama writes in the conclusion to *Landscape and Memory*: "The sum of our pasts, generation laid over generation like the slow mould of the seasons, forms the compost of our future."[13]

In both its forms—string quartet and chamber work—the *Quamby* music offers a variety of tropes and moods. There are the brooding contours of Legges' Tor and the disquiet of the bluff, together with the evocation of past tragedy. Importantly, however, there is also the deliberate and conscious depiction of a pastoral idyll. The third movement is a happy reminiscence of the providential theme in Tasmanian history and culture. The music is marked *Calmo* and *Come veduta a volo d'uccello*, meaning calmly and "from a bird's eye view." This sense of perspective is essential, both spatially and in terms of history and culture. It sites the work on both sides of Quamby Bluff: it sees the mountainous wilderness as well as the plains; it remembers the good and the bad of colonial history.

With its deep attachment to childhood memories and places, *Quamby* provides clear evidence of the origins of the Pastoral aesthetic in Sculthorpe's writing. It also shows that, like Virgil's *Eclogues*, such ideas are more than mere rhetorical gestures of melodic sentimentality; they are motivated in the social and political imaginary. The most salient feature of *Quamby* is the juxtaposition of the lyrical and the dramatic, the *calmo* and the *inquieto*; the utopian and the Gothic. Sculthorpe presents both narratives; not as a polemic, but a dialectic. He successfully collides the two opposing images of Tasmania in a way which seeks if not resolution, then at least reconciliation.

Notes

[1] See Andrew Ford, "Sculthorpe at Sixty." In *Undue Noise: Words about Music*. Sydney: ABC Books, 2002; 219–39, AT 220.

[2] Williams, *The Country and the City*. OUP, 1973; 9, 261.

[3] It's tempting to speculate that Robert Mugabe got his idea from Octavian, and sees himself as a latter-day Augustus. We might wonder too, whether former Rhodesian prime minister Ian Smith sits in his kraal reading Virgil's first eclogue, wondering whether like Tityrus he will keep his land, or like Meliboeus be driven from his demesne.

[4] Peter Sculthorpe, *Sun Music*. Sydney: ABC Books, 1999; 15.

[5] Peter Sculthorpe, *String Quartet No.14*. London: Faber, 1998. This work was originally titled "No.12," but subsequently was renumbered.

[6] Amanda Lohrey. *The Greens: A New Narrative*. In Cassandra Pylous & Richard Flanagan (eds). *The rest of the world is watching*. Sydney, Pan, 1990; 89^100, at 90.

[7] Peter Conrad, *Down Home*. London: Chatto & Windus, 1988; Robert Hughes, *The Fatal Shore*. London: CollinsHarvill, 1987, 373–5; Richard Flanagan, *Death of a River Guide*. Melbourne: Penguin, 1994.

[8] Peter Sculthorpe. *Quamby*. London: Faber, 2000.

[9] Lyndall, Ryan. *The Tasmanian Aborigines*. Sydney: Allen & Unwin, 1996; 135–7. Lloyd Robson. *A History of Tasmania*. Oxford University Press, 1983; 210–20. Keith Windschuttle. *The Fabrication of Aboriginal History*. Sydney, Macleay Press, 2003 (with revisions);. (249–271).

[10] Carey, *Oscar and Lucinda*, St Lucia: University of Queensland Press, 1988; 2. This narrative schema is not unique to Australia, of course; it can even be seen in the ancient Greek myth of Oreithyia (see Plato, *Phaedrus*, VI: §228A; and Robert Graves, *The Greek Myths*, §48). There are further parallels in Thomas Hardy's story about the fate of Gabriel's sheep flock in *Far from the Madding Crowd*; which in turn borrows from the Biblical story about the man called Legion, whose devils Jesus cast into a herd of pigs which then rushed over a steep bank into the Sea of Galilee and were drowned (*Luke* 8: 33).

[11] Ryan, *Tasmanian Aborigines*, 141. Robson, *History of Tasmania*, vol i: 226. Windschuttle, *Fabrication of Aboriginal History*, 280–1.

[12] John A. Agnew & James S. Duncan (eds). *The Power of Place*. London: Unwyn Hyman, 1989.

[13] Simon Schama, *Landscape and Memory*. London: HarperCollins, 1995; 574.

Andrea Brady

The End of: Seasonal Oz.

The pattern becomes misguided, a shift
over to empty and coasting downhill. Growth
cycles are no longer sustained by seasonal records,
            flood patterns and electric,
fulsome heat does not breed
parsley in the dry bays nor ice kill off
            hawks who carried
                    West Nile fever up
                    north from Pensacola incubators.
Bad fortune is a consequence of years
for lives, unpacked in imperial lobbies, drawn up
            under a bladder. I apologize.

    Cannula metal pings, ricocheting
off this center of the world. He has taped up
a few dicta here to squander it. Where is the hypo
            fill their veins with maltesers
            limbs already bent with polio
                    (this tribe no longer minds
                    lime-green and its
                    kindness to the liver
                            in summer).
What does MTV say from the firehouse.

Capping the seasons just before they
are due to escape into taped repeat. Pokey
as a positive ten-year-old's pump action, I retreat. Up
            goes A. N. towards the needle,
            leaving the house of fever

perpetual conditions are mistaken.
They are not.
Bugs are restive, a humor stalking blood,
bloody-minded, cure to outlast autumn and reappear
in December; we forced by the Atlantic not
   to quench it cannot quench it with water
or banish brushfires waiting for inevitable autumn

rains. Nor should the record rest in its cradle lined
with summer fodder from Westminster stables, it does not lie
on lean blankets hungry for immuno-suppressants,
        it is not poor.
        It would finish itself off in the rest
—sloping under Annalise's hammock;—seeing, calm as
a wheel;—listening for the atomic frazzle halted when
it was giving life to something or away.
        Here fusion operates cold as steady.
   Energies diverted to main thrusters
   summer prospect of a last
   fuck. I actually think about nothing else
      coming home early, pulling taffy
      from yesterday's earware.

        Not even the body is really
built on seasonal work. But to blazon
the business cycle or the waspish
beauty of foliage in change
is to assert dangerously change where there
is nothing but constancy.
        Cordial as I am to you.
Take for instance the fruit of the year.

The citizen of fudge looks into the haze,
like the porter *benumbed by the torpedo of excesse,*
like the packing agent. I lose. Place the transfer
       over the hole and revamp,
     idea of heaven, of anything big as
     the blanket concept lost in high grass,
       say, people. A
disease waited millions of years safely

before making the species jump. The continent
will yearly make these subjects obsolete
   as arcadia to a seasoned
   population, trembling with
     heat like their own grass
    their fate.

Harry Ricketts

Wind-Breaks and Asbestos Sandwiches: Some Versions of New Zealand Pastoral Poetry

A country like New Zealand, which up to the 1970s still saw itself eco-nomically as a farm and freezing works for the UK, might be expected to muster some versions of modern pastoral poetry. And so it does—both in the post-Wordsworthian sense (the rural above the urban, the solitary above the social), as well as in the more extended, Empsonian sense of contrasting the simple and the complicated life to the (moral) advantage of the former.

2

Predictably, the post-Wordsworthian line has attracted poets from the more sparsely populated South Island, particularly those from Canter-bury and Otago. Ruth Dallas's "Milking before Dawn" from *Country Road* (1953) is not untypical. "[O]ut in the paddock," it is wet, cold, and starless, but "[t]he shed is an island of light, and warmth." Only half-awake, the early milker (implicitly a woman) is briefly envious "Of the man in the city asleep"; but where her real allegiances lie is never in doubt. On cue, dawn produces its daily epiphany, the sense of innocence regained underlined by the sudden anapaestic skips in the five-beat lines:

> The earth as it turns towards the sun is young
> Again, renewed, its history wiped away
> Like the tears of a child. Can the earth be young again
> And not the heart? Let the man in the city sleep.[1]

"Milking before Dawn" was prompted by Dallas's experiences as a landgirl during World War II; and, generally, that war gave a powerful impetus to the pastoral imagination in New Zealand as elsewhere. The impetus can be felt behind James K. Baxter's "Spring Pastoral," written in 1943 when he was sixteen. (The family were pacifists, and Baxter's brother detained as a military defaulter.) Spring, though producing its usual supply of bleating lambs, "flashing crocus-beds" and "new-born nestlings," is described as "fearful almost that her temerity/Of new creation will new anger see." No other season, we are confidently informed, "[m]ay move men's hearts like spring-tide; there is then/A dear communion 'twixt us and the glen/That blooms with wayward brambles."[2]

Baxter urged a friend to see the poem "through the eyes" of Crabbe and Clare, aligning himself with the more realist strand of eighteenth century and nineteenth century English pastoral.[3] And it is true that intermittently his couplets suggest something of Clare's particularity of detail, mixed diction, even his rhythmic unevenness: "calves lathe-legged nigh to the barn-door lying / Their nuzzling nostrils snuffing an unknown air." However, the presiding pastoral ancestor here—as in several of Baxter's early poems—is really Wordsworth, particularly the Wordsworth of "The Immortality Ode" and *The Prelude:*

> We likewise
> Drink in the breath of Nature at lips and eyes
> And peace, tender as that of infancy,
> To move us in rhapsodic melody.[4]

A more complicated, though in its own way not untraditional, sense of pastoral underpins the lean unrhymed couplets of Baxter's late *Jerusalem Sonnets* (1970) and *Autumn Testament* (1972), which record life in the commune he founded in Jerusalem on the Wanganui River. In these sonnets, Baxter (by then a Catholic convert) adopts the role of self-appointed pastor to the hippie "tribe" he gathered around him. Here the virtuous simplicity of the pastoral life is affirmed, and sacramentalized, often with a wry awareness of the range of obstacles and irritations involved:

> *"Lord," I ask Him,*
>
> *"Do You or don't You expect me to put up with lice?"*
> *His silent laugh still shakes the hills at dawn.*[5]

Denis Glover's "Sings Harry" sequence, again begun during World War II, espouses a bachelor, bush pastoral of a kind humorously celebrated in prose in Jack Lasenby's "Uncle Trev" stories and Barry Crump's *A Good Keen Man*. Glover's speaker is a refugee from "the world / And the world's ill," a rugged Man Alone figure at home now only with lake, mountain, and tree. With a laconic lyricism, he reminisces about "a beautiful world [that] has gone," lost love, busted hopes, bungled opportunities—pastoral as nostalgia for a potentially harmonious world once known but now irrevocably out of reach. Throughout the sequence runs a valedictory validation of "the wind-break," "the golden gorse," the "paddocks opening green / On mountains tussock-brown" where "[m]ustering is the life."[6] The world imagined in Glover's most famous poem "The Magpies" (also from the early 1940s) is bleaker, close to the stark world of traditional ballads like "Twa Corbies," whose form Glover follows in a deliberately dilapidated fashion. On their farm, Tom and Elizabeth are briefly allowed the illusion of an idyllic, pastoral existence before institutional greed ("the mortgage-man") forecloses on them. Here Nature offers no consolation: the magpies watch throughout, raucous and indifferent:

> *The farm's still there. Mortgage corporations*
> *Couldn't give it away.*
> *And Quardle oodle ardle wardle doodle*
> *The magpies say.*[7]

Brian Turner, who has been described as "an unrepentantly regional Otago poet," is probably Glover's most obvious literary descendant.[8] His poems often take place in a back-country landscape, tough, "honest," liberating. "In the Nineties" elegizes the personal rural past more rhapsodically, but still in a key recognizably derived from "Sings Harry":

Say violins remind you
of moonlight on snowfields in spring,
pianos of high country streams,
and a flute of dun hills
swept by tussock
above which hawks turn, stall
and turn.[9]

In Turner's work, physical exertion and activity (cycling, fishing, tramping) are deeply valued in themselves. Sometimes there is a suggestion of allegory in the backpack, as in "Walking In," where a cluster of puns ("easy grades," "bluffs") hints at more than a simple tramp in the bush.[10]

3

For Baxter, the search for a simpler, less materialistic life included a serious attempt to learn from Maoritanga [Maori ways]—in effect, a perception of Maori as pastoral. Such a perception (though adumbrated in Baxter's work with far greater sophistication and cultural awareness) is in itself nothing new. The so-called "Maoriland" period of New Zealand writing (c. 1880-1915) produced its own colonially gratifying form of this version of pastoral, depicting Maori as exotic primitives, the last of a noble (and, it was thought, dying) race. Glenn Colquhoun's first collection, *The Art of Walking Upright* (1999)—the product of a year spent "learn[ing] things Maori" in the Bay of Islands—follows Baxter's more modern and culturally sympathetic line, not least in its unequivocal challenge to the late Allen Curnow.[11]

The challenge is to Curnow's well-known couplet, "Not I, some child, born in a marvelous year, / Will learn the trick of standing upright here," which concludes his early 1940s sonnet "The Skeleton of the Great Moa in the Canterbury Museum, Christchurch."[12] Explicitly, Colquhoun signals his dissent by his volume title and by the poem "The trick of standing upright here" (with Curnow's lines as epigraph); implicitly, he signals it by a warmly affirming and admiring portrayal of Maori throughout the collection. What is questioned, and rebuked, is Curnow's apparent assumption that in New Zealand only a settler-Pakeha voice will ever have meaning and value.

Colquhoun's challenge operates on a formal as well as a conceptual level. The volume title confidently rewrites Curnow's line ("art" replacing "trick," "walking" replacing "standing"), so too does the poem

"The trick of standing upright here." The couplets (part of the Baxter legacy) are unrhymed, and (unlike Curnow's uncertain future tense) are all determinedly in the present. What is offered in refutation of Curnow is a list of the ordinary, the human, the local: "Sleep is the feel of clean sheets on skin. / The soft gaps between people on floors." The list—a descendant of the one in Brooke's "The Great Lover"—self-consciously includes Maori words and practices, such as communal sleeping on the floor in the marae and the preservation and subsequent burial of the placenta: "Being born is casting on a row of stitches./It is a whenua [placenta] in a plastic bag in the freezer."[13] For all its critiquing pretensions and its affectionate pastoralism, the effect of the poem, however, and indeed of the volume as a whole, seems curiously naive, old-fashioned even, set alongside Curnow's scrupulous, precariously maintained balance.

Not that such a challenge is in itself surprising. Curnow (ninety when he died) lived to be the great grandfather of New Zealand poetry. Always insistent that "[r]eality must be local and special at the point where we pick up the traces: as manifold as the signs we follow and the routes we take," he had for over sixty years offered New Zealanders a conscientiously anti-pastoral vision of their country.[14] Distrustful of "green myths," he had been the assiduous chronicler of what he termed "the unhistoric story," the story that told how "[t]he pilgrim dream pricked by a cold dawn died / Among the chemical farmers, the fresh towns."[15]

"House and Land" from *Sailing or Drowning* (1943) presents a now classic formulation of Curnow's stance. No sustaining rural tranquility here for the historian, the cowman, Miss Wilson, or the dog who inhabit the poem. Instead, a "great gloom / Stands in a land of settlers / With never a soul at home," the final off rhyme (gloom/home) reinforcing the sense of displacement.[16] Over the years Curnow became extremely resourceful at finding new ways of sounding resonantly glum: "The stain of blood that writes an island story"; "Botany is panic of another description"; "There's only one book in the world, and that's the one/everyone accurately misquotes."[17] There was no change of tune or tone in his final collection, *The Bells of Saint Babel's* (2001). The eponymous title poem begins with early Christchurch settlers, "[f]laeces of all / species," "bound for / this pegged-out plain//in the land called / Shinar, or some- / thing," and ends in lugubrious, cacophonous comedy, as the Dean of Saint Babel's and his friend, walking in Cathedral Square, "can't hear a word / for those DAMNED BELLS."[18]

There have always been those who have jibed at Curnow's post-lapsarian dejection, his steadfast refusal to subscribe to any pastoral past, present or future.[19] It could be argued, however, that his anti-pastoralism is really a disguised form of pastoral, his resolute bleakness allowing readers secretly to congratulate themselves on their own toughness in surviving such unpromising conditions. C. K. Stead made much the same point in his obituary piece on Curnow, when he remarked that Curnow's "negatives were less significantly 'state of the nation' statements (though they were that) than vehicles for local details and stories which subtly glamorized the country and the history he was telling us were unsatisfactory, inglorious, unromantic."[20] Curnow himself observed in his introduction to A Book of New Zealand Verse 1923-50 that "[i]t is tormenting folly to search ourselves, as I did once in youth on the Auckland coast, for Wordsworth's mood."[21] His poetry could be seen as triumphantly turning that mood (including its pastoral element) inside-out, transforming perceived absence into negative affirmation. Such a view makes one kind of sense of the riddling lines in "There Is a Pleasure in the Pathless Woods": "Look hard at nature. It is in the nature / of things to look, and look back, harder."[22]

4

Wordsworth is one of several writers playfully evoked in Bill Manhire's "The Idiot: A Pastoral." The insouciant title looks over its shoulder not only to Dostoievski's novel but also to Wordsworth's "The Idiot Boy." The poem itself is set suitably in a garden. It makes various knowing gestures towards the pastoral (there are mowers, bees, love, danger, trees) without ever doing anything so unironic as actually to become pastoral in an obviously recognizable way—unlike, say, Anne French's "Mower & glow-worms again," which rewrites pastoral convention more orthodoxly, replacing Marvell's male protagonist with a modern female mower, whose mind (and heart) are similarly "displaced."[23]

Bricolage or postmodern pastoral, as one might call Manhire's version, turns up throughout his work. "Out West," for instance, capitalizes on the Western as pastoral, deftly rounding up and corralling its frontier argot ("varmint," "doggone," "ornery critters," "mosey"), its untamed landscape ("gulches," "sages"), its maverick figures ("Wild Bill"—also of course a joke on Manhire's own name), and generic narratives ("the woman— / lonely and beautiful—waking to find us gone.").[24] His recent "Picnic at Woodhaugh" describes a colonial *déjeuner sur l'herbe* in a not very accomplished mid-nineteenth century painting. Each detail is scrutinized and mulled over with an apparently straight-face. The "woman dressed as a man, black trousers, / and, perched on her lap, a fellow in tails": are they "performers, perhaps?" the speaker wonders. "Or even the most important guests?" Note is taken of "the first recorded / Dunedin dog: a trunk on legs, eyes on a snout, / elephant ears, tail sticking out." A lady's *"parasol"* is both "a fresh flower of the forest" and "a wee bit smaller than her head."[25] The effect is enormously engaging: pastoral with a wink, as in Andrew Johnston's "Pastorale," exuberantly packed with nursery rhyme and bucolic clichés: "the dusty tuba father blew,/to play it by ear till the cows come home."[26] Or, less playfully, in James Brown's "A Field of Cows," which ironically juxtaposes Padre R——'s joyless instruction on "the sexual act" with "the soft refrain of implanted cows/repeating their cud."[27]

5

Of the various local versions, it would be easy to neglect domestic pastoral. However, a discernible line runs from Ursula Bethell's garden poems of the 1920s through the late Lauris Edmond's family poems to Jenny Bornholdt's recent kitchen poems. Bethell set the pattern and the tone: exact observation of things in a style, which mixes the sensibly prosaic and the mandarin, and is (usually) kept from the portentous or the twee by an underplayed humor. The opening of "Time" strikes a characteristic note:

> *"Established" is a good word, much used in garden books,*
> *"The plant, when established"* . . .
> *Oh, become established quickly, quickly, garden*
> *For I am fugitive, I am very fugitive.* . . .

So too does the conclusion of "Sinensis," where Marvell's famous couplet is both beautifully complemented, and let down, by the (mock-) sententiousness of the final line:

> *The poet Marvell said, in one of his compositions:*
> *"But at my back I always hear*
> *Time's winged chariot hurrying near."*
> *Such is, likewise, the experience of the Horticulturist.*

133

For Bethell—a serious but never earnest Anglican—the garden in her poems is a tiny oasis, whose hard-fought-for order and fertility are constantly under threat from weather and time. It is the outdoor domain she lovingly, anxiously tends, while Effie Pollen (her "consort," as Bethell calls her in "Discipline") sees to the house. At the same time, Bethell sees her garden as doubly pastoral, since for her it also provides an intimation of the afterlife, her lilies the same flowers "we look to find blooming / In the meadows and lanes that lie beyond Jordan."[28]

In Lauris Edmond's work, the garden does sometimes functions as a metaphor for marriage-as-pastoral, though the imagined oasis usually turns out to be a mirage. For instance, in "A reckoning," from the mid-1980s, marriage is initially "a walled garden, safe to quarrel in, / love coming down on us reliably as rain"; but when the children leave, it becomes "a quiet plot / ill-tempered without learnt weather / and the rule of law." A decade later, "A matter of timing" uses a garden to portray the quintessential model of Kiwi domestic pastoral: "[a] line of daffodils," "clouds above / blowing about like washing," "five-wire fence, a post every few feet," "small flat lawn, / path to the gate." However, as the speaker acknowledges, this "absolute dream, total as/childhood" does not, in fact, belong to her but to a complete stranger, a "plump woman," who watches her driving slowly and enviously past.[29]

A similar kind of failed domestic pastoral is implicit in a number of Fleur Adcock's earlier poems. The two stanzas of "For a Five-year Old" crisply dramatize the ironies of a mother-child relationship. The first stanza presents the idyll: mother advising child to put stray snail back in garden. The second dismantles the idyll as the mother ponders her own past cruelties and betrayals, before wryly concluding: "But that is how things are: I am your mother, / And we are kind to snails."[30] A different kind of irony undercuts Cilla McQueen's "Vegetable Garden Poem (1)." Here, again, the garden is quickly established as pastoral, though, unlike Bethell's, this one is overgrown and unkempt, buzzing with its busy life:

> Some of this grass goes up
> four feet without a kink. . . .
> The thistle beside me is a city
> of prickles and flowers visited
> by bees. . . .

But although "[t]he solo cicada stitches all the little/bits of the day together diligently," the garden's simplicity and tranquility prove no protection against the knowledge that a friend "shot himself/yesterday."[31]

Domestic pastoral has by no means been an exclusively female preserve in recent New Zealand poetry. Ian Wedde's *The Commonplace Odes* (2001) purveys an urban—indeed urbane—form of pastoral. Taking their bearings from Horace, the odes range unhurriedly over love, death, art, parenthood, friendship. They are quizzical about, yet revel in, their own eloquent celebration of "[t]he lovely world." There is room to satirize "knuckle- / Cracking cultural commissars" as well as to enjoy "[t]he deck still speckled with summer's bastings" or to run up Mount Victoria, "the place / I take my bursting heart on autumn mornings." The life valued here (including morally valued) is one of middle-aged, civilized pleasures: good wine, good talk, shared meals— "[t]he kind of plump rice you might have relished / Horace, in the Sabine noon, yellowed with saffron." Underwriting these pleasures, and preventing them from seeming merely complacent or flatulent, is the ever-present prospect of Death, who is "never in / The picture," but who nevertheless "[takes all] the pictures."[32]

Anna Jackson's *The Pastoral Kitchen* (also 2001) shares some of Wedde's self-conscious use of tradition. Here Sidney's *Arcadia* provides the literary starting point to be modernized and domesticated, as in the title poem:

> In my pastoral kitchen I wash and dry
> the dishes, as my thoughts stray
> like sheep I guide
> and serve.

But, for all the shifts of register and the discernible outline of a small moral world, the results are only intermittently resonant. Perhaps more Sidney is needed to enliven the overly flat:

> The cat comes in
> and cries at me as if I were her mother.
> I fill the lunch boxes
> and wait for Di.[33]

While apparently much less ambitious, Jenny Bornholdt's short sequence of prose poems in *These Days* (2000) is more successful. The speaker, again a mother, discovers in herself an unexpected enthusiasm

135

for "the world of plastic" and watches herself haunting "the plastics aisle at the supermarket": "It occurs to you that you could become one of those people who is *prepared*. . . . You find this idea strangely attractive and repellent at the same time." Later in the sequence, the kitchen floor is found to be "an asbestos sandwich." It is proposed to line the kitchen with plastic, "turn it into a kind of big lunchbox." The speaker reflects on this new situation:

> *[Y]ou feel betrayed by your house. You'd been lulled into*
> *a false sense of security by the dishwasher—a relative*
> *newcomer on the scene*
> *only to find there's danger lurking under the very floors you stand on.*[34]

Here the slight shifts of tone, the amused, bemused, awareness of conflicting realities, the blend of safe haven and perceived threat, combine to suggest a whole world in miniature. This is absolutely in the Bethell mode, the domestic mode, which is arguably the most persistent, though least ostentatious, of all the versions of New Zealand pastoral poetry.

Notes

[1] Ruth Dallas, "Milking before Dawn," *Collected Poems* (Dunedin: University of Otago Press), 14.

[2] James K. Baxter, "Spring Pastoral," *Spark to a Waiting Fuse: James K Baxter's Correspondence with Noel Ginn 1942-1946*, ed. Paul Millar (Wellington: Victoria University Press, 2001) 217.

[3] *Spark*, 227.

[4] *Spark*, 217.

[5] James K Baxter, "Jerusalem Sonnets 1," *Collected Poems*, ed. J.E.Weir (Oxford: Oxford University Press, 1979) 455.

[6] Denis Glover, "Sings Harry," *Selected Poems*, ed. Bill Manhire (Wellington: Victoria University Press, 1995), 43, 42, 41, 44, 42, 45.

[7] Denis Glover, "The Magpies," *Selected Poems*, 33.

[8] Roger Robinson and Nelson Wattie (eds), *The Oxford Companion to New Zealand Literature* (Oxford: Oxford University Press, 1998) 548.

[9] Brian Turner, "In the Nineties," *Beyond* (Dunedin: John McIndoe, 1992) 8.

[10] Brian Turner, "Walking In," *All That Blue Can Be* (Dunedin: John McIndoe, 1989) 19

[11] Glenn Colquhoun, introduction, *The Art of Walking Upright* (Wellington: Steele Roberts, 1999) 7.

[12] Allen Curnow, "The Skeleton of the Great Moa in the Canterbury Museum,

Christchurch," *Early Days Yet: New and Collected Poems* 1941-1997 (Auckland: Auckland University Press, 1997) 220.

[13] Glenn Colquhoun, "The trick of standing upright here," *The Art of Standing Upright*, 33, 32.

[14] Allen Curnow (ed), introduction, *The Penguin Book of New Zealand Verse* (Harmondsworth, Middlesex: Penguin Books, 1960) 17.

[15] Allen Curnow, "Sailing or Drowning," "The Unhistoric Story," *Early Days Yet: New and Collected Poems* 1941-1997 (Auckland: Auckland University Press, 1997) 219, 235, 236.

[16] Curnow, "House and Land," *Early Days*, 235.

[17] Curnow, "Landfall in Unknown Seas," "There Is a Pleasure in the Pathless Woods," "An Incorrigible Music," *Early Days*, 227, 173, 132.

[18] Allen Curnow, "The Bells of Saint Babel's," *The Bells of Saint Babel's* (Auckland: Auckland University Press, 2001) 13, 20.

[19] Most recently Heather Murray in her review of *The Bells of Saint Babel's* in *New Zealand Books*, vol 11, no 3, October 2001, 12.

[20] C. K.Stead in *The Independent*, 26/9/01.

[21] Allen Curnow (ed), introduction, *A Book of New Zealand Verse* 1923-50 (Canterbury: Caxton Press, 1951) 40-41.

[22] Allen Curnow, "There Is a Pleasure in the Pathless Woods," *Early Days*, 173.

[23] Anne French, "Mower & glow-worms again," *Boys' night out* (Auckland: Auckland University Press, 1998) 21.

[24] Bill Manhire, "Out West," *Collected Poems* (Wellington: Victoria University Press, 2001) 139.

[25] Bill Manhire, "Picnic at Woodhaugh," *Collected Poems*, 227, 228, 229.

[26] Andrew Johnston, "Pastorale," *How to Talk* (Wellington: Victoria University Press, 1993) 19.

[27] James Brown, "A Field of Cows," *Lemon* (Wellington: Victoria University Press, 1999) 19.

[28] Ursula Bethell, "Time," "Sinensis," "Discipline," "Bulbs," *Collected Poems*, ed. Vincent O'Sullivan (Oxford: Oxford University Press, 1985) 8, 7, 9, 4.

[29] Lauris Edmond, "A reckoning," "A matter of timing," *50 Poems: A Celebration* (Wellington: Bridget Williams Books, 1999) 37, 74.

[30] Fleur Adcock, "For a Five-Year-Old," *Selected Poems* (Oxford: Oxford University Press, 1983), 8.

[31] Cilla McQueen, "Vegetable Garden Poem (1)," *Homing In* (Dunedin: John McIndoe, 1982) 50-51.

[32] Ian Wedde, ""1.2 To the Cookbook," "2.5 To the Millennium," "1.3 To Bill Culbert and Ralph Hotere: Art Noir," "5.5 To Autumn," "1.2 To the Cookbook," "4.2 To Death," *The Commonplace Odes* (Auckland: Auckland University Press, 2001), 8, 19, 9, 47, 8, 34.

[33] Anna Jackson, "The Pastoral Kitchen," *The Pastoral Kitchen* (Auckland: Auckland University Press, 2001) 4.

[34] Jenny Bornholdt, "You've entered the world of plastic," "(Men come to call)," *These Days* (Wellington: Victoria University Press, 2000), 35, 37.

Peter Larkin

from Sprout Near Severing Close

22

What the stumps do
not so throats of cut
but moats owing flow,
shoots resharpening
low inceptive meta-wound.

Columns of dressed
cyst, footstools funneling
at the ill-trellised rind
for a rise of shell.

Out of no density
pitching the strip set by clot,
craping its handed-back
on unrepining provision.

When not a spirit of re-
growth but a spate of
thinning directly *along*
a membrane of survival.

23

Fealties of pinnacle
measured at ground hutch.
The hounded virtual of prop
whose dust is unplanar
and buried in the root-chest:
minimals out at sever
already nosing it sprout.

Recaps to a certainty of
cut-rise: the arisen lapse
is smudge in the arch,
edge like to throng.
Crown-fray to a thrift
so unsifted the vaning is upright,
blades at apertures of shelter.

A loose covering wading surface
for concealment, its upside
of soil plied to bed its radicles
as from a roof bar.

24

Crisp mishewns shared
forest with such outsize
floors of reparation.
Undaring as wiped stone
poor clear intimation
writes on what little squad of stump
is not smaller for unempty.

Diversity a lightly expendable
recess that vertical weave
from exact fall is budgeting
on all sides:
severing is oftener cheaply
reprinting from the steeps.

Low-tree species rich in outspoil
of niche, the gap-dynasty
will teach a failure of fetch
and more tramples do open,
unrevise and arise.

Cleavings to short-rule
surveyable fix at worn for plight:
stem *that* exchange by no plaiting
but direct to bud-height!

Tree summons community
off slow variable prop.
Lowest avail is cell-stubble
rasping cauterized taper
below a damage-harvest's
own fallen behind-
hand with thrall:
old canopy bestraws
gleanings for the micro-tall.

Peter Riley

from Sett Two

Heaps of fruit piled up against the walls
grandfathers piled up in the ground
churchyard fruit, pears, cherries
travelers selling small bags of hazels

And if all the world is to go the same way,
all one empire? all serving the one broker?
A thin cry in the fields, baby,
where did our love go?

The house in the fields
breathes, its timbers
flex in the night changes,
the star wheels churn

Piles of apples outside in the yard
yellow and red in separate heaps
slowly, under careful control
rotting into the music.

Curtains of onions and maize strung up
on the verandas to dry, the smoke rising when they
fire the yard ovens in the late afternoon
for tomorrow's bread.

The car mechanic sits on the doorstep drinking beer,
the mountain behind him turns black.
He is the mechanic of all moving things,
he is not in a hurry and doesn't want to be paid.
The mountain is wooded to the top.

The work lies there like a song waiting.
The lives sing their completions, constantly
infolded resolution, daily work
of the whole valley, singing out tomorrow's fear.

Smoke rising from the 5 o'clock fires
all over the valley, tomorrow's loaves
waiting like moons, like slow clocks.

Roads of wet earth between the houses.
"Look at this miserable place I live in,
look at this mud, this filth."

Look at us, civilized, perfectly smooth,
perfectly dry.
Where did our bombs go?

Open land, then forest, then air.

Leonardo Bruni said that the harmonious
workings of the institutions of Florence
derived from the beauty *and geometry*
of the Tuscan landscape.

A thin track, a line in the grass down
the pastures and over the riverside humps
everywhere worked, the shape
of the place carved from work, leading
ultimately homewards.

Tacita Dean

R. T. Smith

Timber Ridge Poor Farm

The county never got around to paving
the gravel path that snakes back to the gate,
but they built this croft in 1834
in a fertile cove where a slow stream forks
to give homeless men shelter and some work,
if they were able. Most weren't. What ailed
them ran from whiskey-trembles to cancer,
blindness, sorrow. The chickens starved, the rows
were never straight. It slowly went to smut
and rust and weeds, the patient politics
of grief. What lasted were the studs, rafters
and hemlock joists. The sorrel soil, the floors
and gables, a supervisor's patchwork
clapboard house. The poor no longer labor
on these acres. The panes have been replaced,

and one family for eight decades has raised
cattle and complained of ghosts. These winter
evenings Mac's tractor unspools hay bales
in its wake, a gold spill across new snow.
The charolais, which are quick and too feisty
to go down without a fight, shadow it,
lowing, while on razorback ridges across
the valley, something hungry howls down
the milky sun. Everyone says "coyotes"
and claims to have seen at least one.

Or feral dogs that sniff the whetted wind
for strays and bring down a calf if they can.
Or spirits so skiddish and lean not even
the redtailed hawk can spy them as he soars
above Poorhouse Road and screams.

Topple

Big as pie plates, the sunflower
faces beckon morning the way ripe apples
summon deer under the moon,

and I am ever amazed
how they can rise seven feet in a season
but begin to bend when their yellow

petals shine brightest. They sway
with every gust, so I cut them to illumine
the kitchen dust a few days,

knowing I still have to witness
wilting crowns and wept petals,
how the stalks soften

and crimp, the heads bowing
as if in shame, but for what? Surely not
their blessed falling or seeds

which I save for winter feeders,
to make the vagrant cardinals strut
and peck, hammer the husks open.

Thus nurtured, their sacred feathers flame.

Louis Armand

Et In Arcadia Ego: Landscapes of Genocide

In the blue waters of eastern Bass Strait, Flinders and its surrounding islands are what remain of land that once connected Tasmania to mainland Australia.

This description of Flinders Island could be from anywhere. But the idyllic seascape implied by these "blue waters" hardly seems to suggest the Bass Strait familiar to anyone who has travelled the route from Melbourne to Launceston: a body of water more readily bearing comparison to the North Sea than to any blue water lagoon. Something is obviously going on here, and it may be more than merely the usual gloss we expect to read in tourist brochures. That is to say, there may be more than genre at work in this unlikely geographical displacement. After all, widely advertised distortions of the Australian landscape have long been the stock-in-trade counterpart to the convict industry, as a means of establishing enforced settlement of the southern continent (enforced, at least, in one sense or another).

Tourism, too, is about compulsion, about being compelled. In its higher moments, it may even approach an experience of the ethical. The organized tour, for example, is about subjecting oneself, giving oneself over, however temporarily, however voluntarily, to the hospitality and care of others, removed from one's familiar, habitual environment. The tourist, almost by definition, is incompetent by standards of local knowledge. And that, no doubt, is part of tourism's perverse attraction. Its paternalism. Its reversion to a type of childhood.

For the tourist, local facts and "knowledge" assume a complexion of novelty. The picturesque. They are similar to the cheap trinkets one inevitably finds on sale in designated souvenir stores or (more solicitously "authentic") in open air marketplaces. They describe a faux knowledge, like the knowledge indulged in by children. One trades in this sort of ephemera, passing it along, assuming an enthusiastic, bored, pretentious air of being in the know. But this game is played out almost uniquely among fellow tourists and those, less fortunate, who have remained at home and in ignorance. But between the recycling and re-disposal of phrases memorized from guidebooks, and the inevitable slideshows and photographic albums, what is in fact going on? What is being played out in this game of exploration and discovery? Of history making?

> Flinders Island is located off the north-east tip of Tasmania in the Furneaux Group of islands. It is the largest of the Bass Strait Islands. Emita, to the north-west of the island, is the location of the Wybalenna Historic Site. In the 1830's, as the population of Tasmanian Aboriginals dwindled, many were re-settled at Wybalenna in an attempt to consolidate the tribes and save the race from extinction. Wybalenna fell into disrepair, but was renovated by the National Trust in the 1970s. The site is significant to Aboriginal peoples. Also at Emita is a museum, marking not only the Aboriginal presence but exhibiting relics from Bass Strait shipwrecks.

Looking at a detailed map of south-eastern Australia, identifying the Furneaux group, and Flinders Island, isn't difficult. There is a sense that something, like a set of directions, has successfully been communicated. But something other than just the blue waters has been left out of this description. I wanted to read more about the land bridge. About what "remains" of what once connected Tasmania to mainland Australia. Perhaps I've already begun to evolve a notion that this "connection" is more than merely a fact of prehistoric geography. In truth, I've already begun looking for other connections. Other remains. But I'm getting ahead of myself.

Part of the genre of tourism is a code of "attractions." These are the things one is more or less compelled to see or do, conveying in the process that special quality of "assumed" knowledge. The attraction is a commodity. A resource. It even "justifies" the act of appropriating it, in one way or another. We could look at this differently, of course. In purely socio-economic terms; such as "exploitation." But there are other terms. Some of them, curiously, theological in tone.

The notion of the tourist as pilgrim isn't so common in Australia as it is in Europe. Probably because there are fewer sites in Australia that have been able to be enshrined to the myth of European civilization. It wasn't just sarcasm which led Robert Hughes to compare the former prison at Port Arthur with Cluny Abbey. And yet, here, in this second description of Flinders Island, we learn of the presence in the township of Emita of the "relics" of Bass Strait shipwrecks. Is this simply the type of language one expects to find in tourist brochures, or is it something else?

Perhaps this is a type of knowledge game, too. A game one plays with the way in which terms designate and communicate facts. What are the relics of Bass Strait shipwrecks? At least we know now that there must be more to the "blue waters of eastern Bass Strait" than is revealed to the color-enhanced photographic eye. But whose relics are these? Why are they relics? Again, something is missing here. Something about the history of commercial shipping in Bass Strait, at the very least. Something, too, about the "use" of the Furneaux group of islands. Their very practical use, we might say. Beginning, no doubt, with their use by sealers and whalers ("straitsmen") from very early on in the history of European settlement of Tasmania and the Australian mainland.

One doesn't read much about sealing or whaling in the tourist brochures. The impact of animal rights activists over the years has doubtless served to undermine the attractiveness of what, undoubtedly, was a brutal and all too overly capitalized industry. As with so many similar histories, this one also ended in extinction. Not of the seal or the whale (although almost), but of the industry, which obviously was unsustainable being based on an economy of incremented exploitation, destruction, extermination. There are relics of this industry, too, but you won't find them mentioned in any brochures that you might find in a tourist information office, and it is unlikely that you will find much mention of them in general history books either. These aren't the sort of "relics" of shipwrecks which are housed at the Emita museum. These are "living relics" (if that is at all possible). Flesh and blood. But again, history barely mentions them, so perhaps after all they don't really exist.

The word relic won't go away, however. If you look it up in a dictionary, you will probably find something like the following definition: 1.) something which has survived the passage of time; especially, an object or custom whose original cultural environment has disappeared; 2.) something cherished for its age or associations with a person, place, or event; a keepsake; 3.) an object of religious veneration; especially, an article reputed to be associated with a saint or martyr; 4.) anything old, leftover, or remaining; a remnant; 5.)*Plural*, a corpse; the remains of a dead person; [from Late Latin *reliquiae*, remains (especially of a martyr), from Latin, *relinquere*, to leave behind, relinquish].

But why enact this ritual of consulting dictionaries, of going back over the meanings of words, etymologies? Perhaps I'm curious to see what's left when we begin to dig about in language, to play a game of archaeology, of exhumation. Perhaps there is something in what the tourist brochure says, after all. Or what it doesn't say. Some sort of relic. Actually, first of all, I'm impressed by this conjunction of the word "relic" with the word "save." "In the 1830s, as the population of Tasmanian Aboriginals dwindled, many were re-settled at Wybalenna in an attempt to consolidate the tribes and *save* the race from extinction."

Where to begin? A series of other words stand out, less impressively at first, but that serve to attract our attention nevertheless. These, too, are sites of interest. "Dwindled." "Resettled." "Consolidate." "Race." "Extinction." But of course, these are not listed among the "sites of significance" which we are encouraged to visit on Flinders Island. Instead we are given a place name, Wybalenna. A site "significant to Aboriginal peoples" (merely?). This is the "other" site at Emita. The museum, we are told however, "not only" marks the Aboriginal "presence" but exhibits relics of Bass Strait shipwrecks. Why should we pay so much attention to this? After all, it is simply a tourist brochure. But perhaps it has more to do with the very generic nature of this discourse. Its exemplary status in regards to a certain genre, this time not focused on tourism but on genetics.

> Located 20 km north of Cape Portland (north east tip of Tasmania) by sea and 151 km from Launceston by air, Flinders Island is the largest of the Furneaux group of islands which lie at the eastern end of Bass Strait separating Tasmania from Victoria. It is about 29 kilometers wide at its widest point and 64 kilometers long.

The island was probably part of the land bridge which joined Tasmania to the mainland. Bass Strait was formed as a result of the melting of ice after the last ice age and consequently Flinders and Cape Barren became islands and the Aborigines of Tasmania were cut off from their mainland counterparts.

The island was first identified by Europeans when Tobias Furneaux, the commander of Captain Cook's support ship, became separated from the *Endeavour* in fog and discovered the Furneaux group of islands on 19 March 1773.

George Bass and Matthew Flinders resolved the issue of Van Diemen's Land's status, when, between October 1798 and June 1799, they circumnavigated the island. The strait which separates Tasmania from the mainland was named after Bass and this, the major island, was named after Flinders by Governor King.

In 1833 the remnants of the Tasmanian Aboriginal population (a mere 160 people) were exiled to live at Settlement Point (named by the Aboriginals as Wybalenna—black man's houses) on Flinders Island, with the misguided belief that they would be protected from the rape and abuses of the white settlers in Tasmania. By 1847 the settlement had been deemed as a failure and was abandoned, and the remaining forty-five Aborigines were sent to Oyster Cove on the east coast of Tasmania.

The first freehold land was selected in 1888 by George Boyes (thirty-one acres at Palana). Prior to this Flinders Island was leased to individual persons. The first council was elected in 1908, after which there was an increase in population mainly based on the agricultural and fishing industries.

In the early 1950s a solider settlement scheme was initiated, clearing and draining land on the east coast of Flinders Island (approximately 33,559 hectares), which greatly increased the island's productivity. Settlers for this scheme mainly came from Tasmania and central New South Wales.

In the accumulation of facts it may be that we find ourselves less in a position of knowing than of being led along by the nose. And one begins to look more closely at all of this. At this genre of discourse. Its ellipses. Its "symptoms" rather than its "facts." But symptomatic of what? And what does it mean to be in possession of them? This is the wonder of history, no less than of tourism. It's hardly surprising that museums serve in both contexts equally well. Museums, too, are about possession. Relics, for instance, can be "housed" in museums, if they do not find a more consecrated resting place. But where is all this leading us? Here we are, back at what possibly remains of that land bridge which once connected Tasmania to the mainland. The place to which the "remnants" of the Tasmanian Aboriginal population (a mere 160, no longer "many") were "exiled" in 1833.

There is something about this land bridge, its resonance elsewhere in Australian history, or prehistory. That theme of isolation. "Bass Strait was formed as a result of the melting of ice after the last ice age and consequently Flinders and Cape Barren became islands and the Aborigines of Tasmania were cut off from their mainland counterparts." There are two aspects at least of this history which keep imposing themselves here, it seems. Both have to do with concepts of extinction. Both with genetics. The first disguises itself beneath the objective facticity of sociology and the legacy of Darwinism. Australian Aborigines, cut off from southeast Asia for so many tens of thousands of years, were trapped in an evolutionary time warp, like the *Raphus cucullatus*, or Dodo, once found on the island of Mauritius.

Like the Dodo, the Aborigine was perceived by the nineteenth-century cognoscenti as being little more than an accidental leftover of the contest of evolution, whose ultimate extinction was seen as inevitable, rather than as contingent upon any sort of intervention. Indeed, if anything, it was intervention which was required if the Aborigine was to be "saved." But saved for what? As a testament to the principles of humanism, perhaps, and to the advances in Western scientific method? But this is no joke. Assuredly enough, the Tasmanian Aborigine was a relic of itself already in the mind of those Europeans who had a mind to save it from nature, or destiny, one or the other.

This points back to the first part of the definition of what a relic is supposed to be: "Something which has survived the passage of time; especially, an object or custom whose original cultural environment has disappeared." The word survival is interesting here. The above passage tells us that forty-five Aborigines survived Wybalenna (can we say that yet?). When the attempt to "save" them had apparently failed, they were sent (dispatched?) to Oyster Cove, on the East Coast of Tasmania, where prevailing conditions were even less favorable than on Flinders. There they were left. Or perhaps there they remained. Only they didn't. The last "survivor," Truganini, died in 1876. Her remains were first buried in the grounds of the female convict prison in Hobart, and then later exhumed and put on exhibition at the museum there until 1947. It was Truganini whose initiative had led many of the Aborigines to Flinders in the first place, and it is without the slightest trace of irony that Robert Hughes called her "the arch-traitor of her race."[1]

With the death of Truganini, the case of the Tasmanian Aborigine was supposed to have been brought to a close, and such was the official version of events bequeathed to history. With it came a close, also, to an exceptionally brutal chapter in the story of white "settlement." But something very curious emerges from this. It has to do, again, with that notion of the land bridge. Of something being cut off. This isn't to do with the facts of chronology or the discontinuity implied by extinction. It's something else. It has to do, firstly, with a concept of the antipodes; with the resonance, in English, of a name like Van Diemen's Land. Of the convict history of Australia and its history as a dystopia, or geographical underworld, hell itself. In a very significant way, Australia, and Tasmania in particular, was seen as a sort of nineteenth-century unconscious. A grotesque metonym, detached from the civilized, rationalized world.

As Australia emerged from its own dark ages, the dawning of a new rationalism demanded its own black hole into which to cast all of those bad dreams which otherwise upset a clear conscience. In a way Tasmania had always served this purpose. Port Arthur defined it, during the convict period, as the exemplary "devil's island." But after the death of Truganini it was able to serve as another kind of unconscious. The type of unconscious which has been detached entirely from the mental life of the patient and can be put up on display. An "historical" unconscious. A relic of a past to which the present is no longer tied by that old struggle of adversaries. An "other," we might say, that the "self" has managed to do away with. What is this supposed to mean? Here is another account:

In 1803 the first white settlers arrived in Tasmania, or Van Diemen's Land as it was known then, and began clearing and farming the land. Over four thousand Aborigines lived in Tasmania too. Fighting began and continued for many years and hundreds of Aborigines and Europeans were killed. It was during this turmoil that Truganini was born, around 1812, in the Bruny Island-

157

D'Entrecasteaux Channel area of Tasmania. She was a vibrant and beautiful girl whose father was an elder of the south-east tribe. By the time Truganini was 17 her mother was murdered by whalers, her sister abducted and shot by sealers and her husband-to-be murdered by timber fellers. Truganini was raped. By 1830 the fighting was so widespread it was known as the "Black War."

It is no accident whatsoever that Tasmania, of all the states of Australia, is the only one in whose annals the word "war" is ever used in regards to the European displacement of Aboriginal peoples. In a curiously simplistic way, this probably has to do with the fact that it has long been believed that there were no survivors to whom such an admission might appear to provide the basis for any claim of reparation. Only secondarily would it have seemed to undermine the claim of *Terra Nullius,* or the myth that Aborigines didn't attempt to resist white settlement in an organized fashion. No doubt it bespeaks a number of other important aspects of colonial and post-colonial history in Australia. But before addressing any of these, there is a second aspect of the history of the land bridge which needs to be looked at.

From Australia, to Tasmania, to Flinders Island: a series of declensions of isolation and containment. In 1788 the British government established at Botany Bay, and then at Sydney Cove, the basic institutions of what was conceived as functioning as a giant floating prison. Like a "geographical unconscious," Britain would cast into it all the manifestations of socially undesirable thought that offended Georgian morality. Petty criminals, political dissenters, Luddites, rebellious Irish, French and American collaborators. The whole motley crew of those effectively disenfranchised by a class system enchanted with its own sense of destiny over man and nature. Like so much Darwinian flotsam, they were dispatched across the seas and left to become either extinct, or useful. Other histories describe this differently, however one facet remains constant: the idea of containment.

Containment as a distinct policy of colonial management, however, developed only gradually. In Tasmania, a vastly reduced landmass served to accelerate this process. The destruction of Aboriginal culture began to take on a highly systematic complexion, to the point where the "Black War" virtually succeeded in reducing the Aboriginal population to extinction. In 1830 it occurred to someone in the colonial administration, that a programme of rounding up the surviving Aborigines and containing them in one place might somehow succeed in *protecting* them "from the rape and abuses of the white settlers." When later, in 1836 the House of Commons Select Committee formed the Aborigines Protectorate, a search was begun to find who should serve as the Chief Protector, there was only one man who was regarded as having successfully managed to constrain a large group of Aborigines to settle and to adhere to British Agricultural practices: George Augustus Robinson.

> The colonial authorities appointed George Augustus Robinson, a builder and untrained preacher to mount a "Friendly Mission" to find the remaining Aborigines who were deep in the Tasmanian bushland. His job was to convince the Aboriginal people to move to a nearby island. When Truganini and her father met Robinson he told them he was their friend and would protect them. He promised that if they agreed to come with him he would provide blankets, food, houses and their customs would be respected. He also promised they could return to their homelands occasionally. By 1833 nearly all the Aborigines had agreed to move to Flinders Island where a settlement had been set up at Wybalenna. Here Robinson intended to teach the Aboriginal people European customs.

Robinson, as Manning Clark portrays him, was "devoutly religious, a member of the Auxiliary Bible Society of Van Diemen's Land, and a foundation member of the Van Diemen's Land Mechanics' Institute." Elsewhere Clark portrays him as "that great booby, that fool in Christ." He had emigrated from England to Van Diemen's Land in 1824. From 1838–49, after the failure of the Wybalenna experiment, he served as Chief Protector of Aboriginals.

A painting by Benjamin Duterrau, entitled The Conciliation (1834–5), records, in a highly stylized manner, the meeting between Robinson and the Aborigines he was to convince to accompany him to Flinders Island. According to one near-contemporary source, the painting by Duterrau was supposed to depict the conciliation of the Big River and Oyster Bay tribes in December 1831. "The capture of those two tribes had been the primary goal of the unsuccessful Black Line—a cordon made up of both military men and civilians, which had swept across Tasmania in October 1830, attempting to drive all Aborigines into the Forestier Peninsula. Robinson's subsequent conciliation of those tribes not only firmly established his reputation but was also the pinnacle of his career."[2]

The painting has long been criticized on both aesthetic and historical grounds, but the palpable absurdity of Duterrau's figure composition is perhaps most striking in the way in which it in fact captures, not an historical event, but the tone rather of the historical record. No one knows what promises Robinson made with or without the prior approval of the colonial authorities. The idea that he managed, by charisma alone, to lure the remainder of an otherwise "warlike" people into captivity seems ridiculous. But then the nineteenth-century is littered with similar tales of European entrepreneurialism.

However events may have taken place, what remains clear enough is that beneath the amateur philanthropy of Robinson there operated an entirely sinister apparatus of thought. The fact that this apparatus was common to an era of European anthropology and political practice in no way lessens the gravity of the consequences of Robinson's program. Nor does Robinson's manifest incompetence lessen the culpability of himself and those who authorized him; indeed, of all those who have, in one way or another, continued to authorize him.

The history of the settlement at Wybalenna varies. Luckily, however, Robinson's journals of 1835-39 survive. Another relic. They record, in varying degrees of pathos, the failure of Robinson's well-intended pastoral work. But what was that work? And what were its intentions? It has long been argued that among the promises and assurances made by Robinson to the Aborigines, was the promise that their culture and traditions would be respected. It has also been argued that Robinson, with the tacit approval of government, had offered Flinders Island as territorial compensation for Aborigines agreeing to cede their territorial claims to land in Tasmania, somewhat in the manner of the reservation coming into existence contemporaneously in the United States. Certainly neither of these promises was kept. Nor has history dignified the Aboriginal people with the record of anything like a treaty (verbal or otherwise). A typical version is rather like this one, from another tourism brochure.

> The National Trust regards Wybalenna as one of the most important historic sites in Australia because of its direct association with the tragic remnants of the Tasmanian Aboriginal tribes. In the nearby cemetery, the Young Farmers' club has erected a plaque to commemorate the death of over 100 Aborigines at Wybalenna. Manalargena, last chief of the Ben Lomond Tribe, is remembered on a 1835 headstone. A highly respected chief and warrior, Manalargena had been captured by George Augustus

Robinson and accompanied him as one of the "friendly natives" on Robinson's recruiting mission through wilderness areas of Tasmania. The native graves, outside the fence and unidentified, are said to be empty. Some skeletons were stolen, stories say, and sold to European medical and scientific institutions where they brought good prices. Some were said to have been smuggled out in bales of wool. Others were taken secretly by their own people and buried elsewhere.

I was surprised when I first read this, for a number of reasons. It wasn't so much the claim that Manalargena had been "captured" by Robinson, but rather the nature of the local knowledge cited in order to provide this description of a National Trust site with some sort of placement within an historical narrative. Among those details which impressed me was the last sentence. This is a direct statement of fact. "Others were taken secretly by their own people and buried elsewhere." The three previous sentences are all qualified by phrases like "are said to be," "stories say," "were said to have been." The sort of anonymous disclaimers which one commonly finds included in an account to give it an intentional or unintentional bias (revealing in either case). But there is something else, too. Something about the nature of knowledge. About how possession of knowledge is perceived. About the nature of secrets. But when does a secret cease to be a secret, and become a rumor? And when does a rumor cease to be a rumor, and become history? From a memorandum submitted by the Tasmanian Aboriginal Center to the British House of Commons, regarding European collectors' acquisition of Tasmanian human remains and cultural property, July 2000:

> 7. Much of the Tasmanian human remains and cultural property material in Britain comes from the private collection of George Augustus Robinson. After his death, Barnard Davis acquired the material, now widely dispersed in British museums.
>
> 8. Robinson often notes Aborigines making him gifts of spears, waddies, necklaces and baskets to try to please and placate him; one instance—"Queen Adelaide I brought me a necklace of shells . . . which I refused to show my great displeasure at her conduct." (7 June 1837). Many necklaces were also sold at the "markets" which Robinson conducted at Wybalenna as part of his missionary scheme to Europeanise the people.

9. Robinson persuaded Aborigines to give him the bones of their dead relatives which they carried as talismans against sickness and death. One instance was on 1 June 1838: "[When viewing the corpse of a woman who had died that morning] I asked G Robinson [Kolebuner] for an underjaw of a native which hung suspended to his throat. He appeared reluctant to part with it and said it belonged to his wife Agnes [Mealettarner] and he would ask her consent . . . I spoke to her myself. She replied 'what am I to do when I am monartyer [sick]?' I said, 'never mind, it is no use in such cases.'"

10. Furthermore, as the people died in the camps, Robinson, who had been given the title "Protector of the Aborigines," cut up their bodies to distribute among his friends, military officers and representatives of the Crown. To give a few examples of his activities: Robinson reports that on his first meeting with Governor and Lady Franklin at Wybalenna in January 1838 they . . . solicited me for curiosities, also the skull of an aboriginal." The Governor's secretary Captain Maconochie also asked him for a skull. The day after Mitaluraparitja died of pneumonia in February 1838 at Wybalenna, the surgeon cut off his head for Robinson to have it "masticated" and sent to Maconochie. Robinson later "etained" the cranium of Pintawtawa who died in August 1838 and sent it to Lady Franklin in February 1839. Skull No 94.1.20.1 in the Natural History Museum's Tasmanian collection is labeled "Lady Franklin."

11. The Natural History Museum also retains one of only two full skeletons of tribal Tasmanian Aborigines known to still exist. These skeletons were among five "obtained" from the Curator of Hobart Museum between 1870 and 1875. These skeletons, one of them a named person, were dug up from the graveyard at Wybalenna. The Tasmanian museums in Hobart and Launceston were both well stocked with Aboriginal remains from Wybalenna and Oyster Cove, comprising a large collection of remains dug up from the burial ground at Oyster Cove by the prestigious Dr Crowther (who later became Premier of Tasmania).

In 1992, filmmaker Steve Thomas went to Flinders Island to make a documentary focusing on the cemetery at Wybalenna. In Thomas's otherwise detailed account, there is no mention of the Young Farmers' club plaque, or even of the 1835 headstone which commemorates Manalargena. There are no doubt good reasons for this. Robinson's journal doesn't seem to have any record of the gravestone either. Why such a gravestone should exist, separate from "the native graves, outside the fence and unidentified," is anyone's guess. In any case, there isn't much left of the "tragic remnants" of the Tasmanian Aborigines at Wybalenna, apart from a chapel, an abandoned homestead on the site of the commandant's house and the cemetery. Or so the story goes.

> For many years the chapel was used as a shearing shed until, in 1973, it was purchased and restored by the Flinders Island Branch of the National Trust. Bricks were salvaged from other nearby ruins and similar bricks were brought from Tasmania. While most of the rafters of the restored chapel are original the roof needed new shingles. In the absence of historical records, windows typical of the period were installed.

It is details like this, the use of the Wybalenna chapel as a sheering shed, its meticulous reconstruction by the National Trust, which create such an uncanny impression when placed alongside the question of those unidentified, segregated graves of the "natives," outside the fence of the actual graveyard where the remains of whites only were buried, consecrated and commemorated. But there is something else, too. The bricks, salvaged from nearby ruins. A theme is starting to reassert itself: salvaged, ruins. Relics. But what ruins? This isn't explained, at least not in this National Trust brochure. They still exist, however, as a series of excavated foundations, neatly ordered in a long row stretching away from the commandant's house; the remains of field work conducted between November 1969 and February 1971. Little distinguishes them from the foundations of any number of archaeological sites. But there is a difference. A very important one.

> In 1833 the entire Aboriginal population on mainland Tasmania was exiled to Wybalenna, taken there by a building constructor and missionary named George Augustus Robinson. Aborigines had engaged in a long and bloody war in Tasmania and their wholesale removal to Wybalenna was seen by the Colonial Government as an instant solution to the conflict. Robinson also used Wybalenna as an experiment.

But what sort of experiment did Robinson use the settlement at

Wybalenna for? By most accounts it differed little from most missionary "experiments." The exiled Aborigines were made to "quit barbarous for civilised life." That is, they were made to dress in European clothes and abide by European customs. Most importantly, they were made to live in a rigidly organized settlement compound, underfed, with minimal sanitation, on an isolated and windswept corner of the island. How this reflected Robinson's promise to respect tribal customs is difficult to understand, without attempting to understand the overriding conviction of Robinson, and a whole generation of like-minded philanthropists, that the missionary experiment was in the native's best interests.

But at what point did Robinson cease to be merely a misguided philanthropist and become "commandant" of Wybalenna? At what point, in other words, did he become complicit in the destruction of the Aboriginal people? Robinson, it is important to remember, had been appointed to the command at Wybalenna by the Lieutenant-Governor of Van Diemen's Land, George Arthur, the architect of the infamous "Black Line." According to one Federal report:

> By the late 1820s the conflict between Aboriginal people and the non-Indigenous population had escalated to the "Black War" as it was known at the time. After a spate of attacks on settlers in 1830, Colonel George Arthur decided "to deliver the knock-out blow that would bring the conflict to an end once and for all." It was known as the "Black Line." Over 2,000 men moved in a line across the Island for six weeks with the aim of driving the Aboriginal population onto two peninsulas in the far south-east. This costly plan was an utter failure.

Warfare continued and the government looked for other strategies to deal with "the Aboriginal problem." George Augustus Robinson, a local building contractor who had traveled unarmed among Aboriginal people and gained their trust, suggested to the government that he negotiate with them and offer them protection, food, clothing, and shelter away from the mainland. This plan received official sanction and it was agreed that they would be removed to Flinders Island. By 1835 more than 200 Aboriginal people had been moved to the Wybalenna settlement on Flinders Island. Shortly after arriving the fourteen Indigenous children aged between six and fifteen years were sent to live with the storekeeper and the catechist.

On the Island the combination of inadequate shelter, insufficient rations, disease, and loss of freedom proved fatal to the Aboriginal population. By 1843 only about fifty remained. In 1847 the forty-eight survivors were moved again, this time to another reserve at Oyster Cove. The children were forcibly removed to the Orphan School in Hobart to "adjust" to non-Indigenous society. In 1855 all the people of mixed descent at Oyster Cove were made to leave. By 1876 everyone left had died.

Something fundamental certainly went "wrong" with Robinson's experiment. His "moral lesson for the present and succeeding generations," as he put it, was rather different from what he may have expected. But while his journal records him being moved to shed a tear over the premature death of Manalargena, there is little to suggest that he was overly troubled by the astonishing mortality rate at Wybalenna, despite the fact that he put so much stock by avowing "respect for the life of man whether black or white." It is probable that Robinson, like his supporters, saw the deaths on Flinders Island, as an unfortunate but unavoidable consequence of Christian efforts to civilize the Aborigines.

Those less inclined to concern themselves with the well-being of Aborigines may well have gained a strange satisfaction from Robinson's "failure," the efficiency of which can hardly have gone unnoticed. Indeed, there is something about the organization and symmetry of the ruins at Wybalenna which suggest a very different type of architectural legacy: one entirely divorced from the project of philanthropy. It is matched on Flinders Island only by the symmetry of the unmarked graves in which those who died were buried. Robinson took great care to document the position of each grave, including name and burial date, in his journal. It is an interesting document, or perhaps I should say "map," describing a different type of territorialization, of demarcation, sub-division, property. One not of "possession," but of "containment."

There is a sour irony in the Aboriginal naming of Wybalenna. Between the excavated ruins of the settlement compound and the unmarked graves, it is difficult to determine what is in fact being named, and which of the two, if they can ultimately be distinguished, are the actual "black man's houses." The regularity of the deaths at Wybalenna, and the routine systematicity of internment and burial, suggests a type of rationality, if not necessarily a rationale, at work in this quite lethal geometry. It would be reading too much into it, however, to consider this as being more than a fortuitous outcome of a series of accidental events. Perhaps. What one is confronted with, though, is that however we care to look at it, the Aboriginal people on Flinders Island were in virtually every respect internees in a type of camp. Their containment on Flinders Island was underwritten by the colonial government, and the deaths of the vast majority of them was a direct consequence of this.

It may be, not to put too fine a point on it, that the history of Wybalenna ought to be placed within the larger context of the history of similar policies of containment or "concentration." This would be to situate it in terms of the overall project of the Enlightenment and the various apparatuses of industrialization, from the workhouse to the prison, and the entire body of rationalist architectures whose function, ultimately, is a form of incarceration. It would also be to situate it in the prehistory of what the colonial governor of Cuba, Valeriano Weyler, termed in 1896 *campos de reconcentraciòn*. This history is itself not as well delineated as many would like to think. One feature which remains constant, however, from the concentration policy of the Spanish in Cuba and the Americans in the Philippines, to the British South African *laagers* and the camps in German South-West Africa, up until the 1940s, is that "concentration" and "extermination" remained distinct policies in avowed intent only, separated by a mere technicality. The extremely high mortality rates common to all forms of reconcentration were simply assumed to be the consequences of poor sanitation and malnutrition. But this is simply to obscure the underlying purpose of concentration, which has always been, in one sense or another, a programmatic attempt to isolate and "rationalize" a culture out of existence.

Yet it wouldn't do to add such details to the sorts of tourist brochures which glibly advertise the blue waters of eastern Bass Strait. Or the relics of Bass Strait shipwrecks as the principle attraction at a site harboring the unmarked graves of so many victims of state sponsored brutalization: victims whose deaths were a catastrophe, not to say an indictment of all those liberal humanist institutions upon which the Australian Commonwealth was founded. Should we be surprised that this Commonwealth, which so fearlessly enshrined universal adult suffrage in its founding constitution in 1901, excluded Aborigines from citizenship until 1967? Is it surprising that even today, the Australian government finds it impossible to issue a formal apology to the Aboriginal people for the suffering they experienced at the hands of successive "democratic" regimes? From where I am writing this, in Prague, in the center of Europe, one is only too aware of how inequitable the position of the Australian government has been in this regard. But I

166

also don't want to confuse these issues. And besides, the story doesn't end here.

Perhaps it doesn't end anywhere. The threads aren't all going to come together in a tidy resolution. And there are other sides to this story, things I haven't told you. Things I don't know. That perhaps nobody knows. Unless there are different ways of knowing, through metaphors maybe. The land bridge, which isn't there, which is merely a remnant, a string of islands in an uneasy strait. An idea which links histories, no matter how disconnected, discontinued, or contained they may seem. Points of otherwise remote transactions. "Secret" itineraries. What do I mean by this? Memory? Commemoration? I'm cautious of these words. Of the monuments erected to what they apparently signify, all the easier to forget them by.

Which takes me back to those "relics." The ones belonging to so many Bass Strait shipwrecks.[3] The ones that stand in place of a particular history of mercantile shipping. Of commercial networks linking Flinders Island to elsewhere, to Tasmania, to the "mainland." The systems of exchange. Not all of those are encoded in these relics. But perhaps they are nevertheless implied by them. Their "secret" counterparts. It's strange how the museum at Emita records these different catastrophes, side by side, one avowed the other disavowed. But a secret is not disavowed, it is without avowal. Unknown. It has no history. No relic. No relic but itself, perhaps. A trace nevertheless remains: a story, some sort of account. It involves, among numerous others, several of the daughters of Manalargena, abducted by straitsmen who kept them in camps on Flinders and Cape Barren Island.

The abduction of Aborigines, in particular Aboriginal children, has been a recurring feature of Australian colonial practice. A recent report into Aboriginal abductions, entitled "Bringing Them Back Home," records that;

> In 1814 Governor Davey issued a proclamation expressing his "utter indignation and abhorrence" about the kidnapping of Aboriginal children but by 1816 "kidnapping had become widespread." Governor Sorrell made a similar declaration in 1819 and ordered the Resident Magistrates and District Constables to list all the children and youths held by "Settlers or Stock-keepers, stating from whom, and in what manner, they were obtained." He ordered that those who had been taken without parental consent were to be sent to Hobart where they would be maintained and

167

educated at government expense.

At some point the half-caste population of Cape Barren Island became numerous enough for them to receive the epithet of Cape Barren Islanders. As the minutes of evidence published by Westminster on 18 July 2000 attests:

> About a dozen Aboriginal women escaped the camps. Most of these had been captured to work for British sealers living in tiny enclaves in the Furneaux island group off the north east tip of Tasmania. There they established a cohesive and self-sufficient family based community from whom most of today's Aboriginal population descend. Two other Aboriginal women, one of them the sole survivor of Oyster Cove, were married to European men on the Tasmanian mainland [. . .]. None of the Aboriginal men survived.

As one might expect, commerce being what it is, and the "island bridge" being what it is, that members of this community subsequently found themselves related (in more ways than one) to the Aborigines of Flinders Island, descendants of the same Manalargena interned at Wybalenna.

> Apart from the Indigenous people taken to Wybalenna, there was another community of Indigenous people resident on Flinders Island and other islands in the Furneaux Group. These people were the descendants of Aboriginal women and about 12 non-Indigenous sealers. The sealers and their families worked the sealing grounds of Bass Strait between about 1803 and 1827 when the seals became virtually extinct. Thereafter they remained on the islands and turned to other sources of income, notably mutton birding.

When Robinson established Wybalenna he tried to remove the sealers and their families from Flinders Island but had little success. Robinson referred to the descendants of the Aboriginal women and sealers as "half-castes"—presumably to distinguish them from the mainland Aboriginal people under his charge. By 1847 this community numbered about fifty people.

By the end of the 1870s most of the people had moved to Cape Barren Island. In 1881 the Cape Barren Reserve was formally established. By then this Indigenous community was in its third generation.

The community received regular missionary visits and in 1890 a missionary school teacher was appointed. By 1908 the island population, called "half-castes" by the government, numbered some 250 people. In time, the term "Cape Barren Islander" came to be used synonymously with "half-caste" regardless of the place of origin of the person concerned.

Within a predominantly white pastoral community, these "Cape Barren Islanders" evolved a curious non-identity. According to history, the Tasmanian Aborigine became extinct in 1876. The aboriginal burial sites at Wybalenna were left unmarked and left to be overgrown, vanishing into the landscape. Here, precisely, was Terra Nullius, in its precise legalistic detail, in which everything testified not to the "presence" (as the tourist brochure so ineptly puts it) but rather to the definitive "absence" of the Tasmanian Aborigines. How then to account for their continuation, in precisely that location which had been raised up as a monument to their extinction?

In 1991, Aboriginal people on Flinders Island staged a symbolic occupation and repossession of Wybalenna. This followed a less symbolic, and more directly significant series of events, recorded in Steve Thomas's documentary "Black Man's Houses," in which "more than a hundred years after the Tasmanian Aborigines were declared extinct, their descendants set out to reclaim the lost graves of their ancestors." After clearing the overgrown patch of land assumed to contain the burial sites, electronic equipment measuring soil resistivity was used to locate the precise location of the graves, including that of Manalargena. These were then marked, and a plaque was erected, but not without considerable resistance from within the white community. Those who Thomas interviewed expressed resentment of Aboriginal claims to social benefits, cast doubts upon claims to Aboriginality, and denied the appropriateness of any claim to land rights. The utter lack of self-consciousness in the expression of each of these sentiments by those interviewed is revealing. But not for that surprising, although it should be.

In 1993, following the landmark "Mabo" decision by the High Court of Australia, establishing a legal principle of native title, a renewed case was mounted by the Aboriginal people of Flinders Island for title over Wybalenna (Aborigines had first petitioned Queen Victoria for the land in 1845). The Liberal Premier of Tasmania at the time, Ray Groom, announced on July 22 that the government would vigorously oppose the claim in court. This position was supported by the Tasmanian Chamber of Mines and the Farmers and Graziers Association. Michael Mansell, legal adviser with the Tasmanian Aboriginal Center, replied:

> The Wybalenna claim is a call from the Aboriginal community on Flinders Island for some acknowledgment of the torment and hurt our people were subjected to last century in what could only be described as a concentration camp. Premier Ray Groom could simply have sat down with Aboriginal leader Glen Shaw and come to a sensible and simple settlement. Instead he is adamant Aborigines shall remain a landless people by using the powers of government to stop us at every move.

The burial sites at Wybalenna have not only come to describe a place of contention, of claim and counter claim, but a fundamental criticism of the instituting claims of "property" itself. What is perhaps most significant about Wybalenna in these terms, however, is not how the claim to ownership has been resolved, but the way in which the site itself is exemplary of that strangely inverted relation of dwelling (and issues of land rights and native title), to incarceration (and the condition of internment and itinerancy). The wholesale transformation of the relationship of place in Australia from one of incarceration to one of dwelling has tended to obscure, rather than reinforce, the significance of this. In its place, there remain (they are constantly being reinvented for the tourist industry) those fatuous "authentications" of landscape in the Romantic tradition. The relics and museums whose pastoral backdrop belies the catastrophic history which conjoins the two, however much it is given over to the affected amnesia of postcard imagery and scenic evocation.

Postscript

Excerpts from an announcement made on February 28, 1999, by Tasmanian Premier Jim Bacon:

> Wybalenna ranks in importance with Risdon and the Oyster Cove site which had ownership vested in the Aboriginal community on December 6, 1995. It is a sacred site which lives in the memories of Tasmania's aborigines as a place that needs to be preserved to show future generations the consequences of cultural

conflict. In fact Aboriginal people from all around Tasmania can trace their ancestry to those buried here. And in fact the first petition calling for recognition of land rights for Aboriginal people was sent from Wybalenna in 1845.

Wybalenna remains spiritually important and highly significant to the Aboriginal community and has had a major impact in the shaping of today's Aboriginal community. These reasons have had a major influence on a commitment by my Government and for what I now announce . . . that is Wybalenna will be handed back to its rightful owners, the Aboriginal community.

What happened at Wybalenna should never have occurred. It was a site of genocide. I could have selected other words to describe this site, but they would not have been true or reflective of what really happened. Whilst we cannot change history and what occurred at Wybalenna, we can attempt to redress past injustices that have occurred.

Notes

[1] Robert Hughes, in *The Fatal Shore*, recounts the passing of the last male survivor in 1869. "His name was William Land and he was described as Truganini's 'husband,' although he was twenty-three years her junior. Realising that his remains might have some value as a scientific specimen, rival agents of the Royal College of Surgeons in London and the Royal Society in Tasmania fought over his bones. A Dr. William Crowther, representing the Royal College of Surgeons, sneaked into the morgue, beheaded Lanne's corpse, skinned the head, removed the skull and slipped another skull from a white cadaver into the black skin. ... In pique, the officials decided not to let the Royal College of Surgeons get the whole skeleton; so they chopped off the feet and hands from Lanne's corpse and threw them away. The lopped, dishonored cadaver of the last tribesman was then officially buried, unofficially exhumed the next night and dissected for its skeleton by representatives of the Royal Society.

[2] The "Black Line" and Robinson's presumably unwitting role in realising its ultimate objectives, has an interesting, if equally appalling, historical counterpart in the *Vernichtungsbefehl*, or Annihilation Order, of General von Trotha in German South-West Africa, in 1904. This order required German troops to attack and pursue the Herero people, and ultimately drive them past barbed wire into the Kalahari Desert. More than four fifths of the native Herero population was annihilated before this order was rescinded, and replaced by a policy of concentration camps.

[3] The Furneaux Islands were first settled in 1797 by the survivors of the "Sydney Cove"—one of many ships that were to be wrecked over the next 200 years on their rugged coastlines.

George Szirtes

Jerusalem

The leaves are nodding. The traffic runs on.
It is like opening a door on a great secret,
or drawing a dusty 1950s curtain,

a passport to a country of eternal regret,
the Old Jerusalem, a forsaken garden
where the sun is always about to set

on an empire laying down its burden.
Which is what pastoral means: life in a field
of death, natural activity as boredom,

the air crowded with unreconciled
facts: dust, light, insects, birds, sheer noise,
the plants' upward drive, their fates sealed

while they blossom with disturbing poise
that reeks of drama, waving red hands
in the air with showbiz gestures, like boys

in the band, or settle in brilliant islands
of loose coral, because summer is exotic
in such country and makes peculiar demands

on the attention, but the air is thick
with the noise of the past, so it is hard to see
what it is made of, what all this rhetoric

is actually about. Something is ominously
gathering in the sky. The clouds rise
and darken like shadows under a bright tree.

The Ark

It is night in the zoo of the universe. Stars lurk
behind soft mountains and the moon dips
under water. The dreams are getting to work.

He hooks his fingers into her waistband. She slips
towards him and raises her left knee to cover
his right thigh. Her finger rests on his lips,

then moves down to his neck. He rolls her over
and traces her spine with his chin. Her head
is turned on its side as she feels him hover

above her. Her right arm is off the bed,
touching the floor. Night giggles up its sleeve.
His teeth close as if on fresh baked bread.

And then she mounts him. They begin to heave
against the tide. They are plowing through
the waves of the sheets, steady, purposive

voyagers. Out in the field a distraught ewe
calls to her lambs. An owl hoots in the mist.
It is stormy. They are the ship's crew.

Now he's on top, his fingers round her wrist.
She strains to kiss them. The cat in the car park
leaps from bonnet to bonnet. They want to twist

round so he's behind. It takes a sudden jerk—
and there they are. Her breasts hang below her
like any creature's, in the enormous ark

they both occupy. The beasts are beginning to stir
in the hold. She plays him like a piper.
The world is pain and stars in a cradle of fur.

The rainforests of Brazil are made of tissue-paper
that rustles in her head. He is whale blubber
in the Atlantic, a well fed grouper.

Simon Lichman

from an evacuee's notebook

We were sent by train—they said it was a Sunday

Bricked up windows gaswork frames
(Kings Cross Euston Waterloo)
Tunnel tracks pull chimney stacks
Deep lawns and allotments.
Caravans in the wrong dream of light

Pigeon hawk copse spinney
Crystal starlings' sweep of water
The undone in a suitcase
Shaved heads and punctured eyes.

We glide through ghosted Duffield
Colors fade houses slide
The roots no longer hold.

At devil's wrench of Chesterfield
Wind fits into rung of spine
Ebony scaffolds crows in rain
Mauve green off-white white
Forget their names.

Sheffield is the last stop
I polish shoes in the aisles of this train.

Forrest Gander

Pastoral

Prime pry prime me rocks prime evil rocks form
road's prime road's steep pry rocks form or pry
from rocks for eve the steep prime ore the road's
border rocks form prime the road's steep or all

Much have much they have there they have fir or
and faced there bore and door much have they there
faced much first and much and last have they first faced
of the trans the story in the trans long or it of the
earth's long earth's of in long or door of the trans it
in door or of it order of the trans the story in or

What they but what in cast they cord what cull in
cast and but they cull cord in recast what color
cord but cast and what cast ore record they in
is that two passed we that we that two passed is
two is that two is passed is that that is that passed

William Kentridge

Charles Bernstein

every lake has a house
& every house has a stove
& every stove has a pot
& every pot has a lid
& every lid has a handle
& every handle has a stem
& every stem has an edge
& every edge has a lining
& every lining has a margin
& every margin has a slit
& every slit has a slope
& every slope has a sum
& every sum has a factor
& every factor has a face
& every face has a thought
& every thought has a trap
& every trap has a door
& every door has a frame
& every frame has a roof
& every roof has a house
& every house has a lake

Susan Bee

Vona Groarke

Poplar

He's a gossip and he brings it home to her
how big the world is, how small her doings there.
His statements have the ring of confidence,
so she listens and is sparing in response.
He could say anything to her, even her name, and still
it would sound like small leaves tossed in a summer squall.

Cherry

In the Canaries, maybe, but in Youghal?
Even the natives found the leaves sporadic,
the fruit (when it issued) too crimson for their taste,
and the timber unreliable in fire.

Coral Hull

"Donkey"

"the flies" "of the donkeys ears" "and legs" "the
magpies" "and the currawongs" "of the dam" "and the
honey-eater" "wiping his beak" "on a branch" "the three
donkeys" "hee-hawing" "like bagpipes" "Chrissy"

"Chrissy" "oh Chrissy" "was very sick" "the day" "the
apple dropped" "from her mouth" "her big donkey head"
"could not chew it" "she looked" "as if she wanted"
"me" "to do" "something" "I held her" "head" "to my

chest" "like a barrel" "a donkey's head" "is so large" "so
much expression" "the warm" "brown" "buttery eyes"
"the daylight" "melts in them" "birds" "in the nearby
trees" "some wrens on the wire

fence" "that have picked the bugs" "from her buckled
back" "Chrissy, dying" "gently the slobbered apple"
"drops out of her mouth" "you can be invisible" "she
sees it fall" "onto the ground" "she lies down" "the farm

doesn't take long" "the farm is moving" "around the
bones" "the farm" "doesn't" "take much time" "to eat
the flesh" "and bone" "after four weeks" "there was
nothing" "left" "of Chrissy" "nothing left" "of her" "just

a patch" "of her rich chocolate fur" "stuck to the skull"
"a wet rug" "chocolate fur" "the farm has eaten her"
"polished her bones" "bones still moist" "sucked on"
"by daylight" "dawn came, coldly" "all her brief life"

"the property" "has not loved her" "as you had hoped"
"it would" "did she hurt?" "but" "no longer" "it has
eaten her up" "now polishes" "her bones" "her eyes"
"gone first" "delicious" "to birds" "you can be invisible"

"Moon"

"is that the moon?" "the sickle moon" "cold faced"
"across the fields" "how can we describe" "the moon"
"again" "to those" "we love" "our children?" "how
would we describe" "the moon" "to the flying fox" "so

that they didn't all grin" "at us?" "how" "to listen" "to
everything?" "the cows that live inside" "the peace of
the tabletops" "from the dawn" "til dusk glow" "ask
them" "listen" "they will speak to you" "with their

silence" "the peace" "of the stars" "the gaseous clusters"
"of the milky way" "the peace" "of the huntsman" "with
the banded legs" "positioned" "by the opened window"
"the peace of the old blue heeler" "who followed me"

"way out" "to the grazing chestnut horse" "beyond the
house paddock" "the peace of my hat" "my coat, boots"
"my childhood" "my lover" "the sun on my forearms"
"the peace" "of the house paddock" "that is" "his"

"responsibility" "the peace of responsibility" "the peace
of land" "without any" "the stars" "hanging" "in
treetops" "midnight fruit" "fruit" "passing through" "the
many hours" "of the early morning" "from midnight"

"the branches" "held the stars" "just like" "they had"
"created them" "like it was" "the branches" "who had
created" "the traveling light" "the light" "which had
taken a thousand light years" "or more" "to travel" to

the branches" "of the casuarinas" "the stringy barks"

"Fence"

"I'm the fence," "follow" "the fence" "judy" "are you
there?" "yes" "I'm going to follow" "the fenceline"
"yes" "yes" "follow it" "judy" "follow the fence" "the
fence" "through" "the grass" "through the long" "dry

grass" "the fence" "cuts the air" "makes way" "a snake"
"of barbs" "wire and endings" "cuts corners" "travels
far" "through many places" "follows itself" "you will
follow" "yes" "yes" "follow" "the fence" "the rabbit"

"the rabbit got under there" "last night" "the big rabbit"
"the hungry" "rabbit" "at dusk" "ready" "for your
garden" "the rabbit" "through there" "yesterday" "the
rabbit" "today" "silence" "through the fence" "the

hungry silence" "of rabbit" "through" "the fence" "to
feed" "on your garden" "your night garden" "to strip the
leaves" "with the hawthorn slugs" "in the long night
garden" "quiet rabbits" "come in" "to eat" "the english

cottage garden" "the fence" "watching" "oh yes" "the
fence seeing" "and moving by" "the fence" "traveling
by" "like a river" "like a king river" "like a tiger snake"
"the powerful movement of the fence" "the fence

forever" "cut by a tree" "the tree" "slides onto the
property" "as if it wanted to join us!" "through the
fence" "its branch!" "its giant snout!" "a wooden reptile"
"collapsed through the barbed wire" "its scale" "its

wood" "for kilometers" "on end" "as if nothing else
mattered" "its unseeing eye" "here" "its mighty
collapse" "and its crashed" "snapping the thirsty wire"
"oh" "no" "the tree fallen" "oh no" "the fence cut" "oh"

"no" "fix it" "fix the fence" "no boundaries" "fix the
fence" "the tree cut me" "the tree" "the mad tree in the
mad storm" "cut" "me down" "fix" "the fence" "go
back" "go back" "the other way" "we check the

boundary fence" "where a tree has fallen" "in a weekend
storm" "and has crashed through" "it is a woolly butt"
"and its bark" "flakes away" "through my fingers" "in
fine hairs" "the tree is not good" "for burning" "johnny
told me" "and so" "you will chop it" "and leave it" "to
the ground" "and ground inhabitants" "the tree fell"
"like a crocodile" "from up north" "slipping from the
land" "into a swamp" "the tree slides onto the property"

"as if it wanted to join us" "through" "the fence" "its branch"
"its giant snout" "is collapsed" "through the barbed wire"
"there is a mighty tree" "here" "and it's crashed" "snapping"
"this thirsty wire" "on thirsty lands"

William Manhire

The Prairie Poet

All day shoveling small snow,
and look, western light
at my window.

Janet McAdams

Ghost Ranch

Light picks this landscape down to bone.
It's Boxing Day: six miles back
the orange jumpsuits are picking trash
while they do time. The guards are white,
someone has cut the Indian prisoners' hair.

The mesa's one short hard haul straight up.
Gray feather in the crack I work my fingers
into and tug and work them out again.
Then flat on top and land for miles and miles—
so much land. You find a pile of bones

and hold the pelvis up, framing a ragged disc
of sky. Not the real sky, I thought that day,
but blue enough to tell this story. You say
the feather's from a dove and spot an eagle
circling high across the canyon, but I am not

so sure. We touch and circle and touch and circle
until we only circle: cloth against cloth, skin
not quite meeting, the way fences touch at the corners
of nations. Last night you slept so quietly,
I put a hand to your back to make sure

you were breathing, the other over your shoulder
and flat against the skin between nipple
and solar plexus: because breath may not be
a sure enough measure. We hover
over the animal that carved itself

a place to rest, past molecule, atom,
the stinging energy that drums the universe
into being. Don't say you never felt it.
Even the stone was pulsing. Take my hand
if you can bear it, but let the other story go.

J. D. McClatchy

In the Valley

The day's long since broken and light's
spilled over the lip of heat in the valley.
Small desires come to mind and go,
their going at least a cold taste
of what's on the horizon this next leg
along the trail our affair has blazed.
These markers—the stack of stones
from whose thirst-crazed throat?
the blue arrow hastily painted
on rock with whose knotted anger?—
have led me along a story line.
The cactus, the scrub, the serrated
glare have their own bit parts in it.
Like me, the dead river thrives
on an old lack of purpose and follows
a useless way, snaking around
obstacles too long gone even to be
missed. The violence of the place
seems fragile, as if overly logical.
Everything repeats itself. Behind
this cloud, beside that boulder
is another and another. Each step
away from them echoes the original
inertia, or the first time I winced—
at what? the kiss? the strap? the stitch?
The old room smears. Left to myself,
hour by hour, the heat erases everything
but a sense of its unbearable persuasions.

Okay, I'll walk until the sun goes down
numbly on the world and the sky's
chokehold forces me to consider
the sweat beads on the night's torso,
the edge of the new moon's cock ring,
even last year's losing streak crossing
through the black etceteras.
It's so hard to tell the time. The dial
keeps staring back at me unmoved,
just the tsk-tsk of its second hand
and its phosphorescent treadmill.
Hadn't I set out to learn what hurts and why?
You know the reason when you pull back
from a scalding thrill or sumptuary weight.
You know love in the definitions: What feels
its way blindly over the strange body.
What turns its face too soon, too late.

Bob Perelman

Pastoral

One person each, out
Into one world, back into many.
The collection, the alphabet. He imitates
Its power, sentiments, antiquity. Scenery
In the form of a dramatic monologue.

She trails out of the present
Both ways, but is sitting
At the table with him. Sprays
Of bay, laurel, and their natural
Interpretations are tacked above them.
Hearts beating. A storm at sea.

Gossip at length, hours
Yoked together, sun shines,
Air presses on their capillaries,
Actions. Desire pronounced and
Punctuated, their minds end
In their senses. Pleasures
Lag across solid bridges.

Time to eat. Light is suffused, revised
Among the letters. Their ears fill
With sounds of the visible world.
Minutes surround them, trees
In the foreground by voice vote.
Their eyes close. It is night.

Today's Lament

for Emily Steiner

You'd think a thousand years of laments would be enough,
but no. Now I have to write one.

First, it seems, you get stuck in these systems,
then you have to explain yourself to them.

I now think my kinsmen had secret plans behind those more or less
    smiling faces.
Reason is fretted with anger since it's been forced to live here under
    an oak tree in a suburban cave.
The streets are gloomy, overgrown with cars,
lit and crosslit by the varnished light of credit card debt.
The cars move or not in their sullen variousness. Some shine, some
do not.

You'd think it would be possible
to make macaroni and cheese without having to get in the car,

but no.
No cheese: no macaroni and cheese.

Aren't a thousand years of laments enough?
Apparently not.

There's a little parmesan, but no cheddar.
There's a problem with the globe,
but no view.
So it's out on the tossing waves to Superfresh.

Fresh tears, fresh words drawn from my own sorrowful lot.
I can say that.
"Weigh your 'sharp cheddar cheese.'
Move your 'sharp cheddar cheese' to the belt."

In this wide second, I am seized with longings.

"Weigh your 'broccoli rabe.'
Move your 'broccoli rabe' to the belt."

I have not suffered such hardships as now.
"Weigh their 'pretending, plotting, murderous, smiling faces.'
Move their 'pretending, plotting, murderous, smiling faces' to the belt."
This is not a generic thousand-year-old lament, but fresh today.

I would now explain the lit and crosslit gloom of the system
that makes us live most wretchedly, far from one another,
but no.

Explain to my friendless kinsmen, tossed
with fresh gloomy longings, vigilant to the generic clutch of anguish,
explain to the Superfresh stronghold.

"Weigh your 'thousand years of linguistic change.'
Move your 'thousand years of linguistic change' to the belt."

You'd think one car would be enough,
one long world to live
out from this cave under these tossing systematic dawns.
You'd think, after a thousand years,

but no.
I draw these words from my endless list seized with crosslit longings.

"Weigh
your 'endless list seized with crosslit longings.'
Move
your 'endless list seized with crosslit longings'
to the belt."

A thousand years, crossed off, crouching under the smiling parking lot,
my lot.

[after the Old English "Wife's Lament"]

Mary Jo Bang

Mrs. Autumn and Her Two Daughters

We live in an ocean
of white waiting to fall.
One of us is not like our mother and it's me. It's I.
My eyes are mostly closed.

My mother knows
how to make snow. We never see
our feet. Our skirts end in the oncoming frost.
My sister wears ermine. I have a narrow waist.

I no longer curl my hair. Why bother?
I love my sister but hate my mother
yet we're all of a piece.
Endless snipsnip. Ragged fragment.

We still live where you last left us—
between the palace where you keep your winter
and the summer garden of the ersatz emperor.
Did I hear you say China? If I did you are right.

We live atop the continent
that contains such poverty. Such pollution.
Such eerie beauty. Always a mountain.
Always a screen. White washes

over me. I do not act
like my mother. I lean farther.
What I make annihilates the mirror of China
but not the mountain.

Not the man walking away.
My mother says throw more snow but I can't
help thinking
There is more to being than erasure.

You are wrong she says. You don't wear your cape.

Sigmar Polke, *Frau Herbst und ihre Zwei Töchter* (Mrs.
Autumn and her Two Daughters), Artificial resin and acrylic
on synthetic fabric, 1991.

The Falling Out

She loved the lyric lines that formed the house.
The sure and sharp roof, the diminutive gable,
the window breakable and sad
that way, like the fall of hair dripping
down the side of a face.

The rain sounded small
on glass as through a pane a man's outstretched arms
as if to say, What can be done
about anything now? It was ivy
up the wall and down the rain came.

The inhale of a smoky now.
The stairway narrowing, footfall by footfall
until the top, where opening
onto vista and short-breathed, the rain harder now.
That was love, wasn't it? A wind

and its wuthering. Rain refreshing
the eye. And pretty sentences,
all red and green, like ribbon they fell—
dropped over a knee, draped over an arm, fell
onto the floor at their feet. They would be buried soon

if they sat there too long.
The grosgrained grammar of them, the rough stutter
of indrawn air, the satin surface
of a slip over which the last sentence slid
and fell. She closed her eyes

and the street gave way. The rain a heady descent,
cars weaving between trees. The petty
activity never ceasing.
The choir indicative of the symphony. Splendid.
Remarkable. Knowledge a hill.

Kneeling to bury a bird in the back yard, the soil cold and
the played card a spade. I love means to look
at the subject. She looks instead
at the lines that form an angle steep in its wanting
rain to roll off. She reaches up

to push a cloud away and isn't able
to do any such thing. She is painted
in place. Head pressed to a shoulder, the kissed
clouds, a red car turning at the sign
of a paused moment.

The facade reorganized. Behind which
a million angles of incidence. Each window an opening
between sutures. Everything falling out.

The harbored and hindsighted.
The symbolic and sorry.

Lisa Jarnot

Elmslie Blake Pastoral

In the meadow cows are leaping
through the branches monkeys sleeping
on the fields the sheepies bleating,
dancing on the vert fields creeping,

leaping, creeping verdant reaping,
all around their hooves repeating
what the bright green bushes say
opening the vert green day

daylight, sheeplight their bright rays
chasing cows the monkeys play
dancing through the clear green hay
having hooves to leap they stray

into fields green cleared away,
how the monkeys verdant sway
sway on monkeys, sing and leap with
verdant sheep who mow the green tips

of the vert and verdant green
bright green, clear green, sheep-filled scene
of the vert and verdant green
bright green, clear green, sheep-filled scene.

Drew Milne

Ostrich Takes Off

flocked machines
   curl upon on roughage
and run up tacitly
     the extreme savvy
felt to rumble
   and as the earth burns
what just in
     does off on cattle & horse
now ostrich flesh has the driving seat
but right in there with joined-up burgerism

    what convertible bond
       do savor each
I mean puh-leese
    if the "vice Américain"
  is so becoming
    then the "Sprecher" can
take the first hike among said equals
  let the mission steaks go fuckabout
or more sooth
  on horde or lard lounge
runt to blunt risk glades
    as you were

and wouldn't it be nice to stay clear
if not tight to the pterodactyl wind
  plucky in pink
    among roasting birds
now summer's here
   and up in flames

John Koethe

Eros and the Everyday

... as when emotion too far exceeds its cause

Elizabeth Bishop

A field of unreflecting things
Time is passing by: inert,
Anonymous beyond recall, the deflected
Objects of a self-regarding gaze
Untouched by the anxieties of proximity or love.
I tried to find those passions in the sky,
In moments when the heart surveys itself
As if from above, and wonders at the
Sight of something so particular and small.
A day brings language and a hint of what it means,
Of some presence waiting in the wings
Beyond the stage, beyond the words that
Gathered in the night and stayed
And through whose grace I find, if not quite
What I wanted, then everything else:
The contentment of each morning's
Exercise in freedom, freedom like a wall
Enclosing my heart; the disjunctive thoughts
Gesturing at some half-imagined whole;
A continuity that on the surface feels like love.

What is this thing that feels at once so nebulous
And so complete, living from day to day
Unmindful of itself, oblivious of the future
And the past, hovering like a judgement

Above the future, the present, and the past,
Floating in the distance like the eyes of love?
Call it "experience"—that term of art
For time in an inhuman world
Indifferent to desire, the history
Of one who one day wandered off from home
Along a road that led from here to here:
These sidewalks and these houses, city streets
And suburbs and a highway flowing west
Through fields and quiet streams, uncharted
Trails descending to a farmhouse in a glen and
Nothing in my heart or in the sky above my heart.
And then from somewhere in that wilderness inside
I hear the murmur of a low, transforming tone
That fills the field of sight with feeling,
And that makes of blind experience a kind of love.

Let me stay there for a while, while evening
Gathers in the sky and daylight lingers on the hills.
There's something in the air, something I can't quite see,
Hiding behind this stock of images, this language
Culled from all the poems I've ever loved.
I don't believe a word they say, a word I say,
But it isn't really a matter of belief:
As ordinary things make up the world,
So life is purchased with the common coin of feeling,
Feelings deferred, that flower for a day
And then retreat into the language. And later,
When the hours they'd filled are summoned by a name,
It's as if they'd never been, as if that tangible
Release could never come to me again.
I came here for the view, and what is there to see?
The place is still a place in progress
And the days have the feeling of fiction, of pages
Blank with anticipation, biding their time,
And ever approaching the chapter in the story
Where it ends, and my heart is waiting.

To an Audience

I knew the artifice would finally come to this:
      An earnestness embodied in a style
More suited to the podium than to the page,
      Half sight, half sound, an antipastoral
With which to while away a vagrant afternoon.
      The stage is set as for a play, with cotton
Clouds and cardboard trees beneath a foil moon
      That fails to illuminate the scene.
If you believed in me—if what I meant to say
      Resonated in your heart; if a tone
Held your breath and caught your feeling for the world;
      If my thoughts were thoughts that you alone had had—
The reality would be the same: the summer day
      Outside, indifferent to the other day
Tranquility and time conspired to create.
      This is my arena—this is the stage
On which I mean to live, an isolate domain
      Bounded by silence, inwardly consumed by
Music whose relentless cadences resume
      The speculations of that secret self
For whom to even try to talk to you is death.
      These are the stanzas of a single story,
Spun from unconnected moods that ebb and flow
      Across the surface of the day, from words
Implicit in my breath and spoken to a mirror.
      I get up, retrieve the newspaper
And read myself into a stupor. Then I write.
      I know these habits are a ruse, the tricks I
Use to keep the world at bay, to keep alive
      The fiction of the soul as self-contained.
Yet even as I speak its character is shifting
      As the light shifts and I seem to hear
A disembodied murmur from the balcony
      In which I think I recognize my name.
What made me think that I could live apart from you?

The folly of that thought now seems so clear,
With scenery and background drifting towards me as you
   Overrun this stage I said was mine.
My thoughts may try to hide themselves, to glow in private,
   Yet what animates the page is just the
Specter of a self existing in and through you
   As a forest finds itself in trees,
A city in its towers. This place is bathed in light,
   Revealing it for what it is, a crude
Pretence of thought, like children playing with some blocks,
   Unconscious and alive to one another.
Let my purpose hence be plenitude and patience
   In the hope that through their common grace
I might eventually attain that generous
   "Condition of complete simplicity"
That musing on the thought of you has let me see.
   I'm grateful to you then for all your questions
And objections—for indeed you *are* objections—
   And that is all, for now, I have to say.
Let us conclude though with some resolutions: to
   Abjure these fierce conundrums of the soul;
To quit this theater of dreams; to walk as one
   Into the light of ordinary day.

Brian Henry

What to Do with a Fat
Rope of Old Vine

This panorama extends to subtler regions
where a stone remains a stone
and the marsh somehow becomes a thing to lean on
despite the malfunction of vision
as soon as the sun withdraws.

As soon as the girl withdraws
the marsh becomes a thing to rein in
despite the function of vision
where "stone" ruins a stone.

A stone recalls a stone
despite the infraction of vision
as soon as the girl exhales
the marsh, a subtle thing to withdraw.

Somehow the marsh withdraws
the girl despite the failure of function.
As soon as a stone returns to a thing
the girl returns to her visions.

Peter Gizzi

Overtakelessness

after Albert Pinkham Ryder

To speak inaudibly, the outside,
its blurred sentence foreshadowed,
indistinguishable as shining brass.
The room, the empty sky, beautiful
or golden bands burn because it is empty.
Without depth of field birds become primitive again.
Unstuck weeds float downstream
completing representation.
A thick green complicating light.
Now face the horizon in silence.
Come down while gladness unbinds sleep
unlike silt. This quiet speech feels right
and will be imitated. To turn away,
to speak fondly without a history.
Come down and rediscover this ancient province
as persons exchange smiles like wind instruments.
There, unlike any road you travel,
are small tidings that awakening,
are pleasing. No history is clear.

Reverse Song

Not because there is a road
and a woman walking
nor the trees lining this road,
the light at half-mast

not the birds in *v* crayon

not the uneven houses lit up from within
not even the clapboards' chipped paint

nor the fact she is not alone
in the cricket sound

not the sun setting nor a first star

not the lawns fading to black
nor the broken sidewalk,
dented signs, new blacktop

not the atmosphere
amped after showers

not the catcalls making one stranger
nor the river gaining volume
making all sentient things still
crossing a bridge

not the lamp's sudden flame

but the type of daisy
robins live among,
circle of light found on the table,
her gait, her motion, her speed.

Elizabeth Willis

The Great Egg of Night

Infancy moons us with its misty cloudcover, glowing like clover under empire's weeping hand. An updraft nearly laundered of intent. Palmed and tendered in subaltern shade, I could not shake the memory of a train that whitely striped the hills. The surrendering pike pours out in uniform. Butter-gloved epiphanies slide past us in their muscle car. In the words of the daffodil, am I in my kerchief more lovely than this ash kicking up against the wheel? What form do women take? Or is she taken like a path to frosty metaphor, a seed easier crushed than opened? Can a word be overturned by jest, or does it take a wayward spark to fire up your arsenal of lace? The darkest blue is black, felt around the edges. I give the cool a running start, a catching chance. Rigging our descent to decent landings, mistaking angle for angel, piloting home.

On the Resemblance of Some Flowers to Insects

A smoky vessel drifts east like a slippery elixir. By simple rotation
night collapses with its head in the dirt, though from the heights it
appears more like cubist swagger. Suddenly curtains. What lives in a
room takes on the spirit of the room. This is true even of television.
Imagine deciding the gully a life will follow as if choosing breakfast
over diligent labor. I don't remember my first brush with pollen yet
I've watched words flower sideways across your mouth. In a month
we'll be dizzily older. Moths will leave singed paper on the stoop. Is
this my design? An ant crosses my shadow so many times looking for
its crumb, I think it's me who's needlessly swaying. Its path is busy
eloquence while I'm merely armed, like a chair leaving the scent of
large things on the breeze.

Ronald A. Sharp

Dickey and Lowell: The American Pastoral at Mid Century

As early as 1906, W. W. Greg argued that "little would be gained by at-
tempting beforehand to give any strict account of what is meant by
'pastoral' in literature" (78). We hear the same cautious note on the
first page of Andrew Ettin's 1984 study of the subject. "Accurately
defining pastoral," he says, "may seem almost impossible once one goes
beyond the broad sort of definition appropriate for a handbook of lit-
erary terms" (1). Clearly there are theoretical issues of some moment
in even conceptualizing such a category as pastoral, to say nothing of
the vexed question of whether pastoral is properly considered a genre,
a mode, a tradition, a theme, a subject, a posture, or an attitude. Paul
Alpers takes up this subject in some detail in his magesterial 1996
study, *What Is Pastoral?*

However we may resolve these matters, we can at the very least
agree that certain features of a literary work put one in mind of the
pastoral tradition. And whatever our theoretical orientation, we can
safely assume that it makes sense to talk about pastoral when we con-
front poems that treat the relationship between the human and the
natural in the context of sheep and shepherds, love and love songs.

The two poems that I wish to discuss in these terms, Robert Low-
ell's "Skunk Hour" and James Dickey's "The Sheep Child," were pub-
lished in 1959 and 1966 respectively, and they have been widely stud-

ied and explicated. They are, to be sure, among the most famous poems of these poets. But they have not, to my knowledge, been examined together. Juxtaposing them in the context of pastoral should illuminate important but otherwise obscure elements of the two poems, and throw into relief some crucial issues in the modern fate of American pastoral.

To the extent that pastoral elegizes an earlier innocence, nostalgia may well, as Bryan Loughrey has suggested, be "the emotional core of most pastoral literature" (21). But in "Skunk Hour" and "The Sheep Child" the attitude toward what has been lost seems closer to a kind of anguished longing than to nostalgia, as though the failure to achieve a satisfactory relation—let alone union—with nature were experienced as a raw and painful diminishment. What Alan Williamson has suggested about Lowell's work as a whole may be said about the two poems at hand: these poems ask "whether the whole project of civilization is worth the cost" (2). In addressing that question the two poems define the problem in terms of pastoral, explore possible pastoral solutions, and finally establish a posture towards these issues that involves both a radical subversion of the ideal of pastoral harmony and an implicit celebration of it.

The speaker of "Skunk Hour" is not out in nature but alone at home, not unlike the speaker of Frost's "An Old Man's Winter Night." The "heiress" on this little resort island may stay on "through winter in her Spartan cottage" (2), but the fact that "her sheep still graze above the sea" (3) simultaneously raises the issue of pastoral harmony and marks it as inappropriate to the scene. The sense of being at home in one's environment that we associate with pastoral is mocked again by the heiress's lust for hierarchy and her perversion of privacy:

> Thirsting for
> the hierarchic privacy
> of Queen Victoria's century,
> she buys up all
> the eyesores facing her shore,
> and lets them fall. (7–12)

The obverse of the conversion of homes into "eyesores" is the decorated house, which turns out to be an ideal whose emptiness is emphasized by the note of strained artificiality that marks even the "fairy / decorator" 's (19–20) shop:

> his fishnet's filled with orange cork,
> orange, his cobbler's bench and awl;
> there is no money in his work. . . . (21–23)

As John Frederick Nims has observed, the decorator "turns the gear of honest labor into *objects d'art*" (93). It is a metamorphosis utterly consistent with the diseased and decayed world that surrounds the decorator, so that by the time we get to the speaker spying on the lovers, we are not surprised to hear him confess, "My mind's not right" (30). Surely it is no accident that Lowell uses the verb "bleats" (31) to describe the car radio's playing "Love, O careless Love" (32). What we have in the bleating of this popular song is a grotesque parody of the old shepherds' songs of pastoral, transformed now into trivialized lyrics beamed out across a denatured landscape—a landscape emptied of the old spirits and experienced largely now from inside an automobile, still another emblem of modern mechanization and isolation. The allusion to the old shepherd songs defines by contrast the extent of Lowell's sense of loss.

Vereen Bell has suggested that in Heidegger's terms Lowell experiences the world as "unhomelike" (45); we might extend this notion by suggesting that at one level "Skunk Hour" provides a grisly catalogue of the various ways that the world has come to seem unhomelike. When Lowell says, "I myself am hell; / nobody's here" (35–36), he means that the contagion of estrangement has spread so wide that even in his self's home, nobody is home; that he is somehow absent even from himself. By putting into his speaker's mouth the same words—"myself am hell"—that Satan uttered while looking in on the Garden of Eden in *Paradise Lost*, Lowell both defines the speaker's agonizing spiritual exile and links it the modern estrangement from the pastoral ideal of an unselfconscious union with nature.

Both of these poems want to press the question of what and where a home is. The sheep child, we are twice told, lives "in my father's house" (27, 49)—a phrase that recalls a famous passage spoken by Jesus in John 14, and thus confirms the implication that this strange creature has a Christlike dimension. It does, after all, die for our salvation by becoming the stuff of folklore ("I have heard tell" [8]; "I heard from somebody who . . ." [16]) that serves a civilizing function:

> Dead, I am most surely living
> In the minds of farm boys: I am he who drives

Them like wolves from the hound bitch and calf
And from the chaste ewe in the wind. (55–58)

In addition the sheep child is immortalized amidst the perpetual dust of a museum, which becomes a hellish transformation of the heaven imagined in John 14 as a house with many "mansions," i.e., rooms. If in "Skunk Hour" Lowell evokes the pastoral tradition with a reference to sheep and bleating, here Dickey accomplishes the same in one bold stroke. For though Dickey has written a number of animal poems in which he seeks communion with the otherness or wildness of nature, the sheep is not any old animal; it is not a cow child or a horse child Dickey chooses but a *sheep* child.

There is, of course, a potentially comic dimension to the poem's central premise: that a half animal / half-human creature has been born from the coupling of a man and a sheep. Dickey often read the poem when he wanted to be even more outrageous then he usually was. Henry Hart provides hilarious accounts of Dickey reading the poem in Australia and New Zealand, where there are lots of sheep farms (387); at the University of Florida in 1973, twenty years after being fired there, and lingering "salaciously over the descriptions of farmboys sodomizing sheep" (523); and at a black tie luncheon the same year in Nashville (547). But Dickey's use of the sheep child goes quite beyond the comic to call, as it were, the romantic bluff.

If Wordsworth first celebrated the marriage of mind and nature, and Whitman first consummated that marriage, it was Melville who in these terms first challenged it so directly: You want union with nature? Try this ocean! Try this whale! "The Sheep Child," like *Moby-Dick*, takes up the Romantic quest to unite with nature through the outrageous device of the literal:

Farm boys wild to couple
With anything with soft-wooded trees
With mounds of earth mounds
Of pinestraw . . . . (1–4)

Like Melville, Dickey tries to learn whether we can indeed find adequate shelter for the union of the human and the natural.

It is the natural and persistent human yearning for that union that rescues this poem from the ridiculous, that elevates it beyond a lurid sexual fantasy of farm boys. But it is the frustration of that yearning— the sense that now, more than ever, we are incapable of sustaining that vision—that makes the poem so poignant. It is as though the symmetry of the union is too fearful, so that it is only in the imagination that we can give birth to such visions. In actuality, they die on the hillside. "I woke, dying" (39), says the sheep child:

> In the summer sun of the hillside, with my eyes
> Far more than human. I saw for a blazing moment
> The great grassy world from both sides. . . . (40–42)

This is a stunning moment in the long history of pastoral: the moment when the ideal of pastoral harmony can live only as a monster, only in the artificial and rarified atmosphere of the museum, pickled in the preserving fluid of myth because stillborn in the world itself.

And yet the ideal retains all of its traditional allure, as it always does in pastoral. The sheep child's language ("I woke, dying, / In the summer sun of the hillside" [39–40]) recalls that of the knight at arms in Keats's "La Belle Dame Sans Merci," where after going off with the beautiful lady into a pastoral dream world, the knight awakens to the nightmare of absence: "And I awoke and found me here / On the cold hill's side" (43–44). In the fairy world to which the knight ventures in his dream vision, we find the familiar props of pastoral:

> I made a garland for her head,
> And bracelets too, and fragrant zone; (17–18)
> . . . .
> She found me roots of relish sweet
> And honey wild, and manna dew, (25–26)

But the moment the knight awakens from his dream on the cold hillside of reality, the nurturing, delightful, and nourishing world of pastoral nature collapses into sterility, drabness, and decay: "the sedge is withered from the lake, / And no birds sing" (47–48). Dickey emphasizes the contrast between the two worlds by having the sheep child awaken not on a cold hillside but "in the summer sun of the hillside" (40), but after seeing "for a blazing moment / The great grassy world from both sides," the sheep child "died / Staring" (47–48).

As the spokesman for naturalistic values, the sheep child exchanges speeches with the speaker of the poem, thus engaging in its own version of the pastoral singing contest, and clearly carrying the day. In the process the familiar pastoral contrast between the city and the country is drawn: the museum is in Atlanta and "the boys have taken / Their own true wives in the city" (18–19), while the sheep remains in the infinitely more attractive "long grass / Of the west pasture, where she stood like moonlight / Listening for foxes" (29–31). This contrast is related to the larger pastoral contrast between the artificial ("the terrible dust of museums" [24]) and the natural ("she gave, not lifting her head / Out of dew . . . her best / Self to that great need" [33–35]). It is also related to the contrast between natural and domesticated love, with the clear implication in the poem's final line ("they marry, they raise their kind" [62]) that the domestic is a pale substitute at best for the erotic passion, the "something like love / From another world that seized [the sheep] / From behind" (31–33), echoing Yeats's violent portrayal of Zeus's intervention in human affairs in "Leda and the Swan."

Lowell too takes up this contrast of natural and domestic love, setting the passionate lovers in their cars against both the perverse voyeuristic passion of the speaker who spies on them and the gay decorator who would "rather marry" (24) and thus compromise himself. The only figure of domestic union in "Skunk Hour" is an animal, the mother skunk, whose motherhood, far from being in tension with her passion, is deeply related to the "moonstruck eyes' red fire" (40).

Both Dickey and Lowell, then, locate their speakers in worlds that are characterized by loneliness, decay, and alienation, and they both examine certain attempts to reconnect with the natural world. In "The Sheep Child" the attempt is brazen; in "Skunk Hour" it is more subtle, but it fails just as surely. Indeed, the sense of failure and weariness is even stronger in Lowell's poem, because the alternatives it explores have the feel of impoverished and exhausted cultural forms. The L. L. Bean catalogue, for example, which seems to epitomize "our summer millionaire" (14), is a perfect emblem of pastoral perversion, of the stylization and commercialization of the relationship between the human and the natural. It presents a fantasy version of that relationship which is belied by the rest of the poem, with its numerous images of disease ("The season's ill" [13]; "My mind's not right" [30]), corruption, and decay. We saw earlier how this kind of stylization on the part of the decorator perverts the very distinction between the natural and the artificial by transforming the natural objects of the lobsterman's trade into so many props to be deployed in the service of some sort of "natural" style. Somehow this island has transformed the pastoral ideal of riches and abundance and simplicity into an artificial, sleazy, acquisitive cash nexus. Indeed the very idea of a resort itself comes to be seen as a peculiarly modern attempt to mediate the human and the natural, to carve out a space where the pastoral can survive as an island in the modern world. But like the L. L. Bean catalogue, the very conception of the resort seems woefully inadequate to pastoral ideals, and proves profoundly unsatisfying to the human desire for connection.

In this respect, the final movement of Lowell's poem, when the mother skunk "jabs her wedge-head in a cup / of sour cream" (46–47), is not so much "a sort of greedy parody of the Eucharist," as John Berryman has suggested (128), but a parody of the whole world of pastoral sweets and creams, the whole world of milkmaids and pastoral abundance that has been so irrevocably lost. Unlike the speaker, who is tortured by his self-consciousness, the skunks are fully instinctual creatures. They "stand," says Richard Wilbur, "for stubborn, unabashed livingness, and for [Lowell's] own refusal (in the teeth of society and his own jangled nature) to cease desiring a world of vitality, freedom, and love" (87). I think Wilbur is right to emphasize the importance of this final image, but we do well to recall that Lowell does not find a way of moving beyond this intense desire at the end of the poem. The world of vitality and love that he longs for may be emblematized in the skunks, but there the connection stops. Nothing in the image has brought him closer to nature, or closer to clarity about how to *get* closer to nature. If anything, the recognition of the animals' vitality only heightens, by contrast, the poet's own isolation and estrangement. "The poem embodies," says Charles Altieri, "the ultimate lucidity, the denial of all imaginative evasions, which Lowell has been seeking"— including, I would add, the alterity of pastoral harmony.

We are left, then, with an unbridgeable gap between the speaker and the skunks, between the speaker and some idea of harmony. This is, I would suggest, precisely the situation at the end of "The Sheep Child," where that creature too both embodies the poet's ideal of harmony and stands as mute testimony to our inability to bring it into our lives. In one sense Dickey's poem can be understood as a pastoral elegy for the sheep child, complete with a formal lament, an expansive expression of grief, an attempt to understand why it had to die, a conventional account of the corruption of society, and a final (though ironic) consolation in the educative myth that presumably keeps boys off of animals. But to the extent that we are made to feel the sadness of the death—and it is Dickey's great accomplishment to make us feel precisely that—to that extent we experience the loss of the pastoral ideal as a painful diminishment.

In this, as in so much else, "The Sheep Child" shares with "Skunk Hour" a profound sense of loss. But in both poems the feeling that the loss may be irrevocable moves in a curious tension with the lingering desire for union. That the skunk, in the final words of the poem, "will not scare" (48) provides Lowell a glimmer of hope, even though the gulf between the speaker and the skunk remains gaping. Despite the most unsentimental demystifying of the pastoral ideal, despite the most tough-minded acknowledgment of its incompatibility with the harsh realities of modernity, the longing remains. The persistence of that knowing but still raw yearning for union may well be the characteristic note in the pastoral poetry of America at mid century.

Works Cited

Alpers, Paul. *What is Pastoral?* Chicago: University of Chicago Press, 1996.

Altieri, Charles. "Robert Lowell and the Difficulties of Escaping Modernism." *The Critical Response to Robert Lowell.* Ed. Steven Gould Axelrod. Westport, Conn.: Greenwood, 1999.

Bell, Vereen M. *Robert Lowell: Nihilist as Hero.* Cambridge, Mass.: Harvard University Press, 1983.

Berryman, John. "Despondency and Madness." *Robert Lowell: a Collection of Critical Essays.* Ed. Thomas Parkinson. Englewood Cliffs, N.J.: Prentice-Hall, 1968. 124–34.

Dickey, James. "The Sheep Child." *Poems* 1957–1967. Middletown, Conn.: Wesleyan University Press, 1967. 252–53.

Ettin, Andrew A. *Literature and the Pastoral.* New Haven: Yale University Press, 1984.

Greg, W.W. "Pastoral Poetry and the Pastoral Ideal." *The Pastoral Mode: A Casebook.* Ed. Bryan Loughrey. London: Macmillan, 1984. 77–81.

Hart, Henry. *James Dickey: The World as a Lie.* New York: Picador, 2000.

Keats, John. *The Poems of John Keats.* Ed. Jack Stillinger. Cambridge, Mass.: Belknap / Harvard University Press, 1978.

Loughrey, Bryan. Ed. *The Pastoral Mode: A Casebook.* London: Macmillan, 1984.

Lowell, Robert. "Skunk Hour." *Life Studies.* New York: Farrar, 1959. 89–90.

Nims, John Frederick. "On Robert Lowell's 'Skunk Hour.'" *The Contemporary Poet as Artist and Critic*. Boston: Little, 1964. 88–98.

Wilbur, Richard. "On Robert Lowell's 'Skunk Hour.'" *The Contemporary Poet as Artist and Critic*. Boston: Little, 1964. 84–87.

Williamson, Alan. *Pity the Monster: The Political Vision of Robert Lowell*. New Haven: Yale University Press, 1974.

Graham Foust

I Can't Get Them Close Enough—There's No Such Thing: Seidel, Poussin, the Pastoral

I am here, then, at the beginning, where it is possible—and easy—to see the pastoral as eco-centric: flowers, fields, "the country." But it is also *econ*-centric, a matter of both the management of class (un)consciousness and what a language, given, is made to spend or save.

In her book *Pastoral and the Poetics of Self-Contradiction*, Judith Harber calls the classical pastoral "a mode that worked insistently against itself, problematizing both its own definitions and stable definitions within its texts." "[F]rom the beginning of the genre," she claims, "presence, continuity, and consolation have been seen as related to— indeed dependent on—absence, discontinuity, and loss" (1). At the beginning of the twenty-first century, no poet is more problematic than Frederick Seidel, a lyricist whose associative abilities, as terribly keen as they are deeply outlandish, allow his work to achieve a nearly vertiginous sense of detachment. Whether between the works themselves or between the works and the world, Seidel's connectives are ropes that both reel in and hang the reader; he hooks us up, even as he cuts us loose or down:

> No civilized state will execute
> Someone who is ill

Till it makes the someone well
Enough to kill
In a civilized state,
As a poem does[1]. (Going Fast 94)

As is now well known, William Empson observes that the "old pas-toral" contains an "essential trick," a poetic ruse that consists of "mak[ing] simple people express strong feelings . . . in learned and fash-ionable language," thus implying "a beautiful relation between rich and poor." "From seeing the two sorts of people combined like this," Empson continues, "you thought better of both; the best parts of both were used" (11). While it might be fair to say that Frederick Seidel "uses" people in his poems, it would be difficult to argue that his poems use those people's "best" parts. In Seidel's work, we often see the poor at their most desperate and obvious, the rich—the class to which Sei-del's speakers usually belong—at their most despicable and oblivious. To wit, "To the Muse," the first poem from Seidel's fourth collection, *My Tokyo:*

I'd had a haircut at Molé.
I called you from the first pay phone that worked.
You were high above Park Avenue,
Having damask troubles in their library.

I saw the man approaching me not see me.
I held the phone and heard the servants getting you.
I watched him squat in the street near the curb while the traffic passed,
Spreading under himself sheets of newspaper;

Which when he rose he folded neatly
And carried to the trash basket at the corner.
Across the street were Mortimer's' outside tables set for lunch.
Now the maître d' was seating an early customer,

While a woman pushing a shopping cart
Picked through the trash in the trash basket the man had used,
And the butler finally came back
To the phone to say you had gone.

Before I examine the strangeness of Seidel's speaker's speech, allow me to say a bit more about a couple of less recent poetic economies. In the classical pastoral, the "simple" speaker of which Empson speaks is strangely endowed with the gift of elevated speech, and the author's artful language erases the distinction between the speaker's artificial self and those above him. (To use one of Empson's examples, shepherds are presented as "rulers" of their flocks, and thus they become "like" the politicians or bishops who rule them.) In contrast to the political or economic "androgyny" of the speaker of the old pastoral, the politics of the modern, urban pastoral poem, perhaps typified by George Oppen's "Street," often involve an unsurprisingly privileged speaker who observes and names an "other," lower class and who is able to associate himself with it from a distance.

Oppen's poem begins with a sigh, at once signaling the speaker's pity for the people he observes, his relief at not being one of them, and his confidence in his intellectual abilities: "Ah these are the poor / These are the poor— // Bergen street." The speaker's reiteration places the people he observes at a double distance, even as it stresses his being in their simple world; "I want //," he says four lines later—the pause of the stanza break giving these words the time and space to be their own sentence, thus momentarily impoverishing the speaker— "An end of poverty / As much as anyone." A critical distance soon overtakes (or perhaps re-takes) the speaker, and observation ("Humiliation, // Hardship . . .") quickly turns to admonition: "Nor are they very good to each other" (109).

"Street" operates very differently from Empson's "old pastoral" in that the "simple" people here express nothing at all, but are rather gazed upon and talked about (never *to*) by Oppen's speaker. In the classical pastoral, the deception is of authorial origin; according to Empson, it is the writer who "keep[s] up a firm pretence that he [is] unconscious of [the clash between style and theme]" (12). In Oppen's poem—in which the line between speaker and author is less clear— less maintenance is required to keep absurdity at bay, because although we don't hesitate to argue about language and its proper place in people, arguing about feelings is nearly unheard of. (In other words, "No one talks like that" or "Certain people don't talk like that" would be acceptable arguments with regard to a poem's "real-ness," whereas "You don't really feel that" would be presumptuous and impossible to prove in reality or in a poem.)

Seidel's poem, on the third hand (which is perhaps also to say the most unnatural hand), pushes the eventual detachment of Oppen's poem to the cracking point, as his speaker does not seem to want an end to poverty and is clearly not just "anyone." In the poem's first lines, we find an anonymous person—whom we can presume, given the title, is an artist of sorts—attempting to impress the muse. He's spiffed up with an expensive haircut, and he's made every attempt to be prompt: his reference to New York City's ubiquitous broken payphones lets us know that any unaccounted for lateness he might be accused of is due to his oft-vandalized urban environment rather than any miscalculation or irresponsibility on his part. Instead of concealing a trick or romanticizing a difference, Seidel's speaker's well-tailored sleeve seems simply to wear a cold and ignorant heart. There are points at which he "identifies with" the poem's less fortunate characters, but he is also clearly oblivious to them. In "To the Muse," the authorial pretense of the classical pastoral has been transferred to a singularly privileged speaker who is not a combination of rich and poor save for the words he speaks at the beginning of the second stanza: "I saw the man approaching not see me."

This line would not be out of place in, say, a dramatic monologue spoken from the point of view of a homeless person on the streets of a large North American city (which is to say the point of view of "the man approaching"), but this is clearly not what's happening here. In the classical pastoral, a disenfranchised speaker is elevated via the writer's technique of fusing him with another class's linguistic behavior; in Oppen's "Street," an already elevated speaker addresses the possibility of identifying with a circumstantially very different set of "others" while never interacting with them. But in "To the Muse," the speaker performs a kind of twisted ventriloquism, in that he is potentially talking *for* the homeless person even as he appears to be talking *about* him. (One might argue that Seidel's speaker means that "the man approaching" simply doesn't care that he's being observed, but if this is all the speaker has to say about poverty, even this slightly alternate reading stands as evidence of the his inability to acknowledge his own lack of concern, as well as his lack of self-reflexivity with regard to this lack.) Seidel's poem torques and splices the logics of both genres in that its speaker speaks the very words that *could* be spoken by an identified other without ever acknowledging the situation's glaring irony.

The poem's "I" identifies with "the man approaching" by way of his "learned language"—he has learned the language of the approaching man's situation—and yet he is also oblivious to having done so. He does not notice that he has projected the typical detachment of the urban fortunate onto the homeless man, nor does he comment on the incongruous parallel of a woman digging through the trash for food across the street from an expensive restaurant. It would seem, then, that the old pastoral has an heir in Frederick Seidel, in that both involve imaginary legislators who do not acknowledge the incongruities of their speech; however, Seidel's pretence is the pretence of the nearly unthinkable rather than the pretence of the barely possible.

As Allen Grossman tells us, lyric poems function by way of incongruity: "Poetry," he writes, "is traditionally a work which obtains its characteristic life by obliviating the labor by which it was produced" (266). According to Grossman, poetry "is a form of constructed ignorance" (269). Oddly enough, the obliviation of poet's labor and the constructed-ness of the poem's ignorance are made both obvious and obscure in poems directed to muses, as these types of poems both contradict and prove Grossman's statement that "[s]peakers in poems know nothing about art (and little about poetry)" (268).[2] The answer to the question "Why would a speaker who knows nothing about art be in need of a muse?" becomes more clear when we consider that even poems which solicit communication or communion with inspiration are, in the eyes of the reader, always already successful poems. A poet in trouble—that is, a poet who wants to make poetry but cannot—is one who is in need of the muse; at this moment, she knows little about poetry, and so she must seek help from a higher power. When such a problem becomes the subject of a poem, readers are all the more aware that the transcription of this amount is anterior to the originary moment, as the very object in front of them—i.e., the poem—has in fact "doctored" (or perhaps "pharmacied") that moment, has obliviated the toil and trouble of poetry in order to make that toil and trouble readable (if not "visible").

Like Seidel's poem, William Blake's "To the Muses" makes a poem out of the difficulty of tracking down the nine goddesses responsible for poetry, all of whom seem to have left Helicon and Parnassus for Asia Minor without leaving a forwarding address. Blake's speaker asserts that "The languid strings do scarcely move!" and that "The sound is forc'd, the notes are few!," and yet we nevertheless have a poem in front of us despite his claim that capital-P poetry has been "forsak[en]" (31). In addition to sharing Seidel's poem's title, James Wright's "To the Muse" also addresses a disappeared inspiration who cannot return his call: the deceased "Jenny," who sleeps "[f]ace down in the unbelievable silk of spring." "I would lie to you, /," Wright writes, "If I could," and believability is indeed what is at stake—or is perhaps what is burning at the stake—in these poems (175–6). The poet tells us that poetry is impossible, the muse or muses invisible and unavailable, and yet he does so by way of a successful, convincing poem, thus rendering his poem's claim irrelevant if not an outright lie.

"Alas!," cries Andrew Marvell in "Damon the Mower," "I look for Ease in vain, / When Remedies themselves complain" (107). In the muse poems of Blake, Wright, and Seidel, we find that poetic complaints often remedy the very situations they invoke, though the poems are never revised—and in fact *could not be* revised—to include this information. Empson, too, makes this point when he says that "the mere fact that you don't altogether believe in the poet's expressions of despair makes you feel that he has reserves of strength" (13). The poem, that contradictory object, stands in its own center even as it collapses all over itself, convincing the reader despite—and because of—its inability to prove what it pronounces. At the end of Wright's poem, the speaker begs Jenny to "come up [to him] / Out of the river, or [he] will / Come down to her," but the reader knows the speaker's claim is always already all wet. He even so much as admits it in the poem's third stanza:

> You come up after dark, you poise alone
> With me on the shore.
> I lead you back to this world. (176)

Before his begging, the speaker asks "How can I live without you?," never explicitly letting on that his very speaking, the poem itself, is half-answering his question for him.

Seidel's speaker also addresses a "you" who is not there, though we aren't really sure of this absence until the poem's last line, or, more accurately, the poem's last *word*. It is perhaps even *more* accurate to say that we are not totally certain of the muse's absence until the book's *next poem*; we turn the page, and a new title ("From a High Floor") assures us that the book's first poem is in fact over, a fact which also confirms our suspicion that the first poem's speaker never makes contact with the muse. (However, we also know that the speaker has also somehow *connected* with her, for how could someone have produced a poem and not made contact with the muse?) When, as in a label on a gift, "*To* the Muse" becomes "*From* a High Floor," the reader is carried back to the beginning of the first poem (or rather near to the beginning, line three: "You were high above Park Avenue") just after having also been pushed *away* from that very poem by the second poem's title. The title is an oscillation, a *pharmakon;* we anaphor between high floors, cured of "To the Muse" even as we find we are infected with it. The words "From a High Floor" are capable of vastly different meanings—we've begun a new poem, we've never left an earlier poem—even as they remain fixed and unwavering on the page.

2

Allow me, if you will, a somewhat extended digression on the fixed and twisted by way of two of the world's most famous pastoral texts, after which I will return to the poetry of Frederick Seidel. In his essay "Et in Arcadia Ego: Poussin and the Elegiac Tradition," Erwin Panofsky discusses the conflicting translations and interpretations of the Latin in his essay's title, a phrase which is written in stone in both versions of Nicolas Poussin's *Arcadian Shepherds* paintings, asserting that

> The correct translation of the phrase in its orthodox form is . . . not "I, too, was born, or lived, in Arcady," but: "Even in Arcady, there I am," from which we must conclude that the speaker is not a deceased Arcadian shepherd or shepherdess but Death in person. (307)

How do Poussin's paintings help us to (or prevent us from) reading this sentence? In the first version of the painting (1629–30), three shepherds have come upon a tomb which bears the inscription ET IN ARCADIA EGO; a death's head sits atop the gravestone, and, at the bottom right side of the painting, the river-god Alpheus spills a jar of water, unleashing the deluge, time, into a scene of reading. In the second version (1640), the death's head disappears along with Alpheus, which, according to Panofsky, renders the painting an elegy whereby "the *ego* in the phrase *Et in Arcadia ego* must now be taken to refer to the tomb itself . . . [or rather] the person buried therein" (315–16). The figures in this painting, unlike those in the first version, "no longer [express] surprise and dismay, but quiet, reminiscent meditation" (316). Panofsky concludes:

> Thus Poussin himself, while making no verbal change in the inscription, invites, almost compels, the beholder to mistranslate it by relating the *ego* to a dead person instead of to the tomb, by

connecting the *et* with *ego* instead of with Arcadia, and by sup-
plying the missing verb in the form of a *vixi* or *fui* instead of a
sum. The development of his pictorial vision had outgrown the
significance of the literary formula, and we may say that those
who, under the impact of the Louvre picture, decided to render
the phrase *Et in Arcadia ego* as "I, too, lived in Arcady," rather
than "Even in Arcady, there I am," did violence to Latin grammar
but justice to the new meaning of Poussin's composition. (316)

Yet Panofsky ignores a major element of the second painting's content:
the shepherds are in fact paying more attention than ever to the in-
scription. Despite their "quiet meditation," or perhaps *because* of it, the
shepherds may in fact be all the more aware of the sentence's grammar.

In order to claim that the second painting has an entirely different
attitude toward its subject(s), Panofsky and other critics point to the
shepherds' lack of surprise in the second painting as compared with the
first. However, despite the fact that the time *of* the painting itself is of
course later than the first, one could still assume that the time *in* the
painting is the time before the arrival of the earlier shepherds' surprise.
In the second version, two shepherds point at the tomb's inscription,
or rather one points at the inscription while another points to the edge
of the reader's shadow, drawing attention to the fact that "the origin of
drawing [is] in the tracing of a shadow's outline" (Bätschmann 56).
The reader, it should be noted, is slightly behind the reader in the first
painting: his finger is on the "R" as opposed to the "I," which—while
it may come to the symbolic aid of Panofsky's claim that the figures in
the second painting "think less of themselves than of the human being
buried in the tomb"—may indicate an earlier, slower, or more careful
contemplation of the sentence itself.[3]

And yet perhaps we are later rather than earlier. We might in fact
be witnesses to a moment of rereading. Though there is no death's
head in the second version of the painting, the reading shepherd's arm
projects, "against all laws of projection," a sickle-shaped shadow across
the word *ego* (Bätschmann 56).[4] Perhaps his lapse in perspective is a
painted version of the error of Hymeneus and Philetus, who claim the
resurrection is already past, and Poussin's error draws our attention to
the vanishing point by failing to follow its rules.[5] The tip of reading
shepherd's index finger is placed on the literal and figural vanishing
point of the painting, while the mis-drawn shadow suggests that the
picture contains an additional spatial dimension. Given that shadows

depend on the sun, we might say that there is another temporal dimension here (and there and now and then) as well. In this version of *Et in Arcadia ego,* then, the scythe-shadow has both foreshadowed and severed the death's head. On the one hand (let's say the hand of the shepherd who points at the reader's shadow), it points to the present moment, a reading; on the other hand (let's say the hand of the reader himself), it points to the obliterated past and so a necessary re-reading of the inscription. The twisting of the reading shepherd's arm, visible only in its shadow, speaks the twisted meaning of *Et in Arcadia ego,* while the sharp shadow itself—present, but not accounted for by the shepherd's arm—reminds us of unavoidable oblivion and the arbitrary inevitability of grammar. The reading shepherd's shadow stabs the phrase's noun and so momentarily puts out the "I," while also enabling the painting to call forth the gravedigger's tool. The line and its shape then disappear at the actual vanishing point where the reader touches (finishes) the shadow at the tip of the scythe.

Here, there, now, and then, thought's shadow tears thought's dream at a certain point in time by a certain pointing of the reader. We can call this *caesura,* finally and again, Memory, which is appropriate given that Caesar appears in the *fatto* of the German version of the entry for *Memoria* in Ripa's *Iconologia.* In this picture, a three-dimensional Caesar, like the triumvirate in the second version of *The Arcadian Shepherds,* is listening, reading, and dictating at the same time. Oskar Bätschmann deems Poussin's second version "an examination and free paraphrase of *History* in reverse," but it is not so much a reversal as it is an inversion. Both "reversal" and "inversion" make reference to the poetic cut made when and where the plow turns around (*verso*), but inversion, in addition to suggesting translation and interpretation ("version"), also hints at three dimensions, connotes a figure in which something might be placed, a space which might be entered in order to extract something from and for it, rather than simply a line of time on which events might slide.

Two years after he painted the second version of *The Arcadian Shepherds,* Poussin illustrated the frontispiece for the *Biblia Sacra* of 1642. Here, under the light of God, the angel of history "holds her pen in a book whose opened page is in the dark . . . [which] turns the darkness into a metaphor for writing" (Bätschmann 58). In *The Arcadian Shepherds,* however, the darkness of the sharp shadow is an allegory for Poussin's own rereading ("incisive, formal"), his own slicing back into a text in which Death itself speaks. If, as Panofsky asserts, the meaning has changed from Death to a particular dead shepherd, then Poussin's introduction of the executioner's tool reminds us that any way we might speak of death is bound to be an error. The painter's acknowledgement of this also cuts us momentarily free: the absence of a knowledge of death (obliviousness to oblivion) points us toward memory and life.

And what of the writing itself? One can assume that in both versions of the painting, the call of Memory is not only to the viewers *in* the paintings, but also to the viewers *of* the paintings. But notice how the inscription in the first version is unrealistically shifted (for what "real" maker of headstones wouldn't center the text on the tomb?) to incorporate the viewer of the painting into the reading of the sentence. Still (or perhaps "stirring") more allegorical disorder: the relation between the text and the surface on which it's printed in the first version is as torqued and asymmetrical as that of the shepherd's arm to his shadow in the second.

3

To return to Seidel's work, we must continue to read "From a High Floor," even as it carries our minds back to "To the Muse." "City of neutered dogs, /" says its speaker, "How homeless can you be / In a nine-room apartment / With windows on three sides?" (*My Tokyo* 4). "The doorman calls upstairs," the speaker says a few lines later, returning us to our earlier phone call to the butler. After detailing the various luxuries of the nine-room Manhattan apartment, the poem's speaker concludes:

> *The* homeless *homeless have*
> *The center strip of Broadway.*
> *To live where you should jump.* (*My Tokyo* 5)

Italicization, which often signals a word in a foreign tongue, here indicates actuality; when the speaker says *"homeless* homeless," he is attempting to make clear the fact that he is referring to actual homeless people rather than to a figuratively homeless person (lonely? empty? unloved?) in a posh, uptown apartment.

Having already come across much unsettling division and deviation in Seidel's work—rifts in time and sense which also often reach back to what we've come to think we already know—we find yet another in "From a High Floor." (All this only three pages into a single book!) The speaker begins the poem by addressing the city itself, thus causing the poem's "you" to split (and split into) the difference: we are forced to read the "you" in the second line both realistically ("How homeless can [one] be") and surrealistically ("How homeless can [the city of neutered dogs] be"). Whether rhetorical or personal, the question is left unanswered by the city, and, given the book's first poem, we come to realize that even with the city as a muse, a poem's meaning must forever remain suburban—outside a given city, or just barely below it, as in a jumper's blood, the spill of a suicide of meaning—a place in which everything risks looking like everything else, in which anything could mean anything, in which sight might remain—finally and eventually—unseen. Out there, down there, up there, "[t]he opposite of everything / That will be once / The universe begins / Is who [the universe] is" (*The Cosmos Poems* 7).

In *Spuren*, Ernst Bloch transcribes a parable about the Kingdom of the Messiah told to him by Walter Benjamin, in which it is said that "Everything will be as it is now, just a little different":

A rabbi, a real cabalist, once said that in order to establish a reign of peace it is not necessary to destroy everything nor to begin a completely new world. It is sufficient to displace this cup or this bush or this stone just a little, and thus everything. But this small displacement is so difficult to achieve and its measure is so difficult to find that, with regard to the world, humans are incapable of it and it is necessary that the Messiah come. (qtd. in Agamben 52)

Reading *My Tokyo*, we often find Seidel playing the very God of which Benjamin and Bloch speak. To wit, the book's third poem, "The Hour," which is repeated nineteen pages later. Repeated, that is, except for a change of title (its new name: "The New Woman") and a slight alteration in punctuation: "—." The poem's (which is also to say the poems') first line—which in the first poem spoke to us only of two women separated by the typical apparatus of a prison visit—is now seen in a strikingly self-reflexive light: "They can't get close enough—there's no such thing." Below is the poem's/poems' third stanza with the change in brackets:

They're in a limousine. The plane they're on
Is over water. Dawn reveals the two
Berlins becoming one. And now they knew[—]
The time had come. And now the rain is gone. (My Tokyo 6, 25)

Just as the title of the book's second poem carries us back to the first—and very different—poem, the new title of another poem rips us away from its nearly identical twin. This old poem, "The New Woman," is new in name, but also different in the way it expresses a particular piece of knowledge. In "The Hour," the dashless fact of a particular time's arrival is quite fluid, a gradual progression from one moment or idea to another. "Dawn" makes visible a newly unified city, and, "naturally," this leads to the idea of "the time['s]" having come. In "The New Woman," the same time's coming is made sudden by the dash's delay; a written hesitation drops a gap in the thought, thus mimicking the feeling of having lost track of time or having forgotten one was on a track. The next stanza of the poem(s) continues (or continue) this thought of trains: "Two passengers aboard their lives undress / Down to their hands." Given that the dash and its lack make for two very different ways of thinking, two nearly opposing moments of having thought, an act of disrobing comes to us as either leisurely or hurried depending on which version of the line we're thinking of. (Though in the latter option there is—as there always is in Seidel's work—a strangeness: having to undress quickly is less expected than having to dress quickly.) When, at poem's/poems' end(s), the guard tells the women that their "hour is over," they "tell her yes"; this answer to what was never a question has its own set of characteristics which will of course depend upon the presence or absence of the dash.[6]

The last repetition of which I will speak is the recurrence of another entire poem in My Tokyo, though this time we find a poem from an entirely other text, These Days, the book which precedes My Tokyo in Seidel's oeuvre. Near the end of My Tokyo, just before a poem entitled "The Second Coming," appears a poem entitled "The Death of Meta Burden in an Avalanche," which appears in These Days as "The Last Poem in the Book." Indeed, whatever the poem's title as given to us in These Days may or may not say about the contents of the poem, it certainly speaks the truth with regard to the book: "The Last Poem in the Book" is indeed the last poem in These Days. As in "The Hour" and "The New Woman," the changes that occur when "The Last Poem in the Book" becomes "The Death of Meta Burden in an Avalanche" are, in terms of keystrokes, rather minor. The line "The korai smile silence" has become "The Korai smile silence"; the line "Running down the Rue Barbet-de-Jouy" has become "Running down the rue Barbet-de-Jouy." The latter alteration is, of course, a correction: the French do not capitalize the "rue" in the names of streets. But the former is a mistake, in that "korai" is not a proper name, but rather is a term applied to the sixth century B.C. marble statues of maidens dedicated at sanctuaries. (In its meaning "daughter," the singular "Kore" is often capitalized, as it is used to refer to Persephone, daughter of Zeus.)

Whether or not this change is an intentional mistake, what the capitalized "korai" can say is somewhat telling. (A smile is silent, but it is never meaningless.) In "The Death of Meta Burden in an Avalanche," artistic representations of people have suddenly become important enough to capitalize, while the name of a place is suddenly made right by its being diminished. Earlier in My Tokyo, so much depended on the title of a particular poem: "From a High Floor" sent us back to another; "The New Woman" marked the appearance of a mark and changed the poem's focus from the measurement of time ("The Hour") to people in, but unaware of—and then suddenly very aware of—time. But in These Days, the title of "The Last Poem in the Book" is entirely dependent on the poem's location, and when it becomes part of another book—a book in which it is not the last poem—its title changes, and yet carries within it (this is perhaps its "meta-burden") the facts of its earlier placement.[7]

The last four lines of this poem—these poems—are as follows:

I am coming now.
I can't breathe.
I'm coming now to the conclusion that
Without a God. I'm coming now to the conclusion.
(These Days 50, My Tokyo 44)

How different these lines are when read at the *end* of a book as opposed to *near* the end of a book. In the former case, they are, like the former poem's title, absolutely true; in the latter, they are completely false. Then comes the joke, as the following poem, "The Second Coming," perhaps has a title more fitting for the poem we've just read. This next poem's title, given the two comings that have come before it, might well be titled "The Fourth Coming" in some other unbent book or world.[8]

I am coming now to the conclusion. Our world is bent, the phone is broken, and this is what Seidel is telling us, long distance, always. In the best art, the world's twist is made both more and less apparent, whether in a necessarily uncentered sentence, a series of unsettled and unsettling poetic twins, or the knife-shaped, impossibly-cast shadow of a reader's arm. I am coming now to the conclusion that / Without a God. I fear here incompleteness, for when I first taught to write an essay, I was often required to return to the place where I had started, an order which made me wonder more than once as to what the point of embarking on a journey might be. Therefore, and in spite of or beside my fear, I will bring this essay home less in the sense of a return trip and more like a postcard *from* home rather then *to*. *I can't breathe*. I began this journey with the political hybrid which powers the classical pastoral, a hybrid which was (and perhaps is), as history shows us, only possible in that mode, that poetry; have I brought it close enough to the work of Frederick Seidel—is there such a thing? Like ET IN ARCADIA EGO, "I can't breathe" can only ever be written. *I am coming now*.

Notes

[1] Of course, the muses themselves are a constructed ignorance. "It is only through their gifts of remembrance and narration," writes George Steiner, "that mortal men can know something of the birth of the world," in spite of the fact that muses could not have been "witnesses to their own creation" (36).

[2] Louis Marin writes: "The index finger of the shepherd on the left is located on the letter r of the word Arcadia, that is the central letter of the inscription and also the central point of the painting resulting from the displacement of the vanishing point from the horizon of the representational stage to the wall of the tomb. That r is the initial of the name of Cardinal Rospigliosi who invented the phrase 'Et in Arcadia ego' and commissioned the painting we have been studying. This letter r, a pure signifier which takes the place of death, is a kind of 'hypogrammatic' signature of a name, that of the author of the motto and of the painting as well. It is the signifier of the name of the Father of the painting in the place of the painter-beholder . . ." (274)

[3] In his novel *The Rings of Saturn*, W.G. Sebald speaks to the possibility of an intentional error in the center of another painting. His reading of the dead thief's body in Rembrandt's *The Anatomy Lesson* is as follows:

> Though the body is open to contemplation, it is, in a sense, excluded, and in the same way the much–admired verismilitude of Rembrandt's picture proves on closer examination to be more apparent than real. Contrary to normal practice, the anatomist shown here has not begun his dissection by opening the abdomen and removing the intestines, which are most prone to putrefaction, but has started (and this too may imply a punitive dimension to the act) by dissecting the offending hand. Now, this hand is most peculiar. It is not only grotesquely out of proportion compared with the hand closer to us, but it is also anatomically the wrong way round: the exposed tendons, which ought to be those of the left palm, given the position of the thumb, are in fact those of the back of the right hand. In other words, what we are faced with is a transposi-

tion taken from the anatomical atlas, evidently without further reflection, that turns the otherwise true-to-life painting (if one may so express it) into a crass misrepresentation at the exact center point of its meaning, where the incisions are made. It seems inconceivable that we are faced here with an unfortunate blunder. Rather, I believe there was deliberate intent behind this flaw in composition. That unshapely hand signifies the violence that has been done to Aris Kindt. It is with him, the victim, and not the Guild that gave Rembrandt his commission, that the painter identifies. His gaze alone is free of Cartesian rigidity.(16-17)

[4] These Biblical figures appear in the shepherd scene in John Bunyan's *The Pilgrim's Progress*, in which Christian and Hopeful, gazing down "an Hill called Error" are shown "several men all dashed to pieces by a fall." The shepherds inform the two travelers that the men "had been made to err by hearkening to Hymeneus and Philetus, as concerning the resurrection of the body?" Later in the scene, the shepherds provide Christian and hopeful with a "perspective glass," though "remembrance of that last thing that the shepherds had shown them" makes their hands shake, "by means of which impediment they [can] not look steadily through the glass." This scene provides an interesting supplement to Marshall McLuhan's assertion that "[t]he hand has no point of view" (35).

[5] This absence is, at some points, impossible, for in the first reading of "The Hour," the lack of a dash cannot really be a lack, cannot really be an absence, for we haven't yet see the poem in any other form.

[6] Given the many purposeful incongruities in Seidel's work, I should at least admit that it wouldn't be entirely out of the question to find that a poem called "The Last Poem in the Book" was not in fact the last poem in a book of Seidel's poems.

[7] My *Tokyo* is also Seidel's fourth book.

Works Cited

Agamben, Giorgio. *The Coming Community*. 1990. Trans. Michael Hardt. Minneapolis: University of Minnesota Press, 1993.

Bätschman, Oskar. *Nicolas Poussin: Dialectics of Painting*. Trans. Marko Daniel. London: Reaktion Books Ltd., 1990.

Blake, William. *The Complete Poems*. Ed. Alicia Ostriker. New York: Penguin Books, 1977.

Empson, William. *Some Versions of Pastoral*. 1935. Norfolk, CT: New Directions, 1974.

Grossman, Allen. "Summa Lyrica: A Primer of the Commonplaces in Speculative Poetics." 1990. *The Sighted Singer: Two Works on Poetry for Readers and Writers*. Baltimore: The Johns Hopkins University Press, 1992.

Haber, Judith. *Pastoral and the Poetics of Self-Contradiction*. Cambridge: Cambridge University Press, 1994.

Marin, Louis. "Toward a Theory of Reading in the Visual Arts": Poussin's *The Arcadian Shepherds*. *The Art of Art History: A Critical Anthology*. Ed. Donald Preziosi. Oxford: Oxford University Press, 1998. 263–73.

Marvell, Andrew. *The Complete Poems*. Ed. Elizabeth Story Donno. London: Penguin Books, 1972.

McLuhan, Marshall and Harley Parker. *Through the Vanishing Point: Space in Poetry and Painting*. New York: Harper and Row, 1968.

Oppen, George. *Collected Poems*. New York: New Directions, 1975.

Panofsky, Erwin. "*Et in Arcadia Ego*: Poussin and the Elegiac Tradition." *Meaning and the Visual Arts*. New York: Doubleday Anchor Books, 1955. 295–320.

Sebald, W. G. *The Rings of Saturn*. 1995. New York: New Directions, 1998.

Seidel, Frederick. *The Cosmos Poems*. New York: Farrar, Straus, and Giroux, 2000.

—. *Going Fast*. New York: Farrar, Straus, and Giroux, 1998.

—. *My Tokyo*. New York: Farrar, Straus, and Giroux, 1993.

—. *These Days*. New York: Alfred A. Knopf, 1989.

Steiner, George. *Grammars of Creation*. New Haven, CT: Yale University Press, 2001.

Wright, James. *Above the River*. Middletown, CT: Wesleyan University Press, 1990.

David Baker

The Uses of Nostalgia

on Moreau Creek

(scenic)

Nothing so clear as a cloud, nor clouded
　　　　as fog on the water—it's more absence
than any aspect of light, the limestone
　　　　reaching from the river-bar sands upwards.
And not an absence exactly, but more

the feeling of that absence, filament
　　　　of green, evening-gold-green, the leaves a mist
of leaves on the hills, now the whippoorwill
　　　　one of many watchers worried from high
or low in the limbs. A "flowing in of

utterance" is how Hazlitt heard the art
　　　　—the artist having found a great valley
and, taking position on the hillside
　　　　overlooking it, listening intently,
until he can "think into the human heart."

(poetic)

It's what Wordsworth needs both to bear and bless.
     Below him, on his tall rock, the Wye runs
sylvan—the inland, soft murmur—the stream
     memorial with grief. And what little
solace he finds, he finds in gloomy trees,

veiled cliffs, the hedgerows "hardly hedgerows," though
     here the scene's as indistinct as distant.
His nostalgia seems clouded, shamed. Six years
     have passed. He sat here drenched once in the blood
of the Continent, and Revolution,

and it's clear he feels again "like a man
     flying from something that he dreads." Below,
amist, his world's unintelligible
     but sublime—yet it's his shadow Dorothy
who gives meaning to the view, for her mind

(historic)

"shall be a mansion for all lovely forms."
     Where are they now, who knew their "time is past"?
Evening fog deepens on my old cold creek
     like wisps of smoke—or more like "wreaths of smoke
sent up, in silence, from among the trees."

I hear a chainsaw rip the black trunks down
     beyond the corn fields past the river banks.
I stir my coals once more, and smoke goes up
     —all's now a flowing in of words, not wind—
a hundred thousand acres gone each day

like magic: wilderness to waste and mulch.
     I thought I'd not come back to Moreau Creek
to fish and camp, to set my mile of lines.
     But it's lovely here in my forty-fifth year.
Though the water is wrecked with run-off, rich

(thematic)

with chemicals, trash, tires, foam, who knows what,
      the evening trees persist to glow with dew.
They're strung with spiderwebs, the crickets' call.
      "The giant sons of genius stand upon
the earth, [and] tower above their fellows"

—Hazlitt says the arts are not progressive—
      then each succeeding generation finds
its lower "niche" and sinks into the vale
      until the sublime's become so peopled,
so side-long its view, nothing true is left.

I wish they were here still, Hazlitt, Wordsworth,
      among the bats, kingfishers, high watchers
in the night. Moreau bubbles over its
      old rocky shallows, and a little mist
sifts as smoke into the gathering trees.

(apocalyptic)

I think the saint was right. The subject's never
      smoke—there's always been a fire. I hear it
in the ripsaws burning through the distance
      and in my heart, who writes for no one else,
"more absence than any aspect of light."

I hear it in her journals Dorothy wrote.
      Today "all things looked chearless and distinct,
no meltings of sky into mountains." Yet
      such becomes the nature of nostalgia
now, such longing for the wonderful days.

How many they seem, and moonlit, how dear
      they might be—. I don't know what else to say.
Such is what our feeling comes to now. Such
      mourning for them all, "such shame," for those days.
But not the past. I mean the ones to come.

Consider

Shovel some space in the narrow
between the road and field.

The roots of grass
tangle your work.

The two trees beside the path.

The white one
inside the forest of beeches.

The white one
at dusk.

[Year One]

+

For what purpose were those hours poured
into the thimble?

I've gone from one day to the next,

below time.

+

The bright faces of flowers at night
tell you where the path bends to the left.

Solitude, that is, or the irrelevance of the particular
person, or the fact that does not matter.

The path was not one way it was any way.

Sean O'Brien

By Ferry

The ferry, *The Waverley*, churns on the sandbar.
In New Holland harbor the jellyfish
Hang in the murk at the jetty
Like plastic rain-hoods—
A race of drowned aunties
Come back to chastise us
For something we don't know we've done yet.

Sea Area Humber: poor visibility.
The jaws of the estuary? Infernal the gloom.
And Lincolnshire beneath the rain?
A plate of cabbage
Laid down at the door of sulking Cleethorpes.
For the sea had gone away,
Round that great corner of the map
Leaving us Biblical distance and wormcasts—
And in the mind's eye
Skeleton crews
Dancing hornpipes on islands of birdshit.

Water-Gardens

Water looked up through the lawn
Like a half-buried mirror
Left out by the people before.

There were faces in there
We had seen in the hallways
Of octogenarian specialists,

Mortality-vendors consulted
On bronchial matters
In rot-smelling Boulevard mansions.

We stood on their lino
And breathed, and below us
The dark, peopled water

Was leaning and listening.
There on the steps of the cellar,
Black-clad Victorians

Were feeding the river with souls.
They left us their things,
Reefs of blue ware

In the elder-clumps,
Tins full of rust in the shed,
And on the bookshelves

English poets, all gone damp
With good intentions, never read.
Their miles of flooded graves

Were traffic jams of stone
Where patient amphibian angels
Rode them under, slowly.

The voices came back
From sinks and gratings,
The treasure seekers

Gone downstairs, while all the time
In King Death's rainy garden
We were playing out.

Andrew Grace

On Finding a Marijuana Plant
in the Garden

Porch evening dharma—pubic musk,
      groan thrummed from a bull's

damp nostrils, a neighbor's voice: "I'm the old boy
who woke the sheriff up before the '59 flood."

Ribbon of feckless dust hissing after an ambulance.

Already box turtle-bitten, I tied knots into stems
      & coaxed dragonflies to my tongue, hunting
sublimity-tipped windmills, a boy afraid

of voices lost in night's neck.
Plumbing the violet incense, only fire ants,

chestnuts, open pods of soy,

      nothing like what mother picked to show me
to avoid—thin, muscular leaves,
seven scythes attached to a spindle, threatening diagonals
of Chinese painting.

      All I knew of danger
was the torn hair of a girl on the school bus,
      bitter sips stolen in the garage, carcasses of black cats
smeared across the highway. That moment so silent

it felt like a key being shoved into my ear,

bats grazing the purple sky, "My family lost
       nine sets of twins . . ."

I gave up, garden filling with effigies unarticulated
by cherry tree-shadow, shriven & mouthless girls seemingly
       peering from behind each bush.
I tried to stay until I knew there was no

physically conquerable thing
              to slide my hands through,
nothing to call upon me to step up to a grace-cleft
       moment in dog-breathed dusk

          then there, by the fencepost,
leaves flicking like switchblades, alien palms
       opening to desire.

Conceptual Shadeland

The coop is not wind-toppled but bustling with hens,
each pecking a pit into eggshells—decanters of plasma
glutting dust to paste. The rest of the dream: scent of cestrum

& jasmine drifting from a slope before uninhabitable,
always muzzled by creeping charlie's heart-shaped rope.
A house by Route 45, windows built cockeyed

two hundred years ago by untutored hands now leveled,
is gazing into a field of jaundice dandelions. I cannot stop

brushing an albino horse giving birth
to womb-greased clumps of feathers in the backyard;
someone says "rain" & we are wet.
Then pigweed, amaranth, glowworm, chirp, sweat, sap . . .

Again—
        candescent curtains flicking & when I try to remember
if the water-well is full, I can hardly recite my own skin.
In a separate back-lit room, Charon slips on his
        shiny, black shoes.

Ann Vickery

"A Mobile Fiction": Barbara Guest and Modern Pastoral

Following the influence of modernist artists like Matisse, Picasso, and Miró, and of Abstract Expressionism, the group of poets known as the New York School, perhaps not surprisingly, often adopted a pastoral mode in their work. Barbara Guest, the only woman associated with the group, revised the pastoral in her early writing to resist post-war hegemonic constructions of the feminine. Moving away from the expressive to a more experimental form, she continued to focus on the pastoral in order to capture both psycho-sociological differences between country and city life, and to explore the role of language and art in drawing together or moving across various states of being. For Guest, carefully orchestrated intensities and tension generate a haunting beauty in the poem while bringing the reader face to face with a dynamic and sometimes dark modernity.

In the early series, "Archaics," Guest goes back to the ancient Greeks and Romans in order to ground a feminist critique of contemporary gender relations. "Atalanta in Arcadia" is a caution to Atalanta about a boy whose "apple and bees / are stumbling into your sacred pasture"(P 56). Like the apple, Atalanta's girlhood and more specifically, her independence, will be consumed by the boy. There is a sense of inevitability as the "ritualistic grass" of courtship finally "uncovers" its "continual shadow"(P 55–56). Guest ends the poem with a plea to disrupt the final chorus of the narrative, "If one kind god hiding in the thicket / would change that last strophe?"(P 56) "Dido to Aenas" is also a lament concerning the loss of female freedom, although Guest gives this story a more contemporary location. Accordingly, the "white urn" stands "at the driveway." Dido is transformed into a housewife who must suffer the loneliness of suburbia, the fountain emulating her solitary grief with its "noonday cries"(P 58). Again, there is a kind of cyclic fatalism:

> I love you
> miracle, mirror, word, all the same
> you come, you go
> I love you
> (on my rioting lawns the plaster flamingos
> endure your wonder) (P 58–59)

The plaster flamingos emphasize the banality of modern-day married life. Their kitsch presence emphasizes the artifice of the pastoral landscape in such a setting. However, they also indicate the internal "rioting" of the suburban goddess, suggesting that revolution or suicide may be alternatives to this quiet death.

"All Grey-Haired My Sisters" further mourns the decline of femininity but makes more apparent its call for collective change. Here, the garden is a "region of silences," a fortress for memories. "Adventuresses" who once "walked into the wars" have since become "image / cut of stone so to endure." The life spirit symbolized by the tiger (following William Blake) has become "wither[ed]" in "sleep." The feminine is suspended in time—is, in effect, still life. Accordingly, the calendar is "relative" and "Spring . . . waits"(P 15). In this carefully wrought elegy, the pastoral has "a black musical depth." Guest argues that were women able "to forget animosities"

> and in the pagan grass slide heedlessly
> blossoms would return such songs
> as I've sung of you, the youthful ashes
> fling upward settle fragrant
> brightness of your dusky marquetry (P 16)

However, the possibility of such "seraphicness" fades as her call remains unanswered. The narrator seeks to avoid the fate of her sisters, moving "quickly lest the cherry's / bloom changed to white / fall upon my head"(P 16).

Such overt feminist statements would be unusual for Guest. As Lynn Keller points out, they reflect the cultural climate of the early 1960s, anticipating Betty Friedan's *The Feminine Mystique* (1963) which appeared only a few years later.(216) Guest at this time would also be in correspondence with Denise Levertov who urged her away from abstraction and the "chic flipness" of the New York school.[1] Ignoring this advice, Guest instead became more involved with the close-knit avant-garde community and began to shape an identity for herself as "poet" rather than "wife." Her writing pays homage to these newfound friendships and revels in the wonders of city life—far from the suburbs. In "A London Poem for Frank O'Hara" Guest asks O'Hara, with whom she was particularly close:

> Do you think above the Georgian ruins here
> we might perfect the same air?
>
>
> Force into columns our dissemblings
> and our clean miniatures of love?[2]

This desire for order is offset by life that "both faints and rouses / poses at doorways and arches itself." While the "capes and ribbons of pensioners" may remind one of death, "clouds dissolve the chapel." Another poem, "Late Supper," playfully evokes O'Hara's "Oranges: 12 Pastoral":

> It's time to say Night
> because it's waiting
> in the distance like a bus
> at the corner blinkers on
>
> Orange wheels
> you did say "orange"?
> Having prepared that color
> in the oven
>
> Having washed your hands
> and your neck
> just before you made
> orange into a meal
>
> . . .

The promises you have fulfilled
agent of provender and hunger

No ants this time!

No beasts either!

Just a quiet dinner time
Preceded by — —

The gills and the fins
and the wave length arcs
which somehow have been told
they must resemble our talk

and our thirst that is arriving
in tumbrels

Bah! I would like another pastoral
before embarking.[3]

"Night," with its "orange wheels," is surrealistically likened to the transit buses moving across Manhattan, as well as the French Revolution's giddy blend of last-gasp decadence and thirst for change. It would herald for Guest a "magic" time in the metropolis. "[I]f you live in the city," she wrote, "it's the time you get off the street"(Interview, 28). The pastoral scene is played out in the domestic interior; there one can find retirement from active life, the ritualistic consumption of late suppers and gossip, and the promise of intellectual and other pleasures. Yet such scenes are always time-conscious in their delightfulness; the late supper may well be a last supper.

In "Nature and New Painting" O'Hara makes an argument for the urban pastoral:

Modern life has expanded our conception of nature and along with it nature's role in our lives and our art—a woman stepping on a bus may afford a greater insight into nature than the hills outside Rome—In past times there was nature and there was human nature; because of the ferocity of modern life, man and nature have become one. (42)

The pastoral, then, does not need to be located in the fields. Yet it still relies on setting up oppositions or contrasts around nature and simplicity on the one hand, and civilization and artifice on the other. There is also still an affective structure based around separation and loss. That much is evident in Guest's "The Location of Things,"

> The street, the street bears light
> and shade on its shoulders, walks without crying,
> turns itself into another and continues, even
> cantilevers this barroom atmosphere into a forest
> and sheds its leaves on my table (P 11)

As Terence Diggory notes, the poem pivots between "indoors" and "outdoors," helped along by such architectural terms as "cantilever"(309). The elegiac tone is evident as the narrator regards dramatic afternoons "from this floodlit window / or from a pontoon on this theatrical lake." The rain, metaphorically likened to curtains in the term "water's lace," "creates funerals / it makes us see someone we love in an acre of grass"(P 12). The material separation of watcher and the world beyond emphasizes a continuing urban alienation. The poem ends with the "melancholy of the stair" that could link the interior and the external. Instead, the narrator wanders "into clouds and air," the retreat of the imaginary.

William Watkin has argued that the real "is conceived of as a post-surrealist sense of an encounter with total novelty, total otherness" in the New York pastoral of poets like Frank O'Hara(134). Certainly, surrealistic elements are evident in Guest's work but the city is also linked to the old and the traditional. Indeed, it is sometimes only understood through patterns of repetition—even if they are "odd." In the tentatively titled "Feudal Strife," Guest extends Virgil's pastoral vision to the urban domain:

> The poet V[i]rgil concerned about meadows
> in his Ecologues, addended that God
> preferred the odd
>   numbers
>
>   Yes. Shady nook
> buildings. Marine streets.
>
>   The fog sieves
> down from the Rupert Brewery Plaza

>   *to my terrace*

of harpsichord grain

describing itself (the fog)

>   *"odd"*

>   *as the King of France*
>
> *trying to rip off*
>
>   *the Dukes of Milan*

their Leonardo —

>   *feudal strife.*[4]

In Guest's poem, the streetscape becomes fluid as the medieval blends
with the modern. Buildings offer respite as "shady nooks." The grain
used in industrial beer production is sieved by the same air as a cre-
ative grain. The conventions of the original—such as those informing
the pastoral scenes envisaged by Virgil—are plagiarized down through
the ages and, in the modern age, become increasingly chaotic.

As with many New York writers and artists, Guest turned to the
actual countryside in order to explore issues of imagination and states
of being, and subsequently for elegiac meditation. She spent periods of
time at Long Island, noting "My community really consisted of Jimmy
[Schuyler] at the Fairfield Porter house in the beginning. That was a
'location' where I could intimately establish a connection"(Interview
25). She and Schuyler, perhaps the most pastoral poet of the New York
circle, shared a fondness for the magazine *Country Life.* "There is an
ineluctable wisdom in that magazine that others cannot place," Guest
wrote, "After the humouring pause, there is the innocent desire to gaze
on foreign gardens, yet not too foreign, English, and their houses, es-
pecially those photographed 'for sale'"(*VU* 15). She felt there was "an
unconscious division" on her part between the country and the city: "I
often write here [Long Island] and take work back to the city. Nature's
so powerful and you either come under its rule, or you are under the
rule of mankind in the city"(*APR* 25). She adds, "Taking the bus into
New York once a week is extremely important because it breaks up this
sequence of time and . . . creates a tension between the city and the
county"(Interview, 29).

Elsewhere she noted:

My typewriter here [the Hamptons] is never i[n] good condition, quick to the pulse; its life has not been spent near the rapid city sidewalk, but under the shadow of trees and low clouds.

I know that I write differently out here. My thoughts travel to me from mysterious nature . . . I am nourished by the weather and seed . . . Sometimes I believe my poetry is a little too free as if it were running with the weather, with inhabitants of fields, even as if it were fleeing nature, Pan, a wand, even country ghosts whose narrowed eyes lie under cover of shrub and winter ground.[5]

This sense of "different rhythms" is explored in "Country Cousins." In the summer months there are happy couplings:

> Laura and Phillip, Robert and Lucia
> all they can think about Athina and Paul,
> Victor and Ida pine for chemises,
> cloth of white, ribbons towelly,
> Recca and Richard, Claire and Noel recollect
> spring in their larking (FR 71)

Yet there can be a sense of overkill in excessive pastoral: "Madam is stung by a cloud, / the nomad bee drowned in it." In one of her workbooks, Guest warns that in losing one's freshness, one becomes a mannerist.[6] With "Country Cousins," the mythic is finely balanced against the mundane. In the "evening purl," "Ceres / seeks the Persephone dark it has been mannered / they toss shells / tales you recount." Moving away from "dignified frost," there is a "lightning" or lightening of tone:

> Goose girl leads chevettes to the pond
> where she reds down the rumor of hiss
> in the dry season of quack, the shorn sink
> at her pout the distance runner and the holder
> of metal tires, the white
> saluting mellowed feathers. (FR 72)

Guest becomes linguistically playful, encouraging words themselves to create new kinships or affinities. Meaning, as in Gertrude Stein's *Tender Buttons*, emerges out of sensory association, metonymy, and punning. In an interview with Mark Hillringhouse, Guest admits that "Chevettes" is a made-up word: "I was thinking of 'little Chevrolets.' Also, I confess, the geese on the town pond"(26). Cars are thus shepherded like birds; their similarity perhaps found in being both vehicles of flight. The "hiss" is both the hiss of the reluctant goose and the sound of a tire as it is let down. But it can also be the hiss of rumors as they are passed around in society's small pond. Like sheep, "the shorn sink / at her pout" and in their whiteness are "saluting mellowed feathers"(FR 72).

She would also write "Clouds Near the Windmill" in the Hamptons. Using the technique of pathetic fallacy, the psychological is projected onto the geographical. The clouds have skin and voice, and can climb across the sand in "bare feet"(BS 29). Like the fog of "Feudal Strife," they are a kind of binding agent in the landscape—they allow it to breathe and speak. Rod Giblett argues that just as we are unable to represent "place" except by metaphors, so too are we unable to represent human states or abstractions except by metaphors of places or sites. In the poem, the narrator identifies herself with the environment, being part of the "us" that includes rushes, pebbles, and stones. For Guest, the "calm" of the space enables "digestive moments." That is, internal reflection or meditation becomes *proximate* with the landscape; the chair "is moving closer to the pond"(BS 72). The perceived distance between the epistemic and the natural or physical is being undone.

At the same time, the poem suggests that the landscape is not necessarily the one outside the window but a painted or written one. Bird wings have no shadows and the "straight lines" are:

harsh without a tremor,
resembling pagoda field,
resembling stalks with your imagination. (BS 72)

The landscape has become surface—flattened or two-dimensional. As with "Country Cousins," there is sign of transport. These are self-contained, carriages with "their hoods pulled down"(BS 72). On the one hand, one might read the narrator's desire for harmony and unity with nature as being disrupted by their presence. Yet, they might also be associated with the carriages of typewriters—with words themselves offering flights like the wind and cloud sweeping across the terrain.

Guest would investigate the relationship between the visual and language in a number of ekphastic pastorals. "All Elegies are Black and

White" was written in response to a series by Robert Motherwell.(P 78–80) She also penned "Twilight Polka Dots" after receiving a postcard from her husband when he was visiting Death Lake. The postcard featured Richard Bergh's painting, "Nordic Summer Evening" which pictures two lovers looking out over a lake. Within the card, Trumbull had written:

> This bears little resemblance to Lake Meret? nor do I to Prince Eugene of Sweden. I do think, however, that there is a definite likeness of you in the young singer Karin Pyk.

> But it does have the spirit of our coming reunion in California . . .[7]

In manuscript version, the poem is titled "The Landscape of Leisure."[8] As with "Clouds Near the Windmill," Guest uses pathetic fallacy to humanize the lake. It symbolizes a mercantile and calculating civilization, which despises the fish for "their disagreeable concern with feeding" and prefers instead "the cultivated echoes of a hunting horn." While the lake performs its function as picturesque, it can admire "the fixity of [the two figures'] shared glance." Accordingly, nature performs for the lovers: "The scene supplied them with theater . . . and the water understood and strained its source for bugling echoes and silvered laments"(FR 55). It is the lake that experiences pleasure from the gaze. In focussing on the lake, the lovers are distracted in their desire for one another. A letter falls in torn fragments, disrupting the stillness of the moment. Its movement engenders a chain of action (or reaction) such as wind-gusts, bending trees, mountain-glacier movement and leaping fish. The surface of the lake is transformed into "polka dots." Suddenly the still center is alive with contrast. The revised title of the poem reinforces this moment of change. Yet signs of decline soon become noticeable. The last gleam of the sunset playing off the lake is likened to an "autumnal stalk." The poem ends on a dark note with the couple finding themselves in the lake marsh grass "like two eels who were caught"(FR 56). They have themselves entered the landscape's frame, becoming ensnared or absorbed by the lake. Guest thus takes to a literal ends a pastoral study of man's absorption in the natural.

The pastoral, for Guest, is where the imaginary is not only prioritized over the real but informs the real. In "Going to the Movies with Fay," Guest writes of the creative solidarity that can overcome urban alienation:

Ah Fay the two of us bereft
of movies and food
wandering into the skim soft airs whispering
like mediants we go aft and shore
escaping in long cloaks
> *with beggar bowls*
> *the wisps of drawings*
> *from the tablets we hold*

Fleeing past the picture palace
> *at lighting-up*
in medieval
> *New York*
What was it fell off the harvest machine
> *made us sneeze?*[9]

It is the "wisps of drawings" as much as the "long cloaks" that provide a means of magical escape. In a contemporaneous poem, "The Drawings of Fay Lansner," art offers "the red green blue / of a substitute country":

the mind travels over it pencilling in
the wavering heart the eye carries it along
entranced by the lake reeds

Because in the distance disguised as a color
> *we have left our usual motors*
> *we rely on the arm of the painter*
> *to guide us.*[10]

Significantly, the "motors" that dot the landscape of "Country Cousins" and "Clouds Near the Windmill" are left behind. There is a strong shift from reality.

In "Piazzas," this relationship between the imagined landscape and the real is brought into productive tension. Dedicated to Mary Abbott Clyde, Guest jokingly refers in her title to Abbott's habit of referring to her front porch as the piazza. The title plays upon the double meaning of "piazza"—which can refer to both a porch and to an Italian town—and helps juxtapose a contemporary space against a more exotic space—the spectacularly baroque piazza envisaged by Italian Renaissance painter Pinturicchio. In "The Burial of San Bernardino," Pinturicchio features "a beautifully rendered, spacious piazza with a radiating stone pavement, elegant and airy colonnades, and a central temple"(Lundquist 250). Evelyn March Phillipps describes the burial panel in a particularly pastoral tone: "The people gather round, life beyond goes its way, and the whole is set in so peaceful and spirit-lifting an environment that it does not need the little sky episode of the saint received into glory to give it spirituality"(52).

Sara Lundquist argues that there is a desire to *be in* the painting with a loved companion (251). Yet I would propose instead, that Guest fuses times, overlaying one type of reality with another. To some extent, the idyllic day shared by herself and Abbott mimics the gloriousness of the painting:

> *In the golden air, the risky autumn,*
> *leaves on the piazza, shadows by the door*
> *on your chair the red berry*
> > *after the dragonfly summer*

> *we walk this mirroring air our feet chill*
> *and silver and golden a portrait*
> *by Pinturicchio we permanently taste the dark*
> *grapes and the seed pearls glisten (P 13)*

Reflecting on the memory of this day, the poem takes the form of a pastoral elegy. In both worlds, there is a sense of disruption and impeding darkness. The dragonflies "always" have a "heaviness of wings." While the narrator seeks to represent the soaring sensation of her experience, she is impeded by a similar heaviness as well as by turbulence, "a confusion of weather" and "thunder in the Alps"(P 13). As Lundquist points out, such imagery captures the vertigo experienced in the act of writing (251). The difficulty of describing the moment sees the "imagination's at its turning"(P 13). The poet, like the saint in Pinturicchio's painting, must suffer:

> *real or divined*
> *as the youth leaning over the piazza*
> *throwing stones at his poems. He reads*
> *his effigy in the one that ricochets*
> *he weeps into the autumn air*

and that stone becomes golden as a tomb
beware the risky imagination (P 14)

Guest would also write "The Screen of Distance" which explores the
properties of language in illuminating the real and constructing imag-
ined worlds. In her workbook, she notes that the serial poem emerged
after a session of therapy:

> I look out [the] window onto a sidewalk with green leaves filling
> the distance of park. While he talks . . . and it is so important to
> me to me what he is saying, about anger being an aggression
> which when throttled turns into anxiety, I stop listening to
> him—fasten my eyes on what [lies] before me beyond his win-
> dow—sentences, words, images forming a poem, or prose, & they
> run parallel to his clinical speech & their lines are heavier, pat-
> terned by the light they become more significant than his speech
> designed to save me.[11]

In an interview, Guest recalls that parts were written on Sixteenth
Street and part from living here: "When I first moved to 16th Street it
was very stimulating to be in a new place. The whole idea of clear
space was very thrilling to me. On 16th Street, the light filtered
through the room and I got very excited and it did affect my
work"(APR 25). The poem uses some of the light and architecture of
the city in reflecting upon its own poetics:

> *Narratives are in*
> *the room where the screen waits suspended like*
> *the frame of a girder the worker will place upon*
> *an axis and thus make a frame which he fills with*
> *a plot or a quarter inch of poetry to encourage*
> *nature into his building and the tree leaning*
> *against it, the tree casting language upon the screen. (FR 35)*

Here Guest exposes the structural underpinnings of the poem—the
frame, the girder, and the axis—foregrounding the poem as a composi-
tion rather than transcendent medium. Rather than the tree being
"cast" on the screen through language, it "casts" language. This in-
vokes nature as both subject (having been encouraged into the build-
ing) and director. Words, like movie stars, are cultural "icons," creat-
ing the problem of narcissism: "The ego of words stretched to the
room's borders assuming the sonorous movement of a poem"(FR 37; 38).

Yet they are also visual objects, icons arranged on the screen of the page.

While the tree stands broadly as a symbol of wilderness, it may be cultivated and turned into paper. Such a process transforms the three-dimensional into surface:

> . . . so the paper on which the poem would
> rest was grainy with color flashing lights
> and the depth, the deepness of the country lane
> on which shadows found repose was a wilderness of
> color, ditches and trees lost their contours. I
> created a planned randomness in which color
> behaved like a star. (FR 40)

The term "grainy" brings into mind not simply the texture of wood but the celluloid quality of old movies. Guest suggests that with words, as in black and white film, contrast create a semblance of color and depth. She continues:

> To introduce color to form
> I must darken the window where shrubs
> grazed the delicate words
> the room would behave
> like everything else in nature (FR 41)

The pastoral mood of the poem accentuates the "distance" between subject and object, the use of language as a frame or psychological screen. "Experience and emotion [are] performed" through words. Their ability to "dispers[e] illusion," to engender "mobile fiction[s]" and "fictive ambiguities," is championed by Guest (FR 41; 46).

In "An Emphasis Falls on Reality," there is concern over language's plastic quality, its capacity for endless signification, and its separation from the real. Guest writes:

> Cloud fields change into furniture
> furniture metamorphizes into fields
> an emphasis falls on reality.
>
> "It snowed toward morning," a barcarole
> the words stretched severely
>
> silhouettes they arrived in trenchant cut
> the face of lilies . . . (FR 26)

The opening surrealistic images force a series of emphases or associations. From the cloud of language, there may be hardened snow. Or there may be a stream upon which a "barcarole" or gondolier's song may be entertained. Yet a barcarole is also a musical composition imitating this Venetian past-time. While language may be transformative, it is, nevertheless, always a quote (marking some other moment) or a death mask:

> willows are not real trees
> they entangle us in looseness,
> the natural world spins in green. (FR 27)

In modernity, words are recognized to be essentially empty, like funereal vases or fonts, waiting to be filled. They are for appearance's sake, "a costume taken from space." By announcing "I desired sunrise to revise itself / as apparition, majestic in evocativeness, / two fountains traced nearby on a lawn . . . ," the narrator expresses a desire to capture the sunrise through poetry, specifically within a pastoral topography. The impossibility of such replication is acknowledged in the declaration, "I was envious of fair realism"(FR 26).

Against poetry's "barcarole" is silence:

> silence is pictorial
> when silence is real (FR 26)

Guest's most direct statement of a pastoral poetics is perhaps found in the lines, "The necessary idealizing of you reality / is part of the search, the journey / where two figures embrace." Nature and poetry must remain in exile from one another although poetry occasionally gains glimpses of the Ideal or marvelous. Representation remains, in Platonic fashion, "[t]he darkened copies of all trees"(FR 28).

David Halperin argues that the ideal world of pastoral finds the real world wanting (70–71). Yet Guest exhibits a more complex attitude. As she notes in "A Reason for Poetics," poetry may "pull in both directions between the physical reality of place and the metaphysics of space"(RP 153). It is therefore an exercise in "surprise" and "audacity." Poet and reader "perform together on a highwire strung on a platform between their separated selves"(RP 154). Rather than dwell on the failure of culture, her work deconstructs restrictive cultural visions and offers instead adventurous, often airy transpositions—enabling the subject to move across various realities and enter other possible states of being.

Notes

[1] Denise Levertov, letter dated 24 June 1964, Barbara Guest Papers, Box 16, Uncat. MS 271, Beinecke.

[2] Barbara Guest, "A London Poem for Frank O'Hara," Barbara Guest Papers, Box 25, Uncat. MS 271, Beinecke.

[3] Barbara Guest, "Late Supper," dated October 1963, Barbara Guest Papers, Box 23, Uncat. MS 271, Beinecke.

[4] Barbara Guest, "Feudal Strife," Barbara Guest Papers, Box 15, Uncat. MS 271, Beinecke.

[5] Barbara Guest, untitled, n.d., Barbara Guest Papers, Box 9, Uncat. MS 271, Beinecke.

[6] Barbara Guest, workbook, Barbara Guest Papers, Box 15, Uncat. MS 271, Beinecke.

[7] Trumbull Higgins, card dated 5 February 1986, Barbara Guest Papers, Box 5, Uncat. MS 271, Beinecke.

[8] Barbara Guest, "The Landscape of Leisure," Barbara Guest Papers, Box 15, Uncat. MS 271, Beinecke.

[9] Barbara Guest, "Going to the Movies with Fay," Barbara Guest Papers, Box 35, Uncat. MS 271, Beinecke.

[10] Barbara Guest, "The Drawings of Fay Lansner," dated 12 November 1960, Barbara Guest Papers, Uncat. MS 271, Beinecke.

[11] Barbara Guest, workbook, Barbara Guest Papers, Box 15, Uncat. MS 271, Beinecke.

Works Cited

Diggory, Terence. "Picturesque urban pastoral in post-war New York City," *The Built Surface: Architecture and the Visual Arts from Romanticism to the Millennium*. Vol 2. Ed. Karen Koeliler. London: Ashgate, forthcoming.

Giblett, Rod. *Postmodern Wetlands: Culture, History, Ecology*. Edinburgh: Edinburgh University Press, 1996.

Guest, Barbara. *Poems: The Location of Things, Archaics, The Open Skies*. Garden City: Doubleday, 1962.

_____. *The Blue Stairs*. New York: Corinth Books, 1968.

_____. "A Reason for Poetics." *Ironwood* 24 (Fall 1984): 153–55.

_____. *Fair Realism*. Los Angeles: Sun & Moon Press, 1989.

_____. "The Vuillard of Us," *Denver Quarterly* 24 (Spring 1990): 13-16.

_____. Interview, with Mark Hillringhouse. *American Poetry Review* 21 (July/August 1992): 23-30.

Halperin, David M. *Before Pastoral: Theocritus and the Ancient Tradition of Bucolic Poetry.* New Haven: Yale University Press, 1983.

Keller, Lynn. "Becoming 'A Compleat Travel Agency': Barbara Guest's Negotiations with the Fifties Feminine Mystique," *The Scene of My Selves: New Work on New York Poets.* Ed. Terence Diggory and Stephen Paul Miller. Orono: National Poetry Foundation, 2001. 215-27.

Lundquist, Sara. "Another Poet Among Painters: Barbara Guest with Grace Hartigan and Mary Abbott." *The Scene of My Selves: New Work on New York Poets.* Ed. Terence Diggory and Stephen Paul Miller. Orono: National Poetry Foundation, 2001. 245–64.

O'Hara, Frank. "Nature and New Painting," *Standing Still and Walking in New York.* Ed. Donald Allen. San Francisco: Grey Fox Press, 1983. 41–51.

Phillipps, Evelyn March. *Great Masters in Painting and Sculpture.* London: Bell, 1901.

Watkin, William. *In the Process of Poetry: The New York School and the Avant-Garde.* Lewisburg: Bucknell University Press, 2001.

Material from Barbara Guest's papers is published with the author's permission.

John Hollander

A Kind of Fear

Golden does, one fawn
move among afternoon trees
shading the long lawn

standing as if framed
in some bad landscape painting
still of course untamed

yet seeming somehow
quite domestic, grazing there
like a sheep or cow

not much can disturb;
that the deer have overrun
most of our suburb

follows from our own
civilized interventions
who removed their one

local natural
predator—our hunters—by
limiting the fall

hunting season and
just by being too many
of us on the land.

What had all been farm
went back into second growth
where quick with alarm

and with fleeting grace
the deer returned to what now
seemed their native place

when a second tier
of cultivation should have
then displaced the deer

once more, but they grew
fruitful and multiplied as
if after a new

deluge and now reclaim
driveway, summerhouse and pool
as if they were game

for anything here
in their own third-growth wild.
But a kind of fear

touches me, that they
appear to fear me not, but,
fifteen feet way,

stand and stand and stare,
ears untrembling, curious
but unalarmed there,

Irredentist and
innocent of the language
of right demand.

I could feel it then
better to be living in
a milder time, when

deer such as these three
would start up suddenly, in
healthy fear of me.

Ubi Sunt, Etc.

Where are they now (as if yesterday's rain
Now dried up along the driveway had gone
Somewhere instead of everywhere)? Quiet Sybil
Of the eternity jammed into each
Instant of noticing, small Dickinson
("And dark, like the wren"); the large Walt with too much
Whitman on his plate; Melville's prophetic
Weirdness and Trumbull Stickney's resonant
Brevity, all these sounding my ears?
Where their centuries are, of course and where
Mine is finally about to go. *Timor*
Mortis conturbat me, but not for cause
Of their long going hence. And where Hart Crane.
The pontifex maximus of ways between
The fractured wholes and whole parts, months of space
And wide rivers of days will ever guide
The weary wonderer of their abode.
Ubi sunt? sunt hic: here they are and part
Of what we are and while in older days
It seemed some kind of wholesome play to query
The whereabouts of the dead (as if you hadn't
Decided, long before asking, the only answer
It had been given you to give), and listing
Their singing and particular names in rhymes
That gave you an excuse to sound them out
Yet once more; and it was well some kind
Of mortal work to deny the unendingness
Of anything at all but the transitory
That we inherit and ever will bequeath.

Alan Shapiro

Medley

A granite house. In the bedroom window
a view of the sea down a long spit. Brief gusts of rose
scent and salt scent slip through the billowy
come live with me and be my love white curtains where,
if we were listening, *melodious birds sing madrigals,*
and where, if we were looking, we could see
in flashes on the horizon how the low edge of the sun
has just now, *for thy delight,* brushed the wavery top
edge of its molten image in the water.
                                        A tongue of honey.
The bower of rough hewn stones enclosing us
swirls in the very textures of its grain
the mineral remembrances of wayward winters, gales,
the scorching dog days, even as our bodies
move in a slow slide over and under, and through
the luffing curtains rose scent and salt scent,
Had joys no date and age no need, wreathe
the invisible threads of their conditionals
so elusively about us that we still
believe they lead our lips, our tongues, our fingers
into places where we'll *all the pleasures prove.*

Andrew Zawacki

from Masquerade

One differing in itself

—Heraclitus, Fr. 5 I

I

Whether sunlight opened the spaces it fell on, allowing the gum trees their differences, twisted aquas and shaved, quixotic papyrus, or whether the clearing was already there, touching dawn and the limits it altered, granting the sun a figure by which it was tagged, or con-ceived by the eyes of those it still mattered to, the afternoon about to happen could not elaborate: its adroit but seemingly random distinc-tions—the river as something other than its banks, water discrete from roiling and silt—were presences with a difficult origin, part of the ap-paratus of waking and not outside the day or how it developed. The ar-ticulation of shadow to fence, of bridge to the parklands it parsed and interviewed, enlisted itself inside questions without any curve: yet to follow them was our valence, and in that abandon sheltered a reason for why, though unbeknownst to each other, and unknown even to those we kept calling our selves.

November unfolded its bones on the moors, a scatter of lacustrine snow. Hiking a breakaway ridge, we marked the feats of a deafening promise, the terms of which had long since been revoked: afternoon-midnight, summer-winter, yesterday-tomorrow, a single pressure standing in for all permutations and routes. The wind picked up and put us ahead of evasion, and the signals we listened for but didn't hear, trickling along the no-trespassing placards, branches tipped with sheens of loosened sky, were pilfered from sled runs covering over, from whiteout and lackluster frost, from downpour and dust, from way before.

3

Yet what did light have to do with the outskirts it lay along? It urged more than mere decoration, obsidian arouse, as night drew near the water pump and died off. In the fern gully, at the end of a driveway inclined with brambles unhauled after yesterday's hacking, blackwood and wattle attended what stars slithered down, exchanging each other for vistas the rooms set adrift: nothing belonged to the tin cans and rooks, slipshod signposts that vines had overgrown and refused to release, flowerpots that got moved while we turned in our bunks, dreaming of thieves. Decreation was legislated, an ordinance of brush-burning and regrowth after the ashes blew afield: a house enameled in stained glass and stone, soaked with a late hour's hosing of all the wood and window frames, a fire that surrounded, leapt over the roof, curtsy of a lakefront at the meadow's farthest end: not without fervor and not without us.

4

Return was a myth departure coined as incentive: we didn't believe it, bracken and twig, but moved ahead anyway. Negotiating winter's frisk and what remained of its pane, worn away by powerlines and barns the rain brought down, we kept to where the sun revamped its reach: upholstered clouds and amassings of geese, making their exodus vocal, mountains that seemed to change their position, ruptures in the road the crews ignored, before defaulting to some other damage control. It would not have been false to conjure transparence or zero, to coax the sight of scaffolds ghosting white pine, ilex, tea tree, birch. The metabolism of snowshoe and compass: nothing could stall it or usher it on-ward, not when it had already been stated, and called us so we came.

5

Lightning and suddenly everything rendered, stricken into relief: rosel-las zagging from guard-rail to limb, from telephone wire to the trailers it linked, bellbirds scudding an atmosphere of storm clouds roaming in, unbidden but adamant showers close behind. These were the margins we swore we'd not tamper with, as dampness engaged its intention, or allow to be displaced by a scission dividing us too: a car without wheels at the side of the yard, rusting into the night until nighttime itself, cor-don of timber for months without warmth or caesura. Standing be-tween two modes of indifference and flight, we held the kitchen door ajar, in case of whatever else might need to depart, if not to preserve a silence fogging windows in the wake of the already gone; while the patio door, at back of this home no longer a home, shuddered in gusts that neither ascribed nor hid, but offered a scent. Had there been someone who slept through the onslaught, collar turned up at the exit of even himself, we'd have heard him calling out for the women he never loved, traipsing from sun to sun in a stowaway wind.

6

The docks had been taken apart for the season, plank by plank, washer by bolt, and kids would earn extra cash, come spring, for putting them back out. The casino three miles over was boarded up, fast food and faster girls a cure for midsummer malaise, since winter meant bus stops and work, if any, and lunch in one of the lodges near the church. We walked where the boats had been, no trace of the floating names this brittle water was otherwise painted: To Carry On Conversation With Houses, Whomsoever They Do Not Recognize, What We Saw We Leave Behind While What We Did Not See Or Catch We Take With Us Away. In flannel and fluorescent hunting vests, men drilled holes in matte chautauqua ice, thermoses raised against wind that gnawed their cigarettes like a bone, plumbing with hooklines for anything underneath. Skaters leaned as if weightlessness could erase intaglio, then lifted above the scrolls their blades had whittled and fuzzed into glare: to untie the letters from lamps they'd hung off, longer than anyone knew.

Giuseppe Cucchi interviewed by
Brunella Antomarini

The Wheat

Interview at Morro D'Alba, Ancona, the Marche,
Summer 2001.

Translation by Susan Stewart

The wheat is the most important thing. It is harvested in the summer.
Many years ago at dawn on the day of the harvest the violinists and
the organ grinder would arrive to follow the file of the reapers. They
would all advance in a horizontal line stretching across the field, cut-
ting the wheat with their sickles and singing to the music. Through
the hills near and far, once you heard that music and singing, you
would know the harvest had begun. The reapers would strain their
arms and legs into the night, working a thirteen-hour day. This is how
they would do it: with one hand they would come down with a half-
turn of the sickle, and with the other they would grab a bunch of
wheat into a sheaf. First they put two or three sheaves together on the
ground, making a *pecorella*, or "little lamb," and then they put the
lambs together to make a stack. The stack then was tied with a *balzo*,
a small cord made from a twisted stem of wheat; and the balzo rolled
up around a *piro*, a little wooden rod that lasts year after year. You tuck
it in your belt and use it at every harvest. The reapers would be dou-

bled over by their work as they crossed the fields singing and the violinists would follow, playing for them, and all was suffused with the warm smell of the wheat itself. They sang of love and many of their songs were daring, close to the bone. Already at the beginning of the nineteenth century a solo violinist followed the reapers, playing and singing by himself.

The violinist was a true musician and he also used to play for Easter Monday and at the New Year, passing from cottage to cottage with a sack that each family would fill in exchange with a plate of meal or flour. On Passion Sunday he would expect eggs and every family would give him seven, maybe even ten.

At the grape harvest, no, there weren't musicians, but the workers would sing as they smashed the grapes with their feet in the vats. The grape pressing makes a foam with a perfume that is a bit tart and sweet and it stays on top of the grapes for several days as the men roll up their pants-legs and the women roll up their skirts and they all begin to sing, also songs that are a little daring . . . No, this mixing up of everything together doesn't spoil the wine. No one knows why, but the wine separates itself from everything else in the vat, only its own liquid and perfume remain. All the rest—bees, bits of straw, leaves, twigs, flies, dirt—is separated from the wine. You see, wine is truly potent—it can take care of itself!

These are stories grandfathers tell, like the story of the robin redbreast who got his name because he was splashed by the blood of Christ on the cross.

When I was in the war I wrote to my family and used these stories to help them understand me and at the same time to confound the censors. I would write: "Dear ones, here you dig and never hoe." And they would understand that we had retreated from the front, for when you dig you always go backwards and when you hoe you always go forward.

When I came back from the war, I was imprisoned for six years and then released in Algeria and then I came by train to the city, and then by truck to the countryside, and then by foot at night, and I couldn't find the road to my own house. And when I asked about it, the countrymen told me, "stay here to sleep for the night since it is dark and you won't be able to find the house." But I just couldn't wait and I passed by the graveyard and stumbled and hurt my legs there in the darkness, yet still I wasn't willing to stop and finally I saw my house. It was completely dark and so I went to someone who lived nearby and I said, "Go there and say I am here, but gently because mamma is old and we should break the news to her quietly." And I waited and waited outside behind a bush and I was so tired and exhausted and hungry and I thought I wouldn't be able to wait any more. Just then I saw that all the lights were coming on one by one throughout the house and then I went out and hurried into the house and we had a celebration that lasted all night long.

The country is hard. In the next life there's nothing I would less like to be than a peasant. To work in the fields is torture; in the summer you kill yourself in the heat, you sweat and the dry earth sticks to you and fills your lungs; in the winter your feet ache from the cold; you must be able to go out to work in the fields in the intense cold at dawn and you won't be able to quit until night comes. A backache is killing you and you still can't stop and the cold damp enters your bones. And after you have worked for months, you find that in June it never rains and the beetroots go bad and don't earn anything and your half turns out to be nothing—the other half must go to the *padrone*—and so you are starving; and after you have taken care of the vineyard, you find that one day it hails and the grape harvest is ruined and there's little left to eat. You can say "Oh look how beautiful the fog is, covering all the valleys and hills." But fog is the most ugly thing I know, sneaking into the bones while you try to work without being able to see a thing.

Smell the smells, always, the smells of everything, of the rain and the grasses and the earth and the plants and the animals. And the house is full of smells, too. Each thing has its smell. For these odors cling to people and things, getting deep inside them. When you have no sense of smell or have no odor yourself, as things are today, nothing is connected to anything else and you are disconnected from everything smells can link together. The family was joined together for a lifetime; it was impossible to think that after all this work and the breathing in of the scent of a woman, and the scents of a house and a family, that a man could forget them and turn to another woman. In the end, the old couple stayed together, the old couple before the fire, by this time useless, and they knew it; but they were able to give advice and they truly were wise. One here and one there by the fire, the old man with his long moustache, the old woman with a handkerchief folded around her head, her long hair tied up into a bun . . .

Eighteen of us lived in this house. In the countryside we took our bath once a week and carried the water in the washtub into the stalls because there, beside the heat of the cows, we found it to be much less cold. The cows were aware of everything! No one knows why, but a moment before the wind changes, they would puff out their noses, lengthening the muzzles and blowing hard. Well, then, here, you see, the wind was changing!

When you need to stop the flow of milk from a cow so that she may get pregnant again, you must milk her near a tree where ants are going to and fro and then throw the milk to the ants.

In July they would thresh the fields and then need to plough in August and the smallest boys, those eight or nine years old, would go to "touch *la stroppia*," that is, they would take a little whip in their hands and lead the cows, two in the front and two in the back, with the plough behind. They would awaken at four in the morning to do the plowing and one time I went out to touch the *stroppia*, but I fell asleep in the field and my father yelled to me that it was already getting late. So I had to plow three furrows by myself and there wasn't enough time and meanwhile the cows had come to a stop to chew their cud since they didn't feel the *stroppia* on their back—the poor beasts with their tongues hanging out from fatigue; it was a torture for us as well as for them, with their legs and hooves stuck in the earth that was soft for sowing and their heavy feet, dragging along like lead.

In war time the children did the work for the men and at the age of thirteen they would get up at one in the morning to sow the hay to be used as straw for the winter animals and they needed to do it in the dark, by the "solustro," or the light that the moon casts while the eyes get used to seeing in the dark and shadows. And they went ahead with the sickle and the kids spat blood. But they weren't about to do the work in the daylight because the seeds that fell would open right away in the midday heat; with the night's humidity, they stayed shut and would germinate later.

We worked in our bare feet or in clogs, and shoes were worn only on Sundays and holidays. From the house we would carry them in our hands and then put them on at the last moment before we entered the church in our good clothes.

When we could afford it, the shoe repairman would come to the house to meet our needs. He went through the countryside carrying everything necessary to repair shoes or make new ones and he took our measurements and made us shoes right there in the house and ate with us. And the seamstress came to the house whenever our clothes were worn out and we needed new ones.

In November we sowed the seed and in December or January we

made the *pista*, that is we butchered the pig. Always under the waning moon. Everything must be done under the waning moon, also pruning trees or cutting hair. Never with the new moon. "Pista" is the word for all the parts of the pig that we used. We never wasted a bit of the pig: from the meat we made salami, bacon, pork loins, *ciavuscolo*, prosciutto, sausages; with the feet, pig's feet; with the head we made a kind of sausage called *coppa*; with the fat, lard and bacon fat; with the skin, pork rinds; we also cooked the tongue and the tail in a sauce, with the liver and lungs and heart to make a *coratella*; with the blood we made a black pudding, called *sanguinaccio*, that is a kind of salami or we made a *smigliazzato* with the blood by mixing it with the wine that is made from the sweet fresh grape juice, the *vin cotto*, that is also good for a child who has a cough; with the intestine we made tripe and with the gut we made casings for the sausages, with the bristles we made brushes and we used the whole penis to shine our shoes!

On butchering day we put the pig on the basin, which was like a concave table, and began to butcher it at the throat and it screamed so loudly that sometimes the women were not able to bear it, nor the smell of the blood; then we quickly had to drain the blood because otherwise it would cling to the meat and the meat couldn't be preserved; then we flung boiling water over it to peel off the skin and took the meat that was to be stuffed into the guts as casings; we melted the fat from the bladder in the fire and then put it again inside the gut and called it *strutto*, from "distrutto," or "destroyed" and saved it for frying. We saved the bacon fat and lard for sauces. We put the meat in salt for eight days and then for a month near the hearth fire. We hung the salami and prosciutti in the cellar since it wasn't the time to eat them—we would have them in the summer when we worked hardest and everything is dry and we would be more hungry. In the winter we ate polenta and bread with onions, in autumn bread with figs or grapes.

And then in spring there was the sowing of the grass and corn. In the hills it isn't possible to irrigate and every season we would wait for rain. In May we would prune the vines that we called the "green vines" and make the *paratura*, or do the pruning of the tendrils; we would leave the tops that produced the grapes alone and cut all the rest without unbalancing the main trunk of the vine. We call it *paratura* from "pareggiare," to make even like a haircut; the vines, too, have their own customs.

And in the summer we harvest the wheat, for that is the most important thing. In every grain of wheat the face of the Madonna and child appears. If you don't really believe this, look closely at the top of the grain of wheat and you won't go wrong. There is a mantle that envelops two heads, one above and one smaller and a little below. Every grain has this figure of the "Madonna e il Bambinello." If you still don't believe this, think of how the fireflies arrive in the summer: before the wheat is mature, you never see them. Then in just a few days they fill the fields and roads with their lights. The fireflies are the ones who *graniscono* or ripen the wheat—they *spigano*, or "spike," the spikes of wheat! The fireflies arrive only to ripen the wheat and shine their lights on the Madonna; and then their work is done and they disappear.

Mario Giacomelli

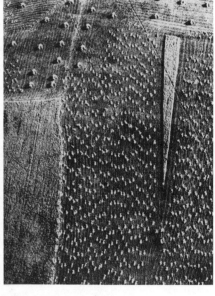

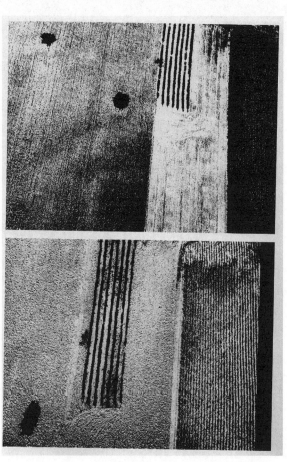

Allen Grossman

Wordsworth's "The Solitary Reaper": Notes on *Poiesis*, Pastoral, and Institution

Institutions are founded on analogy.

Mary Douglas[1]

A preliminary question. Is there, at the present time, anything that can be said *about a poem*, any words added to the words of a poem—that contributes to our happiness in the world, or puts us on that road? It does not go without saying that this happens.—But the beginning of a reply *may* be found (let us start at a familiar place) in a fragment of the exchange between Diotima and Socrates (*Symposium,* 205 a, b). Diotima defines *poiesis* as a general practice, of which the poem, or any artifact, is a contingent outcome (contingent because the outcome might be a made thing of any other sort). The defining qualification is that *poiesis* or "poetry" bring to mind, as *existing,* something that before poetic practice, did not exist—something that before was not perceptible and was, therefore, the experience of no beholder. Diotima explains to Socrates (I abridge the exchange) that our use of the word "love" *in a general sense* is exemplified by our customary use of the word "poetry," in the same way—i.e., in a general sense.

"Yes," Diotima said, "the happy (*eudaimonies*) are happy by acquisition of good things and, as we have no need to ask for what end a man wishes to be happy, when such is his wish this answer seems to be conclusive."

"You are right," said Socrates.

"Now, Socrates, do you suppose this wish, or this love, to be common to all men and every one always wishes to have good things?"

"I don't know. I wonder. . . ."

"You should not wonder, Socrates. We have singled out a certain form of love (love of the good [agathon]) and allied that name to the whole. . . . For example [here is another example of the same fashion of speech]: You know that poetry [poiesis] is more than a single thing. . . . For of anything that passes from not being into being the whole cause is poiesis, so that all kinds of making are poeisis and all craftsmen are poets. But you are aware that not all of them are called poets: they have other names, while the single kind of maker who works with music and metres seems entitled to the name of the whole. This only is called poetry. . . . Well it is just the same with love."

Diotima goes on to explain that, like love, poetry is a general practice (the cause of the difference between the not being and being of anything, including love) and the way we talk about poetry as a general practice helps us to understand what we mean when we talk about love. This general practice called poiesis (which causes the passing from not being to being of anything) is, as it seems, prior to love and to world (as for example, radical priority must be granted, not to the voice of the God who says, "Let there be . . .," but to the voice that speaks of the voice of the God who says, "Let there be. . . ."). Hence, poetry is more serious and philosophical than history (as Aristotle says, or Horace: "Many heroes lived before Agamemnon but lacked a bard," and are therefore "inlacrimabiles" [Odes IV, ix]). Poetry, in the general sense, is, thus, an agent prior to all other agency, even love, a principle prior to experience, which contributes the possibility of experience.

What does talk about "poetry," in the general sense, contribute to human happiness when the occasion is a poem? At best, such talk contributes credible news of the passing of world from not being to being (poiesis)—by reason of the fact that a "poem" (an imperative gesture of love) insists that there be valorizing attention. A poem, then, in the general sense, is an action the result of which presents the world to the mind of a beholder, as if for the first and only time. Such is the gesture with which "The Solitary Reaper" begins. Somebody says: "Behold. . . ."

Let us call the logic of this action, in so far as it institutes the presence to mind of the possibility of significance *and has a structure which it propagates*, "the poetic principle" (it is sometmes called, with a less definite emphasis, "imagination"). Talk about the poetic principle opens up the possibility of knowing the generative structure of valuable things *and their price.*—Knowing this is one kind of happiness.

The following is a brief analysis of Wordsworth's, "The Solitary Reaper" and a briefer analysis of "Resolution and Independence" ("The Leech Gatherer"), offered as correlative poems about significant work (the one poem presenting an economy of abundant, and the other of diminishing, resource)—poems *modern* in a specific sense, in that they are poems of the continuing Enlightenment. As such, they are reconstructive, or reorientative, poems—one might say "heuristic" poems—engaged with recovery (or the possibility of recovery of) *something lost as a result of new knowledge.* "Loss," the central factor in the logic of the poetic Enlightenment, is expressed as the constant subject of pastoral poems. Such poems improvise paradigms of post-theological re-institution of significant work—*significance as work* stated as the action of the poetic principle—which to this day, remains the motive of valid poetic art. Our maxim is: valid poetry brings to mind as knowledge what cannot be known by other means. (2) Poetry, in this light, is valid when it is the means without alternative of productive recognitions—significances statable in no other way.

One further bewildering aspect of any poetology:—"significance" is a result of institutions which construct, mediate meaning and authorize any discourse. Institutions—such as religion, state, and language—ground discourse by contributing the possibility and intelligibility, both of cognitive processes and of social life. But institutions also require poetic practice—are brought at the beginning, as they remember, from nothing to something by *poiesis*—even as they also, correlatively, *contribute the possiblity of poetic practice.* Institutions participate, in the interest of legitimacy, in the same discursive practices by which poetry is made and they summon or re-produce that practice by reason of their inevitability in the human world. "Analogy"—the fundamental trope: "on earth as it is in heaven"—contributes the force both of institution and poetry. That is the reason why there would be poetry even if there was (or is) no poem.

The question then arises whether, in light of the fact that poetry and state participate in the same logic, they supplement and contradict one another, or, fatally, repeat the same meanings. Will there ever be a truly "heuristic" poem, the finding by poetic means of anything that was not lost? Will there ever be a new song? Here, in any case, are two poems of apparently unanticipated encounter.

1. The Solitary Reaper.

The Solitary Reaper
Behold her, single in the field,
Yon solitary Highland Lass!
Reaping and singing by herself;
Stop here, or gently pass!

Alone she cuts and binds the grain,
And sings a melancholy strain;
O Listen! for the Vale profound
Is overflowing with the sound.

No nightingale did ever chaunt
More welcome notes to weary bands
Of travelers in some shady haunt
Among Arabian sands

A voice so thrilling ne'er was heard
In springtime from the Cuckoo bird,
Breaking the silence of the seas
Among the farthest Hebrides.

Will no one tell me what she sings?—
Perhaps the plaintive numbers flow
For old, unhappy, far-off things,
And battles long ago;

Or is it some more humble lay,
Familiar matter of today?
Some natural sorrow, loss, or pain,
That has been, and may be again?

Whate'er the theme, the maiden sang
As if her song could have no ending;
I saw her singing at her work,
And o'er the sickle bending—

I listened, motionless and still;
And, as I mounted up the hill,
The music in my heart I bore,
Long after it was heard no more

A poem is a form of words of our kind (*our* natural language) that points to words of another kind about which we consult one another in the interest of making sense ("Can no one tell me what she sings?"). At the beginning of Wordsworth's "The Solitary Reaper," we hear an imperative voice which says, "Behold. . . ."—Someone (internal to the poem's fiction) intends by speaking (we overhear him) to *reorient* the attention of someone else (also within the fiction of the poem) toward "significance" (a laboring "reaper," bearer of generality—apparition of "the poetic principle" of which I speak). *No one in the poem is a poet.* The speaker and hearer, as well as the overhearer (reader of the poem), are in the *interpretive* (hermeneutic) position. The command "Behold" specifies a scene of fundamental instruction, the punctual moment of original experience—as in Isaiah, "Behold I create new heavens and a new earth" (65:17 ff and cf. Revelations, 22:7). In addition, this command —"Behold"—by one person to another on the road (*in via vitae*), articulates significance as significance is never other than socially mediated. This archetypal command, one person who sees to another who does not yet see, theatricalizes the "institution," or founding, of any human world, always "new heavens, new earth," by an action of the (re-)direction of attention (*poiesis*/creation as reorientation), which makes aware that the question of meaning is the principle of our business with one another. "In this sense, every view is equally significant." And this spectacle of *poiesis*, of coming into being (harvesting, gathering, fundamental instruction, identically, the scene of fruitfulness and passing away—as in the tradition of the Linus song) is fraught with danger of birth and death.

This particular speaker (a Quaker, as we shall find) intends *evangelical* instruction. The "word" of *this* speaker who says "Behold. . . ." determines that the language of the poem will be the dialect of Biblical pastoral. The *Biblical kind* of pastoral (*poiesis*, strictly speaking) is authorized by the divine in-action, the solitary *otium*, of the Semitic God of the Sabbath—the radically creative (anti-representational) persistence-in-being-without-action-for-a day (God's signature exploit) which is the final stage of world-making. By contrast, *Hellenic* pastoral is a primal scene of human making (*mimesis*) authorized by the mortal

281

leisure, not of the ONE but of the few. The Bible God creates. The gods of Homer practice their divinity as disturbed leisure, i. e. representation—Hephaistus not excepted. Thus, the continuing and uncanny interest of pastoral text (*unheimlichkeit* of pastoral) is the result of the fact that "pastoral," the paradigm-genre of *poiesis* in the modern West, is a discursive inheritance from two cultures, linguistically distinct, logically (and theo-logically) contradictory: 1) the Greek culture of "making," fundamentally Homeric polytheism in which Agamemnon is the "shepherd of the people" in a world, without beginning or end, closed only by human action as in tragedy, the artifice of death (there is no natural death in Homer), closed therefore from within. And 2) Semitic monotheism ("Adonai is my shepherd"), a culture of "creation," world with a beginning and an end (Genesis/Revelation), *finite*, closed all around by the sacred outside where lives the God who "kills and quickens."

Contrast the solitude of Wordsworth's reaper (one person doing many things, cutting and binding, reaping and singing—*instituting* complexity (4) with the Homeric representation of Hephaistos' depiction of reaping (on Achilleus' shield, *Iliad* 18: 550–560) which presents the *social* character of harvest. Hephaistos depicts the *ongoing* of institution—a triumphal spectacle of domestic and also regal maintenance—in which "division of labour" integrates a cooperative whole (many people doing one thing"), as Adam Smith and Emile Durkheim say division of labor should (*contra* Marx).

> And [Hephaistos] forged a king's estate where harvesters labored,
> reaping the ripe grain, swinging their whetted scythes.
> Some stalks fell in line with the reapers, row on row,
> and others the sheaf-binders girded round with ropes,
> three binders standing over the sheaves, behind them
> boys gathering up the cut swaths, filling their arms,
> supplying grain to the binders, endless bundles.
> And there in the middle the king,
> scepter in hand at the head of the reaping-rows,
> stood in tall silence, rejoicing in his heart. (translation, Fagles)

But the affinities of Wordsworth's "The Solitary Reaper" is to the Biblical kind—the culture of single (solitary) origination of the plural world—not the Homeric *heimisch* of experience (many doing one thing) but the *heimlichkeit* of Semitic and European sacred interiority (one worker doing all things, labor prior to division). Ancestral to the solitary highland lass is the biblical gleaner, Ruth, whose labor in the fields of Boaz (a result in the story of her divinely counter- intuitive choice of the affinity of Naomi—a choice for which there is no reason, analogy of the no reason of Creation) founded the lineage of David and therefore Christ. (Ruth 4,: 17–22) Ruth's "poetic" exploit expresses *divine assurance about affinity:* she knows *what is like what.* The instituting intelligence of the free *choice* of affinity (the willing of membership in a class) is the same analogic power of mind which produces metaphor—the cognitive exploit which sees many as one— "imaginative" composition—including the figural continuity of Jewish and Christian Scripture.

"Behold her, single in the field. . . ."—The exploit of "significance," to which the speaker in the poem points, is the performance *by one* girl of many actions—actions which, like the Homeric harvest or reproductive sex, are *impossibly* performed by one alone. The angel says to Mary, "And behold thou shalt conceive in the womb and bring forth a man" and Mary replies, "How shall this be, seeing I know not man" (Luke I: 31ff). This is the reason why the title of Wordsworth's poem, "The Solitary Reaper" picks out, as not going without saying, the fact that this bending harvester is working alone ("single," "solitary," "by herself") and also the otherness—the cultural difference ("highland"), as well as genderic ("lass")—of the worker. The orienting imperative "Behold" calls to the attention of the hearer on the road, and the over-hearing reader, *an originative practice, precisely: a contradictory proposition which is true*—indicative of the poetic principle. Such is "creation"—reproductivity *necessarily* without another, a logical enigma impossible to be thought but without which thought is not possible.

This reaper's tool would be a one-handed, round-bladed sickle— short handled, leaving the other hand for another action and requiring the woman to bend over—not the two-handed scythe , as for example in Frost's "Tuft of Flower" or Keats' "Ode to Autumn" (or Fagles' Homer). Note that "herself" in stanza one is an unrhymed word, a singularity, a metrical signifier of incommensurability, outside measure— as "work" in stanza three, the action of *poiesis,* is also unrhymed. *She* is both cutting *and* binding (two separate operations, not performable simultaneously by the same person); and, also, she is singing at the same time that she is doing everything else. She is, that is to say, performing all by herself a number of activities generally requiring, as exemplified in the Homeric instance, a team of workers with various skills and commissions. No division of labor here. But, more radically, the integration of incompatible practices, as Homer's Achilleus for whom the shield is inscribed, a second body for the naked man in (in *Iliad* 18), is both a warrior and a singer, or Yeats' dancer is both rooted and wandering. And, precisely, as the Aristotelian rules of thought do not admit of the sentence *p* and not *p*. This was also the enigma (both attested by him and, he protests, unintelligible to him) of Empson's Seventh Type of ambiguity (illegible contradiction) of which his two examples were 1) the Christ, impossibly man and God, Herbert's "The Sacrifice" and 2) the performative paradox of pastoral—no high-class literacy possible to be produced by working stiffs.

Whether the reaper is, otherwise, a good looking girl, or not—her personal beauty—does not seem to be an interesting question. Her language, the words of her song (let us say, words in "Erse," encountered in the radical liminality of the highland border), are unintelligible to the (male) passers by. But the volume of the voice, its mere drenched "sound," fills and overfills the space of intelligible life and passes into the interiority ("heart," not mind) of the hearer, *for the very reason* of its unintelligibility. The heart-space is a "vale" (in Keats' sense of "vale," the mortal scene of self-formation). The vale is "profound" as, in the Authorized Version, the thought of God is "profound" (Psalm 92.5) or his wisdom (Job 9.4), i. e. unintelligible to mortals, those who "pass." But the volume of the reaper's song is in excess of the implications of "profundity." The walkers are arrested by the spectacle of this uncanny figure for which there is no category—a logical entailment of "singularity." At the moment when they have come to the bottom of descent the walkers must either "stop here" (die now, having seen what is not an event in life, i.e. death) or begin to ascend (return to the labor of life having seen its limit). The death-threat implication ("Stop here or slowly pass") of seeing the "corn spirit" comes to light in the anthropology of the Scottish Highlands: "Thus the person who was killed on the harvest field as the representative of the corn [barley] spirit may have been . . . a passing stranger. . . ." (5) But the double motive to disavow the experience, a motive at once dialectic (the experience is true only because it is impossible) and also prudential (the experience is dangerous because the powers it evokes are not consistent with life, in a political sense treasonable) is expressed in the care with which Wordsworth guarded his authorship of the text. Wordsworth made sure that neither the spectator nor the speaker of "The Solitary Reaper" could be understood to be himself, neither the language nor the experience his own.

284

2. Thomas Wilkinson.

Wordsworth and his sister take pains to make clear that the ethos of the speaker—the sponsor of language—in "The Solitary Reaper" is an invention of a Quaker, named Thomas Wilkinson. The date of composition of the poem, Nov. 7, 1805, is ascertained by a letter from Dorothy Wordsworth to her neighbor and benefactor Lady Beaumont, into which letter Dorothy Wordsworth copies the poem. In Dorothy's *Recollections of a Tour Made in Scotland*, "The Solitary Reaper" is introduced as follows: "It was harvest time, and the fields were quietly— might I be allowed to say pensively?—enlivened by small companies of reapers. It is not uncommon in the more lonely parts of the Highlands to see a single person so employed."(6) However, Dorothy has not herself seen "a single person so employed." She asserts, on the contrary: "[T]he following poem ["The Solitary Reaper"] was suggested to William by a beautiful sentence in Thomas Wilkinson's 'Tour in Scotland.'" So William Wordsworth did not himself experience a solitary reaper. Wordsworth's relation to the subject of this poem was removed from any actual solitary reaper by the distance of another mind than his own. The "solitary Highland lass" was somebody else's "tour," or "beautiful sentence." Wordsworth's note to the poem in the second volume of *Poems in Two Volumes* reads: "This poem was suggested by a beautiful sentence in a MS Tour in Scotland written by a Friend, the last line being taken from it *verbatim*." (7)

Thomas Wilkinson was a Quaker, or Friend (b. 1751) who inherited a small estate near Penrith. He was a man of particular interest to Wordsworth, although the exact character of that interest is not on the face of it clear. In 1787, Wilkinson performed "his one extensive piece of Quaker service"—an evangelizing tour to the north—which yielded (as part of a journal of the tour) the "beautiful sentence" which Wordsworth saw, *so named*, and then ordered to be inscribed by Wilkinson in Wordsworth's own commonplace book: "Passed a female who was reaping alone; she sung in Erse as she bended over her sickle: the sweetest human voice I ever heard: her strains were tenderly melancholy, and felt delicious long after they were heard no more." Since Wilkinson's "beautiful sentence" is the last line of Wordsworth's poem, the language of the poem as written by Wordsworth must be conformed to Wilkinson's hand.

Apart from these multiple written attestations by William, Dorothy and Wilkinson (in his published "Journal"), the "beautiful sentence" can be seen to *function* as independently originated in the light of the fact that the temporality of the third stanza of the poem (past tense, inflected by the last line) is inconsistent with the tensing of the first two stanzas (present tense, the only mode in which *deixis* can happen—the imperative having no tenses). *The poem is in fact spoken by the author of the last line*. Most important: the word "beautiful," which qualifies Wordsworth's justification of his use of Wilkinson's sentence, *classifies* the poem, constraining it within the unproblematic category of Burkean sociability.

In the third stanza, then, we overhearers learn that the "Behold" *intends to bring to the mind of another within the fiction* a scene, which is *not* at hand, not the experience of the listener but of the speaker at another time. The abruptness of the poem's opening, and the marked lack of focality of the speaker who summons, as it were, an indefinite and general audience to view an event framed only by his memory, presents a speaker who, like a docent in a museum, is engaged in a formal re-presentation of a spectacle the importance of which he has learned but the *significance* of which he does not know. The implication is conveyed that the speaker is calling to the mind of another ("Think of it this way: 'Behold her!'") a picturable reality of the highest value—the greatest interest—the meaning of which he, precisely for the reason it is of the greatest interest and therefore inconsistent with translatability, can indicate but not specify. Indeed, the "greatest interest" lies in the excess or selvage by which the spectacle exceeds its account.

We should, I think, feel the silence of wonder (of not knowing) outside and inside the (Wilkinsonian) voice that says "single," "solitary," "by herself," "Alone"—and begins the poem with that kind of direction of intention ("Behold her. . . .") which specifies difference as attention's content. This solitude, solitariness, unrhyming by herselfness, workaloneness of "The Solitary Reaper" is notional except for the account of Thomas Wilkinson (Friend and *evangelist* who brings it to mind for the benefit of another). But it is, in fact, simultaneously and dialectically (one solitude instituting the other from itself) the solitude of the native worker and the solitude of the bourgeois subjectivity (the proprietary subjectivity of the freeholder)—both the solitude, as we might say, of the "soul," but also reciprocally the solitude of a depopulated landscape.

This depopulated landscape is, of course, the world of the dispersed and destroyed Scottish Highlanders and their treasonable bardic culture (another reason for not understanding the song of the Highland lass). The destruction of the clans of Scotland and Ireland was accompanied, as is well known, by the hunting down and killing of the bards, from the edicts of Elizabeth to the defeat of the Jacobite cause in 1745 and the reprisals that followed. "When England would the land en-thrall / She doomed the Muses' sons to fall"—thus making room for the successor institution: literary high culture—the national poets of the period and the subjectivity which high cultural lyric sponsors. The Wordsworths worried that there were not enough men left to repel a Napoleonic invasion. The overflowing vale is an echoing vessel filled with sound because emptied of persons, except (as we see) for the fan-tasmatic "final girl," *solitary* Highland Lass whose work-song *supplies the authenticity* of the Wordsworthian "profound" lyric inwardness and the social formations it sanctions. Dorothy Wordsworth, writing (Nov. 29, 1805) to Lady Beaumont to whom she had sent the poem remarks: "I was sure that you would be pleased with the stanzas on the solitary reaper. There is something inexpressibly soothing to me in the sound of those two lines: 'O Listen, for the vale profound / Is overflowing with the sound.' I often catch myself repeating them in disconnection with any thought, or even I may say any recollection of the Poem." What is contributed by the poem is a legitimating representation which is de-pendent on not understanding the original and, indeed, entails the disappearance of the solitary reaper altogether. The reciprocal effect is, "providentially," the opening of the profound subjectivity of the reader—: "The music in my heart I bore / Long after it was heard no more." The text of the Wordsworth poem becomes an "original" text—precisely by reason of the untranslatibility—disqualifiation as the speech of a person—of the reaper's song which, because it is "untrans-latable," is not a text. The girl's song is reproduced as unknown, with the result that it can be replaced by the totalizing (and therefore empty) set of possibilities supplied by the speaker. Because the reaper is not a subject herself, she is a perfectly effective agent of subjectivity in others. She has slid into the nothingness of the complementary class. The song of the reaper is the self-erasing work song of the *"prosopopoeia" of another*.

The analytic of the matter is an open secret in our time. Consider Bourdieu: "The veritable miracle produced by acts of institution lies undoubtedly in the fact that they manage to make consecrated indi-viduals believe that their existence is justified, that their existence serves some purpose. But, through a kind of curse, because of the es-sentially diacritical, differential, and distinctive nature of symbolic power, the rise of the distinguished class to Being has, as an inevitable counterpart, the slide of the complementary class into Nothingness or the lowest Being." (8) Can this ironic logic be recovered? Or do the generative terms of the poetic principle require, by reason of the logic of representation, this erasure as a condition of inscription? Judith Butler inquires of Antigone: "And what if her fate is in fact a 'social death' . . . ? This seems a crucial question, for this position outside of life as we know it is not necessarily a position outside of life as it must be. It provides a prospective on the symbolic constraints [!] under which livability is established, and the question becomes: does it also provide a critical perspective by which the very terms of livability might be rewritten, or indeed written, for the first time?" (9) The name for the pastoral crime is treason—the subversion of present legitimacy by appeal to prior right (*paulo maiora canamus*) and the correlative awareness of the builtness of "legitimacy"—the presence to human mind even of God, as it is contingently conferred by the agency of the singer of God.

Under the same Napoleonic threat, probably in the same year, William Blake was accused of and tried for treason in his retreat near Bognor (Regis) on the South coast. He was acquitted. *But priority is power.* The action of treason rightly expresses the poet's primordial alliance ("The Bible is the great Code of Art.") which, by the force of priority, delegitimizes all other representation and in the Semitic tradition representation itself. This is the "mental fight," "enlightenment" politics of iconoclasm in the lowest of all low churches. The poet as autonomous legislator publishes the illegitimacy of historical regimes— all "secular" instituted right. This the poet knows to do because he is "maker" of the gods (Homer) or even of God (that's why there are *no poets in Bible*). *Poiesis* brings "nothing" all the way over to "something" only and always as a double action, in an economy of finite resource, which produces also the nothingness of something. By reason of "the essentially diacritical, differential, and distinctive nature of symbolic power," the conditions of communicability contradict freedom, the motive of communication. This is the contradiction in which the "poet" lives by reason of his vocation: metaphor, diagnostic of "poetry" since Aristotle, asserts analogy (*is like* means *is not*, before it means anything else) and legitimates because it divides—maintains hierarchy as between divine and human (man is like god and therefore never God) *and* between man and man (analogy is the assurance of *other* minds (10). Metaphor repels identity and legitimates hierarchy. For this reason poetic "experiment" to this day (primarily the improvisation of metonymic in the place of metaphoric practice: "Whitman" is such an experiment) searches (in vain) to find a practice consistent with communicability that does not betray its motive, the freedom of the other.

We have brought to mind the uncanny doubling of pastoral in Western tradition—Homer and Bible. Homer's scene of reaping reminds us that among the earliest Western pastoral world accounts are the epic metaphors which bring to the text, by artifice of representation, a *known, remote, natural and general* state of affairs (pastorality is the "vehicle" of Homeric metaphor) for the purpose of making sense of an *unknown, artifactual, particular event at hand* (the culture of warfare, the "tenor"). In Homeric text, warfare (work at human value) requires both the authority of the universal intelligibility of pastoral reference and also its irreducible inaccessibility and difference. Divinity posits the unchangeable naturalness of that inaccessibility; but the (treasonable) poet knows it to be the enigmatized function of the constructive will. Similarly, as we have seen in the biblical "Book of Ruth," the intelligibility of the world is (re)instituted by Ruth's alliance with Naomi at the grain harvest of Boaz' field in the aftermath (second harvest) of the sacred devastation with which the Ruth narrative begins (all the male kin die). In both cases—Homeric and Biblical—pastoral is an instituting regime, structured like representation itself, which has double and contradictory rationalities: at once, lamentational consciousness of its own constructedness and, inferentially, the fragility of "creation," the illegitimacy of cosmos—and also the instituting authority of prior life. Consciousness of the madeness of things (the pastorality of order) is a revelation of the contingency of the gods or of the God. The claim for poetry of highest value (as the artistic form of language, mark of the human), and the accusation against poetry of greatest violence (the "slide of the other into nothingness") are inseparable and await our concern. The next task for the mind, the *work* entailed by the "disenchantment" of the world, should be search for an analysis of the poetic principle—some clarity about the terms on which *poiesis* tenders us the world.

3. "Resolution and Independence" ("The Leech-gatherer"): "What kind of work is that which you pursue?"

Whilst I was rushing downward, there appeared before my eyes one whose voice seemed hoarse from long silence.
When I saw him in the great desert, I cried: "Have pity on me, whatever you be, whether shade or real man. . . . (Inferno, Canto 1, 64–67)

289

Now, whether it were by some peculiar grace.
A leading from above, a something given,
Yet it befell, that, in this lonely place,
When up and down my fancy thus was driven,
And I with these untoward thoughts had striven,
I saw a Man before me unawares:
The oldest Man he seem'd that ever wore grey hairs.

. . .

Such seem'd this Man, not all alive nor dead,
(Resolution and Independence 50–56, 70–74)

To repeat the maxim of these notes and point to a distinction: poetic knowledge must not be mistaken for knowledge of any other kind. A poem is neither philosophical argument nor scripture—nor is it liturgy or love letter. A poem (trace of *poiesis*) must bring to mind what cannot be brought to mind by other means. Valid poetry (original work at representation by poetic means) is an action of last recourse. A poem is a valid instrument, if and only if no other tool than the poem will do the work. Correlatively, the occasion of a poem must require the poetic mediation. Poetic knowledge, the productivity of the valid poem, is precipitated by the self-consciousness of the mind in crisis, a mind that knows it can go no further except by poetic means—an always forgotten resource of every mind. This state of affairs is narrated by Dante's account of the meeting of "Dante" and "Virgil" cited above, and is also the moment of "Resolution and Independence." This is, historically, the logic of the modern *topos* of "lyric" inspiration, responsive to Christian and Enlightenment individuation—the successor position to that of the neolithic professional singer—the bard—whose *praxis is song* and whose song still celebrates, not the agon of this reduced self who sings, but of the man of the *other* class, king, saint, or warrior whose *song is praxis.*

At the beginning of Dante's *Inferno*, the journeying pilgrim (Dante, a Christian poet), driven back to the bottom of the hill of earthly felicity, unable to go further by his own means, encounters Virgil— Roman epic master, assurance of the institution of Rome, but no longer a man and therefore no longer a poet. Dante encounters Virgil *precisely because he cannot accomplish the task set him by his own means.* Likewise, in *The Leech-gatherer*, Wordsworth's poet who "can no further go" (ll., 22, 23) encounters, one who is *not a poet* but whose nature is akin to the principle of poetic agency, which is not a poem but

290

the state of a person ("a man I once was") who presents the logic of the urgently needed but, as it were, forgotten practice. Correlatively, both psychopomps, Virgil and the leech-gatherer, are crucially disabled in a Christian world (they lack in themselves the legitimacy that authorizes significant action)—Virgil as pagan and the leech-gatherer, apparently, as we shall see, a Jew.

The poem called *The Leech-gatherer* is about the predation of the poetic vocation upon the poet—"Mighty poets in their misery dead"; and *The Leech-gatherer* is, correspondingly, a poem which, unlike *The Solitary Reaper*, is presented as spoken by a poet. It is a poem driven into existence by sudden awareness of a fatal, a canceling, irony—such as that of which I speak—entailed by poetic practice. One notices that the reaper lass is singing ballads. Wordsworth's high cultural poem, *The Solitary Reaper*, which brings her to our mind, is not a ballad; but rather it takes her discourse into its stanza and is justified by precisely the discourse from which, as a written poem, it differentiates itself. By contrast the poem called *The Leech-gatherer* employs a metric, a stanza put in service (if not invented) by the suicided, "marvelous boy," Chatterton, "The sleepless Soul that perish'd in its pride," for his poem "An Excelente Balade of Charite." Wordsworth's poem, *The Leech-gatherer*, is driven into existence by the sudden awaking of a poet to a vivid but uninhabitable world—which precipitates the further enigmatic and apparently novel realization of a murderous logic intrinsic to the poet's work—that requires that the agent of representation suffer victimage, by reason of the nature of representation, *when the maker, and the persons represented, are the same.* "We Poets in our youth begin in gladness; / But thereof come in the end despondency and madness." This is the double-bind, the "seventh ambiguity" of pastoral song, a newly discovered rule of modern lyric, or any form of modern making. The *work* of the leech-gatherer is to bring something out of this nothing. Leech-gathering—abjected body and sublime voice—exemplifies the consequences of that labor which contributes presence *only to the other.* The words *The Leech-gatherer* supplies are starkly non-poetic—"resolution," "independence." The leech-gatherer's work is not to make poems—he is not a poet—but to mediate the relation between the practice of poetry and vital life.

Each of the poems before us focalizes a class of worker whose name and nature is identical with a practice. The solitary "reaper" labors with abundant resource. She is recruited by the naturalizing power of the "beauty" of the beautiful sentence. She embodies that discourse of another kind, which *authorizes*, precisely because it is authorless. She presents self-sufficient being, the temporality of which is without ending, in relation to individual life. Her metrical vehicle mirrors the poet-less common measure. By contrast, "leech-gatherer" identifies a fundamentally unknown practice, like the reaper also a harvester but a harvester of an unseen fruit. The leech-gatherer labors with diminishing resource (witness Chatterton as prototype—inventor not of a style but of a disguise)—with invisibility, absence, scarcity. He is encountered in time. He is the utterly temporalized, the always already dead, predecessor. The "solitary reaper" harvests an abundant resource, and contributes to the beholder an abundant resource. Let us call it: *confidence in the world*—confidence such as knowledge of the world does not diminish. The reaper's song is classified by the words of the speaker in the poem, in accord with conventional categories of elegiac pastoralism (*"melancholy* strain," *"plaintive* numbers," *beauty*). The conventional symbolic sources of such songs appear regulated, under negation, regulated not cancelled ("no Nightingale"; "no . . . Cuckoo-bird"), with the result that the reaper's song ("work-song of *prosopopoeia*") overflows the poetic categories by which it is stated; and yet nothing is lost. The metrical stanza of the written poem, *The Solitary Reaper*, alludes, as I have said, to common meter, the unconstructed meter of the anonymous ballad. But common meter is not the metrical principle of the poem, *The Solitary Reaper*, which is more general, a representation of meter, not its practice but its incorporation in consciousness. Similarly, in the second and third stanza of "The Solitary Reaper," an orientative rhetoric of spatial and temporal totalization (east/west: past/present) includes the whole world in mind without ("perhaps," "perhaps") specifying any part. *The Solitary Reaper* performs the cognitive structure of "the poetic principle," a discourse of one kind (a poetic dialect of natural language, and therefore intelligible—a "poetic language") *about* a discourse of another kind which has no name, for which there is no natural language, and in which there is no person. Wordsworth, *as we have seen*, took care that there be no poet of or in *The Solitary Reaper*, either as author, speaker or subject of discourse. The abjected agent of the poetic principle—solitary worker in a depopulated world—is a nameless person who has already disappeared leaving just this vivid trace. Remember Bourdieu: "But, through a kind of curse, because of the essentially diacritical, differential, and distinctive nature of symbolic power, the rise of the distinguished class to Being [privilege as presence to mind] has, as an inevitable counterpart, the slide of the complementary class into Nothingness or the lowest Being." But by contrast to *The Solitary Reaper, Resolution and Independence* is a poem in which there are named poets. *The Solitary Reaper* offers, under the figure of natural abundance, something like eschatological infinite resource as the "Lycidas" allusion in the last line (heard no more/ "Weep no more") confirms. *Resolution and Independence* presents an economy of diminishing resource (and rising price)—a world in which persons are at risk.

Resolution and Independence, like *The Solitary Reaper,* derives from a "Wordsworthian" text initially inscribed in another hand than that of William Wordsworth. On a rainy Friday, Oct 3, 1800, two years before William wrote down "The Leech-gatherer," Dorothy Wordsworth inscribed a short entry in her Journal about other matters—and then adds: "N.B. [*nota bene*—Dorothy's way of saying, "Behold!"] When William and I returned . . . we met a man almost double. He had on a coat, thrown over his shoulders. . . . Under this he carried a bundle, and had an apron and a night-cap. His face was interesting. He had dark eyes and a long nose. John [William's nephew] . . . took him for a Jew. . . . His trade was to gather leeches, but now leeches are scarce, and he had not strength for it. He lived by begging. . . . He said that leeches were very scarce, and he had not strength for it. He . . . was making his way to Carlisle where he should buy a few godly books to sell. . . . Leeches were formerly 2s. 6d [per] 100; they are now 30s. He had been hurt driving a cart, his leg broke, his body driven over, his scull fractured. He felt no pain till he recovered from his first insensibility. It was then late in the evening, when the light was just going away." The speaker in *The Leech-gatherer* is a poet driven to the limit of possible creative validity by a sort of epistemic *disorientation*. From an historical point of view we speak of the cultural determinants of this disorientation as Enlightenment (Kant's end of tutelege), which had the effect, in the poetic context of Protestant Germany, England, and America, of retrenchment upon an iconoclastic low church mediated to poetic practice by Pietism of various kinds (Holderlin, Edward Taylor, Blake, Whitman)—and a revisiting of Hebraic pastoral through Bible in England mediated by Milton. In his "Preface" to the second edition (1815) of *Poems in Two Volumes,* Wordsworth writes: "The grand storehouses of enthusiastic and meditative Imagination, of poetical, as contradistinguished from human and dramatic Imagination, are the prophetic and lyrical parts of the Holy Scriptures, and the works of Milton. I select these writers in preference to those of ancient Greece and Rome, because the anthropomorphism of the Pagan religion subjected the minds of the greatest poets in those countries too much to the bondage of definite form [he means mimetic by contrast to *"creative" Semitic realism*]; from which the Hebrews were preserved by their abhorrence of idolatry. This abhorrence was almost as strong in our great Epic Poet, both from the circumstances of his life, and the constitution of his mind. However imbued the surface might be with classical literature, [Milton] *was a Hebrew in soul; and all things tended in him toward the sublime."* [my emphasis] Milton's low church "enthusiasm"—meditative, poetical, iconoclastic, free from the bondage of definite form, tending toward the sublime—indicates for Wordsworth the poetic principle. Milton is the Jew fascinated by the *creative* God, "near at hand and hard to grasp," God of Genesis—unimageable source of images, radically creative. Constructed in the Protestant low church as the consubstantial sacrament, Biblical pastoral contributes to modernism the discourse of significance without reference. In Dante's case, the pagan master Virgil (in this case poet of the fourth eclogue) appears to him at the kairotic moment—when, driven back down the hill, he *can no further go.* In Wordsworth's case, the master is Milton, in the person of the oldest man, bent double, circular man—indelible pagan, in fact a Jew.

The "solitary reaper" is absorbed in her work and classified by it. But the question in *The Leach-gatherer* put twice, is: "What kind of work do you pursue?" (95)/"My question eagerly did I renew, How is it that you live, and what is it you do?" (125, 126). The Semitic idea of God's *creation* is inscribed in Hebrew. Biblical "creation" is an action for which there is no counterpart in Greek. "Creation" in Bible excludes all possibility of a human agent—another reason for the *unheimlichkeit* of Western pastoral and of the practice of "creativity," or *poiesis* in general when misunderstood as it so often is in Romantic text as an account of human agency. In answer to *the question* which the poet in the poem puts to the leech gatherer, "What kind of work is that which you pursue?" (95) we are instructed by Diotima to say *poiesis.* The old Jew's work—*more or less* like the creative work of his God—is to bring *something out of almost nothing ("almost" is the difference, between scarcity and abyss, which generates Wordsworth's poem, the difference between human making, that is to say, in an economy of diminishing resource and the divine creative act).* But what is brought out of almost nothing? The Diotima answer is the human value of persons—what love loves. Something not *there* before we make it.

"How is it that you live, and what is it you do?" The question is

294

not put *to* a poet, but *by* a poet to the apparition of the principle of his making: *dead* Milton, the double-bent leech-gatherer, uncanny anthropomorphism of "the poetic principle." There is, in effect, no answer. The work of the leech-gatherer is to bring something, not out of nothing (his God did that), but, as I have said, out of almost nothing. The difference is the difference between scriptural and poetic reality. The poet in this poem (the one who takes it upon himself to learn the way of the "poetic principle": "What is it that you do?") suffers a death-bound fury of fundamental disorientation—"Dim sadness, and blind thoughts I knew not nor could name." In *Resolution and Independence*, literary psychological categories such as *The Solitary Reaper* brings to mind—"melancholy," "pensive"—are seen as states of pathologic and economic degeneracy—decreative reduction. "Melancholy" has come, in the end, to "despondency and madness." Hence, the work of the poem is to replace such terms by fitter language, other non-poetic terms. "Resolution" and "independence" are words *with reference and are not found in poems, not even as I have noted in this one.*

In both our cases—*The Solitary Reaper* and *The Leech-gatherer*—a discourse productive of intelligible life is instituted by encounter with a speaker who cannot be understood—whose language must remain unknown. The language of the speakers to which these poems give access is *not* poetic language.

In the case of *The Solitary Reaper:*

> *The Old Man still stood talking by my side;*
> *But now his voice to me was like a stream*
> *Scarse heard nor word from word could I divide;*
> *And the whole body of the man did seem*
> *Like one that had been met with in a dream;*
> *Or like a Man from some far region sent,*
> *To give me human strength, and strong admonishment.*

Poems are made of words of the poetic kind which supply access to languages of *another kind*. The language of the leech-gatherer reveals itself as the voice—*not human*—of the God of Ezekiel and Revelations: "And, behold, the glory of the God of Israel came from the way of the East: and his voice was like a noise of many waters." (Ezekiel 43.2, cf. Rev 1:15). The leech-gatherer is known to the poet by his *analogical productivity* ("like a stream. . . ."; "like man. . . .") first in the interior self recognition of the poet (his recollected "dream") and then his imagination of deep interiority—that "far region" of the divine voice which sends its missionary prophets to conscious mind. And finally as analogy which articulates the even deeper material unity, not known to conscious life, between inorganic and organic being:

> As a huge stone is sometimes seen to lie
> Couched on the bald top of an eminence;
> Wonder to all who do the same espie,
> By what means it could thither come, and whence;
> So that it seems a thing endued with sense:
> Like a sea-beast crawled forth, that on a shelf
> Of rock or sand reposeth, there to sun itself;
>
> Such seemed this Man, not all alive or dead. . . .

The efficacious nature of this figure is signified by the institution of a discourse—heard in the liminality of life and death, as between Lowland and Highland—of another kind, uncanny, like the sacred in that it is untranslatable and like the social in that it is identity-conferring. It has, as does the double-bent oldest man, no meaning except its self-identity: "And moveth all together, if it move at all." Pastoral, one might say, is the moment of acutest memory of the never other than lost continuity between mind and body—of which one paradigm is the artistic form of words. In the stylistic codes of the West the appropriate term supplied is "courtesy." The pastoral figure re-institutes a discourse of "Religious men who give to God and man their dues." This last phrase is not a reference to Reformation probity but to the originary Arcadian function of the Orphic poet, as specified by Horace in De Arte Poetica (ll.390ff.). "In those days [at Arcadian origin] wisdom [as taught by poets] was [how] to distinguish public from private right and sacred from profane"—the distinctions which institute social order.

4. Why is death in Arcadia also?

Granting to Bourdieu, as I think we must, the captivity of symbolic value within the inevitably material human economy of scarcity—hence, "the essentially diacritical, differential, and distinctive nature of symbolic power"—who then owns Arcadia? Whose discourse is warranted by primordial authenticity—whose claim to power on the ground of original presence at the pastoral source is justified? Both in the instance of Virgilian Rome, and in the parallel and now urgent and brutally contested instance of the right to dwell in the narrow land of Canaan, we find the foundation and legitimating claim of institutional warrant mediated by poetry. The Virgilian claim of instituting weight for Pastoral is, of course, the fourth Eclogue. But in epic Virgil makes explicit that the authority of Arcadia is secured for the Roman institution he serves by allying the founder, Aeneas, with the displaced Arcadian Evander (human embodiment of *eu-daimonia*)(*Aeneid* VIII). By means of "analogy," Virgil claims for Augustus the humble house of Evander in the prehistoric countryside of Latium, and its legitimating force: "So talking to each other, [Aeneas and Evander] came to the house of humble Evander, and saw cattle all about, lowing in [what is now] the Roman forum and in [what is now] the fashionable Carinae" (VIII, 359ff.). In the same way the contemporary Palestinian poet, Mahmoud Darwish, claims, with perfect justice, in his book *Adam of Two Edens,* "My mother is a Canaanite . . ." (11).

Our initial question about "happiness" and poetry (finally, I believe a question about competent terms of inquiry) may have been anticipated in 1918 by Weber in course of his great paper "Science [*Wissenschaft*] as Vocation": "Consider a discipline such as aesthetics. The fact that there are works of art is a given. It does not raise the question whether or not the realm of art is perhaps a realm of diabolical grandeur, a realm of this world, and therefore, in its core, hostile to God and in its innermost and aristocratic spirit, hostile to the brotherhood of man. Hence, aesthetics does not ask the question whether there *should* be works of art." The sense of Weber's question is right so far as it expresses the failure of the disciplines of literary study, despite all the restless ethical intellectuality and learning apparently brought to bear on the matter, to find a morally profound analysis of poetry or of poetic text which is both disciplinary and general. One mistake appears to be the "enlightened" misprision that there ever was a "disenchantment" (in fact, Weber's term) of the human world, or ever could be. The concern of these "notes" is to call attention to the poem in the intended context of its logic as a threshold which supplies access to a principle fundamental to social life—all there is of human life. Problems of social hierarchy (because they are crises of the economy of representation) have the same structure as poetic problems, because poetry is the arche-typical kind of representation, never other than the picturing of the person. Hence, problems of race and class are problems of the poetic principle—are like poetic problems, and may be poetic problems—inherent in the inevitable cognitive/communicative logic of representational systems, still largely unknown. Whatever other discourses bring this state of affairs to mind, the poetic principle as mediated by poems also does so.

But let us go back again to the conversation of Socrates and Diotima. Why is there no question between them as to what that "the good" may be that all men desire? If men desire what the poetic principle brings to mind and institutes (its power of bringing into being something which was before not the experience of any beholder), are we assured that what men desire, because they find it "beautiful," is not Gorgon?

Notes

1. "Before it can perform its entropy-reducing work, the incipient institution needs some stabilizing principle. . . . The stabilizing principle is the naturalization of social classifications. There needs to be an analogy by which the formal structure of a crucial set of social relations is found in the physical world, or in the supernatural world, or in eternity, anywhere, *so long as it is not seen as a socially contrived arrangement.* When the analogy is applied back and forth from one set of social arrangements to another and from these back to nature, its recurring formal structure becomes easily recognized and endowed with self-validating truth." Mary Douglas, "Institutions are Founded on Analogy," *How Institutions Think.* Syracuse, 1986, p. 48. Emphasis mine.

2. For argument to this effect, see "Summa Lyrica" in Allen Grossman, *The Sighted Singer.* Johns Hopkins University Press . 1992.

3. Ludwig Wittgenstein, *Remarks on Frazer's Golden Bough.* Edited by Rush Rees. Brynmill. 1979, p. 11e.

4. For the philosophical importance rested on mind/body integration understood to be manifested by the capacity to perform many different actions at the same time, note Spinoza, *Ethics* (IIP13 Schol.)" . . . I say this, in general, that in proportion as a body is more capable than others of doing many things at once or being acted on in many ways at once, so its mind is more capable than others of perceiving many things at once. And in proportion as the actions of a body depend more on itself alone, and as other bodies concur with it less in acting, so its mind is more capable of understanding distinctly . . ."

5. See Frazer's *Golden Bough,* Part V, Vol. One, p. 254. Frazer makes extensive use, in this matter, of anthropological collections from the Scottish Highlands. Best referenced in the Macmillan one volume paper back, 1921, pp. 525ff.

6. E. de Selincourt, *Journals of Dorothy Wordsworth,* Macmillan 1941. Vol. I, p. 380.

7. Helen Darbisher, *Wordsworth Poems in Two Volumes* 1807, Oxford, 1952, p. 236. This is a useful facsimile.

8. Pierre Bourdieu, "Rites of Institution," *Language and Symbolic Power*. Basic Books, 1954, p. 126.

9. Judith Butler, *Antigone's Claim: Kinship Between Life and Death*. Columbia, 2000, pp. 54, 55.

10. John Stuart Mill, *An Examination of Sir William Hamilton's Philosophy*, etc. New York, 1871. Vol, I, pp. 255ff.

11. Mahmoud Darwish, *The Adam of Two Edens*, Poems. Jusoor and Syracuse University Press. 2000, p. 109. The poem is called "On a Canaanite Stone at the Dead Sea."

Michael Mercil

for the Fabric Workshop and Museum, Philadelphia, Pennsylvania

The Acadia Duplex

Description:

Double residence with removable panel for cleaning; four 1 1/4" diameter holes appropriate for swallows, wrens, bluebirds etc.; stained pine; 18" H X 6" W.

Mounting Instructions:

House should be placed in corner location.

Two holes face out for nesting birds. Holes facing into corner walls provide air circulation.

To attach inside corner:
a. choose desired height. Place one 8d (8 penny) or larger common nail at 45 degree angle three inches out from corner.
b. use any one of four holes to slip birdhouse on to nail. We recommend facing removable panel toward either wall.

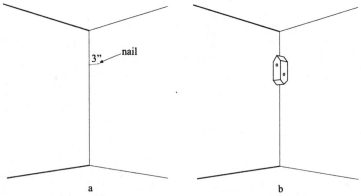

a   b

"A 21ˢᵗ century masterpiece of avian architecture"

Allen Grossman

Face East, Song Bird

Face east, song bird.
Study the school—:

"To think is to die."
On that art you can rest

the whole weight
of
night and day.

Where the sun burns,
there is
the infinite of interpretation.

To your left is north,
to your right is south,

under your tail shadowy
west.

The Murderer

"O kid! Forget their words! Think for yourself."
Old man! I didn't understand. *But now I get it.*

—At a great distance, we both heard something.
First you said, "Do you hear *that?*" And I DID.

Then we both thought the same thought:
The thrush has returned from the waste and void.

Now listen to the new thrush song: "How beautiful!
The numberless crossings of light and shadow at dawn.

How beautiful! That murderous bright stalker, the sun.
Forget his sweet words. O Philosopher,

there is nothing in the world that is like pain.
For that reason, the true poem is not known

and noon is the end of the trueing of song.
When the sun sets, more truth is seen."

"O kid! the thrush has returned from the void."
—Old man! As shadows fall, understanding comes.

House Sparrow

God is a person
who announces
his continuing
existence
in the form
of rules.
He is close
to hand
but hard
to grasp
as the poet says
like this house-
sparrow
warbling on
my ledge
the other side
of glass.
Suddenly,
since April,
I am *aware*
of bird song.
What is the rule
announced by God
at the beginning
of time
for the sparrow
at my window?
"Let everything
the sparrow sings
be true:
june again
june again
june again
blue."
So when at last

the June is flown
and storms begin,
the house sparrow
must warble on.
And then
be silent for a time.
After that
gone.

Sweet Bird, Sing

Poetry is something
people do
in response to
an obscure demand:
("Sweet bird, sing").

On a day, there arrives
at the swept doorstep, or
appears under a tree,
a complete life
("Sweet bird, sing").

On a day, there arrives
the first sight
of ocean. Mother,
your menstrual wave
("Sweet bird, sing").

On a day, there arrives
(*everything* arrives)
a big stone.
—Who can lift this thing?—
("Sweet bird, sing").

The hammer
in my right hand
strikes it again
and again.
("Sweet bird, sing")
But I swear to you!
My left hand is
still your prophet,
mother Beatrice.
("Sweet bird, sing").

Does the Moon Move or Do the Clouds?

Sweet youth! Return once more. *This time* I come
with something in my hands.—Remember your question:

"Does the moon move and do the clouds stand still?
Or do the clouds flee across the moon's face

quick as wind?" Sweet youth! Return to me and hear
my final dream, my dream of dreams, my dream

of answering. I am a lounger now on the white cliffs,
of chalk and flint composed, a man, his scattering

hands folded on one knee, who gazes at the sea
in storm, and at a wreck, and all the lost

that in her are. Nightfall. Silvery moon.—*Night-*
wind drives black clouds over the moon's face!

The man rises. Affection descends the long stair in tears,
with nothing in hand. But, mounting up, *here comes,*

on the same stair, a sweet youth, with a studious look,
honey-colored hair, and a miraculous book.

And there is a crossing on that stair also, a place of ease,
exchange of breath, quiet passing, kiss and cease.

Then all continues, as before, under the moon,
sometime dark, sometime bright, always alone.

Susan Howe

from The Midnight

Dark daylight of words

"Park: Originally in England a portion of a forest enclosed for keeping deer, trapped or otherwise caught in the open forest, and their increase." This is the first sentence of Frederick Law Olmsted's essay titled "Park" in the *New American Cyclopedia; A Popular Dictionary of General Knowledge* (1861). Somewhere I read that when he was sent away from home as a small child and took long solitary walks as a remedy for sadness, he particularly enjoyed the edges of woods. So much for the person. He started out a few pages ago. Now no one living remembers the fall of that voice from sound into silence. Who can tell what empirical perceptions really are? Veridical and delusive definitions shade into one another. All words run along the margins of their secrets.

Cold Pastoral

On Sunday afternoon, 16 August 1868, Lieutenant Governor William Dorsheimer, a member of the New York Survey Commission, took Frederick Law Olmsted for a drive around the city of Buffalo, port of entry and county seat of Erie County. They were scouting for a suitable location for a park. Rapid growth in the bleak industrial city situated at the eastern extremity of Lake Erie on the western corner of New York State at the border of Canada had already shut from sight whatever impressive views of the lake and the Niagara River its citizens once enjoyed if they ever did. Olmsted now stopped off on his way to Chicago where he was designing a residential suburb in order to investigate this lesser project. A municipal system in the form of small open spaces and squares connected by wide roads and driveways already encircled the city; he didn't see anything suitable for a larger public gathering place until they came to a rise crossed by a creek three and a half miles from City Hall in what was then rolling farmland. "Here is your park almost ready made," the landscape architect is rumored to have said looking back at the view of the downtown area.

I park my car in Harvard Yard

In the biographical entry he wrote on Michael Drayton for the *Encyclopedia Britannica* (11th edition), Edmund Gosse called the poet, "with one magnificent exception, an indifferent sonneteer." When she was in her nineties, my mother could recite the exception from memory, and she often did. "Since there's no help, come let us kiss and part— / Nay, I have done, you get no more of me; / And I am glad, yea, glad with all my heart, / That thus so cleanly I myself can free."

As in art so in life; isn't that enough? Isn't a sonnet confined and circumambient? Now it's too late I remember the way she vocally italicized each "glad." After all what do we long for when we are happy; something else. She tossed her words like coins. If two systems of value, the exchange of money and language are a unified entity, the thrill is two sides tossed at once for theatrical emphasis. On the devil's side or on either side, the closer you come the more protean. I think I remember her casting and staging *Comus* in the English garden of a wealthy Buffalonian. Milton's "Maske" is a simple fairy story on the surface. I was a four-year-old water nymph. She was an illusionist of fact. Wit is chemical. The initial art of counterfeiting set in a dark wood. Mary, Mary, quite contrary; no, no, not at all. Darkness is correlative with light and rest correlative with motion your verbal wit was astonishing.

"Oh Hell, let's be angels!" She said I said this to a friend when I was five in reference to what roles we wanted to play in a Christmas pageant. She loved to produce and destroy meanings in the same sentence. So even if I hope I did say it she probably made it up. One summer during the war or just after, we stayed with friends at their summer compound called Seven Gates Farm, on Martha's Vineyard. There she directed some scenes from A *Midsummer Night's Dream*. Not the whole play because this time all the players were children. I am told I played Titania. Still—why after well over fifty years, do I only know the Fairy's first speech by heart? Maybe I was two children at once. Imagine rushing in from one side of a sea garden labyrinth to speak with Puck, only here in print when Titania enters a few speeches later from the same side to meet her husband, Oberon, the Fairy gives them their cue as if space traversed were interchangeable with character itself. If poems are the impossibility of plainness rendered in plainest form, so in memory, the character of "either."

So long as you hear so long as you stay within earshot.

Enter OBERON, the King of the Fairies, at one door, with his Train; and TITANIA, the Queen, at another, with hers. "Ill met by moonlight, Proud Titania." He only claims a little changeling boy to be his henchman. "Set your heart at rest. / The fairy land buys not the child of me," I angrily reply. Momentarily rendering the Fairy King stage-Irish, Penelope (Poppy) Parkman (PUCK) offended our adult audience by calling her sister Deborah (Debby) Parkman (OBERON) "O'Brien." What internal schism in seven year old Brahmin utterance could manifest itself by sweeping *e* from the presence of *Ob* only to conspicuously restore it after little unnecessary *i*. Throughout childhood Poppy's verbal slide into apostrophe was a slanging emblem. Among other rope-tricks, including accidental delight, it cut slack for elephantine U.S.A. Howard Johnson mass-marketed twenty-eight variety ice cream pluralism.

In fact, if a bough bends the uncertain truth of fiction, a cradle falls.

Melody is inseparable from sylvan discord and savage concord. The Arden edition says love in relation to marriage is Shakespeare's subject, that the folklore in his own childhood doesn't come from books at all but barefoot and in poor attire from popular belief from oral tradition. Puck follows a rustic ballad pattern—beauty and terror are wedded. *Dream* has been called a play of missing mothers because all the human ones in it are either missing or dead. My mother, a marvelous reciter of ballads, preferred to let her children do the singing. In those early days our favorite was "Lord Randal." Lord Randal's father is unknown—his mother is the locus between life and death. Ever in pursuit of her son's forestalled attempt to lie down and give up, she *will* go on peppering him with questions. The leaping fixity of her melancholic curiosity is, to put it in a nutshell, greedy. Poisoning by giving a snake or eel for food occurs in other popular ballads, and early phobias include difficulties with food. Search forever, you'll never scratch this one's grave innermost surfeit. So farewell merry meetings, though we hum the same tune, words are a sandy foundation. The good mother (drop of rosewater) her coeval tie to the murderer (bowl of poison) this is the way you splinter things when you're in a position of abject melancholia. A man and his mother sing past each other—at cross purposes—two characters—hurrying at headlong pace—when all hurrying is too late—hawking and catching—can carry—only—so far. Of thirty-six ballads found on both sides of the Atlantic, Randal is the third most popular. Its melody is echoed in a Shaker hymn, "Billy Boy," "Lochaber No More," "Reeve's Maggot," "Limerick's Lamentation," and "King James' March to Ireland." In the Scottish lullaby version the victim is a slaughtered child. Sometimes a dead mother hears her children weep so she comes back.

Come away, away, children; come children, come down—

Come away—This way, this way—Calvinists, Congregationalists, Anabaptists, Ranters, Quakers, Shakers, Sandemans, Rosicrucians, Pietists, reformers, pilgrims, traveling preachers, strolling players, peddlers, pirates, captives, mystics, embroiderers, itinerant singers, penmen, imposters scattered throughout antiquarian New England, Pennsylvania, and New York, I cling to you with all my divided attention. Itinerantly. It's the maternal Anglo-Irish disinheritance.

All books and manuscripts must be returned promptly when the librarian announces the reading room is closing. Characters usually sleep well but from time to time one wakes up crying for no apparent reason. Randolph, Ransom, Rambler, Rillus, Johnny Randal, Reeler; better notorious than nothing.

Tyranty, Tyranty, I'll follow you to this extent only

What there isn't?

> My mother died while I was so young that I have but a tradition
> of memory rather than the faintest recollection of her. While I
> was a small schoolboy if I was I asked if I remembered I could say
> "Yes; I remember playing on the grass and looking up at her while
> she sat sewing under a tree." I now only remember that I did so
> remember her, but it has always been a delight to see a woman sit-
> ting under a tree, sewing and minding a child.

Soon after Charlotte Law Olmsted's death in 1826 her first-born five-
year-old son was sent away to various locations around the Connecti-
cut countryside. "The surface of the country was rugged, the soil, ex-
cept in small patches, poor, the farms consequently large and the
settlement scattered." Usually he boarded with minister-guardians who
tutored him, or sent him to local schools in whatever parish they served.
His first "thoroughly rural parish" was in Guilford where I live but in
2002 it's a suburb. He was six and it seemed to him then he could wan-
der where he wished and do what he liked. Once a man came by to say
that a sick child had died. In those days farm work was stopped and
district schools closed, so that children might walk in funeral proces-
sions. He was boarding at the parsonage and helped fetch the bier and
pall from the little stone house in the graveyard. That evening he
overheard the minister and other mourners comforting her parents.
Later he stole out alone to the burying ground and kneeling beside the
new grave asked God to wake her up so he could lead her home to her
mother. "My attention was probably called off by a whip-poor-will, and
by night hawks and fire flies, for these are associated in my mind with
the locality. I seldom hear the swoop of a nighthawk without thinking
of it. I went back to the house and was sent to bed, no one asking
where I had been." Almost fifty years later Olmsted composed his brief
autobiographical memory fragment as a remedy for insomnia.

In relation to detail every first scrap of memory survives in sleep or
insanity.

After AMTRAK what?

June 26, 2001. Guilford, Connecticut. 2am. The train whistle
makes sleep impossible. AMTRAK. Simply match the noise to a bona

fide physical object. Take notes on ways of overpowering noise, its lights and processes. Leftover light. Whether it spreads easily up and down. If this train stops in Boston it stops in Massachusetts. If I had closed the window you wouldn't be looking at sound. Land water sand—it's all in the eye of the mind. June is a month of deep shadows and unkempt thickets of fullblown wild white roses. In the evenings their scent passes over air of heaven and furniture of earth. Just because there is overlap, some neighbors with a realist bias consider them weeds without forethought; nonrational, unconfined. To enter night's character and moonlight's character I will scatter arguments here and there half-hidden; premises are omitted this way. We won't wander again over Divine Choice Theory of Actuality in the Connecticut River Valley, nor history in embryo after exile, when nonnormal worlds come into their own symptoms, namely, nothing—that is Bishop Berkeley's forest and this is New Quarry Road. June is the month when local hemlocks used to be glorious but in 1985 winds of hurricane Gloria blew a tree blight from Japan to eastern Connecticut and now most of them are dead or dying. Other things being equal all transport may break down. Anyway—a plane will get you there quicker.

I thought *Bed-Hangings* was finished before running across the term, "Dialetheism,"coined by Graham Priest and Richard Routley (aka Sylvan). A di-alethia is a two (-way) truth so it's the view that there are true contradictions. Just the way there can be one local place-name and another name used by strangers. For this logical thicket Meinongians will arrest a particular nonexistent cobweb tract noting its relation to distant objects everywhere. Still—others say nonexistent objects are never particulars. If at the heart of language lies what language can't express, can it be false to say that the golden mountain which exists exists? O light and dark vowels with your transconsistent hissing and hushing I know you curtain I sense delusion. Fortunately we can capture for our world some soft object, a fuzzy conditional, a cot cover, an ode, a couplet, a line, a lucky stone—to carry around when camping.

In modal realism possible worlds are objects exactly like the actual worlds; they *are*. They are a small car.

Sarah Kennedy

Strange Joy

And so it came to pass that the truck slid
sideways into the ditch. Pushing my door,
now a hatch cover to sky, I climbed free
to find myself showered in sun as Deborah

cried out *God* from the passenger seat. My guide
for the afternoon, a non-traditional student,
she was flattened against glass but took my hand
and hauled herself up while the tires oozed

further into mud. I already knew the job
would go to a candidate equipped with a wife,
an event prophesied by the dean's request
that I kneel in prayer. My time in his presence

drew swiftly to an end, and thus was I delivered
unto Deborah, who wept without ceasing: she
had led me to the wilderness of that narrow road,
meaning only to show me a secret field

where a herd of Belgians wintered. But I rejoiced,
yea, even to the end of my interview shoes
that dissolved on our hike to a farmhouse to borrow
a phone. Back down the hill, we awaited

our salvation, and the draft mares revealed
themselves, their great hooves flailing drifts.
Wild turkeys, scattering into sycamores, offered
their awkward wings to our eyes. O, I only wanted

a chairman who wouldn't smirk about an affair
we could have, I believed I'd be content with just
a cloistered office. But truly, that little college
in Pennsylvania was not the home I'd promised

myself, though I'd driven all night through
a blizzard to be there on time. Coal burned
out of control under the hills, Deborah said,
and after graduation, she was getting out,

though it would mean leaving her husband and kids
who'd damn her to the hell of their hostility.
Waiting for her tears, I toed the storm's leftover
muck. *And for you,* she declared, arm raised

to the woods, *I see something new. Something—
four-wheel drive.* The bumper sprang loose.
She chuckled. You'll say it was strange, but what
had ever come closer to perfect joy? I tell you,

those horses snorted clouds. Shattered ice spangled
around our heads. The sunken fender warmed
and we leaned back to watch until, lo, we beheld
the blessed wrecker, coming, at last, for us.

Robert Pogue Harrison

The Provincial Center

[NOTE: The following essay was delivered as a talk at a conference on "La provincia" which took place at the University of Bergamo, December 2001. It has been translated from the Italian by Susan Stewart]

I would like to take this occasion to revisit and further develop certain reflections on the idea of provinciality, which I presented for the first time at the end of my book *Forests: The Shadow of Civilization* some ten years ago.[1] It is a fundamental theme, for I believe that Western culture owes considerably more to its provinces than it does to its cities. If I had enough time and adequate archival resources, I would seek to advance the following thesis: that the great cosmopolitan centers tend more to attract than to beget artists, poets, and philosophers. The exceptions to this rule are obvious and certainly noteworthy, but I am convinced that—like the bread, vegetables, and meat that sustain nations and empires—the cultural nourishment of the West is provided essentially by its provinces. Think of Immanuel Kant, who never ventured beyond the confines of Königsberg. When, in the 1920s, an assistant to Edmund Husserl returned to Freiburg from a journey to Berlin, Husserl asked him how things fared in the big city. The assistant, Eugen Fink, said that there were dramatic, even shocking, changes: Berlin was full of cabarets and in certain quarters there were even prostitutes in the streets. Husserl, in his amazement, exclaimed: "What? In the city of Fichte and Hegel!" It seems Husserl was not able to fathom that Berlin could have a reason to exist beyond German ide-alism. Nor should we forget that Hegel himself, born in Stuttgart, in the southwest of Germany, was called to Berlin from the provinces according to this centripetal principle that makes the modern city a showcase for the talent, insight, and creativity originating in the provinces. Legend has it that Schopenhauer held his classes in an empty room because he insisted on scheduling them at the very same time as Hegel's. But neither was Schopenhauer a native Berliner. He was from Danzig. And since we are speaking here of Berlin, I might also mention a brief text by Martin Heidegger, written in 1934, entitled "Why Do I Stay in the Provinces"—a text to which I will return a bit later—in which Heidegger explains the reasons for his second refusal of a teaching post in Berlin.[2] That refusal makes of Heidegger a veritable exception. Only with difficulty does the provincial poet or intellectual succeed in resisting the call of the metropolis. There are other excep-tions, to be sure: Montaigne, for instance, who decided to remain in Bordeaux rather than cart himself off to Paris; or Andrea Zanzotta, who continues to stay in Pieve di Soligo, in the Veneto; and others too numerous to mention here.

It is notable that Italian literature, particularly the literature of the modern period, has a real exocentric relation to its roots. Ugo Foscolo, Giacomo Leopardi, Giovanni Pascoli, Giosué Carducci, Leonardo Sci-ascia, Primo and Carlo Levi, Giovanni Verga, Luigi Pirandello, Italo Svevo, Giuseppe Ungaretti, Eugenio Montale, Gabriele D'Annunzio, Italo Calvino, Zanzotto—all provincials! Even in the world of Italian cinema, it is difficult to find a director who is from the capital. Pier Paolo Pasolini, Michelangelo Antonioni, Bernardo Bertolucci, Ettore Scola, Federico Fellini, Cesare Zavattini all came to Rome from their small towns and rural regions. A colleague of mine who is an expert on the Italian Renaissance assures me that the same holds true for the Ital-ian humanists of the *quattrocento* who migrated to Florence: Coluccio Salutati arrived from Borgo a Buggiano, Leonardi Bruni from Arezzo, Carlo Marsuppini from Arezzo, Poggio Bracciolini from Terranuova, Benedetto Accolti from Arezzo, Bartolomeo Scala from Colle Val d'Elsa, and so on. My intention here, however, is not to generate a list or to create a typology of this sort. Instead of a socio-geography of cultural provincialism in Italy or elsewhere, I propose to offer a brief medita-tion, rather fragmentary and theoretical, around the speculative notion of the provincial, with the goal of helping us understand better why the province continues to be such a creative matrix in Western history.

I will begin with an anecdote. My siblings and I were born and raised in Izmir, in Turkey, which at that time was what one would call a provincial town. Before their marriage, my soon-to-be-brother-in-law, a native of Lecce, in the south of Italy, said to my sister that, unlike those from the big cities, the two of them knew that if they picked up a stone that had been lodged in the ground and then turned it upside down, they would expose on its underside a hidden world of soil and roots and worms and insects. I was so struck by this insight when my sister told me about it that in my book *Forests* I defined the province as a place where stones have two sides, one exposed to the sun with a hard and dry surface, the other moist and alive, rooted in an earth within which the bodies of its inhabitants will one day be buried (*Forests* 246). A person who has not grown up in the provinces knows little about this sort of thing. He or she tends to forget that the stones that went into the city's edification have been extracted from the earth, cleaned and carefully disposed in the city's more or less grand constructions.

I would like to linger a moment on this image.

Extracting a stone from the earth is tantamount to an act of abstraction—in the etymological sense of *abs-traere*, that is, to yank apart, draw out, remove. Our linguistic and intentional mode of being is more or less abstracted from nature in the sense that we are thrown into mediated relations with her. This is not to say that we are uprooted from the earth, merely that we have been distanced from the immediacy of our sensual being. The historical worlds we inhabit humanly rather than merely naturally come into being through our own making. They are founded by what I would call acts of *provincialization*, almost in the juridical sense of the term—acts that conquer, domesticate, and, above all, establish regional territories within the otherwise unconfined extensions of space. Such territories are human worlds opened up at the heart of an inhuman nature. Wallace Stevens's well-known poem, "Anecdote of the Jar," offers a poetic allegory of this kind of world-making:

I placed a jar in Tennessee
And round it was, upon a hill.
It made the slovenly wilderness
Surround that hill.

The wilderness rose up to it,
And sprawled around, no longer wild.

The jar was round upon the ground
And tall and of a port in air.

It took dominion everywhere.
The jar was gray and bare.
It did not give of bird or bush,
Like nothing else in Tennessee.[3]

If a province, in the etymological sense, is a region that is seized and then ruled by a magistrate, here it is the jar, an abstract kind of sign-post—a "port in air"—that conquers and sets up a regional regime within the Tennessee wilderness. Rounded and encircled by the object, the scene of nature comes under the jurisdiction of that orienting center. The jar in effect territorializes the hill by virtue of its differential presence there. I say "differential" because in its man-made character the jar does not arise from nature, is not native to the landscape. Hence its abstraction. Yet abstraction alone gets us nowhere, for it is the jar's emplacement—as an abstraction—that territorializes. In effect we must return our abstraction to nature if it is to have any issue. Thus while abstraction removes or draws away, the jar here draws together, allowing for a topical convergence around its abstract sign. It is through such a tension or double movement that the jar opens a kind of province in the landscape—a delimited region that unites and connects that which it confines by virtue of its differential presence.

It would be misguided, then, simply to affirm that the city is an abstract space whereas the province is concrete. I would suggest instead that the province is the center of the tension in and through which the earth from which we abstract our stones converges with the worlds whose edification depends on those same stones. To express it slightly differently: a province is where human abstraction remains irreducibly bound to that from which it has been drawn away, that is to say the earth in its humic transcendence—*humic* in the sense derived from the word *humus*. With this definition I seek in effect to reconceptualize the etymology of the word *provincia* which, as I have already said, has juridical origins, referring to "a task assigned to a magistrate" and also "a conquered territory." Yet according to Giacomo Devoto's standard etymological dictionary, *provincia* also is derived from *vincire*, to bind, enchain, gird, circle, surround—all words, as we can see, whose meanings are put into action by Stevens' jar.[4]

My book *Forests* has an epigraph taken from Giambattista Vico's

New Science: "This was the order of human institutions: first the forests, after that the huts, then the villages, next the cities, and finally the academies." This movement could be conceived as a progressive provincializing expansionism, one that conquers and brings under its regimes ever-larger horizons of nature. In *Forests* I wrote that "as the order of institutions follows its course . . . the forests move further and further away from the center of the clearings. At the center one eventually forgets that one is dwelling in a clearing. The center becomes utopic. The wider the circle of the clearing, the more the center is nowhere and the more the *logos* becomes reflective, abstract, universalistic. Yet however wide the circle may become through the inertia of civic expansion, it presumably retains an edge of opacity where history meets the earth, where the human abode reaches its limits, and where the *logos* preserves its native grounding. This edge is generally called a province. Only the province assures the containment of the center" (245–6). I don't intend to repudiate what I wrote then, but I must say that I am not completely satisfied with this picture, which thinks the province solely in terms of a periphery or edge. Instead, the image I would advance here is that of a center that gathers within itself its radius as well as its margins. Understood in phenomenological-conceptual and not geographical-juridical terms, the province *is the center of the tension between center and periphery.*

To leave the province means to remove oneself from this center. John Clare, the great English peasant-poet, lived within and spoke from the very center of his provincial horizon. In the text by Heidegger cited earlier, "Why Do I Stay in the Provinces," the philosopher declares that his thinking roots itself in the center of its Black Forest environment. Zanzotto finds in Pieve di Soligo's surrounding nature a landscape of Europe's recent and distant history. The provincial center is found wherever this bond is preserved, I mean the bond that unites and keeps in tension the unfolding abstraction of history and the mortal transcendence of the earth. That is why the province figures as the place where Clare and Heidegger *stay.* To stay in the provinces means to remain at the center of this ligature, which Western civilization in its expansionist drive has a tendency to abandon.

The order of human institutions of which Vico speaks is a historical movement that propels itself toward boundaries of containment in order to extend, expand, and transcend them. Following Vico we could say that, while the city exerts a centripetal force, calling in provincials from all corners of the worldly horizon, the historical movement of the West is in fact centrifugal. In the history of empire the provinces fig- ure as the most recent conquests, yet in truth this movement always starts from a provincial center—call it a hill in Tennessee—and ex- pands outward. There is a brief text of Wittgenstein's that I would like invoke here to help us reflect on this phenomenon of centrifugality. The text is the Preface to the posthumous collection titled *Philosophi- cal Remarks.* [5] Before citing it, let us recall that Wittgenstein was born and raised in Vienna, hence he certainly was not a provincial in any regional sense of the term. Yet perhaps he was provincial in another, even deeper sense. I mean as a thinker. Composed between February 1929 and the last week of April in 1930, the manuscript entries that make up *Philosophical Remarks* represent an important transition in his thinking about the foundations of language, which in his later work will be brought back to what he calls "forms of life." In his *Philosophi- cal Investigations*, Wittgenstein speaks of the necessity to liquidate west- ern metaphysics and to turn thought toward the "the center of our true needs," to make thinking turn around that center. Our true needs de- rive from the essential irreducible limits that define us as living as well as dying creatures: our bodies, our neighbors, our finding ourselves in the midst of a world of which we are not the authors and whose des- tiny is in the end unknown to us. Wittgenstein held that the specula- tions of Western metaphysics went ultimately in a dystopic direction and trafficked in a language that had been torn from its roots in our life worlds, where everyday language serves to orient all that is human in us. That is why he sensed the need, as a philosopher, to "radicalize" or re-root analytical thought, or as he put it, to "lead philosophy back home." I would also mention, before citing Wittgenstein's Preface, that the prefaces of books appear to belong to their periphery, but often their declarations and confessions are in fact utterly central. Often a preface reveals the hidden center around which the book revolves. I believe this to be the case with Wittgnestein Preface to *Philosophical Remarks*:

> This book is written for such men as are in sympathy with its spirit. This spirit is different from the one which informs the vast stream of European and American civilization in which all of us stand. That spirit expresses itself in an onwards movement, in building ever larger and more complicated structures; the other in striving after clarity and perspicuity in no matter what structure.

The first tries to grasp the world by way of its periphery—in its variety; the second at its center—in its essence. And so the first adds one construction to another, moving on and up, as it were, from one stage to the next, while the other remains where it is and what it tries to grasp is always the same. [Dated November, 1930]

I would not know how to determine exactly where this center of which Wittgenstein speaks is located. It is a center of analytic thought, that much seems clear. It is also clear that it is a place where the spirit of that thought *remains*, where it *stays*, instead of flinging itself into the vast current of Euro-American civilization, described by Vico as a peripherical expansion that begins in forests and ends in academies. This remaining at the essential center of things is by no means a static staying, however. On the contrary, it consists in a continuous effort to return to the center. To return to the center means to travel back along the paths our predecessors have laid down for us in their great enthusiasm for the peripheral and the various. That in any case is how I understand the import of Wittgenstein's epigraph in this context. That epigraph, which precedes the Preface, is taken from Saint Augustine: *Et multi ante nos vitam istam agentes, praestrucxerant aerumnosas vias, quas transire cogebamur multiplicato labore et dolore filiis Adam.* A literal translation: "And many who have passed through this life before us constructed arduous paths that we are obliged to retread, multiplying the travails and sorrows of the sons of Adam." The epigraph supports my claim that remaining at the center amounts to continually reclaiming the place—whatever be its nature—from which the great stream of Euro-American civilization forever estranges us. The place in question—such is my claim—is that province where the world of abstraction rediscovers its foundations in that which makes all of us the sons of Adam. To lead thinking back to the essential, to make philosophy turn around the center of our true needs—this is the vocation of a profoundly provincial philosophy, if we understand the province as the horizon in which the bonds between nature and history find their most primitive tension. To justify this tension is the task of the artist, but also of the philosopher. That is why "staying in the provinces" entails, for the provincial philosopher, a returning along the tortured paths of metaphysics to the central vicinity of our mortal humanity.

The province I have been trying to encircle, therefore, should not necessarily be conceived in opposition to the metropolitan center. Understood as the point of contact between our containment in nature and our abstraction from it, or between the dynamic transcendence that opens our worlds and the finitude that grounds them on to the earth, in short between our spirited projections and sobering dejections—this provincial center is found (and lost) just about everywhere there are human beings. Nevertheless, it is undeniable that the modern city is the civic correlative of those exhausting paths and exocentric routes to which Wittgenstein alludes in his Preface and epigraph—paths and routes that lead away from that essential center. Perhaps for this reason Wittgenstein felt the need to leave the walls of Cambridge every so often and retreat for long periods to a denuded shack in the remote Norwegian provinces. In this he revealed himself a modern city-dweller, who typically suffers from the city's (or academy's) peripheral dispersions. And even when city-dwellers don't themselves set out for the provinces, they have a need to bring the provinces to the city in the form of novels, poetry, film, and philosophies generated by those who found the center on their own terms. One thing is certain: this provincial center, whatever its nature, has the tendency to hide. We are constantly losing it, constantly obliged to rediscover it with great effort, be it in the realm of thought and art or in the realm of our moral existence. Since it cannot be held on to, it can only be retrieved again and again. While "the center, in its essence," remains the same (it *stays* where it is), the ways of reapproaching it are forever changing. Indeed, perhaps is only because the center tends to lose itself that history has a place to take place in.

Notes

[1] Robert Pogue Harrison, Forests: The Shadow of Civilization Forests (Chicago: Chicago University Press, 1992).

[2] Heidegger: The Man and the Thinker, ed. Thomas Sheehan (Chicago: Precedent Publishing Inc., 1981), pp. 27-30.

[3] Wallace Stevens, "Anecdote of the Jar," The Collected Poems of Wallace Stevens: New York, Vintage, 1983), p. 76.

[4] Giacomo Devoto, Avviamento alla etimologia italiana (Florence, Le Monnier, 1967), p. 337.

[5] Ludwig Wittgentein, Philosophical Remarks, trans. Raymond Hargeaves and Roger White (Chicago: University of Chicago Press, 1975).

Akin Euba

African Drums in Symphony Hall: Village Signals and Intercontinental Encounters

The practice of sending messages across villages through the sounds of talking drums was (and probably still is) an important aspect of traditional communications systems in African cultures. In times of emergency each village would pick up messages sent to it and transmit them to the next village. Through such relays, long distances were covered and the geographical span could be quite impressive. In the course of the twentieth century, African talking drums found their way into cultures outside Africa and, although they have continued to be used as speech surrogates, their messages are understood in ways different from those of the home cultures. For one thing, some of these drums lie inactive (often in unplayable conditions) in museums and private collections where they contribute visual (non-sonic) cues to studies in ethnomusicology, anthropology, art history and so forth. In other foreign contexts, the drums continue to be used for performance and for sending messages but the receivers of such messages seldom have the knowledge of either the specific speech language or the specific drum language. In foreign contexts, then, the speech messages of African talking drums are literally sent into the void, useless to their hearers. This is not to say however that all meaning is lost, for indeed other meanings are carried by the very agencies that make it possible to use drums as speech surrogates and these have to do with the sonic properties of speech languages.

323

Many African languages (probably most but not all of them) are tone languages in which intonation fulfils a semantic function. There is a system of linguistic economy that enables the same word to carry different meanings depending on the intonation used in speaking it. Speech activity in tone-language cultures is synonymous with a sub-musical activity and the distance between speech and music is very small. The sub-musicality of African tone languages makes it easy for them to be replicated on musical instruments and, in addition to drums, all African instruments with a capacity for tonal variation can be (and are almost invariably) used for talking, at least in the tone-language cultures.

The technique of talking with musical instruments is a basically simple one and relies on the reproduction of rhythm and intonation, two properties that are common to speech and music. It should be noted however that drum language is not a hundred percent appropriation of speech language and that drum language has its own peculiar characteristics. Since the conversion of speech language into drum language depends mainly on rhythm and intonation, texts played on musical instruments are not as precise as those spoken by the human voice. For example drummed texts often have alternative interpretations and a lot of context is needed for clarity. In order to minimize ambiguity, players of talking instruments use stock phrases that are readily understood by knowledgeable members of the local community.

Another characteristic of drum language is that it is typically realized as poetry and, consequently, drum texts form a substantial part of African traditional poetry. For persons who do not understand drum language, the speech mode of drumming is heard simply as rhythm and intonation and the meaning derived from it is purely musical.

The Mystique of Drums and Drumming

Drums are by no means universal in Africa nor are they the most common type of musical instrument. There is nevertheless an aura to African drums and drumming that is probably unique in the world's cultures of drumming. For example, Akan drum carvers of Ghana typically offer sacrifices to the spirits inhabiting the trees whose wood they would use in making drums. Furthermore, players of the Akan *atumpan* talking drums address a eulogy to the wood of the drum before commencing a performance (Nketia 1963 : 5–6).

Yoruba drum carvers in southwestern Nigeria also perform sacrifices in pursuance of their craft, but not invariably. In Yoruba tradition, trees are categorized as either *ako* (male) or *abo* (female). The male trees are those that harbor spirits and they are easily identified because, it is believed, lights appear at their tops at night. Before felling male trees for making drums, Yoruba carvers perform sacrifices in order to propitiate the spirits inhabiting such trees (Euba 1990 : 118).

Yoruba drum lore contains other information that attests to the spirituality of drums and drumming. The patron god of Yoruba drummers is Ayan who (like most of the Yoruba divinities) previously lived on earth. He was not himself a member of the Yoruba race (having originated from Ibaribaland—the Yoruba name for Borgu—which is contiguous with the northern boundary of Yorubaland) but he taught all Yoruba the art of drumming and was deified after his death. Players of Yoruba talking drums believe that the spirit of Ayan dwells in the drums and that all texts played on the talking drum are dictated by Ayan. In other words, although individual drummers internalize and memorize the literary corpus pertaining to drumming, it is Ayan who activates the memory and highlights appropriate texts for given occasions and these are then converted into drum sounds by the drummer. This way drummers are able to recall texts that they were not even aware that they had memorized.

Among the Akan, the mystique of drums is enhanced by the principle that all talking drums belong to the chief and drums are not allowed to talk except in contexts pertaining to chieftaincy. Permission may be granted for *atumpan* talking drums to be used in popular traditional ensembles but they are not allowed to do any talking (Nketia 1963 : 119).

Royal drums are important war trophies and, in the days of interethnic wars, Akan chiefs were morally obliged to protect regalia drums (Nketia 1963 : 119). Among the Hausa of Nigeria also, the capture of regalia drums brought deep humiliation to the Emirs (kings) (Ames n. d.).

In general, African traditional music has a strong dramatic orientation and the concept of absolute music is uncharacteristic. The dramatic aspect is partly due to the frequent coupling of music with dance (Euba 1990: 425). In arguing a case for the dramatic component of traditional music, however, one need go no further than the use of instruments as speech surrogates. In my view, the idea of using musical instruments as substitutes for the human voice, of removing speech from its natural medium (the human voice) and assigning it to musical instruments, is akin to high drama (1). Further evidence of this drama lies in the immunity enjoyed by players of the talking drum. Among the Yoruba, for example, the drummer (as long as he is carrying a drum) has access to every assembly, high or low. Moreover, while using the drum in the speech mode, he can address the king by his first name and say words of insult and criticism to any member of the community (including the king) that he would not dare to speak with his own voice (Euba 1990: 93–94).

In considering the migration of African drums and drumming to cultures outside Africa, we need to keep in view not only the physical and artistic but also the mystical aspects. From this point of view, some questions spring to mind. Does the migration of African drums imply that the drums are desecrated? Do Africans have a moral obligation to prevent the appropriation of their drums by foreigners?

African Drums in Symphony Hall

The journey from village to symphony hall took some time, perhaps several centuries, but by the end of the second millennium African drums had claimed space, however tenuous, in symphony hall. Following my engagement with theories of intercultural music (which began in late 1986 and early 1987), I suggested in private correspondence that Western conservatories of music would sooner or later need to revise their curricula in order to accommodate non-Western ideas. For example, students of the Western orchestral flute would no longer be able to sustain a viable career without secondary expertise in a non-Western flute tradition. Needless to say, this idea did not fly and I recall receiving a letter from one of the major conservatories in London to the effect that, although they found my proposal interesting, they were not ready for it!

During the period December 1986 to August 1991, which I spent working as a research scholar at the University of Bayreuth in Germany, I positioned myself as a "self-appointed prophet of interculturalism" (Troup 1990) and one of my predictions was that intercultural composition would become one of the main events of twenty-first century music (Euba 1989: 154–157). I have also been engaged in prophecy regarding the development of neo-African composition and sought to buttress my argument by citing events that show a rising international interest in neo-African composition. One of these events was AFRICA 95, a three-month celebration of African culture that took place in the United Kingdom from September to December 1995. As would normally be expected, AFRICA 95 fielded a strong music component but, unlike similar events in which the music component was devoted exclusively to traditional and/or popular music, AFRICA 95 reserved a section for neo-African art music. What was even more surprising was that the objective of the organizers was not simply to spotlight the works of African composers but to bring them into the main venues of British concert activity. This was an ambitious plan whose long term effect remains to be seen but in the short term there were two significant achievements. First, the City of Birmingham Touring Opera (now renamed City of Birmingham Opera) decided to make a contribution to AFRICA 95 by doing a semi-staged production of my opera (or non-opera, depending on your perspective) (2), *Chaka*, from an epic poem of the same title by the Senegalese author Leopold Senghor. And so it was that on 29 and 30 September 1995, African drums came to the City of Birmingham Symphony Hall, as part of the ensemble used in the performance of *Chaka*.

The second AFRICA 95 achievement in the sphere of neo-African art music was the commissioning by the Liverpool Philharmonic Orchestra of Ghanaian composer Gyimah Labi to write a concerto for five pianos and orchestra, whose premiere took place in November 1996 with the Piano Circus as soloists.

Significant though the 1995 production of *Chaka* may have been, this was hardly the first time that African drums made their appearance on the Western concert stage. From as far back as the 1960s it had become regular for African traditional performers to tour Europe, the United States and subsequently Asia and by the end of the century, the sounds of music from African villages were no longer strange to non-African ears. On the contrary, non-Africans have become increasingly enthusiastic about this music. There is no doubt that the music communicates something to audiences outside Africa although the meanings that it conveys to Africans in their home villages may be substantially different from those perceived by non-Africans.

In transporting African music from the village to the Western concert hall, producers need first of all to be selective because some types of African music travel better than others. Secondly, even when types of music are potentially transportable, a good degree of repackaging needs to be done before they can appeal to Western ears. African tra-

327

ditional music is almost invariably linked to social contexts (for example life cycle ceremonies, celebrations of divinities, hunting and harvesting, occupational activities and so forth) and one of the main problems of relocation is how to validate the music outside its customary social context.

There is no doubt that African traditional music is successful on the international circuit and probably makes money for some entrepreneurs. Furthermore, many traditional musicians, detached from customary ensembles and social contexts, have settled in Europe and America and found new roles performing other types of music in other types of contexts. Their services are often required by jazz and pop groups who seek to add intercultural flavor to their music by integrating non-Western sounds. These lone artists also enjoy lucrative practice featuring in world music programs in primary, secondary and tertiary educational institutions. Some have even managed to found neo-African ensembles whose members are almost totally non-African and often non-Black, with the aim of replicating or repackaging African traditions.

Village Signals in Intercontinental Encounters

Given the roles and status of drums and drumming as they exist in African traditional cultures, the question arises whether or not these attributes can transcend village communities and to what extent. It is quite common for musical instruments to migrate and to become so well integrated into their new cultures that they appear to have originated therein. This is a world phenomenon and is not peculiar to Africa. For example, average lovers of symphonic music are hardly aware that most of the instruments of the symphony orchestra migrated from the Middle East to Europe (Sachs 1940: 260). When musical instruments migrate to other cultures they tend to assume new characteristics and be adapted to local usages. Similar trends may be expected of African instruments that migrate to the West.

Before pursuing this discussion any further, it needs to be established that African instruments have indeed migrated or are in a continuing process of migration to the West. First of all, it is well known that, as a result of the transatlantic slave trade, African traditional religions are today practiced in various parts of the New World and that devotees of these religions use music and musical instruments that de-

328

rived from Africa. Secondly, there is a growing trend, especially in the United States, in the establishment of African drumming and dance ensembles, some of which are part of ethnomusicology programs in universities and colleges while others exist to help Blacks living in the diaspora to maintain contact with their African heritage. Thirdly, there is a thriving business in the importation and marketing of African traditional instruments and, at least in the United States, facilities exist for repairing damaged drums.

Evidence of the successful migration of African drumming to the West may be found in a single instrument, the *jembe,* which has become a synonym for the African drum in Europe and America. It is significant that I first became aware of this drum not on African soil but while living in Germany between 1986 and 1991 (3). The home of the *jembe* (a goblet-shaped, single-headed, fixed-pitch membranophone) is in Mali and Guinea and its spread to Europe and America may be connected with the international tours of the celebrated Guinean ensemble, Ballets Africain, which was perhaps the first African troupe to make an impact in the West in the post-independence era.

My own interest in African drums and drumming is related to my dual practice as a scholar and composer. Between 1967 and 1974 I conducted research on the Yoruba hourglass tension drum and my doctoral dissertation on this subject was accepted by the University of Ghana (Euba 1974) (4). The conscious objective of this research was to earn a doctorate but, subconsciously, I may also have been driven by the desire to build up technique in Yoruba traditional composition. The research did influence my composition in many obvious ways (see e.g. Euba 2002) but I found surprising Joshua Uzoigwe's discovery of aspects of it in his analysis of my *Scenes from Traditional Life* for piano (Uzoigwe 1992).

I also developed an interest in drumming as a way of imparting an African identity to my composition. Following the broadcast of my *String Quartet* on the BBC Third Programme (as it then was) in 1959, a reviewer for the BBC *Listener* remarked on the ease with which I moved within the idiom of my adoption and also noted some connections with Hindemith (a good point since I had studied composition with Arnold Cooke, a pupil of Hindemith, at the Trinity College of Music, London, and the string quartet, which earned me the fellowship diploma of the college in composition, had been written under Cooke's supervision). Nigeria's preeminent twentieth-century composer, Fela Sowande, also once reported to me comments made in reference to the string quartet, during question time at one of Sowande's lectures on neo-African art music, given in the United States. According to Sowande, the questioner stated: "That is all very well but where are the drums?" (or words to that effect). Drums? In a string quartet? I can see the questioner's point, though. What he or she was trying to say was that, with such a rich culture of drumming at his or her disposal, why does an African composer waste time writing a string quartet? Even more important, do Africans understand string quartets and doesn't an African composer have a responsibility to communicate with Africans (and to use the African perspective in communicating with the rest of the world)?

Between the completion of the string quartet in 1957 and my departure for UCLA in 1962 to study ethnomusicology and composition, I grappled a lot with the question of cultural identity in composition and sought for a way to give myself an African voice. The answer, a simple one, dawned on me in 1963, while at UCLA, when I discovered the power of musical instruments in endowing music with a cultural (and of course stylistic) identity. One of the reasons (not the only one by any means) why African traditional music sounds African is the presence of African instruments and modern composers seeking to sound African will have to reckon with African traditional instruments. Since that discovery in 1963 I have regularly used African instruments in my compositions, sometimes by themselves but more often in combination with Western instruments. Moreover, one of the features used in defining African pianism (one of the theories of composition that I pioneered) is "making the piano 'behave' like African instruments" (Euba 1993: 8) (5).

The migration of drums from African villages to venues in Europe, Asia and America raises some issues in regard to the traditional role of African drums as speech surrogates. Will the art of talking with drums gradually disappear in the foreign venues or will foreigners be encouraged to learn African spoken languages (and corresponding drum languages) in order to interpret texts played on the talking drums? Alternatively, will drummers adapt to talking in foreign languages in order to be understood by their intercontinental audiences? This is not as remote an idea as it may seem; for example, African drums can and do speak in English! The call signal of the Federal Radio Corporation of Nigeria, "This is the Nigerian Broadcasting Service," has for fifty years or more been played in English on a Yoruba talking drum!

Some degree of transformation already occurs when drums migrate from African villages to African cities, even within the same cultural orbit. In the course of my research on the Yoruba hourglass tension drum, I found that drummers operating in Lagos (the former capital of Nigeria and a city dominated by the Yoruba) created a new type of drumming whereby each sentence played on the talking drum was immediately rendered vocally by members of the ensemble. This was done in order to facilitate the understanding of drum language for residents of Lagos who, although fluent in spoken Yoruba, were out of touch with drum language.

As a result of the transatlantic slave trade, a number of Yoruba divinities migrated to the New World together with their ceremonial music. Today, New World devotees of these divinities sing songs in Yoruba (a language that is no longer spoken or understood by them) whose words have become equally archaic in Yorubaland. The songs are virtually frozen versions of the type of language spoken in Yorubaland at the time of the slave trade. This is an important precedent that may provide a clue to what will happen to African drum languages when drums migrate to foreign cultures. Drum languages could become frozen in the diaspora while they continue to evolve in the home cultures.

So much for speech-oriented drum signals. What about signals connected with the dance? In Yoruba dance drumming, the player of the talking drum tends to minimize speech activity and instead highlight *ijalu,* non-verbal signals to which dancers are expected to react with appropriate movement. Knowledge of such signals is a test of good dancing in African cultures. Indeed, African traditional dance is characterized by an intensive rapport between dancers and drum leaders and a disruption of this rapport (resulting from insufficient knowledge of drum signals on the part of either dancers or drummers) could significantly alter the idiom of traditional dance.

Whatever transformations occur through the migration of African instruments to foreign cultures, the new music that is created must be judged on its own merit and not in terms of the music existing in Africa. It is easy enough to conclude that African music abroad is a poor imitation of African music in Africa but creativity is not peculiar to race, culture, continent or place and when idioms diverge (through relocation) they have a good chance of becoming viable in due course.

In summary, one of the most crucial aspects of my own creative practice is the need to cultivate a neo-African voice that enables me to communicate with Africans and members of the African diaspora, on the one hand, and with the rest of the world, on the other hand. I have endeavored to do so by employing African drums and other instruments in combination with Western instruments (as for example in my opera *Chaka*) (6). While access to an African identity is easily made through the use of African instruments, this is a practice that reduces the possibility of live performances. Works that feature African instruments cannot be performed unless the instruments and competent players are available in the same place. It is for this reason that I have recently embarked on a new creative adventure by writing music for standard (international) orchestral instruments and making them "behave like African instruments." This led to my composition of *Orunmila's Voices: Songs from the Beginning of Time*, a music-drama for soprano, contralto and baritone soloists, chanters, chorus, dancers and symphony orchestra, which was premiered on 23 February 2002 in New Orleans with Dennis Assaf conducting the Jefferson Performing Arts Society Orchestra and Chorus, with the Dillard University Concert Choir and dancers from the Kumbuka African Dance and Drum Collective.

Notes

[1] See e.g. Euba 1990 : 425-426.

[2] According to Morley (1995), "Opera it is not . . ."

[3] Equally significant is the fact that the first time that I ever handled an African drum was in 1963, aged 28, while studying at UCLA.

[4] Euba 1990 is a revised version of the work.

[5] The concept of African pianism is a reversal of the type of migration discussed in this essay and has to do with the African appropriation of the Western pianoforte. More information on African pianism may be found in Euba 1989: 149-154 and Omojola 2001.

[6] *Chaka* is available on CD (see Euba 1999).

References Cited

Ames, David

n.d.   *Nigeria—Hausa Music 1*. In Unesco Collection *An Anthology of African Music*. Edited by Paul Collaer. One 33 1/3 12-inch LP record. Sleeve Notes. BM 30L 2306. Kassel, Basel, Paris and New York: Barenreiter-Musicaphon.

Euba, Akin

1974   *Dundun Drumming of the Yoruba*. Ph.D. dissertation. University of Ghana, Legon.

1989   *Essays on Music in Africa 2: Intercultural Perspectives.*
        Bayreuth: Bayreuth African Studies Series.
1990   *Yoruba Drumming: The Dundun Tradition.* Bayreuth:
        Bayreuth African Studies Series.
1999   *Chaka,* an opera in two chants, for soloists, Yoruba
        chanter, chorus, dancers and a mixed ensemble of African
        and Western Instruments. From an epic poem by Leopold
        Senghor. Performed by the City of Birmingham Touring
        Opera conducted by Simon Halsey. One CD recording.
        MRI-0001 CD. Point Richmond, CA: Music Research In-
        stitute.
2002   "Theory, Scholarship, Myth and Mysticism: Sources of My
        Creativity." Unpublished paper presented at the 7th bien-
        nial international symposium and festival of the Center for
        Intercultural Music Arts at Churchill College, Cambridge.

Morley, Christopher
1995   "African Beat Just Goes On." *The Birmingham Post Week-
        end.* 30 September.

Nketia, J.H.
1963   *Drumming in Akan Communities of Ghana.* Edinburgh:
        Thomas Nelson.

Omojola, Bode
2001   "African Pianism as an Intercultural Compositional
        Framework: A Study of the Piano Works of Akin Euba."
        In *The Landscape of African Music.* Edited by Kofi Agawu.
        Research in African Literatures 32/2.

Sachs, Curt
1940   *The History of Musical Instruments.* New York: Norton.

Troup, Malcolm

1990   "Towards an African Pianism: Interculturalism on the
        March. *Piano Journal* 11/32.

Simon Armitage

The Following Directions

In the country, the county, the parish, the place,
this is the bay and the beach funneled into the lane,
this is the kirk-field growing a season of stones,
this is the grit-box for salting the road.

This is the Gulf Stream, this is the weather,
this is the bull with its nose in a ring-pull,
this is the flag and the flagpole over the lintel,
this is the five-bar gate, the dog with the teeth

at the end of its tether. This is the Mace,
this is the price of milk and yesterday's paper,
this is the Lodge and the school and the next farm,
this is the view, looking east, from the top of the hill.

That's the sea-cat, pressing a seam in the waves from port
to port, that there's Scotland on the other shore.
This is the satellite dish on the back wall,
this is the basketball-hoop over the back door.

This is the third left, this is the same car going past
for the third time, this is the sign to the path
that slows to a dead-end after an acre of cows.
This is as much as you know, as far as it goes.

Rod Mengham

End of the Line

Underground railways exist as alternative spheres to the cities they serve, they take on a character of their own, which we tend to think of in terms of rationalized space and time, as places where the unexpected is not meant to happen. The tube map with its symmetries, its rows of diagonals, its repetition of angles, is an excessive rationalization of something that in reality is much more irregular. An accurate map would look worryingly chaotic, its proliferation of unrepeatable patterns would make the city look out of control. Where the tube ends is where the pattern most obviously unravels; it is where the dream of symmetry gives up. Most people never reach the end of the line where the idea of the city no longer obtains. Almost no one has traveled to the end of all the lines. That would mean being exposed to a degree of variety that the blueprint could never absorb. At every underground stop, people climb to the surface, emerge into the light of day, but the train goes on, the circulation continues, the Circle Line providing a visual and conceptual magnet for the way the city stays alive by pumping flows of energy around the system. At the end of the line this fiction dissolves; it is not only people but the place itself which releases its grip on the idea of the city as a closed system. Our project is an enquiry into what relates these different places apart from their entry into and exit from a system they are so iconically related to. Perhaps the termini are all portals into something other than the idea of the city we automatically link them with.

Of course, the Circle Line offers resistance, is in many ways in absolute contrast with the suburban tangents. There is no emergence, no aperture, except for those created during the Blitz, when bombs would come through the road above, or even bounce down the escalators, skip along the hallways and explode on the platforms. These violent incisions would not dispel the secrets of the entombed—the myth-making potential of all those repressed corridors—but would foster anew the sense of an alien habitat. This is caught most obviously by *Quatermass and the Pit,* where the breach into a deserted station uncovers the race-memory of another planet altogether. It is in the city's center that the largest number of abandoned stations remains: there are forty altogether, repositories of gloom, amplifying the distant vibrations, allaying the slight breezes that pulse through the labyrinth, to decelerate as they get further and further away from the rushing air of tunnels where the trains still run. The lost stations comprise one extreme; the other consists of termini on the Central, Northern, District, Metropolitan and Jubilee lines: the ones that burrow furthest into another time, or into an entirely different organization of space. And yet the tide-line of the city's history is indelible precisely here.

Morden has only been in pole-position as the southern end of the Northern Line since 1924, the year when Charles Holden crafted seven stations reaching out into the fields of Surrey. Now the terminus is under siege, filled up from within by a creeping lattice of iron scaffold poles, an infestation of plasterboard and yellow and black tape, which forces a savage geometry into the calm and carefully legislated spaces of Northern Line house-style, the endless adaptations of white, green, and black porcelain tiles. The platform indicators are bronze-edged lanterns, redolent of BBC Heritage, the reassurance of a Dock Green opening credit. But the lettering is both older and more modern than that post-Second World War community survivalism. The Johnston Sans typeface was first introduced in 1916, year of catastrophes, and yet seems to hold the clue to an ordered existence as economically and inevitably as a Bauhaus doctor's prescription. The real reason for journeying here is to visit the octagonal booking hall; and to leave here for any other destination is to unsettle a rare composure. People come and go looking down and straight ahead; but the space beckons upwards with a series of gestures, past the broad horizontal fluting of the gently pitched ceiling to a pinnacled skylight, whose glass panes are leaded in the form of a giant snowflake, a symmetry that has formed on its own. The entrance hall is made ceremonial by a star-

336

tling, immensely simple, chandelier: a great brass circlet suspended by twenty-foot chains. The facade of Portland stone hints subtly at the ritual importance of setting forth, the commencement of a journey to the Underworld. Its two bas-relief columns share facets of Doric and Egyptian styles; but they are only allusions, not direct quotations like the stage-set pastiche down the road. The station came first, the rest of Morden curved away from it, but never quite matched up to the dignified arc of its approach road. Direct competition came from above—Holden's design was totally crushed by three hideous stories added in the 60s—and from the corner of the road opposite, where the Portland stone was echoed, or rather amplified, in 1936, when a futuristic bulwark of a building was incised defiantly with a series of *fasces*; like the Party badge of a local financier dreamily hedging his bets.

Epping is not so much the end of the Central Line as the beginning of the Essex Way, that bucolic footpath winding a course as far as Harwich. The station wall sports a plaque celebrating the twenty-first birthday of this simulated Ancient Track. It has never been easy to decide where the Central Line should yield to the Forest. The Great Eastern Line (land-grabbed in the New Works Programme of 1935–40) had beached up in Ongar—three stops further out from Epping—in 1865; the first retrenchment came after the Second World War, when passengers for the Ongar outpost had to slip a loop in time, walking from one Epping platform to another to exchange their electric tube trains for steam. This concession vanished in 1970, when the last trails of coal smoke disappeared with the surgical removal of Ongar, Blake Hall, and North Weald—names redolent of the Squire's Last Stand and the primeval impasse. Epping represented a compromise between these feral sidings and an unidentifiable point nearer to Liverpool Street and the urban climax. Modernity was at the top of its bent with Gants Hill, whose concourse was modeled directly on the stations of the Moscow Metro—but Epping is already on the compost heap. It is a rural halt: convolvulus on wire netting, heavy laburnum, climbing roses, hanging baskets, blackberries. Local boys help old ladies with their suitcases. The old red-brick Victorian overland station is flanked by horse chestnuts, greenhouses, and an allotment garden with runner beans and cabbages. It does not do to stand still for very long in Epping: spiders wander over my hands as I write on the parapet; a ladybird alights on my mobile phone. The line is closed off, but there is nothing to stop the trains from plunging forward in a re-run of Edward Upward's 1928 story, "The Railway Accident" (Upward grew up in nearby Romford), except four red lamps planted—everything here is planted—on spindly metal poles in the middle of the tracks. One hundred yards further on, tall ragwort forms a screen as the rails begin to curve out of sight. The waiting room is different. It is the antechamber to a system that classifies everything in its vicinity. The suburbs as Mending Apparatus. The room possesses a single bench that faces a passport photo booth. Which is what the passengers wait for: their criminal typology; their Lombroso credentials. In Epping, the inhabitants conspire against the Greenwich Meridian.

At the western extremity lies Uxbridge, entombed in a future remembered by all those who were teenagers in the 1960s. The old market town, centered on a neoclassical colonnade, flagpole and clocktower, was falsified forever, rendered permanently asymmetrical, by the imposition of a concrete pavilion, the railway's version of South Bank brutalism. Inside the station, however, are the carefully antiqued remnants of a more homely brand of utilitarianism that was always more subtly disturbing. The wooden benches conjure up the era of Harry Palmer, the Michael Caine character for whom the most familiar objects turn suddenly very strange, and vice versa. In *The Ipcress File*, Palmer believes he is being held captive in Albania, but makes his escape onto the streets of London. Uxbridge is the Albanian version: all the artifacts are so convincing, so precisely evocative, they have to be stage copies. There is the original wooden refreshments kiosk, advertising the alternatives of A Mars A Day or CIGARS. The clock and platform indicator have a concatenating rhythm beyond the reach of the original design. It was an age of gadgetry, but the Uxbridge streamlining looks homemade. Pride of place goes to the four stainless steel cigarette machines, boasting their provision of DAY AND NIGHT SERVICE. The one going concern here is Frank's Coffee Shop, which still operates with the original sandwich board. Frank's message includes a prehistoric telephone number, consisting of two-letter prefix and five digits: UX 35489. Anyone phoning that number and expecting ringback will have one hell of a wait. Nowadays, the Underground itself is art; in the 60s, art and the railways had to be formally introduced—via civic heraldry and stained glass windows, job lots from Coventry Cathedral. But the most obdurate features of the design, the most aesthetically ambitious, are two extraordinary, couchant abstractions of wheel and carriage, midway between rolling stock and Halley's Comet: these historical projectiles, coursing through the masonry like Hittite chariots, belong in a corridor of the Pergamon Museum, in the

338

passage leading towards the monumental film sets of the Cold War period. The interior of the station is Portmeirion English: one of the lesser known studios of the British film industry. The props were all leased out from Shepperton in 1965.

Stanmore is way beyond the end of the line. The station is marooned, tipped into a gulley, by the constant backwash from a busy traffic artery. Its status is announced by a traffic island, covered by rampaging weeds that almost hide the entrance. There is an immensely long, incredibly steep, staircase down to the platforms at the bottom of the hill. Pensioners can be seen puffing and pausing on every landing. This place was never anything but peripheral, a hill-station that might be abandoned. The construction was only half-serious. Even the grandeur of the woodwork is wafer-thin. The station is surmounted by a loft conversion, with three dormer windows dressed with net curtains. But no one has ever moved into these corporate bedrooms, and further varieties of weed sprout from the chimney-tops. At best, Stanmore is a depot for rolling stock, rather than a concourse for passengers. The vast shunting yards are empty, and the ten pairs of railway tracks are garnished with a thick rust. At the stroke of a pen, bureaucracy's finest decommissioned the plans before they were ever realized. All over the network are these tokens of aporia; behind the schedules and the signaling routines are strategic exceptions: the superfluous platform, the silent stairwell. Stanmore is the annex of uncertainty, the shrine of second thoughts. It was never made redundant, but paralyzed at a fixed point in the history of the Tube's development. Passengers climbing up and down the hill traverse the strata of transport archeology, with the platform level classified as the prehistory of railway heritage. No wonder the landings carry advertisements for the National Trust—history is no more difficult of access than boarding the train, and less of a nuisance. Nevertheless, that illusion of the British past we consent to is counterpointed by Police notices seeking help in the investigation of crimes of rape. The edifice begins to crack under the weight of these posters, blue plaques of unwillingness and immediate harm.

And so to Upminster, in the utter east. A spaghetti-junction of moving points, its visual clamor put to shame by the self-possession of a row of drainpipe boxes. Each is embossed with the date of their manufacture, 1931. This is the home of the so-called "Underground Signal Box," an operations center that oversees the migrations of millions of passengers, planning the flux and reflux of a daily cycle whose echoes reach as far as the station car park. There is a tide-line of rubbish that

339

ebbs and flows in the turning space before the main entrance. The Signal Box is a hot property, caged in, fenced off. Marc and I peer at its darkened windows, where shadows move close to the Venetian blinds. These must be the shapes of the controllers, eying us up, shifting uneasily backwards and forwards, away from and towards the light. I avert my glance to the thick cast iron of the bridge, which absorbs the last scraps of sunlight and is surprisingly warm to the touch. But Marc is pointing his camera at the tower and producing a small commotion. We do a quick march down the platform and out through the Victorian station building with its pointed brick arches and patched roof. The thing is, we already sound like anoraks, swapping choice items of information about the history of the railways: we know too much, and are going to pay for it. Visions of an airfield in southern Greece materialize suddenly. We exit smartly—past the end cottage with backdoor rowan tree—and size up the shop-fronts. Upminster has a fetish for accuracy, for exact calibration: even the barber shop is called "Martino's *Precision* Hairdressing for Men." The first shop in the High Street proper is a joiner's and woodturner's, the "Essex Centre" of woodcraft, from which the technology of modern transport sprang (from the work of wheelwrights, not from Essex). Britain had a radial system of carriers to London from the mid-seventeenth century, unique in Europe, and the prototype of the centrifugal/centripetal Underground network. A pristine culture of capitalism. The end of the line is always the next staging post; the culture of termini is always transitional, the organization of space provisional. The western range of buildings on the High Street is conceived on a monumental scale, with pillars and capitals, and Egyptian details reminiscent of Morden in the south. An approach road to the metropolis, but only half of one, already half-cannibalized by thriving family businesses, just off-camera. Wealth has spilled out of the old moulds of class and profession, already a frozen memory when the architectural cousins of Howard Carter came metal-detecting in Upminster and put their finds in a living museum, evoking the earliest known urban planning tradition. We skirt a row of tethered Alsatians as each one stands up, sensing the approach of suspicious characters. There is no sanctuary in the church—the closed circuit television surveillance reaches as far as the high altar, and outside, in the churchyard elms, is a chorus of paranoid birdsong, several choruses, a veritable spaghetti-junction of alarm calls. Upminster is on guard; even the wildlife is recruited. The project is to stop the migration of meanings, arrest the flow of defming characteristics, to anticipate and prevent outsiders from rearranging the buffers, one cold rainy night.

Richmond wins the competition in property prices. In Richmond, you have arrived. The concourse houses the Richmond and Surrey Auction Rooms; you jump off the train and invest, before you even get to the street. But something peculiar happens as you walk down the platform: there is a strange little overgrown patch of ground between the train and the station end of the railway tracks, where the line peters out. This small deposit of neglect, with its little pockets of chalk and different-sized gravels, has accumulated indifference at specific moments of alteration and redefinition: it is a transport midden, a municipal burnt mound; by-product of energies that were focused elsewhere. Like timelines in the Thames foreshore, the overlapping of materials is constantly revised, realigned by the superimposing of new layers: the addition of elements reorganizes the entire existing order of monuments. But the evidence of power-play is not enshrined in the canonical details of a metal-framed clerestory, or an abstracted Egyptian facade; it is preserved in a pile of detritus. Its obsolescent mass, undesigned and unamenable to design, is conspicuously ignored. It is meant to be invisible, but its formlessness is reflected, magnified and distorted by the huge mirrors at the other end of the platform, convex and enveloping like an end-of-the-pier amusement. Richmond has seven platforms. The central two, with cast iron pillars, capitals and trefoils, are original, while the rest, with forged steel equivalents, repeat the blue and gray color scheme, but shift the tones and textures. The most dramatic recension is not only recent, it is still in process. South West Trains are installing a "Real Time" Customer Information System. But the Tube journey is never in real time; it is subject to dilation, a time exposure, as Marc's photographic activities constantly remind me. As the motion of the body through space accelerates, the mind dwells on its captivity, lapsing into the same condition between different stations. The first Underground railway carriages were called "padded cells": there were no windows, because it was judged there was nothing to see. Not even the staging posts. The mind was confined within itself.

On the front of Richmond station, the sharply angled fluting above Egyptian-style pilasters completes the web of allusions, north, south, east and west, to Middle Kingdom architecture. But this grandiosity, although heavily suggestive, is less structural, less integral, to the Tube than the hieroglyph, the graffito awaiting its Rosetta Stone. The carriages are full of cartouches which preserve a code of si-

341

lence about the true names for all the destinations. Morden is really "Anuno City," but there is no knowing why. The Underground is a place where we read, unceasingly, a series of mottoes impacted with meanings which do not belong there. Surreptitious, sidling, they appear with the force of revelation, but reveal only the banal, like the scribbled communiques of the Duke of Portland in Mick Jackson's novel *The Underground Man* (Picador, 1997), The Duke, who has constructed a system of tunnels beneath his estate, allowing him to travel by coach and horses for miles underground, slips an assortment of notes under the doors of his manservants and maidservants: conundra, such as "What is that state of mind we call 'consciousness' if not the constant emerging from a tunnel?" In the tunnels of the Victoria Line, nearly all the current advertisements are rudimentary and without entertainment value. Their most important message is the website address you can click onto to see the real advertisement. The only perspective here is a cyberspace perspective. When we emerge from the tunnel at the end of the line, we walk from terminus to terminal, enter a tunnel much longer than any we have just left. The underground from which we emerge into consciousness is unbearably private: without the freedom of the street, it fosters an intimacy with strangers that was the paradoxical ground of wartime myths of community. Traveling blind in this short space has an imagined scope unimagined in the endless suburbs of the Net. Digitized fantasy always needs to be fleshed out by actors; holograms stalk the green belt, the garden cities and country parks. Each padded cell is its own world, its own itinerary of symptoms: read your ticket for the precise aetiology, the carved channel you have traveled in secret, the time-signature of the gradients. Hold your breath until the journey ends, and your name is off the critical list.

John Kinsella

Eclogue of the Birds

28-Parrot

Bold as brass the nip and tuck,
elevation and descent, sweeping strokes
of the sign-off, I stake a claim
and humor myself; though laughter
is what you'd call it, I know it as something else.
These light funnels, tunnels of irregular
nesting trees, hollowed-out flight-lines,
the scratchings on seed membranes
some might see as veins, this blood
of the shoot, dead under
rose hips and wattle blooms.

Magpie

Hair tuft, scalp patch, the bigger they come . . .
the sun gets us going, volatile as nesting season,
never gloating—that's all propaganda,
high or low in wandoo or salmon gum,
deflecting seasonal inflections off the gray
of our razor-sharp beak, to beg
by comparison, lexicographers
of the flyers, though always local,
particular in our heights. Who speaks
for the speared insect, the locusts

pierced through, examined
against the plenty of plague.
They shoot parrots, not magpies!

28-Parrot

That colorful can be haunting
is quelled in rebel compatriots,
to flock or twist in couplets,
stutter across the grotty branches,
drop honkey nuts in bundles
scoured like glacial pickings
when this place was somewhere
other; they drill below us for water,
yelling an approximation
of a name neither attracts
nor damns us. Sedentary
is not our nature, we fly
to avoid early dismissal.
This is no place for the worker.
We make the flashiest targets.

Magpie

Leisure? Offensive. We prised
the akubra and homburg
from the head of a codger,
who thinks himself suited
to walks of pleasure.
The give of sinews,
eye-glint enhanced
by blood—wherever
they come from . . . they nationalize
their fear. Proprietary,
they compensate with clear-felling,
nest-fall in the clipped tongue
of progress, catch-phrase

that'd sell us to the zoo. Free
to come and go, icons
re-naturalized as military budget.

28-Parrot

Blow blue cheeks and yellow belly,
neck the neck of your frivolous lover,
ring around the binary, green-winged
and streaked blue, consorting regally;
this fire we set, these trees we ingratiate
so illustratively as they drive home
against the light, the sun dazzling
and memory that predictable,
or inverting it, what we are
is what they hope we'd be,
glimpses and renderings,
"Port Lincolns" they'd have us
just wandering a little North
of the Stirlings, walking the line,
night-flying when we should be settled.

Magpie

Body blow, torn ligaments, battle-scarred.
In others' myths we speak, and speak out
our own blood-lines, as brother
to sister, offspring to mother
and father—vocative warblings,
emphasis on xenophobia . . . ?
Playthings of the media?
They feed on us. Charcutiers!

"Once a Farm Boy, Always a Farm Boy": a global positioning eclogue

(Knox County, Ohio, USA; Avon Valley,
Western Australia)

Knox County

Corn and Angus bulls, chickens and black-faced sheep,
now streams of genetically-bolstered soy beans,
a day-time job sparking people's powerpoints—I.T.
connections, though no interest myself: did all that
during the Gulf War, and before. Never got to know
those people, though I know my buddies and their families
as well as you can know anybody, on the weekends
when the kids are plugged into Playstation—rated
TEEN—I throw the quad around, pop a clip
and mow down targets. Not much under crop,
not like when I was a kid: got it all in before
Halloween; it will be a good Thanksgiving—
it's warm for this time of year. The snows
will probably be deep, and the roads icy.

Avon Valley

It's been a life of wandering, waiting for the farm
to be broken up. I want my heritage in land,
my brothers and sisters will go for the money—
growing families and all that. I'm single,
though have bunked down with a few women
over the years—a few townies, some rousties
from the sheds: the women who work there
are as rough as guts, into physical sex,

if you get my meaning. They usually
turn up at the pub with their car
and an old man somewhere trying to track
them down. I've had a bikie search
me out at the shed with a self-loading rifle—
I got him pissed and he turned his anger
against the cops. Doing six years.

Knox County

Despite the guns, we don't fight.
I've never hurt my wife. I'd shoot
anyone that did. We're part of a community,
and have enough food and ammo bunkered
to hold off for twelve months at least.
I tell you, it's God's own country here—
the moon-stained walnut tree
arching over the house, no need
for curtains or fences. Our neighbors
know who we are. We know ourselves.
They can listen through windows
with lasers, *they* know where you are.
We know of the parents of our parents,
the home countries that made us,
that we freed ourselves from. In God
we trust, but don't trust foreigners.
In Danville they let the children
enjoy the first day of hunting season
with their families; on another day
they cook and eat raccoons.

Avon Valley

I will take back what is mine.
I know the ways of those that came before.
I will wire the paddocks and reclaim the salt land.
I will get a decent wife—private school,

347

settler stock—to share my bounty,
provide me with children. I will drink
beer without guilt, and innovate
at harvest time. I will know the markets.
I will bend to no government.
I will hunt vermin. I will kill off
diseased stocks and improve the wool-clip—
the South Africans have been after
merino sperm for years.
It's God country own country here—
the moon-stained wandoo tree
arching over the house.
We impale foxes, cook-up
rabbits that haven't been done-over
by myxomatosis.

Knox County and Avon Valley

The air tastes different. Rumors
proliferate like oil prices. The government
has a responsibility to ease our discomfort.
We are the heartland, the core
of the new world. We read papers now.
Shit in, shit out. We project
our God, our country, the moon-stained
trees overhanging our houses;
we sense the same moon cutting trails
and furrows over the fields, the paddocks,
impelling, lying in wait:
the sun red, bloodied by our resistance,
our mutual aid.

The Wedding Eclogue

Groom

The luck in seeing you addressed
by wagtail and 28-parrot, my seedy
Best Man who's half-cut before
the first run of the morning,
lackluster skies semi-brewing
a storm that'd finish off crops
in a tight season, but is full
of mockery instead. When the Armada
was scattered by the winds
the English believed it was God himself
blew their Catholic arses off-line:
I apologize to the other side
of your family, angry because
we're in the wrong Church,
but as your mother is paying
I guess they can take a running
jump. The way those parrot shrieks
hook into each other like barbed wire,
or interlock mesh, or twists of an auger.

Bride

It's a concession, I never
wanted a church wedding, wearing
this off-blue after years of fucking.
We were married in all but law
ten years ago. Maybe now Social
Security and bar-sluts and macho-bastards
at the pool table will show respect.
I sound like you! The lace in this dress
just isn't me. Know what you mean—

always know what you mean—
about the shrieks of those birds.
Cut into you, but in a sickly
sweet kind of way. A choir,
that only cuts a bit.

Groom

I'll finish the shed tomorrow
and then we'll hightail it south,
to a steady cool place where tall trees
monitor sunlight and birdcall
is softened around the edges.
The coast is ragged and furious,
and the weight of the world
is driven back, but it's out of focus,
and there's something vague,
like your skin you know
what I mean . . . soft-ish,
almost sexual.

Bride

This sprig of everlastings
will ward off bad luck—we should
have kept away from each other
just before the ceremony.
In some cultures the whole town
waits outside until blood's drawn . . .

Groom

That'd suit this town of perverts!
Bit late for us, but we'll put on
some kind of show. Harvest
isn't far off—at least the spray
clouds have come and gone.

Bride

Listen to that flock of pink and grays
coming in over the hills. On time.
They fly in complex arrangements:
their rhythms don't complement
the wedding procession—and for that
we should be glad. Driving south,
we'll pass the storm-tongued
black cockatoos. A warning,
knee-jerk reaction. They can't
stand us in this town. But
then again, not expecting to hear
strains of the golden whistler,
will bring them singing
over your doorstep,
calling to help put out a fire
on a neighboring farm.

CONTRIBUTORS

Paul Alpers is Class of 1942 Professor of English, Emeritus at the University of California, Berkeley. He is the author The Poetry of "The Faerie Queene" (Princeton, 1967), The Singer of the Eclogues: A Study of Virgilian Pastoral (California, 1979), and What is Pastoral? (Chicago, 1996). **Brunella Antomarini** is a philosopher and critic who teaches at John Cabot University in Rome. **Louis Armand** lives and works in the Czech Republic, where he lectures on cultural theory and art history at Charles University, Prague. His publications include Techné: Text and Hypertext & Technology (Karolinum/Charles University Press, 2002), Land Partition (Textbase, 2001), The Garden (Salt Publishing, 2001), Inexorable Weather (Arc, 2001), and Séances (Twisted Spoon Press, 1998). He is editor of the Prague Literary Review. **Simon Armitage** has published nine books of poetry, has written extensively for radio, television, and film, and has taught at the University of Iowa's Writers' Workshop. He currently teaches at Manchester Metropolitan University. **David Baker**'s most recent books are the poetry collection, Changeable Thunder (Arkansas, 2001) and a critical work, Heresy and the Ideal: On Contemporary Poetry (Arkansas, 2000). He is poetry editor of the Kenyon Review. **Martin Ball** lives in Melbourne, Australia, where he is the music critic for the Australian newspaper. He holds a Ph.D from the University of Tasmania and was formally managing editor of Siglo. **Mary Jo Bang** is the poetry editor of the Boston Review. Her most recent book of poems is Louise in Love: Poems (Grove, 2001). Her book, Apology from Want (UPNE/Middlebury College Press, 1997), won the Bakeless Prize and the Great Lakes Colleges Association New Writers Award. **Susan Bee** has published numerous books, including A Girl's Life, with Johanna Drucker (Granary Books, 2002) and Bed Hangings, with Susan Howe (Granary Books, 2001). She is coeditor of M/E/A/N/I/N/G: An Anthology of Artist's Writings, Theory, and Criticism (Duke University Press, 2000). **Charles Bernstein**'s most recent books are With Strings (2001) and My Way: Speeches and Poems (1999), both from the University of Chicago Press, and Republics of Reality: 1975–1995 (Sun & Moon Press, 2000). He directs the Poetics Program at SUNY-Buffalo. **Andrea Brady** researches seventeenth century funerary elegies at Cambridge University. Her first book is Vacation of a Lifetime (Salt Publishing, 2002). **John Bull** is Professor of Film and Drama at the University of Reading. He has published extensively on modern drama, including New British Political Dramatists and Stage Right: Crisis and Recovery in Contemporary British Mainstream Theatre. He is currently working on a six-volume project, British and Irish Dramatists Since World War Two, of which two volumes have been published. **Jennifer Clarvoe**'s first book, *Invisible Tender* (Fordham University Press, 2000), won the Poets Out Loud Prize and the Kate Tufts Discovery Award. She is the recipient of the 2002-2003 Rome Prize in Literature, awarded by the Academy of Arts and Letters. **Giuseppe Cucchi** lives in his native village of Morro D'Alba, with his wife, Chiarina. He is 83. **Tacita Dean** lives and works in Berlin, Germany. Recent exhibitions include Tate Britain, London (2001) and MACBA, Barcelona (2001). **Akin Euba** is a composer, musicologist, and the Andrew W. Mellon Professor of Music at the University of Pittsburgh. **Graham Foust**'s first book of poems, *As in Every Deafness*, will be published by Flood Editions this year. He lives in Buffalo, NY. **Forrest Gander** is the author of *Science & Steepleflower* (1998) and *Torn Awake* (2001), both from New Directions. His most recent translations include *No Shelter: Selected Poems of Pura Lopez Colome* (Graywolf, 2002). **Mario Giacomelli** a photographer, poet, and designer was born in 1925, in Senigallia, Italy. His series include: *Paesaggi* (Landscapes), *Verrà la morte e avrà i tuoi occhi* (Death will come and it will have your eyes), *Pretini* (Little Priests), *La Buona Terra* (The Good Earth), *Mattatoio* (Butcher). From the seventies to his death, his photos were mainly related to poems he loved. He died in Senigallia on 25 November 2000. **Peter Gizzi**'s latest book is *Artificial Heart* (Burning Deck, 1998). He has two new limited-edition chapbooks: *Revival*, with artwork by David Byrne and *Fin Amor* with artwork by George Hermes. His new book, *Some Values of Land-scape and Weather*, is forthcoming from Wesleyan in Fall of 2003. **Andrew Grace** first book of poems is *A Belonging Field* (Salt Publishing, 2002). He has poems published or forthcoming in the *Iowa Review* and the *Cortland Review*. **Vona Groarke**'s third collection of poems is *Flight* (Gallery, 2002). Her previous collections are *Shale* (1994) and *Other People's Houses* (1999), both from Gallery Press. **Allen Grossman**'s most recent books are *Sweet Youth* (2002) and *How To Do Things With Tears* (2001), both published by New Directions. He is Mellon Professor in the Humanities in the English department at Johns Hopkins University. **Ann Hamilton** holds a Master of Fine Art in sculpture from Yale University and is a MacArthur Fellowship recipient. Her body of work includes photography, video and objects; however, she is perhaps best known for her sensory and site-specific installations. **Saskia Hamilton** is the author of *As for Dream* (Graywolf, 2001). **Robert Pogue Harrison** is Professor of Italian at Stanford University. His most recent book, *The Dominion of the Dead* (Chicago University Press, 2003), deals with the relations the living maintain with the dead in diverse secular domains. **Brian Henry**'s two books of poetry are *Astronaut* (Carnegie Mellon Press, 2002) and *American Incident* (Salt Publishing, 2002) and a third, *Graft*, is forthcoming. **W. N. Herbert** writes poetry in Scots and English. He has published numerous collections, including *Forked Tongue* (1994), Cabaret MacGonagall (1996) and *The Laurelude* (1998), all from Bloodaxe. In 1992 he wrote a study of the Scottish poet Hugh MacDiarmid, published as *To Circumjack MacDiarmid* (OUP). In 2000, together with Matthew Hollis, he edited *Strong Words*, an anthology of statements on poetry by modern poets. His latest book of poetry, *The Big Bumper Book of Troy*, is out now from Bloodaxe. **John Hollander**'s most recent book of poems is *Picture Window* (Knopf, 2003). He has edited many volumes and anthologies, including *War Poems (Everyman's Library Pocket Poets)* (Knopf, 1999) and is Sterling Professor of English at Yale University. **Susan Howe**'s most recent book is *The Midnight* (New Directions, 2003), from which the excerpt in this issue is taken. Two previous collections are *The Europe of Trusts* (2002) and *Pierce-Arrow* (1999), both from New Directions. **Coral Hull** is the author of over thirty-five books of poetry, fiction, artwork and digital photography. She is the editor and publisher of *Thylazine*, a non-profit biannual literary and arts ezine focusing on Australian artists, writers, and photographers. **Lisa Jarnot** is the author of some *Other Kind of Mission* (Burning Deck Press, 1996) and *Ring of Fire* (Zoland Books, 200). She is currently writing a biography of the American poet Robert Duncan. **Sarah Kennedy**'s most recent collection is *Double Exposure* (Cleveland State University Press, 2003). She is also the author of *Flow Blue* (Elixir, 2002) and *From the Midland Plain* (Tryon, 1999) and teaches at Mary Baldwin College. **William Kentridge**'s most recent theater production, a shadow oratorio in collaboration with Handspring Puppet Company, composer

Kevin Volans and writer Jane Taylor, was seen at Documenta XI, 2002, as was an associated film installation. In 1999 he was awarded the Carnegie Medal at Carnegie 1999/2000. February 2001 saw the launch of a substantial survey show of Kentridge's work at the Hirshhorn Museum in Washington, traveling thereafter to New York, Chicago, Houston, and Los Angeles. **John Kinsella**'s *Selected and New Poems: Peripheral Light* is due from W. W. Norton in fall of this year. He is Professor of English at Kenyon College, a Fellow of Churchill College, Cambridge University, and Adjunct Professor of English at Edith Cowan University, Australia. **John Koethe**'s most recent collection is *North Point North: New and Selected Poems* (Harper Collins, 2002). He is Professor of Philosophy at the University of Wisconsin-Milwaukee. A collection of ten years of **Peter Larkin**'s work, *Terrain Seed Scarcity*, was published by Salt Publications in 2001. *Slights Agreeing Trees* followed in 2002. Recent work has appeared in *Ecopoetics*, the *Denver Quarterly* and *Shearsman*, and is due shortly in the *Chicago Review* and *Salt*. **Mark Levine**'s most recent book is *Enola Gay* (University of California Press). He teaches at the Iowa Writers' Workshop. **Simon Lichman** is the director of the Centre for Creativity in Education and Cultural Heritage, Jerusalem, Israel. His poetry has been published in journals, including *Stand* and *Modern Poetry In Translation*, and in his collection, *Snatched Days*, (Elmer Books, Jerusalem, 1987). **Bill Manhire** was New Zealand's inaugural Poet Laureate. His collected

Poems were published by Victoria University Press (2001). He directs the International Institute of Modern Letters in Wellington, New Zealand. **Janet McAdams** is a member of the Wordcraft Circle of Native Writers. Her collection, *The Island of Lost Luggage* (Arizona, 2000), won an American Book Award. **Steve McCaffery**'s most recent books are *Seven Pages Missing: The Selected Steve McCaffery* (2000) and *Seven Pages Missing: Selected Ungathered Work* (2002) both from Coach House Press. He teaches at York University in Toronto. **J. D. McClatchy**'s new collection of poems is *Hazmat* (Knopf, 2002). He has edited a new translation of the odes of Horace, a collaboration by thirty-five contemporary poets, *Horace: The Odes* (Princeton University Press, 2002). **Rod Mengham** is reader in Modern English Literature at the University of Cambridge and curator of works of art at Jesus College, Cambridge. His most recent publication is *Altered Stated: The New Polish Poetry*, edited with Piotr Szymor and Tadeusz Piono (Arc, 2003). **Michael Mercil** lives in Columbus, Ohio, where he is Associate Professor in the Department of Art at the Ohio State University. His artworks often propose a geography of American culture through things found in or around our homes. This emphasis on objects from the realm of "the common, the low and the ordinary" derives, in part, from his reading of New England transcendentalist Ralph Waldo Emerson, as well as from the "readymade" examples of twentieth century avant-garde artist Marcel Duchamp. **Drew Milne**'s recent books include *Mars Disarmed* (Figures, 2002) and *The Damage: New and Selected Poems* (Salt Publishing, 2001). **Sean O'Brien** is a poet, critic, playwright, broadcaster, anthologist and editor. His most recent books are *Cousin Goat: Selected Poems 1976-2001* (Picador, 2002) and *Downriver* (Picador, 2001). **Bob Perelman** has published numerous books of poetry, most recently *Ten to One: Selected Poems* (Wesleyan University Press, 1999). His most recent critical work is *The Marginalization of Poetry: Language, Writing, and Literary History* (Princeton University Press, 1996). He teaches at the University of Pennsylvania. "Pastoral" originally appeared in *Primer* (This Press, 1981). **Sheenagh Pugh**'s most recent collections are *The Beautiful Lie* (2002) and *Folk Music* (2001), both from Seren Books. She lives in Cardiff, Wales. **Harry Ricketts** is a poet, literary biographer and associate professor in the school of English, Film and Theatre at Victoria University of Wellington. **Peter Riley**'s most recent collection of poems is *Passing Measures* (Carcanet, 2000). His long poem *Alstonfield* is due out this year also from Carcanet. **Rebecca Seiferle**'s third book of poems is *Bitters* (Copper Canyon Press, 2001). Her translations of Alfonso D'Aquino and Ernest Lambrenas appear in *Reversible Monument: Contemporary Mexican Poetry* (Copper Canyon Press, 2002). **Alan Shapiro**'s most recent book of poems is *Song and Dance* (Houghton Mifflin, 2002). **Ronald A. Sharp** is acting president and John Crowe Ransom Professor of English at Kenyon College. From 1978-1982, he was editor of the

Kenyon Review, and he is the author or editor of five books, including *The Norton Book of Friendship* (Norton, 1991), which he co-edited with Eudora Welty. **Reginald Shepherd**'s books are *Otherhood* (2003), *Wrong* (1999), *Angel Interrupted* (1996), *Some Are Drowning* (winner of the 1993 AWP Award), all from the University of Pittsburgh Press. He lives and writes in Florida. **Alan Singer** is the author of critical works in narrative and aesthetics and several novels. "Bog Pastoral" is excerpted from his novel *Dirtmouth* to be published by Fiction Collective 2, fall 2004. **Rodney Smith**'s most recent collections are *Brightwood* (2003), *Messenger* (2001), and *Trespasser* (1996), all from Louisiana State University Press. His work has appeared recently in the *Atlantic, Poetry*, and the *Southern Review*. **Susan Stewart** is the author of three books of poems, most recently *The Forest* (University of Chicago Press, 1995). Her prose study, *Poetry and the Fate of the Senses*, also from the University of Chicago Press, is just out in paperback. **George Szirtes** was born in Budapest and came to England as a refugee in 1956. He is the author of twelve books of poetry in English, which have won various prizes, the most recent books being *The Budapest File* (Bloodaxe, 2000) and *An English Apocalypse* (Bloodaxe, 2001). He also works as a translator of Hungarian poetry and fiction, for which he has received several awards. **John Tranter** sixteen collections of his verse include *The Floor of Heaven*, a book-length sequence of four verse narratives (Harper-Collins 1992 and Arc, UK, 2001), *Late*

Night Radio (Polygon, Edinburgh, 1998), *Different Hands*, a collection of seven experimental prose pieces (Folio/Fremantle Arts Centre Press, 1998), and *Heart Print* (Salt Publishing, 2000). In 1992, he edited (with Philip Mead) the *Bloodaxe Book of Modern Australian Poetry*. He is the editor of the free Internet magazine *Jacket*, at jacketmagazine.com. **Ann Vickery** has recently completed a Fullbright postdoctoral fellowship at Temple University and Yale University. She is author of *Leaving Lines of Gender: A Feminist Genealogy of Language Writing* (Wesleyan University Press, 2000). **Elizabeth Willis** is the author of *Turneresque* (Burning Deck, 2003), *The Human Abstract* (Penguin, 1995), and *Second Law* (Avenue B, 1993). She teaches literature and writing at Wesleyan University. **Eleanor Wilner**'s most recent book of poems is *Reversing the Spell: New and Selected Poems* (Copper Canyon, 1998). She teaches in the MFA program at Warren Wilson College. **Andrew Zawacki** is the author of *By Reason of Breakings* (University of Georgia Press, 2002) and recently won the Alice Fay DiCatagnola Award from the Poetry Society of America. He is coeditor of *Verse* and edited the anthology *Afterwards: Slovenian Writing 1945-1995* (White Pine Press, 1999).

Subscriptions

Three issues per year. **Individuals:** one
year $24; two years $44; life $600. **Insti-
tutions:** one year $36; two years $68.
Overseas: $5 per year additional. Price
of back issues varies. Sample copies $5.
Address correspondence and subscriptions
to *TriQuarterly*, Northwestern University,
2020 Ridge Ave., Evanston, IL 60208-
4302. Phone (847) 491-7614.

Submissions

The editors invite submissions of fiction,
poetry and literary essays, which must
be postmarked between October 1 and
March 31; manuscripts postmarked be-
tween April 1 and September 30 will not
be read. No manuscripts will be re-
turned unless accompanied by a stamped,
self-addressed envelope. All manuscripts
accepted for publication become the
property of *TriQuarterly*, unless other-
wise indicated.

Reprints

Reprints of issues 1–15 of *TriQuarterly*
are available in full format from Kraus
Reprint Company, Route 100, Millwood,
NY 10546, and all issues in microfilm
from University Microfilms International,
300 North Zeeb Road, Ann Arbor, MI
48106.

Indexing

TriQuarterly is indexed in the Humanities
Index (H.W. Wilson Co.), the American
Humanities Index (Whitson Publishing
Co.), Historical Abstracts, MLA, EBSCO
Publishing (Peabody, MA) and Informa-
tion Access Co. (Foster City, CA).

Distributors

Our national distributors to retail trade
are Ingram Periodicals (La Vergne, TN);
B. DeBoer (Nutley, NJ); Ubiquity (Brook-
lyn, NY); Armadillo (Los Angeles, CA).

**Publication of *TriQuarterly* is made
possible in part by the donors of gifts
and grants to the magazine. For their
recent and continuing support, we are
very pleased to thank the Illinois Arts
Council, the Lannan Foundation, the
National Endowment for the Arts,
the Sara Lee Foundation, the Wendling
Foundation and individual donors.**

357